Praise for Olivia Twist

"A brilliant reimagining of *Oliver Twist*! The prologue hooked me immediately. Langdon deftly plunges the reader into Dickens's world of loveable orphans fighting to survive on the darker streets of London. Their plight is set in stark contrast to the sumptuous backdrop of Victorian England's high society. *Olivia Twist* deals with treachery in both worlds and proves a spirited heroine worthy of admiration, while Dodger is the perfect bad boy hero. Sigh, I've fallen in love."

—KATHLEEN BALDWIN, bestselling author
of *A School for Unusual Girls*

"Captivating from the very first page to the very last! *Olivia Twist* is an enchanting story, brimming with eclectic characters, intrigue, and a romance that is certain to leave you weak at the knees. Not to be missed!"

—JEN TURANO, *USA Today* bestselling author

"When I learned Lorie Langdon made a foray into historical romance, I couldn't wait to get my hands on this book. And she didn't disappoint. Langdon expertly balances historical detailing and plot, the voice sparkles, and the characters were so endearing, I couldn't wait to escape into this book each night. Lively and transportive, *Olivia Twist* is a romantic and clever take on a classic that will leave readers yearning for more from this author."

—HEATHER WEBB, author of *Last Christmas in Paris*

"Delectable romance, spine-tingling danger, and an indomitable female lead make Lorie Langdon's *Olivia Twist* an addictively exquisite romp. One that kept me up far past midnight!"

—MARY WEBER, author of the Storm Siren
trilogy and *The Evaporation of Sofi Snow*

OTHER BOOKS BY LORIE LANGDON

Doon Novels (with Carey Corp)
Doon (book one)
Destined for Doon (book two)
Shades of Doon (book three)
Forever Doon (book four)

Gilt Hollow

OLIVIA TWIST

LORIE LANGDON

BLINK

BLINK

Olivia Twist
Copyright © 2018 by Lorie Moeggenberg

This title is also available as a Blink ebook.

Requests for information should be addressed to:
Blink, *3900 Sparks Dr. SE, Grand Rapids, Michigan 49546*

ISBN 978-0-310-76341-3

Cover design: Kirk DouPonce
Interior design: Denise Froehlich

Printed in the United States of America

18 19 20 21 22 /LSC/ 10 9 8 7 6 5 4 3 2 1

For Tom—
Because you would do anything for me, even fisticuffs.

PROLOGUE

1841
Holborn, London

For long minutes, there was considerable doubt as to whether the child would survive to bear a name at all.

Although being born in a workhouse was not the most fortunate of circumstances, in this child's case the alternative would have made for a much different story; likely a very short one.

Extended moments passed as the babe lay on a thin, flocked mattress, struggling to find that first, essential, life-giving breath while the parish surgeon warmed his hands by the meager fire and the nurse slipped into a dark corner to find fortification within a tiny green bottle.

Oblivious to the disinterest of those gathered in the room, the baby gasped and proceeded to declare, to anyone within hearing distance, her choice to live.

Her mother, on the other hand, lifted her head and croaked, "Let me see it, so I may die."

The surgeon rose from his position by the fire and hovered over the woman. "Oh, Miss, you must not talk like that."

The nurse tucked her bottle away and approached. "Lor', no, there's a dear young lamb 'ere. And there's a place in the werk 'ouse for ye both."

Apparently, her prospects held little appeal, because the young mother gave her head a weak shake and held out her hands toward the child. The surgeon placed the babe in her arms, and the mother pressed her cold lips to the baby's downy fluff in a lingering kiss before falling back with a gasp, gone from this world.

"Ah, poor dear!" The nurse took a quick taste from her green bottle before scooping up the child.

"The baby's frail and likely to give you some trouble," the surgeon said, slipping on his gloves with great consideration. "No need to call for me. Just give it some gruel. That ought to strengthen it up." He paused to take a long look at the young mother resting in repose, the graceful arches of her dark-gold brows and the sweep of her curls across the pillow. "She was a lovely girl. Where did she come from?"

"She was brought in last night," the old nurse replied as she juggled the squirming child in one arm while digging in her pocket with the other. "The overseer found 'er in the street. Likely she'd walked some distance. 'Er shoes were wore to the nub. But where she came from, no one knows."

The surgeon leaned over the body and lifted her left hand. "Ah, no wedding ring." He stared thoughtfully for a long moment. "Nurse, raise this one as a boy."

The old woman's arm froze mid-swig. "Sir? But she be a female."

"Give her a fighting chance. If she grows up to look anything like her mother, the horrors she'll be subjected to"—he straightened and looked the nurse in the eye—"will be unimaginable. Tell everyone she's a male child." Stuffing on his hat, the surgeon turned and walked out into the night to find his dinner.

8

The old nurse sank into the chair by the fire and proceeded to dress the infant, contemplating the seven babes of her own, five of which she'd held as they died. This world was hard enough for any child, let alone an orphaned baby girl. With a damp smile at the babe's perfect head covered in golden curls, she watched it twisting and rooting in her lap.

"Yer a feisty one, me beaut," the nurse whispered in conspiracy as she cupped a tiny balled fist in her workworn hand. "That trait will serve ye well. But yer goin' to need more to make it." The old woman's eyes clouded with the image of her firstborn child, a son with hair the color of harvest wheat who'd passed before his second birthday. Mayhap the name would bring this one better fortune.

A single fat tear fell and splashed against the baby's round cheek, startling both woman and babe. Leaning down, she spoke into the pink seashell ear, "I'll no' let ye perish this time, my little Oliver Twist."

CHAPTER 1

Eighteen years later
Grosvenor Square, London
The Platts' Annual Autumn Dinner Party

The sounds of clinking china and animated chatter faded as Olivia's cheeks warmed, and the rhubarb tart she'd consumed moments before threatened to disembark. And yet, she continued to stare. The gentleman in question raised his glass in salute, sharp blue eyes glittering as they locked on her face. His lips tilted, and the smile swept through her as a spirit might pass through one's body, leaving her breathless.

The young man's uncommon good looks assured she would have remembered if they had met before. So why then did the planes of his face, the way he flicked his dark hair out of his eyes, and the restless tap of his fingers against his thigh send jitters of recognition through her chest?

Olivia took a step forward, her gaze never wavered. Energy radiated around him, as if it took every ounce of his self-control to remain still. He tugged at the velvet lapel of his forest-green jacket and then shoved his hand into the pocket of his trousers as he spoke to his companion. Olivia's heart skipped a beat and then raced forward, a memory just beyond her grasp swirling through her mind.

"Olivia! Look who I've found lingering by the warm punch." A familiar voice cut through the line of Olivia's thoughts, knotting them into a jumbled mess. She tore her gaze away from the gentleman across the room to find her cousin, Violet, approaching on the lanky arm of Maxwell Grimwig. Violet tucked a stray crimson curl behind her ear, her lips forming words that to Olivia sounded like gibberish. With a lurch, the room tipped and slid away from Olivia's feet, and she grasped Maxwell's jacket sleeve for leverage.

"Miss Brownlow!" Maxwell exclaimed as he took her by the shoulders and steered her to a nearby chair.

"Good heavens, should I get the smelling salts?" Violet's ruffled kerchief smacked Olivia in the face like a lavender-scented laundry bat.

With an exasperated yank, she captured the offensive cloth from her cousin's hand and fixed her with a death glare. "Not hardly." Fainting was not something Olivia made a habit of, and she wasn't about to start now.

"No need to get testy. I was simply attempting to revive you." Violet pouted, bending to peer into Olivia's face, as if searching for signs of a fatal malady. "I believe I warned you against that fourth tart."

"I'm perfectly fine." She huffed out a sigh and then softened her tone. "I promise." Since Olivia had no mother yet living, Violet had a tendency toward over protection. Most times, Olivia found her friend's cossetting lovable, but when she dared a surreptitious peek over Violet's chartreuse-clad shoulder, and saw the mysterious gentleman had moved on, her frustration spiked.

"You don't look fine," Vi proclaimed, hands gripping her corseted waist.

Olivia narrowed her eyes at her closest friend, noting the yellowish tinge underlying her rosy, freckled cheeks. There was no getting around it; the ghastly lime gown would have to be tossed at the first opportunity. Violet was a master at choosing shades to best complement Olivia's caramel-colored hair and odd, yellowish eyes, but when it came to her own vivid coloring, she seemed at a loss.

Olivia rose to her feet and smoothed her gold-and-cream-striped skirt. "In any case, the tarts were worth it. They were truly the best I've had all year."

Violet giggled. For Olivia, the food was the main attraction at every party—at least that's what she led others to believe. In truth, she would swim the length of the Thames for a slice of chocolate cake, but her ultimate goal at these events had little to do with her culinary obsessions.

"Miss Brownlow," Maxwell panted as he rushed to Olivia's side, sweat beads dotting his hawkish nose. "I brought you refreshment."

Olivia accepted the warm mug as a bell tinkled, announcing dinner. "Why, thank you, Mr. Grimwig." She took a small sip and lowered her lashes. "I am much restored."

The sharp slopes of his cheekbones glowed. "May I escort you to the dining room, Miss Brownlow?"

"Of course, Maxwell." She'd known Maxwell Grimwig for ages, therefore his neck only reddened slightly at her breech in proper address. Olivia detested the formal nature of dinner parties. She'd much rather meet with friends in a more casual setting. A picnic under the trees with her pup by her side, an intimate tea where no one counted the number of cakes she consumed, or a friendly game of cricket would all be preferable. Although these large social gatherings did have their advantages.

Olivia rose and placed a hand on her friend's offered elbow. "Max, are you acquainted with that gentleman in the forest green coat?" She craned her neck as she searched the departing crowd for the dark-haired man, and spotted him walking the young Widow Thesing through the doorway. "Just there." Olivia stood on her toes and pointed.

With a squeak, Violet grabbed Olivia's hand and yanked it down. "Olivia! He might see you," she hissed in outrage.

Olivia recovered her hand from Violet's lethal grip and then shrugged a shoulder as she arched a brow at Max. "Well?"

"Yes, I . . . er . . . believe that is Jack MacCarron." Max stuck a finger between his throat and his collar.

"I've never heard of him." Violet, who prided herself on knowing everyone who was anyone, peered across the room searching for the gentleman in question.

"That may be because he is fairly new to society. Moved here from Ireland a couple years back, I believe." Maxwell glanced around as the last few stragglers filed out of the room, and then sank down onto a chair and motioned the girls to sit on a brocade sofa across from him. "The circumstances were quite extraordinary, I hear."

Loving nothing more than a good story, Olivia perched on the edge of the divan beside Violet as Max pitched his voice in a whisper. "Jack's aunt took him in after his parents were found murdered—his mother stabbed to death and his father shot in the head."

Olivia arched back, chills running down her spine. "Truly?"

Maxwell's lips thinned as he waggled his caterpillar-like eyebrows. "As it may be believed, young Jack was nothing more than a half-wild ruffian when he showed up on his aunt's doorstep. Took her *years* to civilize him."

"Who is his aunt?" Violet whispered, gripping Olivia's arm.

"The old Widow March."

Olivia exchanged a wide-eyed glance with Violet. Lois March had a reputation for being eccentric. Everyone said she had lost her mind when her husband of forty-five years passed on, but Violet, having been acquainted with the woman since infancy, claimed she hadn't had much of a mind to lose.

Olivia leaned in and cupped her hand around the side of her mouth. "I've heard it said the Widow March buries something in her back garden at the light of every full moon. What do you suppose it could be?"

"I've heard 'tis the bones o' dead children," whispered a melodic, Irish brogue, so close the tiny hairs by Olivia's ear stirred. With a gasp, she rotated in her seat and almost collided with a solid shoulder covered in forest-green broadcloth. The gentleman in question leaned down, as if in conspiracy, a grin tilting his mouth, his blue eyes as frosty as a December morning.

Olivia shot to her feet and Mr. MacCarron straightened, his smile broadening.

Her cheeks burned as she stared up into a face that made her heart leap into her throat, but with a determined swallow she propped a hand on her hip and demanded, "Has anyone ever taught you that it's impolite to eavesdrop?"

"Has anyone ever told ye that it's cruel to gossip?" Jack MacCarron's smile never wavered, but something in his gaze forced Olivia back a step.

"Now, MacCarron, we were just having a bit of fun. No need to take offense." Maxwell's voice shook only slightly as he moved to Olivia's side.

"None taken." Jack's eyes narrowed dangerously on Olivia for several beats, dredging up fears she thought she'd long outgrown. Something about the curve of his mouth, the shape of his face drew her back into her long years of destitution—begging on the streets, robbing to survive—but such a connection was impossible.

He took a step forward. "I don't believe we have met." Olivia suppressed the urge to flee.

"My apologies," Maxwell said. "Allow me."

After a rather stilted round of introductions, Jack retrieved a woman's reticule—presumably the reason he had returned to the drawing room—and made his exit. Shaking off her recollections, Olivia watched his broad back until he disappeared, and then turned to find her best friend, lips parted, staring at the now empty doorway.

Despite the rainbows and butterflies reflected in Violet's gaze, the knot in Olivia's gut had little to do with romantic dreams and everything to do with a growing awareness rising within. Jack MacCarron was indeed no stranger to her.

Olivia glided down the dark corridor, slinking from shadow to shadow in a dance she'd performed more times than she cared to number. Her excuse for trespassing in the living quarters of the Platts' home held validity—this time. Presumably, she'd left the party to "lie down."

She could not believe she'd almost fainted. Her momentary weakness made her stomach clench with disgust. But Max Grimwig had come to her rescue in his sweet, bumbling way. His proposal was forthcoming any day now, and although she viewed him as no more than a friend, her uncle's declining health and dwindling finances assured her swift, if not enthusiastic, acceptance. She ignored the cold that spread through her chest at the thought of marrying. Eighteen was an acceptable age to become a wife, but for Olivia it signified responsibilities she had no inclination to take on, and more remarkably, it meant the end of her freedom.

But she would do what needed done. As she always had.

Violet made her disapproval of the match clear, but true love simply did not exist outside of fairy tales and her friend's ridiculous gothic novels. The Grimwigs' wealth would bring her security, allow her to support her uncle, and, she hoped, subsidize her charitable mission.

Olivia paused to open a massive armoire, but only finding stacks of fresh linens, continued down the hallway.

Last month while in the garden at the Drewforths' ball, Max had snuck a kiss. His lips were warm and gentle, pleasant. But it had left Olivia questioning why other girls compared the kisses of one gentleman to another. How different could they possibly be? Unbidden, the image of ice-blue eyes and a slow smirk filled her mind.

"Ouch! Blast it—" Olivia clamped her mouth closed, her heart racing as she grabbed her smarting foot and glanced up and down the hall. Still alone, she searched the floor for her assailant and found a squat frog balanced on the edge of the carpet runner. Cursing her own clumsiness, she moved to step around the doorstop, when a metallic glint caught her eye. She bent and plucked up the tiny statue for further examination. Hefting it in her hand, she noted the weight and the tarnished spots in the creases where the polish had missed. A triumphant grin spread across Olivia's face. Solid silver.

The idiotic trinket would bring a fair amount of coin at market. "No one shall miss you, my little darling," Olivia whispered as she slipped the amphibian into the pocket of her skirt, its added weight pulling the fabric taunt.

She turned to go back to the party when slow footsteps, so light she almost didn't hear them, signaled someone approaching. Keeping her gaze glued to the landing at the top of the stairs, she backed up then reached behind her to turn the nearest doorknob, but it wouldn't move. Her pulse galloping ahead of her, she tiptoed to the next door, finding it locked as well.

The footsteps continued, and a tall shadow stretched across the landing. Olivia turned and ran. A stream of weak light indicated a cracked door near the end of the hallway. She raced toward it, and without thought slipped inside. Pushing the door to, she leaned against the wall and let out a long breath, willing her heartbeat to slow. The light of a single lamp on the bureau illuminated burgundy bed coverings, dark leather furniture, and the implements of a pipe spread on a low table by the window. Mr. Platt's bedchamber. If anyone found her there, she didn't dare contemplate the consequences.

At the Wolfbergs' party the previous week, she'd nearly been caught nipping chinaware from the kitchens. The butler had walked in on her the moment she'd plucked the gold-rimmed saucer from its velvet-lined drawer. As luck would have it, one of the maids approached and, in a ringing voice, Olivia demanded to know where she could purchase the dishware for her uncle's household—as if they could actually afford such finery. After being informed that the china had been passed down in the Wolfberg family for generations, the butler had taken Olivia's arm and escorted her back to the party.

If the servant had arrived a second later, he would have witnessed Olivia slipping the saucer into the custom-made pocket of her skirt—and her mission at every extravagant, overdone soiree would have screeched to a tragic end.

The footsteps grew closer. Olivia pressed her back into the wall and sucked in her chest, as if not breathing would somehow make her invisible. The footfalls paused right outside the door, followed by an odd scrape and click. Her hands gripped the wall like talons, and she peeked around the edge of the door, just as a dark-haired gentleman with broad shoulders slipped into the next room.

Mr. MacCarron? She jerked her head back into the room. What could he possibly be doing in the Platt family wing?

Olivia pressed against the wall and clutched the locket resting beneath the neckline of her dress, worrying the smooth metal against the fabric, an unconscious habit that brought her comfort. Like a word on the tip of her tongue, she could almost grasp what eluded her about Jack MacCarron. Before she could contemplate further, a muted banging made her jump, and the exposed skin of her upper arm scraped against the wooden chair rail at her back. She wrapped her gloved fingers around her stinging flesh as another muffled thump from the next room drew her attention to the connecting door. Of course! Mr. and Mrs. Platt would have adjoining bedrooms.

On her tiptoes, she crossed the room and turned the knob slowly. Careful not to make a sound, she eased the door open a crack. Silence.

Turn. Run! her mind hissed. But she didn't. She stayed. She had to know.

Opening the door, she peered inside. The bedroom was dark save for the muted glow from the open window.

Standing stock still, she trained all her senses on the room. A flash of light left black spots dancing before her eyes, and then she heard a low curse. What on earth was he doing in there? Easing open the door a bit more, she leaned forward until she spied a dark form hunched near the foot of the bed. Heart racing, she stepped inside.

As if pulled by an unseen force, Olivia took another step and another. A cloud shifted outside and a beam of moonlight painted the curve of his stubble-covered jaw and strong nose. Bent over a metal box beside an open hole in the floor, he maneuvered the tools in his hands with quick, deft movements. And that niggling that she'd experienced the moment he'd smiled at her reared up and screamed the answer into her mind.

The floorboard creaked under her heel and she froze, her breath seizing in her chest. The man looked up and their eyes met for a moment that stretched into an eternity, and she knew she was right. "Dodger?"

His shocked expression turned fierce, and he sprang from his crouch like a big cat she'd seen once at the Regent's Park zoo. Faster than she could have thought possible, he grasped her arms and pushed her up against the wall. "Where the devil did you hear that name?" he ground out between clenched teeth.

Olivia blinked. The thin scar on his right cheekbone, the vein that pulsed in his throat when he was angry, the outline of dark lashes around light eyes—*Dodger*. She longed to confess, "It's me, your erstwhile friend, Ollie." But he'd never believe she was his long-lost chum—the orphan boy he'd taken under his wing some nine years past.

"I asked you a question," he growled. The solid weight of his body pressed closer, forcing her to tilt her chin to meet his violent gaze.

The tiny hairs on her arms rose, sparking the survival instincts from her youth. *Never back down.* Stiffening her posture, she spat, "Whyever would I answer such a great brute?"

His eyes widened and she pushed against his hard chest. Seemingly caught off guard, he stepped back. Olivia inched toward the door. "I thought you were *Dozer* . . . er, Mr. Dozer, the footman." She arched an eyebrow and slid her mouth up on one side, allowing him to come to his own conclusions regarding why she would seek out a footman in a dark bedroom. He frowned.

Olivia walked backward, quickly. "But I can see I was mistaken. My apologies." She dipped her head in a respectful nod. She'd seen too much, and she wasn't about to stick around to find out what the grown-up Dodger . . . er . . . Jack—whatever his blasted name was now—would do to keep her mouth shut.

"Wait." His voice deep and commanding, Jack took a long stride forward. Olivia turned on her heel and fled out the door and down the hall as fast as her feet would carry her. When she reached the staircase, she dared a glance over her shoulder and breathed a sigh of relief that he hadn't followed. She attempted to descend the stairs at a respectable pace, her mind whirling with memories. After escaping the workhouse, her prospects had been slim.

Olivia had slept curled up in a field, been chased by soot-covered chimney sweeps across Blackfriars Bridge, and hadn't eaten for days. She'd never felt more alone in her life. So when a little old woman had promised her lodging and the easiest work she'd ever do, Olivia had been ready to follow the woman anywhere. But a boy with a ragged top hat, wide smile, and grubby cheeks had looped an arm around her shoulders and steered her away, informing her *that* sort of work would lead to an early grave. *"I'm Jack, better known among me mates as the Artful Dodger."*

Then he'd invited her to be the master of her own fate.

She'd followed him off the crowded street of Cheapside through a maze of sewers, rickety walkways, and a cockroach-infested apartment building, before they'd emerged in a massive third-story attic filled with mismatched furniture where children laughed and played games while sausages smoked on the fire. If life got any better than that, she didn't know how. In comparison to the toil-eat-sleep schedule of the workhouse, the bone-numbing cold, the beatings, and the rats—*God save me from nibbling, stinking rats*—Dodger's gang of ragamuffins were a revelation.

Fagin, the old kidsman, had taken one look at Ollie's face,

proclaimed her *the perfect angelic distraction,* and without an inkling of her true gender, presented her with a pristine, blue sailor's suit as a welcome to the crew.

That night, the Dodger had offered her a soft pallet under the eaves of the roof, removed from the chaos of the other boys. Her belly full of smoked meat and day-old rolls, she'd grinned dreamily as he'd tucked her in, promising to teach her a trade that would keep her full and protected for the rest of her days.

When one of the older boys had complained about her prime sleeping spot near the fire, Dodger had punched him sound in the nose, and then pulled his pallet next to hers so that she laid nestled between him and the wall. A few moments later, he'd produced a brightly wrapped piece of candy and handed it to her. "This lot don't know 'ow good they got it, Ollie."

With trembling hands, she'd unwrapped the gold cellophane and popped the confection into her mouth. The buttery-sweet taste had brought tears to her eyes. She'd had candy once in her life, on Christmas the year before her nurse passed on.

With his head propped on one hand, those canny blue eyes searched hers. "But you do know, don'cha?"

She'd nodded, swiped at her wet cheeks, and sucked on the sugary goodness melting on her tongue. Dodger had flopped onto his back, one hand behind his head. "Don't you worry none, kid. After I've trained you, you'll never 'ave a reason to leave our right little nest."

He'd turned to face her again, blinking at her wet cheeks. "Lesson one: Friends are just enemies in disguise. Don't let the others see ya bawlin'. Tha's a good way to get trounced."

That was the day he'd become her champion. Brash, confident, and brave, he'd been all the things Olivia wanted to be.

Her heart light, she skipped down the rest of the stairs toward the sounds of the dinner party. Against all the odds, that daring, clever boy had fought his way off the streets and into the upper echelon of London society. But if he'd truly left the life behind, whyever would he rob the Platts?

Olivia paused in the darkened hallway and stroked the silver treasure in her pocket. Why, indeed.

CHAPTER 2

❧

*J*ack donned his old hat and ran a hand over his face as he stepped out the back door of the townhouse he called home. There was only one person in the world for whom Jack would be up and about at this ungodly hour, and she happened to be the woman who'd changed his life. Lois March may look like a half-baked old granny, but when she set her mind to something, not even that cold-hearted bludger, Edward Leeford, could've denied her.

Thoughts of the man who'd terrorized his young life set Jack's feet moving faster. The scar on his right cheekbone throbbed, as it did every time he thought of Leeford and the beating he'd given Jack when he refused to take a five-year-old boy to steal from the most corrupt whorehouse in the city. At thirteen, Jack had seen it all and had no qualms about robbing the old flesh peddler, but the job required a tiny body. Jack had taken the boy halfway to Seven Dials before he'd been struck by a rare moment of conscience and turned back. Everyone had their limits, even orphan thieves, and Jack had reached his. When he returned empty-handed, Leeford, who was several years Jack's senior, had beat him so badly that he still bore the scars. And when Jack had stepped in to protect the little one from the same fate, Leeford had pulled a knife.

Fagin, his old kidsman—the man who'd been like a father to him—hadn't said a word as Leeford stabbed Jack between the ribs and took the child to complete the job himself. Jack left that day and never looked back, taking half of Fagin's gang with him.

He'd heard Leeford had met a tragic end, his story one of Jack's motivations for finding a new life. *Violence begets violence.*

He rolled his shoulders as he turned onto Piccadilly Street, the coarse shirt he reserved for his trips into the city scratchy against his skin. *Saints!* The old biddy had transformed him into a right dandy.

Jack had yet to decide if Lois March was his savior or his one-way ticket to Newgate Prison, but regardless, her intimate acquaintance with every well-off family in London— and more importantly, all their most valuable treasures—had led to his current vocation. He almost smiled, recalling how Lois referred to some of society's most elite families by the jewels they owned. The Platts' were "the Rubies," for the exquisite set of ruby earbobs, bracelet, and necklace Mrs. Platt had inherited from her grandmother. Lois viewed them as the perfect mark because she'd only seen the woman wear the jewels once in twenty years. All the same, he'd argued against the crack. Heirlooms were the type of loot that would be missed, and the paste-jeweled bauble he'd left in their safe wouldn't fool a blind man.

As Jack turned a corner, he approached a maid from the neighbor's household carrying a basket of fresh fruit. With a tip of his hat and a grin, he snatched a gleaming apple off the pile.

"Jack!" The girl—who could not have been more than ten and five—slapped his arm and gave him an evocative smile over her shoulder as she passed. "Stop by later and I'll make ye a nice tart."

Biting into the crisp, sweet fruit, Jack watched the exaggerated sway of the maid's hips. The girl really should take more care in who she propositioned. An apple in the wrong hands could spoil her forever. And Jack was most definitely the wrong hands for any sort of intimate association. Jack contemplated going back and putting a definitive end to the flirtation, but the weight of the bracelet in his pocket pushed him onward.

With any luck, the Platts wouldn't notice the missing piece for a few weeks, and by that time the rotation of guests flowing through their home would make it impossible to implicate him in the theft. Although the rumors circulating about him—like that bloomin' git, Grimwig, calling him a half-wild ruffian—wouldn't help his cover. Jack reached around and squeezed the tight muscles at the back of his neck. It rankled to admit, even to himself, that particular rumor to be true. The day he had picked Lois March's pocket, he'd been an animal of the streets—a leader of many, and a master of nothing. That was the day the Artful Dodger died. And after many, many months of Lois's patient but vigorous tutoring, the gentleman Jack MacCarron was born.

Nonetheless, the girl with the autumn-wheat curls and tawny eyes could ruin everything. Had his ears played tricks on him when he heard her whisper the name Dodger? Even so, that didn't explain why she'd looked at him with the hope of the world in her gaze.

As he turned onto the Strand, a sausage vendor caught his eye, and the aroma of the spiced, roasted meat caused his mouth to water. Sharp hunger pains—his constant companion and master for the first sixteen years of his life—clenched his stomach. With effort, he pushed away the phantom ache. There wasn't any part of his past he missed less than that constant, gnawing emptiness.

An overloaded chicken cart barreled toward him, and he ducked into a shadowed alley. Soon, the smell of food faded away as the undulating reek of the Thames and the stench of human filth overpowered everything else.

He passed a group of children huddled by the backside of a chimney, tattered clothes hanging from bony shoulders and feet black with filth, their hollow, spectral-like eyes beseeching. Jack dug in his pocket and flipped a handful of shillings in their direction, turning away as they scurried on hands and knees fighting over the money.

But as much as he pushed his feet to move, the sight of a tiny child in his peripheral vision kept him rooted to the spot. Tackled by the others, the boy—no more than five years old—rolled into a ball, his fist clutched tight to his chest as the older children hammered him with fists and feet in an effort to get the coins he clutched to his chest.

"Give us that, ye little rat!" The largest of the boys landed a jab to the child's kidney.

Jack had to admire the little one's tenacity as he clutched his prize, not making a peep throughout the beating. In two long strides, Jack reached down and grabbed the back of two filthy necks and lifted them into the air, fists still swinging.

"Leave off!" the child in his right hand screeched.

Jack turned away from the scuffle and dropped them both to the ground. Towering over the pile of children, he demanded, "Clear out, the lot of you!" When they'd scrabbled back, he helped the now bloodied child to his feet. "You're a fast little thing, eh?"

The boy stared up at Jack with defiant blue eyes and nodded.

Looping his arm around the kid's frail shoulders, Jack led him away from the group. "Do you know St. Christopher's in Southwark?"

"Ye . . . yes . . . my lord."

The title tightened something in Jack's chest, cutting off his breath. Kneeling, so that he met the boy's gaze at eye level, he said, "I am no lord. Do not bow to any man, toff or thief. They're no better than you. Do you understand?"

"Yes, sir."

Satisfied with the lift of the boy's chin, Jack gave him directions to the nunnery behind St. Christopher's and instructed him to offer his service for room and board. The nuns didn't take in many orphans, but for one so young, Jack thought sure they'd make an exception. They had for him. "If they want you to peel potatoes, scrub the privy, or polish their shoes, you do it without question, eh?"

The boy grinned, his teeth stained the putrid brown of the Thames. The nuns would take care of that too. Jack ruffled the kid's greasy hair. "Now run, and don't stop until you get there. Be sure to tell 'em Dodger sent you."

The shillings still clutched tight in his fist, the child took off like a shot. Jack resumed his course down the alley, but as he passed the children crowded by the chimney, he clenched his jaw and tried to block out their pleas. *"Please, sir. We're starving. Can ye spare a bit more, sir?"*

He couldn't help them all; that was no longer his job. Shoving his hands into his pockets, he gripped the gems waiting to secure his future—worlds away from this hell.

⁓

Olivia threw the stick so hard that she spun in a circle with the effort. Brom raced after it in excited leaps, his multihued fur quivering in glee. Most would not consider her great, mixed-breed dog a proper escort, but no one who cared would be out of bed at this hour to judge. Olivia exhaled a cloud of fog into the crisp morning air and sank onto a nearby bench. Tucked back into a stand of molting trees, she breathed in the scent of decay, of green life leeching from foliage, leaving behind the vibrant colors of change.

Sleep the night before had been impossible as her thoughts turned over the evening's events again and again. It had been no great surprise when Dodger did not return to the party after their confrontation, although his absence would make him a prime suspect if anything significant were to turn up missing.

Olivia slumped against the back of the bench. Her initial joy at finding him well and alive had soon faded as she recalled the last time she'd seen him. If Dodger had robbed anyone other than her Uncle Brownlow that day, she would have hung for his crime . . .

"There's our mark now, Ollie," Dodger whispered as he inclined his head toward an older gentleman browsing through a street vendor's assortment of books. The man wore a coat of the deepest red, the snowy ruffles of his shirt peeking from beneath his cuffs, his tall Hessian boots shining in the sun. Dodger gestured toward the table, indicating Ollie should attempt a distraction.

Ollie swiped the crumbs from her mouth with a dirty sleeve, approached the bookstand, and squeezed in between the white-haired gentleman and a less-affluent customer. Her hands clammy and shaking, she selected a brown leather tome and opened the cover, moving her finger along the letters as if she could read them. She turned the page, repositioned her foot, and stomped on the toff's boot. When the man harrumphed his displeasure, Ollie apologized and grinned up at him, using her dimples to their full advantage. The man did not return her smile, but met her gaze and held it, blinking several times before his mouth fell open. Ollie's smile faltered, the book falling from her hand as she stared into honey-colored eyes, the exact shade of her own.

Then the man jerked and spun about. "Thief!"

Dodger froze in shock, before whirling on his heel and taking off, the man's wallet clutched in his fist. Ollie dashed after him, her heart galloping into her throat. This was not supposed to happen! The Artful Dodger never got caught.

Shouts of "Stop the boy!" and the pounding of boots followed them as they raced through the streets. Dodger slammed into a vegetable cart, sending the produce spinning over the cobbles behind him. Ollie stumbled over a rolling potato, and before she could right herself, arms grabbed her from behind. She struggled, pulled, and kicked, but they held her fast.

"That is the wrong boy," insisted the white-haired toff as he bent over and tried to catch his breath. "It was . . . the taller . . . dark-haired one."

"I saw this one hand off the wallet with me own eyes.

This be yer thief, sir," a gravelly voice claimed behind her. She twisted around to see the cop's belly protruding far over his boots. Likely he'd never catch his true target, and figured one tooler was as good as another.

"No! It wasn't me!" Ollie knew what they did with thieves. It was death by hanging or deportation to the Colonies, which was a drawn-out death at sea. She stopped struggling and implored the gentleman who was her only hope. "I didn't do it. I swear it on me mother!"

Ollie stared up into the man's kind face, pleading with her eyes. And then, as if his voice echoed through a long tunnel, she heard him say, "Release the boy."

"But sir, we cannot abide law breakers. This be for the magistrate to decide." The beak wrenched her arms tighter behind her back.

As the toff argued with the constable, Ollie spied a familiar crooked top hat peeking up from behind a wagon. She let out a slow breath. Dodger would come up with something. He was clever enough to save them both.

Dodger rose up and met her eyes. But then the boy's face hardened, all emotion leaching out of his expression, and in the blink of an eye he was gone, taking the man's wallet with him. All the air whooshed from Ollie's chest, like a kick to the ribs. An unfamiliar sensation stung the backs of her eyes, and her throat constricted. Blast it! She hadn't bawled since she was a toddler in nappies.

She swung back toward the white-haired gentleman, but he wouldn't meet her stare. He'd lost the fight. Her breath coming in shallow gasps, she stumbled over her feet as the copper led her away to face her sentencing.

It wasn't until Brom trotted up and sat at her feet that she realized her fingernails were digging crescent-shaped ridges into her palms. Her dog, ever the gentleman, tilted his head, one of his ears cocked in concern. "I'm all right, Brom. Give me that." She reached out, and he dropped the damp stick into her hand. Olivia surged to her feet and hurled the branch halfway across the square. She'd trusted Dodger with her life! And he'd rewarded that faith with betrayal.

Brom bounded after his prize in reckless abandon, and Olivia longed to race alongside him, to pump her legs in time with the indignation flaring through her chest. Curse her absurd skirts, anyway. If she'd been wearing her trousers and cap, she and Brom would sprint across the square and down to the river.

That's when she noticed the dog—his stick forgotten— watching a dark-haired man striding briskly through the square. "Well, how about that." Olivia set off to retrieve her errant pet, when she noticed the man stumble, then dance to the side with inherent grace. Something in the man's movements made her walk faster. He turned to stare at her dog, and the newsboy cap pulled low over his eyes did nothing to disguise his square chin or the determined angle of his jaw.

Dodger.

Olivia jogged to Brom, clicked his leash into place, and, ignoring the warnings in her head, followed her quarry at a distance. After adjusting the angle of her hat to partially cover her face, and tightening the sage-and-lime-striped ribbons under her chin, she quickened her pace.

She almost lost Jack when he cut in front of a chicken cart and ducked into a dark alley, and again when she came across a cluster of children huddled against a chimney. She stopped at the sight of fat tears streaking through the grime on a sandy-haired boy's face. He sat away from the others, nursing a bloodied lip. Olivia approached and handed the child a pound note. Wisely, he tucked the bill into his pocket, a secret smile on his face.

Olivia swallowed hard, said a prayer for the children as she continued on her way, and repeated in her mind: *I cannot save them all.* But she could get to Saffron Hill that night, and deliver the loot she'd collected over the last week. Those kids depended on her. Archie and Brit would keep the younger ones fed, but Chip's cough worried her. It had gone from a dry tickle to a wet bark, overnight.

Ahead, Dodger slipped around a corner, and Olivia picked up her pace. She lifted her skirt and stepped around a pile of refuse, yanking Brom's leash when he stopped to investigate. But when she turned, Dodger was gone. She rushed past a pair of young women pushing red roses in her face, two blooms for a penny, and spied a shop door closing with the clang of a bell.

Rushing forward, she stopped short and read the words painted on the shop window: *Paul's Pawnbroker Shop.* The cracked letters partially obscured her view as she watched Jack follow a squat man in an old-fashioned powdered wig behind the counter and out of sight. Brom sniffed at the opening where the door hadn't closed all the way, but Olivia pulled him back. She didn't even know what she hoped to accomplish with this little bit of sleuthing. So she stood outside and endeavored to look as if she belonged.

The shelf in the window displayed a random ensemble of cracked pottery, a plebeian calico shirt on a form, and a dusty garnet brooch. Shelves of merchandise lined the walls from floor to ceiling and racks of clothing divided the middle of the room. A perfect place for a young woman, such as herself, to shop and listen. Olivia led Brom inside and moved to browse a selection of threadbare dresses. A few moments later, the bell rang again and two rough-looking young men pushed into the store. Jerking her eyes back to the garish purple silk in front of her, Olivia attempted to remain unnoticed, but a low growl vibrated from Brom's chest, drawing the ruffians closer.

One was tall and angular, wearing a knit cap pushed back on his shaved head. The other one appeared almost as wide as he was tall, with brown curly hair and eyes the color of mud. Brom's rumble took on a menacing note as the men moved around the clothing racks and stopped, one on either side of her.

"Oh, tha's a nice poochy, now." The short one extended his hand to Brom's nose.

Olivia turned to find the tall one standing less than a foot away from her. "Well now, whot's a pretty lady like you doin' in old Paul's shop?" He picked up a silk ribbon from her hat and rubbed it between his fingers as he spoke. "You lookin' to make a trade?"

The glint in his eyes made Olivia's stomach constrict. She stepped back and turned toward the short one. "Just browsing, but my gentleman is meeting me here in a moment."

"Oh, is 'e now?" the tall one questioned, his eyes raking over her from head to toe.

"Me thinks the lady's skirt looks awful light. How 'bout you, Critch?" The short one chuckled at his own wit.

Olivia rolled her eyes. She may be a lot of things, even some unpleasant ones, but she was certainly no prostitute.

When the thugs began to pluck at the fabric of her dress, she knew it was time to make her exit. Narrowing her eyes, she stared the short one in the face and said, "Excuse me, sir, but I must be going."

"Not just yet." The one called Critch put a hand on her shoulder and spun her around.

Brom's bark exploded from his chest, his sharp, white teeth snapping. Moments later there was a blur, followed by a sickening clang, and the dog was silent.

"Brom!" Olivia bent and grabbed his muzzle between her hands; his soft brown eyes were open, but dazed. She glanced over her shoulder to find the short one holding a skillet and grinning. She surged to her feet, an inferno rising inside her, never before so grateful she was tall for a female. She towered over him as she hissed, "You slimy little toad! How dare you touch my dog?" The thug backed up, his eyes darting toward the door. Hysterical laughter echoed behind her and she whirled on Critch with a glare that could break glass, but he only looked more determined.

"I'm not done with you, little dolly," he muttered as he grabbed her by the shoulders and pulled her to his chest with a thump. Grasping his arms for leverage, Olivia hiked her knee up, and smashed it between his legs. With a groan, all the color drained from his face and he doubled over, his knit cap falling to the floor. When he raised his head, the viciousness in his expression trapped Olivia's breath in her throat. She stumbled back as his hand shot out and locked around her wrist.

"Fancy meeting you here, Miss Brownlow." The voice cut through the room like sharp-edged steel. With one glance at its source, the short one's mouth dropped open marionette-style, and he catapulted out the door with a harried clang of the bell.

"D-d-oddger?" Critch straightened and dropped her arm, his eyes flaring wide. He was taller than Jack, but his spine seemed to shrivel before her eyes, his neck almost disappearing into his collar.

Dodger leaned against the counter behind him. "I'm sure I don't know who ye mean."

Jack's appearance and the two thugs' transformation made Olivia long to head for the door herself, but her feet seemed to have grown roots. Brom nudged her hand, and she patted his furry head, gripping his leash like a lifeline.

"Dodger, man, it's me, Critch." He opened his hands in an imploring gesture. "I'd heard you got transported. But if you're back in town, I'm wit' you. That bloomin' Monks is takin' over everything. I'll pledge to you right here, man. Half of whot's mine is yers."

The shift in Dodger's expression reminded Olivia of shutters locking tight against a storm. In two strides, he crossed the room and slammed Critch against the shelves, china cups and dishes crashing to the floor at their feet. His face inches from the sniveling Critch, Jack rumbled, "The Dodger's dead and buried, you hear?"

Critch nodded, a droplet of crimson drawing a line down the pale skin of his throat where Dodger pricked him with a knife that seemed to have appeared out of nowhere.

"And if I hear of you even whispering that name in your sleep, Critch—" Dodger's face appeared flat as stone, but the vein in his neck pulsed visibly as he snarled, "You'll be joining him."

Dodger gave the terrified Critch a final slam against the shelving, sending a ceramic bowl smashing to the floor, and then turned his flame-blue gaze on Olivia. Her racing pulse stuttered to a halt as he stalked toward her, grasped her upper arm, and steered her toward the door. Brom growled low, digging in his feet. But before she could feel relief at her dog's heroics, Dodger poked the side of Brom's neck with two fingers and commanded, "Quiet."

All the tension left Brom's body as Dodger took the leash from Olivia's stunned fingers and led them both into the street.

So much for her loyal guard dog.

"No need to pout, Miss Brownlow. Your mutt merely senses I'm no danger to you."

Yet. He didn't say it, but the implied threat in the tone of his voice sent a series of chills skittering down Olivia's spine, making her knees go weak. He tightened his grip on her arm, supporting her weight until she regained the strength in her legs. What had she been thinking to follow him?

Long gone was the charming Irish gentleman, fake accent and all. Her survival instincts kicking in, Olivia squared her shoulders and spoke over the clatter of horse's hooves and squeak of wagon wheels against cobblestone. "Where are you taking me?"

"Somewhere we can talk."

Dodger steered them around a pair of street peddlers. One shouted the virtues of rat poison, while the other pushed rag dolls in Olivia's face, until Brom snapped at her and she scurried away. They turned onto a side street and passed a row of women washing bottles outside a tavern, two of the three stopping their work to stare openly at Dodger. Olivia couldn't say as she blamed them. She chanced a glance at his profile, the distinct slope of his nose, his black hair resting against the sun-kissed skin of his neck, firm lips relaxed in a perpetual smirk. Olivia shook her head. It would never do. "You're going to need a better disguise than a beat-up hat pulled over your eyes if you hope to convince everyone you're dead."

A muscle clenched in his jaw, and Olivia felt his entire body tense. But honestly, she should know. She'd learned a few things spending the first nine years of her life masquerading as a boy.

"People see what they want to see," he replied as they turned down a side street.

"Precisely. And it would seem quite a few people wish to see you."

They turned another corner and stopped. He still held her elbow as he looked down at her, something flaring in his gaze. Respect? Anger? Recognition? He stood so close she couldn't think, except to notice she only had to tilt her head a bit to see the blue of his eyes. He was barely half a head taller than she was, but his athletic build and the way he carried himself made him appear much larger. His fingers tightened on her arm, burning into her flesh. Brom gave a mournful whine, and Olivia stepped back, yanking her arm from Dodger's grasp.

They were in a narrow, dead-end passage surrounded on three sides by brick buildings, and, according to the smell, very near the river. Olivia grabbed Brom's leash and watched as Dodger moved to lean against a wall near the mouth of the alley, crossing his arms over his chest.

He watched her for several seconds before asking in a level voice, "Why were you following me?"

Olivia clenched her hand into a fist and threw out a question of her own. "Why were you robbing the Platts?" Her conscience pricked a bit as she thought of the silver frog. But she had her reasons.

He shrugged one broad shoulder. "Because I can."

It was so typically Dodger that Olivia bit her lip to keep from smiling. He'd once picked the pocket of an on-duty constable, simply because one of the other boys insisted it could not be done. He'd not only taken the copper's wallet, but his baton and cuffs as well. "Dodger . . ."

He pushed off the wall, his eyes chips of ice. "It's Jack." He stopped in front of her, arms still crossed over his chest. "How is it you think you know me, Miss Brownlow?"

For a fleeting moment, Olivia considered telling him the truth. But the impassive look on his face stopped the words from forming. Instead, she curled her lips and arched an eyebrow in a flirtatious expression she'd seen her cousin, Francesca, use to her advantage with men on several occasions. "What, you don't remember me?" She tilted her head. "I'm hurt."

He closed the space between them in a single step. His legs brushed her skirts, and Olivia drew in a startled breath. His scent filled her senses; crisp and clean like the air after a hard rain. In a quick, fluid motion, he untied the ribbon holding her silk cap in place and removed it from her head. His eyes roamed over her face, and her heart beat so hard she felt it in her throat. He leaned forward, bracing one hand against the wall above her head and bent close, his breath tickling the hairs by her ear. "I would never claim to be a saint, Miss Brownlow." His voice, soft and rich, melted her insides like butter. "But *you*, I would've remembered."

CHAPTER 3

Heat flooded Olivia's veins, and her vision dimmed, causing her to grip the rough brick wall at her back. Jack hovered over her. Too close. She caught the sweetness of apples on his breath as he leaned in, and her skin tingled in response to the movement. All they would need to do was turn their heads a fraction and their lips would meet. Anticipation sparked down her spine. But when several moments passed and he didn't move to touch her, a realization hit Olivia like a bucket full of icy water.

He's playing with me!

He hovered, waiting and ready to pounce as soon as she took the bait. As soon as she made the first move. Just like one of his marks.

Steeling her spine, Olivia turned her head toward him and moved a hand beneath his coat with deliberate slowness. She grasped the solid heat of his waist. "Perhaps . . ." she breathed into his ear.

He cocked his head, and when their eyes met, the ferocity in his blue gaze almost caused her to lose her nerve. Ignoring the twisting in her gut, she leaned in close, her mouth a hairsbreadth from his as she dipped her hand into the warmth of his pocket. ". . . I could refresh your memory."

He drew in a sharp breath and lowered his mouth to hers. But in that moment, Olivia ducked under his arm. She skipped away, waving the thick roll of pound notes she'd just pulled from his waistcoat.

Jack's eyes flared. "What the devil—" His expression turned dark, and he stalked toward her.

Olivia's fingers numbed, and she almost dropped her prize. She hadn't thought her plan through. There was no way she could outrun him in her blasted skirts. Jack advanced, his face set in hard, angry lines. She backed away, searching the alley for some kind of weapon. With a snarl, Brom leapt forward and sank his teeth into Jack's thigh.

He yelped and grabbed Brom's muzzle, trying to pry the animal off his flesh. "Call off your beast, or I swear I'll . . ."

"Brom, come!" The dog unclamped his jaws, narrowly avoiding a swipe of Jack's fist, and ran to her side.

Olivia glanced around the corner. Her path clear, she backed up several quick steps.

"Stop!" He tried to follow, but only succeeded in limping forward before reaching down to clutch his injured leg. "Dammit!"

Olivia shot Jack a triumphant grin, spun on her heel, and ran down the alley before she changed her mind and helped the bloomin' git.

⁓

Jack slammed into the townhouse, the door banging against the jam so hard a china plate slid from the wall and crashed to the floor.

"Mister MacCarron." Clyde, the March family's butler,

hobbled into the room, his stiff legs only able to carry him a few inches at a time. "Are you quite all right, sir?"

Remorse flared in Jack's chest, and he turned to gather the pieces of the shattered plate. "I've got it, Clyde." Jack bit the inside of his cheek, the pain in his leg flaring as he straightened and turned to face the old man. "But Lois won't be too pleased, eh?"

Clyde returned Jack's smile with a gap-toothed one of his own. "No worries, Mister MacCarron. I'll replace it straight away with another plate." He leaned in, and said in conspiracy, "She'll be none the wiser."

"That's a good man." Jack gave the butler's rail-thin arm a pat as he moved toward the stairs, concentrating hard on not limping. "And for the last time, call me Jack," he instructed over his shoulder before he mounted the first step.

"Yes, sir, Mister Jack."

Jack shook his head in bewilderment as he watched the butler shuffle out of the foyer. Upon his death, Lois March's husband left her with nothing but a household to run and debilitating gambling debts; and when the funds inevitably dried up, Clyde had been the only servant to stick around. As a result, the butler had witnessed Jack's transformation from street urchin to gentleman, making him very well aware Jack possessed no lineage, and that, in fact, he was no better than Clyde himself. Nevertheless, the old man insisted on treating him like bloomin' royalty—which only confirmed Jack's theory that people see what they choose to see.

And it would seem quite a few people wish to see you.

The words echoed in his head as he leaned heavily on the banister, ascending one slow step at a time. What did Olivia

Brownlow want from him, anyway? Just the thought of the girl made his blood boil. He *never* lost control. It was the first rule one learned on the streets—fail to restrain your emotions, and the desperation takes over. But, blast, if he hadn't almost kissed her on one of those same streets, his muscles shaking with the effort not to touch her.

Jack paused on the stairs, took a deep, mind-clearing breath, and dug his hand into his jacket pocket, pulling out the lacy bit of fluff and ribbons he'd taken off her head. Suppressing a growl, he shoved the delicate cap back into his pocket. He couldn't allow himself to care about the girl. She knew too much, and he needed to find out what she planned to do about it.

"Well, if it isn't the favored nephew. Been hitting the bottle early today, Jack?"

Oh, good grief. Jack resisted the urge to roll his eyes as he gripped the newel post and pulled himself up the last step, meeting the calculating gaze of Christopher March, Lois's grandson. Also known as a royal pain in his bum.

Crossing the few feet that separated them, Jack ignored the sharp ache in his leg and stopped in front of the tall, thin gentleman. "When did ye get into town, Topher?" Jack crossed his arms over his chest and leaned against the banister, just remembering to turn on his Irish brogue. "And more importantly, when do ye plan to leave?" Topher divided his time between Oxford and his mother's home in Hampshire, with the occasional perfunctory visit with his grandmother. But now that he'd finished his university studies, Jack feared the prat would become a more permanent fixture in his life.

Topher shoved his hands into his pockets, lips curving up

at the corners, his gray eyes as flat as coins. "Sorry to disappoint, old man, but I'm here for the winter season. Mum and Gran think 'tis high time I selected a bride." He arched a pale brow. "You know, to produce an heir and all that."

Christopher never let an opportunity pass to rub in the fact that he was the sole heir for both sides of his family. His father, Lois's only child, had passed years ago, and Topher had no other siblings, making him his mother's heir as well. Little did he know the fortune he'd be inheriting from his grandmother Lois would be nonexistent without Jack's nefarious skills.

"Excellent. Best o' luck with that." Jack pushed off the banister and moved past Christopher, headed for a good soak to cleanse his wound and ease the throbbing ache in his leg. *If I ever see that devil dog again . . .*

"Oh, and Jack?" Topher's hand snaked out, catching Jack's arm, causing him to flinch and spin, his fingers already gripping the hilt of his knife. Every nerve in his body urged him to return the unanticipated physical contact with deadly force. Luckily, his brain caught up before he could follow through and unsheathe his weapon. He forced the tension out of his shoulders and met Topher's gaze with a lazy smirk. "Aye?"

Topher had the intelligence to appear taken aback, but unfortunately that didn't stop his next string of accusations. "It's funny, but I was looking over some of Father's papers and came across a record of the March ancestry." Topher raised his chin, his usual unfounded confidence returning. "There's no record of Gran Lois having any siblings."

The smile froze on Jack's face, but he forced his next

words to be light. "One would think"—Jack shrugged away from Topher's grasp—"the heir to not one, but *two* bloody fortunes would have a better use for his time than trying to discredit his only cousin."

"I don't trust you," Topher hissed, his near-colorless eyes narrowing into slits.

"Of course ye don't. If you're so worried, take it up with Auntie Lois." He started back down the hall. "I'm sure she can clear the whole thing up for ye, laddie," Jack added, laying the accent on thick.

"Jaacckk!"

"Speak o' the devil," Jack muttered at the sound of Lois's birdlike shriek. He picked up his pace, and fire shot up his leg. Now he'd have to come up with a plausible excuse for losing the advance money for the Platts' bracelet, since the truth was too humiliating to repeat.

Jack clenched his teeth. Olivia Brownlow was going to pay.

Haze draped the skyline of the city like the oozing, yellow center of a stale egg. Peels of fog slithered and curled over the cobbles, striking at Olivia's heels. She turned north, passing by the apartments of Furnival's Inn on Holborn, her stride brisk and determined. The key to masquerading as a boy, besides the costume, boiled down to the walk—Brom's leash in loose fingers, shoulders back, chin up, hat pulled low.

When Olivia first began her nightly forays into the hells of London, her hair had proved the biggest challenge, but the heavy mass was now safely obscured in a net—obtained at an exorbitant price from a traveling theater company— covered by a short wig of muddy brown hair and topped with a newsboy cap for good measure. To complete her costume, she scooped dirt from her uncle's garden and smeared it with abandon on her cheeks, nose, and chin.

Grasping the top of her coat closed against a sudden damp chill, she turned up Chancery Lane, the lamps glowing dimmer and farther apart.

"Hullo, boy . . . only a half crown for you!" The call came from a group of young women huddled in front of Krook's Rag and Bone Shop. Olivia took them in with a glance: thick face paint, skirts tucked up to reveal dingy petticoats and torn stockings.

Olivia grunted a firm no and crossed to the other side of the street, ignoring the insults and bawdy propositions that followed her rejection. Her stomach clenched in sympathy for these women, their dead eyes beyond desperation.

But for the grace o' God, there go I. The words of her old nurse popped into her mind, reminding her if it hadn't been for the woman's perseverance in raising her as a lad, Olivia's fate may not have been different than the poor women ped- dling their wares for a pittance.

The sack of stolen knickknacks clinked together as she shifted the weight onto her other shoulder, reminding her of her task. She hoped the dishes, random pieces of flatware, mother-of-pearl hand brush and, of course, her friend the silver toad would feed the children for at least a week. The bread, quarter wheel of cheese, and pears she'd nabbed from the pantry should help too. She didn't dare take more, for fear of the quick accusations of their meticulous housekeeper, Mrs. Foster.

With a deep breath, she ducked into the network of alleys that would take her to Saffron Hill. The irony that this dilapidated slum was where she'd lived with Dodger for those pivotal months in her youth was not lost on her. Olivia grinned as she recalled the look of outrage on Jack's face that afternoon. Ah, revenge was sweet. The pound notes in her pocket were an unexpected boon, and would go far to prepare her boys for the winter months.

As Olivia passed behind the old workhouse, she lifted a lavender-scented kerchief over her nose and mouth in an attempt to filter the foul air. She skirted a pile of sleeping bodies, empty bottles strewn around their nest, a black rat sniffing the discarded trash.

Almost there.

Brom pulled ahead, sensing the proximity of his friends. Olivia glanced behind her one last time to ensure no one paid any mind to a boy and his oversized dog. When they reached the barricaded doorway, Brom sniffed the opening and then hopped through the narrow gap in the boards. Olivia dropped her satchel inside first and squeezed in behind him. Muted light from two glassless windows illuminated the abandoned home as they navigated around piles of filth and broken floorboards to a ruined staircase, the bottom stairs ripped from their moorings. Olivia pulled down her kerchief, pursed her lips, and whistled a short tune into the quiet. A few bangs followed by footfalls racing across the upper floor preceded the appearance of a single candle flame. A small blond head jutted over the edge of the landing.

"Ollie's 'ere!"

Olivia waved.

"Chip, you're supposed to ask for the password!" an older voice scolded before Archie's freckled face appeared beside Chip.

Olivia bit back a grin and nodded her agreement with Archie.

"All right," little Chip said in an exasperated tone. "Whot's the password, then?"

"Ichabod Crane," Olivia pronounced with clarity. A favorite story, "The Legend of Sleepy Hollow," spawned an inordinate amount of the boys' passwords.

"Get the board!" Archie ordered.

With a flurry of bangs and chatter, a slab of wood no wider than Olivia's shoulders lowered down the broken staircase. The moment the board connected with the floor, Brom scurried up. Olivia passed her knapsack to Archie before making her own ascent.

Moments later, they all gathered around the fireplace, a nice blaze dispelling the chill in the barren room. Moving their pallets, half the children huddled around Brom, lavishing him with affection, while the other half crowded around Olivia. With the exception of Brit, who stood, arms crossed, legs braced wide as if on the deck of a rolling ship. The unofficial leader of the Hill Orphans, as they called themselves, Brit took his responsibility with proper seriousness. Olivia estimated the dark-haired boy at eleven or twelve years of age, but his height and almost regal bearing made him appear much older. His feet and fists were the size of a grown man's, reminding Olivia of Brom when he was a pup, his huge paws portending his adult size. Tonight, she could see the weight of some unseen burden pushing down Brit's shoulders, trouble haunting his dark eyes.

Olivia lifted Chip's warm weight from her lap and began removing food from her bag as the boys continued to chatter about their exploits of the previous week. Archie squatted beside her, took out his knife, and cut the pears into equal portions as Olivia did the same with the bread and cheese. After she'd finished distributing the meager meal, she took a portion to Brit, who now leaned against the window frame, gazing up at the stars.

"What is it, Brit?" Olivia roughened her voice. Even though she suspected some of them guessed her secret, she kept up the pretense. Brit remained silent as she handed him the food, and she noted he'd grown again; the top of his head was even with her eyes.

He finished off the food in two bites, leaned against the sill, and then traced a letter *B* on the frost-coated glass before wiping it clean and beginning on an *R*. Olivia's chest ached as she stared at the brilliant boy's profile, his jaw tight with anxiety. Leadership followed him, whether he chose it or not. He'd been born with that indescribable quality that drew others to him. Much like someone else she knew.

Brit wiped away the last letter of his name and then looked down at his feet, his long, dark lashes brushing the apples of his cheeks. He worked so hard to hide his own needs, but for all his bravado, he was still a child. She longed to take him and all the others home, clean them up, feed them until they could eat no more, and tuck them into a row of cozy beds, just like Snow White and her tiny men. But her uncle had denied that request long ago. Perhaps he didn't believe he had the funds, but she would do everything within her power to help these lost little boys.

Olivia cleared her throat and punched Brit on the arm. "Talk, boy. I don't have all night."

Brit responded with a wry half grin. "Where ye off to in such a hurry, Ollie? Have a fancy waitin' for you?"

"That hurts my heart, it does." Olivia put a fist to her chest in mock outrage. "Do you think I'd put a lady before my dearest friends?"

Brit chuckled at the floor and shook his head.

"How has Chip's cough been?"

Brit's mouth set in a grim line before he met her eyes and answered, "Improved. But sometimes when he sleeps, he sounds like he's got chains rattlin' in his chest."

Olivia glanced behind her at the child, his golden curls bouncing as he rode Brom's back like a jockey on a racehorse. Brom rested his triangular head on his crossed paws and endured the humiliation admirably. Over a year ago, she'd been volunteering at St. Bart's and met little Chip. Hacking and pale, he'd been crouched on the front steps of the hospital in tears. She'd stopped to speak to him, wishing to help anyway she could, when a tug on her shoulder made her spin around to find Archie nabbing her purse. Instead of calling for the beaks, she'd followed the thief covertly and discovered a group of boys residing by the docks, freezing and half starved. She'd returned that very night disguised as their benefactor; the working class young man, Ollie.

Chip's energy had returned since last she'd seen him, but he remained a bit pale. "Keep an eye on him, Brit. We may need to get him to a doctor."

"We don't need the help of no blasted crow." Brit crossed his arms tighter over his chest. Olivia had forgotten his deep aversion to doctors and wondered, not for the first time, what caused it.

"What's got you so riled up, anyway?"

"Could be nothin'. There's a new thug roughin' up some of the street kids. Tryin' to make a name for himself by takin' what ain't his. I heard he's vamping on some of the orphan groups. Sending them on jobs and takin' the loot." Brit shrugged. "You know old Fawks?"

She thought for a moment and then remembered the salty veteran missing his left hand. He told different stories about how he lost it every time someone asked. He'd worked the streets around St. Bart's since she'd been part of Dodger's gang.

"Sure, distracts with his stump and robs with his right."

Brit captured his bottom lip between surprisingly straight teeth before continuing. "He was found murdered two nights past. Rumors have it, he wouldn't give Monks a cut."

"Have you seen him around here?"

"Not yet." He turned to Olivia, eyes blazing. "And we better not. We don't need no kidsman. I can protect this lot on my own!"

All the playful chatter by the fireplace stopped. And Olivia turned to see the other boys watching them with wide eyes. Archie, who'd been sorting through the treasures in Olivia's bag, shot to his feet. "Aye, we don't!"

Then fifteen other voices chimed in agreement. Boys jumped to their feet, pumping their little fists in the air, sending Brom to scurry away from the hubbub.

"Quiet now, boys," Olivia commanded as she moved in front of the fire. "No need for a riot. I agree with Brit." The boys calmed. "Brit, what'd you say this bludger's name is?"

"He goes by Monks."

"Monks," she repeated, wondering where she'd heard that name before.

She was still repeating it when she waved goodbye to the boys and started home.

Turning onto Pall Mall, her feet aching and eyes drooping, she counted the fourth booming chime of Big Ben in the distance. Her eyes widened as the memory snapped into place. In the pawnshop, that bald ruffian Critch had said something about needing protection from Monks.

"Come on, Brom," Olivia whispered, yanking him away from a pile of horse manure in the street, and picking up her pace. "Mrs. Foster will be out of bed soon."

Before she'd left the Hill, Olivia had pulled Brit and Archie aside, giving them half of the cash she'd taken from Dodger, with instructions to purchase clothing, boots, and blankets in preparation for winter. She'd planned to give them the entire amount, she trusted them enough, but after hearing about this Monks character, she knew copious amounts of cash flow could draw unwanted attention.

Olivia breathed a sigh of relief as they approached the dark townhome. Four in the morning was cutting it too close for comfort. Rounding the corner of the house, they entered the back garden and shimmied behind the bushes. Olivia froze. The pantry window, which she'd left cracked, stood wide open. Her pulse jumped to double time as she boosted Brom into the house, climbed inside, and quietly shut the window behind her. Had Mrs. Foster found her missing and left the window open in warning? Considering the healthy dose of laudanum Olivia had slipped into the woman's tea, it seemed unlikely.

She removed Brom's leash, letting him find his own way to bed, and then removed her boots and tiptoed through the quiet house. Running her fingers along the wall to guide her through the pitch-dark hallway, Olivia finally made it to the sanctity of her room. She shut the door softly behind her and moved to light a single candle. As the flame grew, Olivia moved to sit on the bed and then jumped back up with a gasp.

Perched on the middle of her snowy coverlet, the green silk ribbons tied in a deft bow, sat her missing cap. The one Jack had removed from her head that very morning.

CHAPTER 4

Francesca Lancaster swept into the Cramsteads' drawing room as if she were taking tea with Queen Victoria. Her black curls bounced becomingly against blue silk-clad shoulders, and Olivia wondered, not for the first time, how the sausage-shaped ringlets stayed so springy. The distinct fragrance of roses and lilacs tickled Olivia's nose as her cousin flounced into the chair beside her.

"Hullo, my darlings." Francesca tilted her head in greeting, sending the feathers, lace, and gewgaws adorning her enormous hat into a riotous dance. Olivia suppressed the urge to throw her arms over the tea and cakes for their protection.

She hadn't realized she was leaning forward and staring into the forest atop her cousin's head until Violet grabbed her arm and yanked her back into her seat. Olivia sat back, her eyes still glued to the woodland scene. "Good gracious. Is that a stuffed owl?"

"What a lovely fascinator, Francesca. Is it new?" Violet crooned, talking over Olivia's question and shooting her a silencing glare.

"Oh, yes! Isn't it divine?" Francesca settled her skirts around her chair and then touched the hat reverently. "Madam Fanchon says they are all the rage in Paris."

"I'll bet," Olivia muttered, earning a swift kick from Violet's pointy boot. She shifted her legs out of range, arched an eyebrow at her good friend, and saw the corner of Violet's mouth twitching. Violet and Francesca's mothers were sisters, while Olivia was a cousin on her mother's side. As a result, she endured Francesca for Vi's sake. But when the girl showed up wearing hats the size of a small village—that likely cost enough to feed one—Olivia's tolerance strained its boundaries.

Violet poured as Francesca rattled on about the wonders of her dressmaker. Like a hawk sensing prey, Fran turned her assessing stare on Olivia. "You must accompany me to Madame Fanchon's shop this afternoon, Olivia. The woman can do miracles with even the dullest coloring."

Ignoring her cousin's not so veiled insult, Olivia glanced down at her pale yellow frock without much interest. As with all her dresses, Vi had helped her make the selection, and it suited her as well as any other. Image was important to her uncle, or she'd likely be wearing the same three dresses in perpetual rotation.

"You ought to wear colors that play down that ghastly tint to your skin." Francesca's eyes swept over Olivia's face and neck. It was true that Olivia loved the sun, its warmth too delicious to resist. "I mean really, Olivia, you ought to use a parasol. You look as if you have been working alongside the gardener!"

Francesca paused in her tirade to nibble a pink-frosted petit four, and all Olivia could think about was how Chip's face would look if she managed to smuggle some of the square-shaped cakes to the Hill. But there weren't enough for each of the children, and in any case they'd be smashed beyond recognition if she stuffed the remainder in her small reticule. But if she stopped off at the kitchen before she left, perhaps they would have enough.

"Olivia Brownlow! Are you listening to me?" Francesca demanded as she set her cup on the saucer with a resounding clink.

Olivia blinked at her cousin and dropped her hand from the egg-shaped locket around her neck, not wishing Fran to notice her nervous tic. "Of course, Fran. I'll accompany you to your modiste. I haven't purchased a formal gown in ages. In fact, I'm in need of something to wear to the Grimwigs' ball."

"Well, that doesn't give us much time, does it? The ball is in less than a fortnight." Francesca tapped a fingernail against her lips. "But I'm certain Madam can come up with something suitable, even if it is not custom."

That settled, the conversation shifted to various subjects that didn't involve Olivia's inadequacies as a properly turned-out lady. Topics that only required her occasional nod or monosyllable agreement, until a single word pulled at her attention.

". . . MacCarron."

Olivia froze, the dollop of Devonshire cream meant for her scone landing on her plate with a plop. She'd been unable to get more than a few hours' sleep since he'd snuck into her room and deposited the cap on her bed. Her trepidation forced her up multiple times during the night to ensure the window and door were locked tight.

Francesca's face flooded with color as she continued, "He's quite glorious. And those eyes! Good gracious, he stares as if he can see one's deepest, darkest secrets." The throaty giggle that followed scraped across Olivia's brain like a knife against china.

"Last week at the Dells' musicale he shed his coat, took

the stage, and played the most haunting melody on the violin." Francesca propped her chin on her fist with a heavy sigh. "I thought I would swoon at the sight of his strong hands so expertly manipulating that delicate instrument."

Olivia choked, almost spewing the tea from her nose. After several moments of Vi pounding her on the back with enthusiasm, Olivia regained her ability to breathe. Dodger's skills with a beat-up fiddle had driven away the cold and boredom many nights on the Hill, but Francesca's recollection implied quite a different type of warming.

"Honestly, Fran!" Violet exclaimed, her freckled cheeks flushed red. "Mr. MacCarron is quite handsome, but . . . but . . . he is not in the least suitable," she sputtered. Olivia had to agree, considering what she knew of Jack's background and his current penchant for attending high society events with the sole purpose of robbing the family blind.

"Don't be such a prude." Francesca waved her hand as if dismissing her cousin's concern. "Whoever said what I have in mind is suitable?"

"How perfectly revolting," Olivia remarked in her most blasé tone.

Francesca narrowed her gaze at Olivia in challenge. "You've never thought about a dalliance with anyone? Isn't there some gentleman who makes your blood boil? A man who could compel you to throw caution to the wind?"

Violet, her eyes wide as green saucers, sat straight up in her chair.

Olivia met Francesca's stare. "I am not dead, Fran. But there is such a thing as duty. Not to mention morality—"

"You can't tell me," Francesca's words trampled over

Olivia's, "that flop Grimwig makes butterflies dance in your belly?"

Memories of the one disappointing kiss she'd shared with Maxwell filled Olivia's mind, followed swiftly by visions of Jack's warm body surrounding hers in the alley. An odd heat spread low in her stomach as she recalled how close his lips had come to hers. Olivia cleared her throat. "It's nearly four. Oughtn't we be off to Madam Fanchon's?"

A tiny smile curved the corners of Francesca's mouth. "Of course. I want to commission a gown that will ensure Mr. MacCarron's unrelenting attention."

Olivia set her napkin on the table and stood abruptly, prompting her cousins to follow suit. But Francesca wasn't finished. "He simply could not take his eyes from me at the musicale."

Ha! Her jewels, more like. Francesca never left the house without some form of extravagant bauble. The sapphire earbobs she wore now would be worth her life to someone like Dodger. But a tiny doubt niggled through her mind; Jack would be drawn to the challenge her gorgeous, well-to-do cousin presented.

And there is no earthly reason why I should care, Olivia chastised herself.

❦

It was a fool's errand, and Jack could freely admit that he was the fool. He knew little of soliciting acquaintances or courtship rules, and even less about phony ones. But here he was, strolling—or limping, as the case may be—down New

Bond Street, toward Cavendish Square, a calling card tucked in his pocket. Clyde, God bless him, had come up with one of Mr. March's tall, black umbrellas. The old brolly allowed Jack to lean upon it as he hobbled, affording him a modicum of dignity.

The heart of Mayfair pulsed with energy. A rare afternoon of sunshine had turned New Bond Street into a crush as hundreds of the wealthiest people in London ambled with languorous, sophisticated grace down the main thoroughfare past decorated shop windows, searching for a place to part with their money. The street thug in him reared his ugly head, happy to oblige, but the gentleman Jack MacCarron limped on.

Snippets of Chopin flooded from the open doors of an upscale dining room, where the scents of rich sauces and slow-roasted chops made Jack's mouth water. Men in high hats and tailed coats escorted their women, tempting them with all manner of luxuries from rich chocolate to the latest bonnet style to glittering jewels. Clusters of ladies in water-colored silks twirled parasols and gossiped behind gloved hands. A girl with familiar honey-colored hair, wearing a jade-green frock, strolled down the other side of the street with lively grace. But as she drew closer, Jack could see that it was not the woman he sought.

Lois had not believed his concocted story of a street robbery. Jack was unsure if she thought him incapable of being accosted in his own element or if she'd read the subterfuge on his face, but the shadow of distrust that lingered in the woman's faded blue eyes stabbed him in the heart. True, the Platt bracelet brought a larger advance than anything they'd attempted to hock thus far, but Jack would never swindle Lois. She'd been far too good to him.

The scents of fresh biscuits and sugared fruit tarts filled the air as Jack approached the striped awning of a teashop. On such a beautiful day, the windows were thrown wide and the tables were filled with women wearing all manner of extravagantly trimmed hats. Eyes followed him, and he endeavored to straighten his stride as he touched the brim of his top hat and nodded to a group of posh young ladies. He was rewarded with blushes and giggles, a reaction that never got old. Jack felt his chest puff, and the ache in his leg faded just a bit. Living on the streets, dignified women looked through him on the daily. All it had taken for them to see him was a well-fabricated lineage, the right clothes and manner, and suddenly their doors—and safes full of valuables—were wide open to him. And in many cases, their regard.

His new way of life was in mortal danger, however, because of one fearless girl: Miss Olivia Brownlow. Admittedly, sneaking into her home in the dead of night just to deliver an enjoyable little scare had been all kinds of madness, but finding her bed empty drove him to distraction. Questions had circled his mind ever since. Where could she have gone? And had she been alone?

That lovely little thief had thwarted him, yet again. So he'd decided that if he could not get to her his way, he would play the toff, as he'd become so blasted good at.

Turning onto Oxford Street, Jack quickened his pace. Grinding his teeth against the pain, he envisioned the confrontation to come. He would find out exactly what the girl knew about his past life and regain his capital, or she would not enjoy the consequences. A tremor beneath his fingers alerted him to loosen his grip on the umbrella handle he clutched in a death grip.

Steady on, Jack.

He took a deep breath and focused outside himself. As he exhaled, he noticed the shadowy patterns on the sidewalk, created by the sun shining through the shifting leaves. A lady and her two daughters approached, their skirts sweeping against the cobblestones like a thousand whispers. Jack tipped his hat, his shoulder muscles unclenching as he relaxed into an easier stride. The townhomes in this section of the city were more narrow and less grand than in St. James, with a few small businesses sprinkled in amongst the residences. The occasional carriage rumbled past, but overall, Cavendish Square seemed a peaceful little quarter.

After finding the correct number on the neat, brick brownstone, Jack walked carefully up the steps to the cheery blue door and engaged the knocker. As he heard footfalls approaching, he dug out the calling card in his jacket pocket. A stately man opened the door and inclined his head. "May I help you, sir?"

"Is Miss Brownlow at home?" Jack inquired, fairly certain that if the girl was at home, she would not be at home for *him*.

"Why, no, sir—"

Unwilling to take no for an answer, Jack thrust his card at the butler and stepped into the entryway, forcing the man to take a step back. "I'll wait." He swept off his hat and pressed it into the wide-eyed codger's chest.

"Sir, I have no inclination when the lady will return. But I would be glad to pass along your card." He clutched the rectangle of paper, holding it between them like a tiny shield.

"That's quite all right." Jack stepped farther into the house and turned toward the open doorway of a sunny room, decorated in shades of yellow, gold, and white. "The drawing room, I presume?" Jack glanced over his shoulder to see the butler's tight nod. "I'll be comfortable here."

"Yes, sir." The butler shot him a glare before he turned his back and stomped down the hall. Jack imagined the old man was likely off to shred his hat in the meat grinder.

Hats were replaceable. With a shrug, Jack moved across the room to the front windows. The overstuffed chairs called to him, but if he sat, he was unsure he could get back to his feet without the pain showing on his face, and he refused to give *her* the satisfaction. Turning away from the window, he wondered if the hell-beast was in the house or if she took him everywhere she went.

As he perused the comfortable elegance of the room, he was drawn to a portrait hanging over the unlit fireplace. At first, Jack assumed it was Miss Brownlow—waves of dark-gold hair swept up from the graceful bones of her face, mischievous eyes the color of bronze in the sun. But no, the chin was a bit weaker, the smile too demure, the lips not quite as full. He moved closer.

Olivia Brownlow was a mystery. Without doubt, she was beautiful—even more so than the woman in the painting. But it was more than her beauty that drew him like a moth to a blasted flame. There was something about her that brought out a fierce side of him, something primitive that made him want to throttle her one minute and protect her the next. In the pawnshop with Critch hovering over her, it had taken every bit of Jack's self-control not to rush the bloke and knock him out cold.

A rhythmic clicking caused him to spin away from the painting. The devil-dog sat in the doorway, tongue lolling out of his large, triangular head. "Ho, Brom. Back for seconds, eh?"

The mutt stood, trotted over to Jack, and sniffed his pant leg in the precise spot where he'd sunk his teeth into his flesh.

Jack stiffened, but Brom gave him a sheepish look and licked his trousers, leaving an enormous wet spot behind. "So you want to make up, do you?" Jack arched a brow at the dog's huge, liquid eyes. "I'm not sure I'm ready to forgive and forget."

The sound of male laughter echoed toward him, and Jack's head snapped up. Giving Brom a pat, Jack moved to position himself so he could see the entryway. An older gentleman, stooped over a cane and wearing a house robe, faced a tall, stringy man whom Jack recognized from the Platts' dinner party. Maxwell Grimwig, the bloke who'd introduced him to Miss Brownlow. Jack stood as still as a statue, listening.

"Max, my boy, I knew you would come through. Olivia is like a daughter to me, and I will see her happy and settled. Thank you for giving me that peace of mind." The old man choked, and then coughed so hard it sounded like he might break a bone.

"Mr. Brownlow, can I get you anything?" Maxwell patted the old gentleman on the back, quite unhelpfully, until the butler entered and handed Mr. Brownlow a cup of steaming liquid.

After taking a restorative drink and wiping the moisture from his eyes, Mr. Brownlow said, "I am fine."

"Sir, be assured I will be the best husband in the world to your niece. I've cared for her for a long time."

The word hit Jack like a blow to the chest. *Husband?* He could not imagine a wildcat like Olivia married to the staunch, ever-proper Grimwig.

"I know you will, Maxwell. Olivia is headstrong and not always"—the old man paused as if searching for the right words—"decorous. But it reassures me that now you know of her past, you will have a better understanding of her ways."

Grimwig glanced down, and a frown pulled at the corners of his mouth. But when he turned back to face Brownlow, his smile was back in place. "Of course, sir."

"I must rest now, son. But Olivia will be thrilled." Mr. Brownlow turned and began shuffling back down the hall. "Come by for dinner soon."

"I will, sir," Grimwig called as he took his hat and umbrella from the butler.

Jack sunk back out of view, his mind racing with questions. Why did old man Brownlow sound as if he were apologizing for something in Olivia's past?

He heard the front door shut and turned to see Grimwig strolling down the street, his lips pursed in a whistle. What was it about the bloke that made Jack want to punch the tune from his mouth? Jack looked down and found Brom gazing out the window, following Maxwell's progress. "He's hiding something, isn't he, boy? And I aim to find out what."

CHAPTER 5

Mrs. Pickney Price requests the pleasure
of Miss Olivia Brownlow's company at
a Dinner Party, on Monday, October 29.

AN ANSWER WILL OBLIGE.

Dancing.

O livia glanced at the card one last time and tucked it
inside her reticule as the coach pulled up to the glowing mansion. For some inexplicable reason, she felt it
necessary to carry the proof of her invitation on her person.
This, unfortunately, did not go unnoticed by the other occu-
pants of the vehicle.

"I find it extraordinarily diverting that you continue to
read that card as if the words may have changed in the last
two minutes," Francesca commented as she tugged on her
gloves and pressed the seams between each finger. "Is there
some code in the writing which you are trying to decipher?"

Before Olivia could concoct an adequate reply, Mrs.
Lancaster remarked, "Olivia is simply being thorough. Something you could take a lesson on, dear." The distinguished
older woman fluffed her salt-and-pepper curls as she pinned

her daughter with a stare of reproach. "You put entirely too much reliance on the servants, Frannie."

"That is what they are for, is it not?" Francesca lifted her chin and stared at her mother as the door opened. A crisp breeze carrying the tang of wood smoke swirled into the carriage, ruffling the hairs around Olivia's face. After several uncomfortable beats, Fran dropped her gaze from her mother, and then turned to the footman, taking his extended hand.

For the tenth time, Olivia wished her aunt Becky could be her chaperone that evening. But Violet and her mother were on the other side of town attending a party Aunt Becky proclaimed would result in Violet's imminent betrothal. Poor Vi. Her mother carted her out in front of every eligible young man like a pony at auction. With a sigh, Olivia smoothed her peach-colored skirts and followed Aunt Katrina out of the carriage.

Olivia viewed the moment of arrival at a dinner party as if it were a brightly wrapped package. Each guest was handpicked by the hostess for either optimum equanimity or maximum drama, and not knowing the mix created a moment of salacious anticipation. The instant she walked into the Prices' drawing room and spied the widow, Lois March, she knew what sort of party this would be, and the knowledge sparked a flutter of excitement in her chest. Harmony was overrated, and deadly dull.

With a lift of her chin, she began to mingle. She exchanged inanities with several acquaintances before pausing in a cluster of Francesca's friends. "Then, I told him he was quite the wittiest thing in all creation." Frannie's voice, half a pitch higher than normal, cut through the chatter around them, drawing the attention her cousin craved.

Not wishing to contribute to her narcissism, Olivia turned and searched the room to find Mrs. March laughing with a young, blond gentleman with whom Olivia was not acquainted. Tall and thin, but broad of shoulder, he wore his black-and-white formal attire as if he had been born in it. Their eyes met across the room, and the young man raised his pale brows and nodded in her direction before he turned back to the still guffawing older woman.

"That's Topher March, Lois's only grandson," said Francesca's plump, brunette friend, who Olivia thought might be named Marcie or Maggie, or perhaps Mildred. Something with an *M*, she was quite sure. But having met the girl more than once, she simply could not ask. This sort of conundrum was exactly why she needed Violet by her side.

"Yes, and Mr. March is the sole heir to not one but *two* fortunes. I simply must be seated with him this evening," Francesca asserted.

"Must you, Fran?" Olivia arched a single brow at her cousin. "Are you quite certain he is the *most* eligible bachelor in the room? Perhaps you ought to wait and see who else will be in attendance before staking your claim."

Francesca's lips stretched into a tight smile before she replied, "How very thoughtful, Olivia. You are absolutely right. I shall await all of the arrivals before pressing my case with Mrs. Price."

Olivia met Fran's dark eyes and accepted the unspoken challenge. "Whomever your escort is this evening, dear Frannie, I'm quite sure he will be infinitely . . . appropriate. Now, if you will excuse me."

With a nod, Olivia turned and made her way across the

room, smiling along the way, but not pausing in her quest to reach the Marches. When she glanced over, she noted that Mr. March tracked her progress. Barely resisting the urge to check and see if Fran had noticed the gentleman's attentions, she completed her rounds, and when she finally reached Mr. March's side, he greeted her with a short bow.

"Mrs. March." Olivia bobbed a curtsy to the hunched, yet somehow regal, old woman.

"Why, Miss Brownlow, how very lovely to see you, dear. You are looking quite . . ." She paused, her faded, hazel eyes flowing over Olivia from head to toe then returning to her face with a twinkle. ". . . trim."

A short laugh burst from Olivia's throat at the woman's subtle reminder of their first meeting, when she'd commented Olivia ate like a pregnant cow. "Yes, I've been somewhat negligent in my culinary pursuits of late."

Mrs. March's cheeks lifted as she met Olivia's eyes, a new appreciation glowing there. "Miss Brownlow, may I present my grandson, Mr. Christopher March."

"Mr. March, I am so pleased to make your acquaintance." Olivia curtsied to the attractive gentleman, all the while watching out of the corner of her eye for Francesca. When she met Mr. March's gray gaze, she lifted her brows and quirked her mouth in an attempt at flirtation. "Why is it we have never met?"

"Topher's just completed his education at Oxford. Isn't that right, my boy?" Mrs. March spoke several decibels above normal conversation, the feathers on her puce hat trembling in response.

"Yes, my certification was a dual focus in finance and

business. Top of my class." Mr. March clutched his jacket lapels and leaned in as if he spoke in confidence. "Rather necessary when one will soon be managing *two* landed estates."

"Yes, quite." Obviously, Mr. March's wealth had been recently gained, otherwise he would not find it necessary to proclaim it. New or old money was of no consequence to Olivia, but if this braggart was the most eligible bachelor at the party, she'd rather sit with the butler. She began to search the room for her cousin's dark head in earnest, hoping to arrange an introduction.

"My mother's family estate, Woodcreek Park, is over a hundred acres in Hampshire. She is planning a lavish house party during Christmas. I'd be glad to add you to the guest list, Miss Brownlow." Mr. March's odd, pale eyes swept over Olivia's face, one corner of his mouth curling. "If you're so inclined, that is?"

The invitation was clear, but Olivia had no desire to spend any length of days confined with this gentleman. "I—"

"Being inclined would imply the lady had an interest, Toph." Jack's cool voice caused an instant heat across Olivia's skin. "And it is clear she does not."

Propriety forgotten, her head swiveled in search of the speaker. Jack, handsomely turned out in a navy blue coat, appeared at Mrs. March's side as if out of thin air.

"Oh, Jack!" Mrs. March practically yelled. "I am so pleased you changed your mind about attending."

With Jack's presence, the room brightened, as if several more candelabras followed him into the room. A smile that seemed to originate deep in Olivia's chest stretched her lips without her consent. And froze there as revelation stopped her breath. She'd been searching for him—for Dodger—all these years. In every dirty face, every outstretched hand and orphan she helped, she'd searched for her childhood mate, the boy who'd taken her under his wing when she'd had no one. But why?

She watched his left hand where he rubbed his thumb across the pads of his fingers in a nervous tell he'd had since childhood. His shoulders straight, his lips pressed into a casual smirk, it was the only indication of the vast emotion brewing inside him.

It was true he'd left her to her fate that long-ago day. But as a result, hadn't she been taken in by her uncle, whilst Jack had been left to muck out a living on the streets?

Perhaps she'd been the one who had left him behind, not the other way around.

Ridiculous. Before he could see, she straightened her spine and flattened her expression, but her external control did nothing to calm the galloping of her heart.

"Jack, old man." Topher punched Jack's upper arm with a bit too much force to be considered companionable. "Your plans at the gaming hell fall through?"

"Something like that." Jack dismissed Topher's barb and turned to Olivia. Barely restrained ferocity lurked beneath his ice-blue eyes as they fixed on her face. "Miss Brownlow, how very good to see ye again."

"And you, Mr. MacCarron." She sounded breathless as she dropped into a rigid curtsy.

Jack cocked his head to the side, his eyes narrowing on Olivia's head. Without thinking, she touched a gloved hand to the green and coral garland of flowers woven into her hair, hoping the elaborate coiffure had not fallen.

"What a flattering hair ornament, Miss Brownlow. But I do believe I prefer that ruffled cap ye wore the other day." Jack paused as if searching his memory. "Cream with green ribbons, I believe?"

Olivia sucked in a breath. Would he give her away? Accuse her of stealing? He couldn't possibly confront her without the risk of implicating himself. *Could he?* She should have anticipated this moment.

Fighting to regain her polite countenance, she quipped, "Why, Mr. MacCarron, how observant of you. I had no idea you had such a burning interest in fashion."

"Nor I," said Topher with relish. "But it explains quite a lot."

The two men exchanged heated glares, and Olivia worried that they might come to blows.

"Excuse me, Mr. MacCarron." The hostess, Mrs. Price, rushed to the edge of their little group with Francesca hovering by her side. "I believe you have met the lovely Miss Lancaster. Would you mind terribly escorting her to dinner this evening?"

Fran directed a smug grin at Olivia before her face fell back into its usual pouty, yet enticing mien. The transformation from spoilt brat into sensual temptress almost made Olivia laugh. Almost.

"Indeed." Jack turned and bowed over Francesca's hand, his lips lingering a moment too long on her gloved knuckles. Something bitter rose in Olivia's throat as Fran curtsied to Jack, a pretty flush pinkening her cheeks before she took his arm and he led her away.

"Dear Miss Brownlow." Mrs. Price bustled forward,

fanning her blotchy face. "I've been informed Mr. Grimwig has been detained. Which is good, since Mr. MacCarron's arrival would make an odd number. But I think Mr. March shall suit as your dining partner, yes?"

"Yes, of course." The words had not finished leaving Olivia's lips before Mrs. Price flitted off to organize another pairing.

Olivia glanced at Topher March and then over at her cousin, who stood so close to Jack that her dark curls brushed the midnight blue of his coat. Jack leaned into her with a chuckle, clearly amused by their conversation. Fran's wishes for a "dalliance" with Jack fresh in Olivia's mind, she turned away from the couple and set her jaw.

It would seem her cousin had won this battle after all.

Jack watched the amethyst-and-diamond earbobs wink from between Miss Lancaster's dark curls, teasing him like a can-can dancer's ankles. The chit had babbled nonstop between every bite of the last seven courses. But all Jack could think about was getting her alone, quieting those chatty lips, and slipping her jewels into his pocket. Well, that and the atrocity occurring at the other end of the table—his blasted "cousin" charming the devil out of Miss Olivia Brownlow.

Jack leaned back and shot a glance down the table. Topher was making a clownish face and wiggling in his seat, presumably doing some sort of impression, while Olivia grinned, a single round dimple appearing in her right cheek. Something about her face tugged at long-buried memories of his youth, stealing his breath. But how could that be? Anything reminiscent of his childhood would find him living in the streets, far, far from Olivia's glittering world of privilege.

". . . MacCarron? *Mr.* MacCarron!"

The air returned to Jack's lungs in shallow degrees. He turned to the woman batting his arm as if she were trying to kill an insect and snapped, "Yes, Miss Lancaster?"

The woman froze mid-swat, her eyes widening and cheeks flushing. With effort, Jack relaxed the muscles of his face and offered a smile. "Is everything all right, lass? Could there be a fly in your meringue, perhaps? I'll notify a footman posthaste." Jack lifted his arm, pretending to search for a servant, until Miss Lancaster tugged his arm down by the sleeve.

"Stop, sir! My meringue is perfect." Her delicate hand lingered on his arm as she lowered her lashes and then gazed up at him with inviting dark eyes, the violet jewels at her ears catching flames of candlelight.

Jack calculated the size and value of the gems as he met her gaze. One missing earbob could be easily explained, and the theft would be quite a pleasant one to execute. Now, how to get her alone? Once he found a quiet corner, the act itself would take a matter of moments.

A servant reached between them to set a glass on the table, breaking their connection. Jack brought the flute to his lips, the sweet nectar gliding down his throat as he glanced around the table noting the glazed eyes, overly loud laughter, and flushed cheeks around him. Perhaps getting Miss Lancaster alone would not be so difficult.

A boisterous laugh drew his gaze down the table, past

Olivia. Lois met his stare through the shimmering candelabras and sparkling crystal, the levity of her regard resetting
Jack's priorities in an instant. A pleasant encounter with Miss
Lancaster, no matter how lovely her jewels, could not replace
the advance money he'd lost to Miss Olivia Brownlow, or the
trust it had cost him with his benefactor.

Getting to Olivia, however, might prove a challenge.
Topher appeared quite enchanted by the girl. In that exact
moment, he was leaning over her, whispering something in
her ear, and Olivia's full lips slanted in an expression Jack had
once mistaken for enticement. Right before she'd ripped the
money from his pocket. Topher appeared similarly seduced.
As far as Jack was concerned, the conniving duo could have
one another. But his unfinished business with the girl simply
could not wait.

After dessert, the party made their way into the hall, and
the hostess explained they would be forgoing the custom-
ary separation of the sexes for some after-dinner dancing.
The woman was considered progressive in her views, which
served Jack's purposes precisely. Seeing no need to prolong the
inevitable, he maneuvered Miss Lancaster through the crowd
until they were directly behind Topher and Miss Brownlow.

"Excuse me, old man," Jack placed a hand on Topher's
shoulder just as he was about to lead Olivia to the dance
floor. "But Miss Brownlow promised this first dance to me."

Topher spun on his heel, his jaw set in a mulish line. "And
when exactly did this promise take place, *cousin*?"

Olivia's burnished-bronze eyes clashed with his, one of
her brows rising in a graceful arch. Without missing a beat,
she said, "I lost a bet to Mr. MacCarron, you see. And the

prize was of his choosing." Olivia dropped into a quick curtsy, her eyes never leaving his. "If this is your reward, consider our bargain fulfilled."

"Well, I suppose I am relegated to wallflower status," Miss Lancaster harrumphed.

"Not at all. I'm positive my good cousin would be glad to oblige ye." Jack smacked Topher on the back, returning the blow the git had dealt him earlier in the evening. But before Toph could take offense, Jack introduced him to the petite beauty at his side. With several rather pathetic glances at Miss Brownlow, Topher bowed to Miss Lancaster and asked her to dance.

Side by side, Jack and Olivia watched the other couple make their way into the melee. Jack offered his arm and, dropping his accent, commented, "Very smooth, my dear. Wherever did you learn to lie like that?"

A cross between a choke and a laugh sputtered out of Olivia as she placed her hand on his sleeve. "Only from the best, Mr. MacCarron, I assure you." She held his gaze with a self-satisfied smirk.

"Is that so?" He took her hand, spun her into the dance, and yanked her toward him with a bit more force than he intended. Her body smashed into his, the smug grin melting from her face.

"Quite," she squeaked, taking a step back and positioning her hands for the waltz.

They began to move to the music, and the residual pain in his leg—left by her blasted mutt—fueled something dark in Jack's chest. How was it that this spitfire always seemed to get the best of him?

As they turned, Jack caught Olivia's eye and raised a brow in question. "Clearly, lying is not your only nefarious skill, Miss Brownlow. Perhaps you'd care to enlighten me on any others I should know about?"

Her cheeks flushed bright even in the dim candlelight. "I assumed you would appreciate my skills of deception, Mr. MacCarron, since you seem to be a master yourself." Her words were a whispered hiss, her eyes shooting fire.

"Honestly, my dear, I have to concede the title of master to one who deceives those around her into believing her a lady, when she follows men she just met into the bowels of London and robs them blind." Her fingers dug into the muscles of his arm, but he ignored the warning and leaned closer. Her scent of sunshine and vanilla flooded his senses as he murmured, "Not to mention, she slips from her bed in the dead of night, for what intention I cannot possibly imagine."

Olivia sucked in a breath, and Jack met her startled gaze, letting his lips slide into a slow leer. "Actually, I can imagine all sorts of thought-provoking possibilities."

With a jerk of her head, Olivia lifted her chin. "Mr. MacCarron, it does not surprise me that you would accuse me of impropriety. However, I would not be so quick to cast the first stone. The only way you could possibly have the intimate knowledge of my sleeping habits is if you are a deranged prowler."

Their gazes locked and held as they spun around the room, moving in perfect time. Tension coiled tighter in Jack's gut until he thought he might snap. Provoking the girl was not advantageous to his cause. Besides, there were far more enjoyable ways to sway a lady to his intentions.

"Miss Brownlow, your lovely face is only surpassed by your brilliant wit." Unintentionally, his voice had dropped low and soft, and with a start he realized he meant every word. Recovering, he wiped the besotted look off his face and quipped, "What a sparkling treasure you are."

"Nice try, Mr. MacCarron. Just tell me what it is you want and I'll consider whether to grant your request."

"You have something that is mine, and I intend to have it back."

"Considering the source, it seems it was never yours to begin with."

Jack pulled back and watched her under lowered lids, calculating how far he could push. "The money you took may seem a trifle to you, but 'tis of the upmost importance to me. Ask anything of me and it's yours." Tightening his hold on her waist, he pulled her closer and breathed in her ear, "Think carefully. What is it you want, Miss Brownlow?"

A proper lady would have slapped his face and left him on the dance floor long ago. But this vivacious girl had not. That's how Jack knew he had her hooked.

CHAPTER 6

Olivia searched Jack MacCarron's heavy-lidded gaze, a slim crescent of crystal blue visible under the fringe of his raven lashes, and felt as if she were under a magician's hypnosis. What did she want? Her eyes wandered down the strong line of his nose, to his finely sculpted mouth.

Just being in his arms—the solid heat of his grip on her waist, his large fingers enveloping her gloved hand—made her more aware. More alive.

More.

But she wanted more answers. How had he gone from brilliant street thief to sought-after gentleman?

She wanted more of this thrill coursing through her veins. How was it that every point where he touched her felt amplified by a thousand?

What she wanted popped, unbidden, into her mind.

She wanted *more* of him.

Olivia sunk her teeth into her lip to keep the words from spilling out and lifted her gaze to his. Jack's stare flickered from her mouth to her eyes and back. She released her lip and realized they stood still in each other's arms, no longer dancing. "I want—"

"Excuse me, Mr. MacCarron. Might I borrow my . . . er . . . Miss Brownlow for this next quadrille?"

At the sound of Maxwell's voice, Olivia jerked and pulled

out of Jack's arms. Max hovered behind Jack's shoulder, his hands clasped behind his back, his face an emotionless slate.

Jack took a smooth step back and dipped into a shallow bow, his stare boring into hers as if to say, *This isn't over.* Olivia dropped a quick curtsy, daring to give him a brief nod of acquiescence. Then Jack turned and addressed Max. "Ah yes, Grimwig, isn't it?"

Max nodded, digging his finger between his stiff collar and his blotchy neck before offering his hand to Olivia. "Miss Brownlow, would you care to dance?" Max's posture was so erect as he bowed, Olivia worried he might snap in half. Guilt dropped like a stone into her gut.

Olivia curtsied deeply to Max, and as she straightened, gave him a wide smile she knew displayed the dimples in each of her cheeks. "I appreciate the invitation, Mr. Grimwig, but I find it uncomfortably warm. Shall we take a turn about the garden instead?"

"Certainly," Max said with a spark of pleasure in his eyes. "Shall I fetch you some punch first?

"If ye'll excuse me, I'll be off to other amusements." With the crooked smirk of a pirate, Jack turned and made a beeline through the crowd to a waiting Francesca.

The spell broken, Olivia had no idea what she'd been thinking to want more of anything from that devil. He was still the same self-centered swindler he'd always been.

"Errrherm." Max cleared his throat beside her, and she realized she was watching Jack as he bowed over Frannie's hand.

Olivia turned to her companion. "Shall we have that fresh air, then?"

"Yes, of course." Max grinned and offered her his arm.

Outside, a crisp breeze tugged strands of Olivia's hair across her eyes and cheeks, loosening the elaborate coiffure it had taken Fran's maid over an hour to concoct. Olivia didn't care. She longed to tug the pins from her hair and let it fly in the wind. To spin and dance. To live.

Autumn always stirred a restless urgency within her that she couldn't've explained to anyone. Except Jack, she admitted with reluctance. Only someone who'd lived on the streets could understand that the advent of winter was like the coming of death. The months leading up to it the last hurrah before every second was spent evading the lethal blow of the reaper's staff.

She'd have to get out to the Hill, and the sooner the better. Not only did she need the outing herself—free of the encumbrance of heavy skirts and propriety—the boys would be feeling the same impatient energy, and she didn't want them doing anything reckless.

Under the harvest moon, she strolled arm in arm with Max through the decaying garden. Leaves skittered across the path, crunching beneath their shoes. Olivia breathed deeply of the musky scent of dried foliage on the cool night air, and leaned into Max's slight warmth. Always attentive, he inquired about her day, her uncle's health, and even Brom. Remembering that she'd found Brom four years ago on this date, she reminded Max of the rather intense debate they'd had over Brom's name the day after she'd found him.

Max chuckled before answering, "Ah yes, that scruffy little mutt. I think I only argued to distract you from his dilapidated state. I was fairly certain he wouldn't live through the night."

"He was pretty beat up, wasn't he?" Olivia shook her head as Max led her to a bench tucked into a stand of trees, their brilliant orange and crimson wrappers shivering in the wind. "But he was scrappy! I knew he'd fight his way through."

"That he did," Max commented as she tucked her skirts around her legs to make room for him on the narrow seat. She patted the cool stone, inviting him to sit, before he settled his lanky frame beside her.

"Oh, but you hated that I chose to name him after Brom Bones." Olivia pictured that tiny pup, large chunks of his black-and-brown fur missing, blood soaking the rest. He'd captured her heart from the moment she'd found him shivering in the alley behind Millie's Bakery.

"If you were going to choose a name from "The Legend of Sleepy Hollow," with those skinny legs and giant paws, Ichabod would've been a preferable appellation. I could never understand why you'd want to name a pet after a villain." Max shook his head, as if he were still in disbelief.

"But Brom Bones isn't a villain at all. He's simply misunderstood."

"That's what you said then too." Max plucked a scarlet leaf from his coat, his thoughts seeming far away. "That was the day I knew I wanted to marry you."

Olivia's breath hitched, and she had to force herself to meet her friend's gaze. "Why?"

"Because as I watched you tend that battered little mutt, you were the most beautiful thing I've ever seen." He swallowed, his throat bobbing convulsively as he took both her gloved hands in his. "Olivia Brownlow, will you do me the honor of becoming my wife?"

He lowered to one knee before her and she searched his face. This was Max, with the same neatly combed brown hair and lanky limbs he'd had since they met at twelve. He was kind, had impeccable manners, and always wore just the right cravat to complement his waistcoat and jacket. She admired Max. She even loved him, but she didn't feel fluttery inside at the prospect of seeing him, or find excuses to touch him, or long for his company. She wasn't *in love* with him.

Olivia was unsure what she wanted for her future, but a lifetime as Max's wife—designing the perfect place settings for dinner parties, keeping his house running with precision, throwing extravagant balls—didn't appeal to her in the least. Especially now.

If she said no, she would not only crush the hope in her friend's eyes, she'd lose the opportunity to support Uncle Brownlow when he needed her most. At their current rate of expenditures, Uncle feared they would need to downsize homes again and lay off the staff within six months.

But as she remembered Max's thin lips on hers, a shudder scraped across her skin. "Max, I—"

"I know you see me as a friend, Olivia. But I believe in time that I could be more. Your uncle shared with me your past . . . that your mother ran away with your father, a low-born inventor." Olivia shifted on the bench, the cold of the stone seeping through the layers of her dress. "It was a bit of a shock, as you can imagine. Especially how your mother died. Horrible stuff."

Unable to understand why her uncle would share this part of her past, Olivia sat frozen, Max's words like nails driven into her brain. Decorum and social standing were everything to the Grimwig family. How shocked would they be if they knew she'd been raised in a workhouse and then lived as a thief on the streets?

He moved back to sit on the bench beside her, keeping her lifeless hands in his. "But I've worked through it, and there's no reason why Mother and Father need to know. No one needs to know. It can be our secret."

"Secret?" she muttered. "And you'd still stoop to marry me?"

"Well, yes. Your unfortunate birth is not your fault. I understand, since your mother died in labor, that your occasional breaches of comportment are due to your lack of feminine influence." He smiled with confidence. "But not to worry; my mother is an excellent teacher, and I'm sure she'll take you under her wing."

"Unfortunate birth?" Olivia pulled her hands from his and stood.

"Olivia?" Max shot to his feet and reached toward her. Olivia stumbled back, grabbing on to a branch to break her fall. She moved away from the tree and continued to put distance between them, walking backward and shaking her head in denial.

"No, you don't understand." Max followed her. "Olivia, I swear I won't tell anyone . . ."

Olivia picked up her skirts, turned, and ran blindly down the path.

He couldn't do it.

Jack stalked down the darkened hallway, too annoyed to keep to the shadows, as he knew he ought. There had been no mark planned for this party, but he needed a distraction from what surely was about to transpire below stairs.

He had known for days about Maxwell's intentions and couldn't do anything to stop the inevitable, but he'd rather pull out his fingernails one by one than join the engagement celebration and act as if it was a match made in heaven. *A match made in hell, more like.* That bloomin' tosser couldn't fight his way out of a wet paper sack, let alone keep up with a force of nature like Olivia Brownlow.

A noise up ahead caused Jack to stop and press back into a doorframe. He sucked in a breath and stood very still. There it was again; a clattering followed by a voice, singing, or laughing, he couldn't tell. He let out a breath. Likely a servant or a maid, but he'd investigate before continuing.

Creeping forward, he ran the pads of his fingers along the wall to feel for vibrations—footsteps, doors opening and closing. He grew closer to the noise, and words began to reach his ears.

". . . unfortunate . . . I'll show . . ." *Slam!* "Blast it!" in a furious whisper.

Jack reached a door rimmed with faint light and stopped. He glanced over his shoulder, and finding it clear, eased the door open enough to peek inside. A woman hunched over a dressing table, presumably searching for something, while muttering. "I suppose I should be thanking my lucky stars for such a *generous* offer."

He knew that voice, and recognized the elegant drape of peach silk from narrow waist to delicate lace hem that, as she reached to grab a gilded brush set, lifted to reveal trim, stocking-covered ankles and delicate heeled slippers. She turned in profile and shoved the grooming implements into her reticule. *Olivia.*

Jack slipped into the room and shut the door soundlessly behind him. This was not her room. She could not possibly be staying here, since she lived not four blocks away. But here she was, pocketing some unknown lady's personal items. He watched as she weighed a costume-jeweled hairclip in her bare hand and tucked it into her bag.

". . . that waxed string bean will be lucky if *I* ever speak to *him* again!"

At that, a spark of light ignited in Jack's chest. There could only be one "waxed string bean" in their mutual acquaintance and, if her rant were any indication, he was *not* her newly betrothed.

Silently, Jack moved farther into the room and leaned a shoulder against the bed frame. "I wouldn't bother with that clip if I were you."

Olivia started and spun around.

"Paste jewels won't bring more than a tuppence." He shrugged one shoulder. "Of course, if you want to wear it yourself, that's a different matter. But I wouldn't recommend it. Especially if you run in the same circles with its original owner."

"Mr. MacCarron . . . ah . . . this isn't what it looks like." She hadn't moved a muscle, just stared at him as if he were a ghost.

He couldn't guess why she felt the need to steal, but apparently the money she'd taken from him was not an isolated case. Jack pushed off the bed and moved toward her. "Oh, I think it's exactly what it looks like." He didn't stop until he was so close that she had to tilt her head to meet his eyes.

"Truly. My friend asked me to fetch her . . . her things." He watched the delicate muscles in her throat contract as she swallowed.

Slowly, he reached out, took the second hairclip from her trembling fingers, and set it on the table. "What are you doing, Olivia?"

She was silent as her gaze drifted over his face and settled on his mouth. Heat rushed through his veins.

Jack reached out and fingered one of the curls that had escaped her coiffure. She watched the motion of his hand, but didn't swat him away or tell him to stop. "Have you decided what you want from me?"

Her eyes blazed into his. "No," she whispered.

"Oh, I think you have." He stepped closer.

"Jack—"

His name on her lips broke his self-control. Before she could continue speaking, he cupped her head, wrapped his arm around her waist, and took her lips. She melted into him, her fingers threading through his hair.

Her body burned against his, and her mouth tasted like the flesh of oranges, luscious and sweet. The floor, the walls, the ceiling, every solid thing seemed to gravitate into the heat of their kiss until they were the only living things in the universe.

Jack ran his hands up her back and cupped the soft skin of her neck. The room spinning, he gripped the dressing table with his other hand. But even as he lost his head, his sharply honed instincts began to sound. If they were caught, the consequences would be marriage. And he had no intention of shackling himself to this girl, or any other.

When she pulled in a soft, mewling breath, he let go and pushed her away.

Olivia slumped back against the dressing table, her chest expanding with her breaths. Jack turned away from the alluring sight and shoved a hand through his hair.

"Olivia, you need to go," Jack ground out between clenched teeth.

"But I—"

"Now." He turned to her with a warning glare.

Hurt flashed in her eyes. She touched her lips. Then she pushed off the table and ran out the door without a backward glance.

Away from the temptation of her presence, Jack could breathe again. He blew out the candle on the bureau. He'd lost his taste for thievery this night. The treasure he'd found in this room proved infinitely more amusing. Too bad he could never allow it to happen again.

He kicked a pair of ladies' boots under the ruffled bed skirt as he stalked toward the door. The chit still had his money, and he wasn't one step closer to getting it back.

CHAPTER 7

W e're in danger, Ollie. We 'ave to move." Brit paced in front of the crackling fire, his shadow throwing monstrous shapes around the room.

"There's nowhere *to* move!" Archie insisted from his perch on the windowsill. He hopped down and joined the gathering by the hearth. The bruise on his right cheek molted his freckles into a map of purple and green. "Where can we go? Other gangs own every piece of this city."

A barking cough drew Olivia's attention to where Chip lolled on the floor, his head resting on Brom's furry back. She squatted beside the little blond boy, whose skin had taken on a disturbing gray tinge. She rested a hand on his head, but he felt cool and dry.

"Well, what do you suggest?" Brit asked. "We can't just let that dinger Monks take everythin' we've got!"

"I say we fight!" Half of the boys cheered at Archie's suggestion, while the other half stared wide-eyed at the two older boys.

"Arch," Brit said, "you know I'd never back down from a good brawl, but look at your face. And you saw Turner after Monks's boys finished with him. What chance do we 'ave if they got the best of a bloomin' blacksmith?"

"Those prats jumped me from behind and you know it! Let 'em come at me fair and see what happens to 'em," Archie snarled, rising on his toes to get in Brit's face.

Olivia jumped up and positioned herself between the two boys. "That's enough!" She put a hand on both of their chests and shoved. "Monks can't be everywhere at once. We've just got to outsmart him."

"Outsmart him, how?" Brit asked as he shot Archie a glare.

Olivia shoved a finger under her hat and covertly scratched beneath her wig. "I haven't figured that out quite yet." There was honor amongst thieves, a code that they all lived by: your score, your prize. Those who broke the code were brought down quickly. All except this Monks character.

Needing time to think, she opened her bag and let the boys converge on the apples and fresh bread inside. She'd brought the rest of Jack's money with her, but she was having second thoughts about giving it to the boys. She told herself that reluctance had absolutely nothing to do with Jack's heartfelt plea on the dance floor, or the amazing feeling of his lips on hers. *Damn his blue eyes, anyway.*

When they finished eating, she motioned for Brit and Archie to follow her to the far side of the room. "Does Monks know about this place?" she whispered.

"No. And he ain't goin' to find out, neither," Archie insisted, throwing a look at Brit. "We'd do anything to keep this place secret. All the boys know it."

"It's true, Ollie. A couple of us slept in the street a few nights back, to throw Monks's bludgers off the trail." Brit shook his head, the corners of his mouth turned down in a deep frown. "But he's getting closer, I can feel it."

"Brit." Olivia put a hand on his broad shoulder. He appeared to have grown another inch in the last week; the ragged hem of his trousers barely covered his calves. "You know you can't protect them all. You've trained them well. You have to trust they can take care of themselves."

Brit met her searching gaze. "I've forbidden Chip and the younger boys from working the streets. I try to take 'em for an outing once a day, to tire 'em out. But I can't stand the thought of any of them . . ." His mouth clamped shut, and a muscle worked in his jaw as he turned away to face the window.

Olivia exchanged a knowing glance with Archie. Suppressing the urge to pull the boy into a hug, she settled for roughing up his shock of red-orange hair and sent him to check on Chip.

She moved to lean against the window frame, opposite Brit. A weak stream of moonlight highlighted the shadows under his eyes, making him appear years older. He looked as if he might implode at any moment, but Olivia knew a way that she might reassure him that he wasn't alone. Lowering her voice to a whisper, she asked, "Do any of the other boys know . . . that I'm a girl?"

Brit's lips compressed as he tried unsuccessfully to hide a grin. He'd confronted her about her ruse less than a week ago, and she'd admitted to him she was female, but hadn't shared any further details about her life.

"Hey." When he looked at her, she pushed the dirty brown wig off her forehead. Then with a full, dimpled grin, she gave him a saucy wink.

Brit's reaction was instantaneous. He laughed—something she hadn't heard him do in weeks. The grin on his face was a beautiful sight to behold. "Stop, Ollie. What if they see you?"

Olivia tugged her wig back into place. "It's time I shared the truth with you. My real name is Olivia Brownlow. You can find me anytime, night or day, at Number Four, Cavendish Square. If you ever need me, send word, and I'll get to you as quickly as I can."

Brit's wide brown eyes blinked repeatedly. "Yer a *proper* lady?"

"Shh!" Olivia glanced over her shoulder at the other children, but no one seemed to notice Brit's outburst. "Yes, that is true. But I was once just like you, living on the streets, until providence intervened and my uncle took me in."

He narrowed his eyes at her and accused in a harsh whisper, "You're a lady, living in a proper house! I ain't gonna show up on your doorstep in me filthy coat and short pants, like some stinkin' beggar."

"I don't give a fig about that. Nothing has changed. I'm still the same old Ollie." When his skeptical expression didn't change, she captured his gaze and lifted her chin. "You've seen me fight. I can hold my own."

Brit tore his eyes from hers and stared down at his foot as he moved the toe of his shoe through a layer of grime on the hardwood floor.

Olivia waited, holding her breath, until he lifted his head with a grin.

"You're a right brawler." He shrugged a shoulder. "For a *lady*."

She punched his arm, hard. "For anyone!"

"Yeah, all right. I'll give you that." He rubbed his bicep where she'd hit him. "So, what's the plan?"

Olivia pulled the rest of Jack's money from her pocket. The boy's eyes grew huge as she handed it to him. "Only use this a little at a time. Finish getting supplies for winter and add to the food supply where needed. When you work, go out together. Send two groups of three, preferably with you or Arch in one of the groups, and stay within shouting distance of each other."

Brit nodded solemnly as he folded the money and tucked it into his pocket.

"And for saint's sake, get yourself some blasted trousers that fit."

Jack hiked the few blocks to Cavendish Square in a downpour. Even with his collar turned up and hat pulled low, icy water found its way down his neck. Big Ben's resonating clang sounded once in the distance and he picked up his pace, his boots squeaking and splashing as he traversed the deserted walk.

At the risk of his good home and occupation, that morning after church services, he had confided in Lois the truth of the lost advance money. After several long and humiliating minutes of her cackling laughter, she had asked him what he planned to do about it. When he'd reminded her that day's sermon had been about forgiveness, all he'd received was an icy glare. So here he was dressed in black from head to toe, like some villain in a penny dreadful.

Jack stopped under the canopy of a dripping tree. Number Four Cavendish Square was dark as pitch, intermittent flashes of lightning illuminating the blank windows like ghoulish eyes. The conditions were not ideal for a nocturnal jaunt, but if he hoped to get his money back and solve the mystery of Miss Brownlow, he would need to take her by surprise.

As if by some invisible signal, the rain stopped and a series of soft sounds echoed through the night. Smoky fog rose from the cobbles like steam as Jack crossed the street, hopped over the front gate, and ducked behind a hedge. The scents of wet leaves and dirt mixed with something musky and less pleasant. Through the branches, he could make out patchy black-and-brown fur. Brom.

Dragging a hand over his face, Jack counted to ten in his head and then peered around the hedge. A dark-haired youth with a sack slung over his back led Brom on a leash down the street. What the devil? Or rightly, *who* the devil? Why would a servant take the dog out in the middle of the night?

After giving the lad a head start, Jack followed at a distance. He'd planned to tail Olivia to her destination, but instead, he'd get what information he could from the boy before heading back to climb the trellis outside Olivia's window. The thought of finding her sleep-mussed and snuggled into her bed heated his blood and quickened his step.

They neared a tree-lined park at the end of the square, and Jack picked up his pace. The wound in his leg gave a pull and twinge, which he ignored. As he closed the distance between himself and the boy to a few yards, Brom dug in his feet and swung his massive head in Jack's direction. The boy scolded the dog and tugged on his leash, but Brom spun, bearing his teeth with a menacing growl.

Jack walked straight at the dog and pulled his hat from his head. He'd made peace with the beast—he just hoped Brom felt the same way. As he entered the light of a streetlamp,

Brom's posture relaxed and his tongue lolled out of his head. Jack took a few cautious steps before the boy made an odd, high-pitched squeak. Jack's gaze jerked up to a face that struck him as familiar. Before he could figure out why, the lad made an inarticulate command, yanked the leash, and ran.

Saints. If there wasn't so much at stake, he'd let the kid go, but instinct spurred him to give chase. Smashing through the underbrush and dodging branches, he came out in an open space, winding paths intersecting at a circular fountain. Ahead, the boy skirted the fountain and then deftly jumped over a stone bench. Jack ran faster, pushing through the burning pain in his thigh. His greatcoat flapping behind him like a giant bird, he made a flying leap and tackled the lad to the ground. They landed in the wet grass and rolled. As soon as they stopped, the boy scrambled away from him on all fours, quick as a flash.

"Oh no, you don't!" Jack caught a flailing arm in one hand, and then clamped his other on a thrashing leg and flipped the boy onto his back. Crawling, he knelt on hands and knees over the boy. "I'll not hurt you, kid—" His voice stuck in his throat. Hat gone, a brown wig sat askew, revealing strands of dark-gold hair escaping a net. Jack's gaze flicked to the boy's face. Narrowed and shooting fire, were a pair of very fine honey-colored eyes.

"Olivia? What the devil do you think you're doing?" Jack demanded.

"That's none of your concern! Now, let me go!" She kicked out with both legs, and he swiveled, narrowly avoiding a boot to the ribs.

"Damn it, Olivia. Hold still or I'll lie full on top of you!"

That stopped her. She panted beneath him, her lips pressed into a stubborn line, her curves imperceptible in the ragged boy clothes. Jack hovered over her and stared at her face as the clouds shifted past the moon. Streaks of dirt covered her creamy cheeks, and the short wig framed her face in a way that sparked a long-buried memory he'd been trying to kindle for weeks—a memory of a *boy* who followed him everywhere and looked at him with the hope of the world in his eyes.

Jack released her as if she'd burned him and leaned back on his haunches. She sat up, but neither one of them spoke. Their gazes locked. The answer to why Olivia knew his true identity hit him like a punch to the throat. Visions of a little curly-haired boy with an angelic, dimpled smile transposed over the girl who sat before him now. "Ollie?" He almost choked on the word.

She nodded, and he knew it must be true. But his brain battled against his gut, questioning which identity was real—the little orphan boy he'd taken under his wing or the society miss who was undoubtedly female. The *female* he'd kissed until neither one of them could breathe.

For a moment, Jack thought he might cast up his dinner.

The creature before him nodded again. "Aye, Dodger, it's me."

Brom, who'd stayed in the periphery of his vision, but, thank God, hadn't intervened, gave his hand a thorough lick. But Jack couldn't move. An inferno sparked inside his chest. Olivia Brownlow and Oliver Twist were one and the same? The ball of fiery rage dropped into his core and he shot to his feet, his hands curling into fists.

She scrambled to her feet and backed up, but before she could run, he stalked toward her and grabbed her arm. "Who the hell are you underneath all the lies?"

She tilted her little round chin and met his gaze, her gold eyes shimmering. "I could ask you the same question."

Blast if she didn't have a point. He certainly wasn't who he'd been all those years ago either—his toff mask in place on the daily.

His voice softened as he asked, "Why didn't you tell me?"

"Why should I?" Her countenance hardened with anger and perhaps hurt. "You left me, Dodger! Or don't you remember?"

"Ho, there! Lad, do you need assistance?"

Jack dropped her arm and stepped away as a constable strolled toward them, his night club drawn.

"No, sir," Olivia answered in a deep tone of voice Jack didn't recognize. She plucked up her hat and shoved it on her head, then hoisted the bulging sack over one shoulder, her scorching gaze searing into his. "This toff and I were 'aving a difference of opinion, but we're *finished*."

Her emphasis on the word finished was not lost on Jack. The copper moved between them in a threatening manner. For a heartbeat, Jack debated taking him down, gripping Olivia by the shoulders and shaking answers out of her, but the unpleasant emotions churning his stomach drained him of his anger. Without another word, he turned on his heel and stalked away.

Finished, indeed.

Not bloomin' likely.

Chapter 8

Olivia twirled her spoon through the dollop of cream atop her soup, creating a swirl of white in the burnt orange. An earthy tang of nutmeg with a hint of cinnamon tickled her nose, but she had no inclination to lift the spoon to her lips. Four days had passed since Jack discovered her identity. That night, in the moonlit park, she'd read his handsome face like a tragic story. The shock and anger were understandable, but when his lips distorted as if something horrid had passed beneath his nose, it had felt like a kick to the belly, a shot at her most vulnerable place—the fear that she didn't fit in. *Anywhere.*

She propped her chin on her fist and watched the cream completely dissolve into the steaming soup. Jack hadn't attended the Dunfords' soiree the previous night, and according to Christopher March, no one had seen him for days.

But Jack wasn't the worst of her troubles. The night before last, a couple of goons had followed Brit and Archie back to the hideout on Saffron Hill. They'd demanded a payoff, threatening to disclose the orphans' location to Monks if none was received. Their silence had cost over half of the cash she'd given to Brit for winter supplies, leaving nothing left to purchase the clothing the boys needed. Or for the doctor little Chip required to treat a sudden fever spike.

"Do you expect to divine some great secret from your

soup, my dear? I've finished mine and, although it was quite delicious, there are no surprises hidden within." Uncle Brownlow picked up his bowl and brought it close to one wide eye and then the other.

Olivia chuckled at his antics, her heart squeezing in her chest. The day she'd robbed her uncle on the street had been the best of her life. He'd seen something in her eyes that fateful day—something of himself, perhaps—and had followed her to the courthouse, where he'd witnessed her faint when the magistrate sentenced her to death. Hours later, after her uncle had bartered to clear her name with a bottle of aged Scotch and a box of costly cigars, she'd awoken in a fresh night rail, surrounded by clean linens and the scent of lemons . . .

Ollie glanced down at the soft white gown covering her from neck to wrist, sat up, and screamed.

"Oh my, no." The woman beside the bed patted her back. "We'll have none of that now."

But Ollie could not stop the blind panic from rising in her throat and blasting out of her mouth. No one could know her secret. Her old nurse had told her in vivid, terrifying detail what would happen should anyone find out the truth. Being a male orphan was hard enough, but females suffered a far worse fate . . . especially lovely ones. At least that's what nurse had said. And Ollie had believed every word.

Scooting to the other side of the bed, she jumped to the floor and ran toward the door, grabbing for the handle just as it opened. The toff she'd robbed barreled into the room, caught her by the arms, and held her tight. "What is the meaning of this?" he thundered.

Ollie swallowed her screams, and the tears took over,

streaming down her face in great rivers. Could this man, with eyes so like her own, harm her? She wanted to believe she was safe in this clean, beautiful place. But at what price?

So much kindness shone from Mr. Brownlow's face, that when he pulled her to him and wrapped his arms around her, she sagged against his sturdy frame, her entire body shaking with sobs.

"Shhh, it's quite all right now," he soothed, stroking her short curls. "I have some important questions for you, but you cannot answer them if you are crying, can you?" He pulled back and smiled.

Ollie shook her head as she met his gaze, sniffling up her tears.

"Now then, what is all this screaming about?" The man led her back to the bed.

Like a wrung-out ragdoll, she climbed under the covers and let the maid wipe her face. Mr. Brownlow pulled a chair up and sat looking at his folded hands. It was several minutes before Ollie realized he waited for her answer.

"I-I am sorry, s-sir." Her speech broke on the sobs shuddering through her chest. "N-no one knows I-I'm a g-girl." She took a steadying breath before continuing in a whisper, "At least they didn't."

"I see." The man gave her a small smile, but his eyes were sad. "Your fear is understandable. But you need to know something." Slowly, as if her bones were made of the finest porcelain, he took her hand in his and met her gaze. "I will never allow anyone to harm you. Ever."

The man's lined face swam before Ollie's eyes, and a tiny spark of hope leapt within her.

"In fact, I believe you and your friend robbed me for a reason. That God brought you to me after all these years."

She wasn't sure, but she thought she saw his chin tremble.

"When Nanny took your clothes to the laundry, she found this . . ."

Her breath caught as he lifted a golden chain from his pocket—Ollie's only possession, her mother's locket. Her old nurse had found it on her mother's body and saved it for her until she was old enough to keep it herself.

She reached out and Mr. Brownlow set the necklace in her hand, where her fingers closed around the oval, a perfect fit in the hollow of her fist. "I don't understand." What could her locket have to do with God wanting her to rob this man?

Mr. Brownlow leaned forward. "Do you know whose locket this was, my dear?"

"Yes. It was my mother's."

The old man's eyes closed and tears leaked onto his weathered cheeks. When he looked at her again, his smile was wide. "Her name was Agnes Fleming, and she was my niece. My beloved sister's daughter. Which makes you my great-niece."

Ollie was speechless as she stared at this man's familiar honey-colored eyes, the confirmation that he did not lie. But she'd been on her own since her nurse passed on. Suddenly, she had family? She wasn't altogether sure what that meant.

"My dear, I know this is a lot to take in, but I was hoping you would consider living here with me." He gave her hand a quick, warm squeeze. "I'd resigned myself to living the rest of my life alone. But if you'll consent to stay, we can take care of one another."

Ollie swallowed the lump in her throat. "Truly? You want me . . . to stay here, forever?"

Mr. Brownlow laughed softly. "If you so choose. Clothes, food, books, toys . . . a proper education . . . I could provide all of those things for you."

She glanced down at their joined hands, his skin papery and spotted against her small, reddened fingers. Slowly, she raised her eyes to find the man waiting, patient and still. The choice was easy. "Yes. I would like that . . . very much."

His arms came around her, enveloping her in the scents of soap and spicy tobacco. She'd never smelled anything so sweet.

When he released her, his face grew serious. "There's just one more thing. I understand why you pretended to be a boy, but now that you can live as a female, I think a new name is in order. How does Miss Olivia Elizabeth Brownlow sound?"

She repeated the name under her breath several times before answering, "I like it!" She cocked her head to one side. "But do you think you could teach me how to spell it?"

Her uncle's rich laugh filled the room. "It would be my honor, little one."

Olivia almost choked on the unexpected emotion clogging her throat. Without thought, her fingers grasped the spot under her dress where the egg-shaped locket rested against her skin. Her reassurance and strength. But there was nothing except a hollow there. The only piece of her mother she'd retained all these years, gone to finance a single physician's call. And worse, in her rush to help Chip, she'd forgotten to remove the tiny portrait of her mother that her uncle had given her.

God, what have I done?

"Olivia, what is it?" Her uncle's trembling hand grasped her fingers, his skin warm and thin as paper.

Olivia met his faded gaze and shook her head in silence. Tears filled her eyes. She didn't resent selling the locket—it was a worthy sacrifice for the health of a child—but she still ached with loss. And fear. Stealing a few trinkets at parties wouldn't be enough to ensure her boys' safety this time. She didn't doubt the thugs who had blackmailed Brit would be back for more. And who was this Monks character terrorizing the Hill? What could she do against a seasoned crime lord?

"Is it Maxwell's proposal that has you flummoxed? I'm aware you have yet to give him an answer."

Olivia pushed away her soup, pulled her fingers from her uncle's grasp, and folded her hands in her lap. *Max.* She'd all but forgotten he awaited a response. Another situation she'd thoroughly mucked up. A tremor shuddered over her shoulders and down her spine at the memory of that night. Being in Jack's strong arms, the solid heat of his body, his mouth. Olivia cut the thought short and reached for her water goblet, taking several long swallows.

"Do you have feelings for him, dear?"

Olivia almost jumped out of her chair, water sloshing over her fingers as her gaze swung to her uncle's wizened face. "Why would you say that?"

"You and Maxwell are friends, are you not?"

Olivia nodded and then turned to stare at the flicker of the candles in the center of the table. Of course her uncle wasn't referring to Jack. They had never met. Well, except for that long-ago day when he'd accused Dodger of robbing him on the street. The irony tightened Olivia's throat.

"I see no other reason why you should delay. Maxwell Grimwig is a well-respected gentleman, his family is above reproach, he is kind and . . . will support you in a manner—" A sharp cough cut him off. He took a gulp of brandy before continuing in a rough tone, "A manner in which I am no longer able."

Her uncle's words confirmed every logical reason why she should accept Maxwell's offer with haste before he changed his mind. But a pair of lethal blue eyes haunted her until she could see no other. Her traitorous heart didn't care a whit about propriety or material possessions; it longed for passion and adventure.

Flames still dancing in her vision, she turned back to her uncle. His shoulders slumped inside his bottle-green coat, his neck so thin, he looked like an ancient turtle. Her heart ached to see him so diminished, the robust uncle of her youth just a memory. She rose and enfolded him in a quick hug. "Uncle, I'm so sorry. I've been a selfish cad."

Olivia returned to her seat, and dug into the roasted squab and buttered turnips on her plate. Why hadn't she thought of it before? Maxwell could be the answer to all of her worries. She would accept his proposal and explain about the Hill Orphans. He would have to help them. Wouldn't he?

"Does this mean you'll be accepting Grimwig's offer, dear?"

"Yes," she answered, her mind consumed with how best to arrange a meeting with Max. She simply couldn't wait until the Carters' dinner party, two days hence. Waiting would be torturous. And besides, the boys needed their help *now*.

"Olivia?"

She had not seen or heard from Max since the night of his proposal. What if he didn't show to the Carters' either? The next event was the following week . . . the Grimwigs' ball. They would need to make the engagement announcement that evening.

"Olivia Elizabeth Brownlow!"

Olivia jerked, dropping her fork with a clatter. She turned to her uncle, whose white brows were connected over his sharp nose, his mouth a stern slash. She hadn't seen that particular expression on him since he'd caught her smoking his pipe.

"Sir?"

"Is it too much to ask that you attend the conversation?" His face softened, his mouth turning up in bemusement. "You've always been a little dreamer, my girl. But this is important."

"Yes, sir."

"Why have you hesitated to accept Maxwell's proposal? Do you have feelings for another?"

"Feelings for another?" she repeated, buying time. She had many feelings for Jack—anger, fascination, resentment, desire—none of which signified a future.

"No, Uncle, my hesitation was not due to anything but my girlish fantasies of romance. I was momentarily . . . distracted by the attentions of another. But I've come to see the futility of that . . . er . . . relationship." She clenched her teeth, clarifying pain radiating through her skull. Wanting and needing were two exceedingly different things. What she wanted was of no consequence. Everyone she loved would benefit from her match with Max. Jack MacCarron was nothing but a liar and a thief.

"Do you not love him?"

"Love?" Olivia blinked at her uncle for several moments before she realized that for the second time that evening she'd been thinking of Jack when he spoke of Max. She cleared her throat and arranged the napkin on her lap. "Max is an honorable man, who I'm sure I can come to love over time. Please do not worry yourself, Uncle."

"I see." His narrow shoulders slumped impossibly lower, his chin dipping into his starched cravat. "I find I'm too fatigued to eat." He rang a tiny bell by his plate, summoning the butler.

Thompson arrived and helped Uncle Brownlow to his feet.

"Please finish your meal, my dear. We can talk more of this on the morrow."

"Of course." Olivia nodded. Her uncle seemed to be weaker than usual as he leaned on the butler's arm and they left the room.

She would not give him any more cause for concern. She would arrange a meeting with Max, and by tomorrow, she would be a *happily* engaged woman.

❧

"Whiskey, govnah?" A serving girl leaned into Jack's face, her ample bosom blurring as it threatened to spill out of its laces. His gaze flicked from her chest to her face, and he reared back in his seat. The woman's pockmarked skin and crusted, empty eye socket sobered him in an instant.

"None for me, thanks."

The girl moved to the next gentleman at the round table, and Jack turned his attention to the pair of tens in his hand.

He'd bluffed his way into a small fortune tonight, but it didn't make up for what he'd lost the night before. Somehow, he couldn't bring himself to care.

"I'm all in," the portly man with heavy muttonchops announced as he pushed his little pile of coins and trinkets into the center of the table, and then puffed on a fat cigar.

Jack watched the bloke scratch the side of his meaty nose, his eyes shifting between the center of the table and the cards in his hand. Jack almost smiled. Some people simply shouldn't attempt to bluff.

Through a thick haze of smoke, Jack watched the man next to him fiddle with his cards. The reddish-brown stains under his fingernails and the vague, rotten stench surrounding him pegged him as a butcher. After several glances between his cards and money, he folded.

Next was the old man. Jack had never traded with him, but judging by his mismatched clothing and the random baubles he wagered, Jack guessed he owned a pawnshop, and not a very successful one. He slapped his cards down. "I'm out too."

Perfect. Jack pushed his pile into the center of the table. "I'm in. Show yer cards."

Sweat popped out on the fat man's forehead as he lowered his quivering hand. A pair of eights. Jack slapped his tens down and raked in his winnings.

"Aw! Ye blasted blighter! Me wife's gonna kill me."

"If you didn't have a wife, you wouldn't have that problem, now would you?" Jack muttered.

The portly man continued to sputter until a hand yanked him out of his seat by his collar. "You had yer turn," the newcomer growled as he gave the stout man a push, sending him to his knees.

The new gent was barrel chested, his arms corded with the muscle of a dock worker. His dark, alert eyes darted to each player at the table before he sprawled in the newly vacated seat and pulled out an impressive wad of bills. "Deal me in."

As the butcher dealt the cards, Jack watched the newcomer. His clothes were of average quality, clean but mended in spots. Incongruous with the roll of money he flaunted. Perhaps he played for a benefactor who didn't wish to dirty his hands.

After several rounds, Jack was forced to abandon that conclusion. The newcomer played with a recklessness that a sponsor would not appreciate, almost as if money were not the object of this particular gent's aim. Jack forced himself to focus. A gambler with no interest in money could only mean trouble.

Jack folded and watched the newcomer take the last of the pawnbroker's earnings. Jack gathered the cards and shuffled the deck. "You out, old man?"

The pawnbroker shook his head and dug through his pockets, presumably searching for something to wager.

The cards distributed, Jack glanced at his hand. He hadn't been around this much smoke in ages, and it was giving him a raging headache. Or, mayhap, it was his lack of sleep and food. But every time he thought to return home, to his soft feather bed, meals served like clockwork, and his responsibilities to Lois—which would include attending parties at her whim—something deep in his chest ached. It had taken him at least a full day to realize it was his heart. He'd let his blasted guard down with Olivia. He actually felt something for the girl.

He checked his pocket and noted the sad state of his funds. Lifting his free hand to his forehead, he squeezed his temples; but the moment his eyes closed, a honey-gold gaze stared at him in accusation, and the anger inside him sparked fresh. *She* was the one who had deceived *him*, not the other way around.

A sudden shift in the energy at the table yanked Jack's attention back to the game.

The newcomer leaned forward, his body as taut as a fiddle string. The pawnbroker was in the process of setting something in the center of the table. An oval locket, engraved with an intricate filigree design, attached to a long, gold chain.

"Too rich for my blood." The butcher threw down his cards. "I'm out."

Jack's gaze shifted from the necklace to the man across from him, who snatched the locket from the old pawnbroker. "Let me see that."

Jack sat straighter in his chair as he watched the man click open the locket in his wide palm, his eyes narrowing in satisfaction.

"What's your price, old man?" the newcomer demanded.

The pawnbroker blinked owlishly. "'Tis a wager."

"Blast that. I'll buy it outright. What's your price?"

Understanding seemed to dawn on the old man's face, a smile multiplying the wrinkles of his cheeks. "What'll you pay, chap?"

Jack watched with renewed interest as the big man

offered an amount that far outweighed the value of the piece, and demanded to know where the locket had been acquired. But before the pawnbroker could answer, Jack cut in. "I'd like to see the locket."

The possibility of a bidding war caused the old man's eyes to glow with triumph. Jack extended his open hand. Waiting. The big man glared, the necklace clutched in his fist, a muscle working in his jaw.

"The necklace was placed as a wager." Jack leaned forward and met the man's vulpine gaze, unblinking. "If you plan to take it off the table, I'll have a look, or you'll put it back in the pot."

The man's attention shifted to a blond gentleman near the bar nursing a mug of ale, and then he turned to Jack, the tension leaving his shoulders with a shrug. He reached across the table and let the necklace drop from his fist by slow degrees, the chain still clasped in his fingers.

Jack grabbed the locket with a swift yank. The big man came out of his seat glaring, and the butcher pushed back from the table so quickly he almost toppled in his chair. With deliberation, Jack leaned back in his seat and flicked out his coat, revealing several knives strapped against his chest. "Relax, gentleman. I'll have my look."

Out of the corner of his eye, Jack spied the bloke with the ale moving to stand behind him. His muscles tensed for a fight, but he forced himself to appear relaxed and crossed his ankle over his opposite knee.

He unclasped the locket. It took every ounce of his considerable self-control to hide his reaction to the portrait within. Dark-gold hair, a dimpled smile . . . *Olivia*. He blinked. No, not Olivia: the chin was too weak, the jawline less defined. It had to be her mother, the woman in the painting above the fireplace in the Brownlows' parlor.

Jack quickly calculated the money he had left. It was less than what the big man had bid, but he offered every last pence to the pawnbroker. "However, I do not require the source of the sale. You can maintain the privacy of your clientele." Jack held his breath as the old man's eyes darted between him and the locket and then to the man hovering at his shoulder. It was the first time since leaving the Dodger behind that Jack wished for the notoriety he'd lost. A good scare could go a long way in such situations.

Extending a shaking hand, the pawnbroker requested the locket back. Jack handed over the piece and wondered why on earth the big man had such a strong interest in a seemingly benign object. Did he know Olivia? What were his intentions? Blackmail? From what he'd gathered, she and her uncle were close to broke.

"I've decided to sell . . . er . . ." The old man swallowed and glanced at Jack and then back at the man behind him. The git took a menacing step forward. But it was unnecessary. As usual, greed won out. "To the highest bidder."

The vile grin that split his opponent's face caused Jack's fingers to curl into a fist. He watched the big bludger take the locket and tuck it into his breast pocket, then count out the promised fee. The bills clutched in his fist, he prompted, "And the information?"

Clearly, the source of the locket was of equal importance to the trinket itself. Jack could not allow these goons to sense his personal involvement, so he crossed his arms over his chest and settled back in his seat, even as his every sense strained toward the old man.

The pawnbroker's gaze never left the money as he answered, "One of the Hill Orphans brought it in. Dark-haired kid . . . believe he goes by Brit."

With a nod, the big man handed over the cash. The harsh plains of his face revealed nothing as he pushed his chair back and left the table. The other man fell in beside him and they made their way to the bar. Jack gathered his winnings, donned his hat, and rose from the table. Pushing his way through the crowded, smoke-filled room, he positioned himself at the corner of the bar. If not in fact her mother, the woman in the locket had to be Olivia's close relation, so why would a street kid have it? Likely, it had been stolen—just like so many he'd lifted in years past. An accidental trip, a quick yank, and the ladies were none the wiser.

Jack motioned for the bartender and paid his tab, keep-ing one eye on the men with the locket, who were toasting their boon. The man who'd hovered behind him at the table tipped back his drink and faced Jack full on, and the room gave a sharp tilt. Jack gripped the tacky wood of the bar and stared. Tall, broadly built, and a few years older than Jack. His hay-colored hair pulled into a tail at his neck only accen-tuated sharp features and close-set eyes.

His old nemesis, Edward Leeford. Ice skittered across Jack's shoulders and burned through the scar between his ribs. But it couldn't be. Leeford had died at the hands of a band of coppers who chose to extract their own justice from his evil hide.

But there he stood, laughing and drinking. Very much alive.

Jack inched closer. Did Edward wish Olivia ill? Despite Jack's jumbled feelings for the girl, he couldn't abandon her to Leeford's machinations. Even if getting involved was all kinds of madness. He moved around the packed bar and insinuated himself within hearing of Leeford and his goon.

"Did ye see that bloomin' prat when I stole the locket from under his nose, Monks?"

Monks? Jack knew that name. As the men ordered a second drink, Jack struggled against the exhaustion clouding his brain, a memory finally surfacing. *"That bloomin' Monks is takin' over everything. I'll pledge to you right here, man."* That day in Paul's shop, Critch had been terrified. Now Jack knew why. Leeford and Monks were one and the same.

Jack ordered a mug of water and downed it in two gulps. Leeford must've taken on the name Monks in order to escape his past sins—and enemies. But it would seem he was intent on making all-new ones. After a second glass of water cleared his brain a bit, Jack knew what he had to do.

When Monks and his cronies headed for the door, Jack followed. Turning up his collar and angling his hat over his eyes, he tailed the men out onto the street. He kept a discreet distance, but he couldn't hear any of their boisterous conversation. As the two neared the path that ran along the Thames, a dense fog rolled in off the river, allowing Jack to move closer. Leeford's growled words began to carry through the haze.

"Whoever heard of putting such asinine terms . . ." His voice dipped too low for Jack to hear.

"Whot did it say?" the big man asked.

"Some rot about his offspring with this whore." Leeford lifted the locket and flipped it open to reveal the portrait within, his words cutting out again. ". . . that little whelp never should've been born, I tell you."

"Why not just take 'em out of the picture all together, Monks?"

Leeford was quiet for several moments before he snarled, "Death is too easy for my precious sibling."

Leeford's words pressed down on Jack like an invisible weight slowing his steps. Was that balming git talking about *his* Olivia? Could Leeford be her brother in truth? It sounded as if he was looking for his sibling, and not for a pleasant reunion. God only knew what horrible thing his deranged mind had planned.

An impenetrable wave of fog drifted across the path, and Jack inched closer, desperate to hear more.

"Hmm . . . that sounds like somethin' you'd want to be keepin' quiet," the big goon commented with a bit too much nonchalance.

Jack stiffened as Leeford growled, "What do you mean by that, exactly?"

"Nothin' at all, Monks. Just that certain mates can be trusted with information and certain mates can't. Those trusted gents would be worth somethin' to you, I imagine. Somethin' extra."

The smog thickened to the point that Jack could no longer see the men. A warning churning in his gut, he picked up his pace and pulled his largest blade from its holster. Leeford, the snake, was about to strike. He could feel it in his bones.

Jack needed to get to him and deflect his attention from Olivia. Every ounce of his energy focused, he stalked forward, tendrils of mist churning and coalescing around him, narrowing visibility to a handsbreadth.

A thump sounded up ahead, like bone hitting flesh, followed by a groan. Blindly, Jack rushed forward as a muffled cry rang out, followed by a series of quick stick and hiss sounds. Jack slowed his gait. Knifing through cloth and flesh made a very distinct noise.

He stopped to listen and turned in a slow circle, the roar in his veins filling his ears. Quick footfalls pattered against the path and Jack tensed, gripping his knife, before he realized the sound moved away from him. Cautiously, he stepped forward. His boot collided with something warm and solid.

He bent down, blade at the ready. The big man from the poker table stared straight at him, prone at his feet. Jack lurched back. Dropping his weapon, he caught himself before he fell, his hands landing in warm fluid. He smelled the acrid tang before he lifted his palm.

Blood.

The big man was dead. Multiple stab wounds in his stomach and chest still pumped blood onto the stone path.

Jack's heart slammed in his chest. He shot to his feet and spun around, searching for the killer. If Leeford would murder his own man to protect his secret, he wouldn't hesitate to take Jack out too. A deep bellow thundered through the night, and he stumbled back before spying the swing of gas lanterns on the water. A barge cut through the waves near the shore.

It could be the Watch out for nightly rounds. And here Jack stood beside a dead body with blood on his hands. There was no saving this bloke now. Swiping his hands on his pants, he snatched up his knife and ran.

CHAPTER 9

Olivia's ribs strained against her corset as she took several deep breaths and followed Max down the cobbled garden path. A kaleidoscope of russet and tangerine leaves swirled through the air in seamless accord with Olivia's restless spirit. She'd paid Max a morning visit, forgoing the idiotic ritual of leaving her card and then waiting for him to call on her at his leisure.

Her escort had posed a bit of a dilemma. Olivia did not have a lady's maid, and most of the time she preferred it that way, but today she'd had to resort to bribing one of the kitchen staff away from her duties. Olivia glanced over her shoulder and found the girl hunched in her wrap, following at a discreet distance, a worried look pinching her face. The housekeeper, Mrs. Foster, would have both their hides if she discovered the girl missing.

Facing forward, Olivia tucked a stray strand of hair back into her chignon. She had dressed with extra care that morning, wearing her sky-blue day dress and velvet sapphire overcoat that cinched in at the waist and flowed over her hips. With the matching royal blue hat pinned at a saucy angle, even Francesca would have been proud.

Max plodded along the winding path ahead of her, not speaking. She could only hope he would give her a second chance. But a tiny part of her still wished that he wouldn't.

She'd lain awake half the night fighting her demons and praying for guidance, until she'd worked herself into a knot of anticipation and foreboding.

She followed Max under a vine-covered trellis, heavy with bell-shaped yellow flowers, and almost immediately the cloying scent of late-blooming jasmine tickled her nose. The Grimwig garden was immense. She, Max, and Violet had spent many hours here in their youth, so she could guess Max's ultimate destination.

As she'd anticipated, they rounded a bend and the carousel-like gazebo came into view. Its white-and-pink-striped columns and powder-blue gabled roof were exactly as she remembered. Olivia almost laughed at the memory of a long-ago spring afternoon when a toad had hopped out of her pocket and into Violet's tea. It was a wonder Vi still consented to be her friend.

They reached the steps of the candy-striped gazebo and Max bowed with a sweep of his arm toward the interior. "After you, my lady." His lips were pressed tight and lines radiated from his eyes. She had done this to him. He more closely resembled his stuffed-up father than her happy-go-lucky friend. Suddenly, it didn't seem such a chore to make him smile again.

Olivia sat on one of the rounded benches and grabbed Max's gloved hand as he settled beside her. She let the words spill from her unchecked. "Max, I was wrong to run away from you the night of your proposal. I was confused, but I'm not any longer. Pray, please forgive me?"

"Of course, I forgive you." His eyes softened, and the unguarded expression gave Olivia the courage to charge ahead.

"I accept. I would be proud to be your wife." She gave his hand a squeeze and watched his eyes light up like fireworks.

"Oh, Olivia!" Max wrapped her in a tight hug, and then pulled back and planted a quick kiss on her lips. "I hadn't dared hope. I imagined you wanted to speak to me in private to tell me you'd accepted someone else's proposal."

Olivia shook her head, keeping the smile on her face as a breathtaking image of raven hair falling over ice-blue eyes filled her mind. With determination, she pushed Jack out of her thoughts and focused on the man in front of her. Jack had no place here.

"We'll make the formal announcement at the ball next week. Of course, we'll need to let Mother and Father know immediately. They will be so pleased!" Max hugged her again. "How does a Christmas wedding sound?"

Olivia grew still, her airway constricting as if a noose were tightening around her neck. "So soon?" She'd hoped to have at least six months to become accustomed to the idea— six more months of freedom.

Max's mouth pulled down in a deep frown, and Olivia scrambled to reassure him. "'Tis only that it's less than eight weeks away. Eight weeks to organize a ceremony and find a gown . . . It's not enough time to prepare."

Max's brows shot up and he shook his head "Oh, no need to worry on that account. Mother could pull it together in *two* weeks if need be."

"Yes, I'm sure she could." The mental image of the formidable Mrs. Grimwig, costumed in a general's uniform, directing a battalion of caterers and livered servants made Olivia grimace. She rose from the bench, walked to the other side of the gazebo, and stopped at the lattice railing. The late-morning sun danced on the surface of a nearby pond, and beside it willow reeds swayed in the breeze. As she watched, a gardener emerged from the trees with a net on a long pole and proceeded to scoop fallen leaves out of the water. What kind of life had she committed to, that there were servants to perform such a task?

She felt Max stop behind her. "Remember that day when you reached into the pond to pick up a turtle and Violet pushed you in from behind?"

Olivia laughed. That's why they were still friends. Violet had not taken the toad incident lying down. But she'd had no idea that Olivia never learned to swim. There had not been much opportunity for aquatic recreation living on the streets, and even less in the workhouse.

"Yes, and you had to jump in and save me because I thought I was drowning." They both laughed at the memory of Olivia floundering and screaming, her dress and petticoats floating around her arms. In actuality, the water had only been up to her chest; she'd needed only to put her feet down to save herself.

She turned and looked up into Max's familiar face, his brown eyes shining with mirth. Perhaps being married to this man wouldn't be so disagreeable. He lowered his head, and his mouth brushed hers in a lingering kiss. Olivia closed her eyes and leaned in, letting him take the lead, longing to be swept away. But his lips on hers were tentative, wet. When he lifted his head, she found herself relieved and wishing to wipe her mouth with her sleeve. No heat rushed through her veins, no desire to pull him back for more.

Olivia blinked up at Max and wished she didn't have another's kiss to compare his to.

"Let us go share the good news with my parents," Max whispered into her hair. He took her gloved hand in his and tugged her toward the arched opening.

"There's something I wish to discuss with you first." She batted her lashes up at him, only feeling a small twinge of guilt at his dopey smile and dazed eyes. The orphans were worth any amount of manipulation.

"Of course, darling."

The endearment felt strange, and she longed to pull her hand from his. But instead, she followed him back to the bench seat and arranged her skirts around her as she gathered her thoughts. She'd rehearsed this speech all night.

"Max, I need your help. There are a group of young boys, orphans, whom I've gotten to know through my . . . volunteer work at St. Bart's." It was a small lie, but better to lie than risk his derision, or, worse, his refusal to help.

"St. Bart's is in Cheapside, is it not?"

"Yes, but—"

"Olivia, that part of the city is much too dangerous! I must protest—"

"Please allow me to finish." Olivia placed her hand on his knee, effectively silencing him.

"These boys were all abandoned at a young age and make what living they can on the streets. But with winter coming, they are in danger of starvation . . . or . . ." Olivia swallowed, genuine tears gathering in her eyes. "Or freezing to death in the streets."

Max's brows drew together over his nose. "Surely, there

is some organization for these children, such as the local parish?"

Olivia shook her head. "No. There are just too many street children. The churches can barely make ends meet. They can't afford to offer charity to them all, so they offer it to none."

"What is it you are asking?"

"They need our help, Max. Their lives are unimaginable! We have so much, and they have so very little. I would ask you to prayerfully consider making a financial contribution to the cause."

Max shifted his legs away from her, leaving Olivia's hand to fall onto the bench. He stared out at the vivid garden for several moments, a muscle in his jaw clenching. "Olivia, I've always admired your kindness and compassion. But by giving these boys a handout, you're only making them dependent on you. They need to learn how to earn an honest living. Even a workhouse has to be preferable to starving on the street."

Olivia begged to differ. She still had the scars on her back and legs from floggings she'd received for infractions as innocuous as tripping on the stairs. One of her most severe beatings had come after she'd been caught giving a smaller child her ration of bread. And the constant bone-aching cold and gnawing hunger never fully left her mind. She'd gladly abandoned that life of abuse for the freedom of the streets. The first time she'd nipped a meat pie that'd fallen off a street cart, she thought she had died and gone to heaven.

But she didn't share any of her memories; instead, she spoke as an outside observer. "I've heard the conditions in those workhouses are deplorable. The children sleeping with rats. Being beaten for not working fast enough. What kind of life is that, Max?"

Max searched her face, and she could almost see the gears churning in his brain. When he spoke, his voice was hushed. "When I was eight years old, I found a baby squirrel. It was tiny and fuzzy, but Mother would not allow pets, so I kept it in a box in the solarium. I lined the box with an old blanket and brought him milk and biscuits every day. Once he grew bigger and could get out of the box, he would climb the ficus trees and scamper around the room, but he would always come when I brought his food. Summer came and it was time for us to travel to our country house, so I let the squirrel go in the garden, confident that when I returned, he would be waiting for me."

Max paused and swallowed, the knob in his throat moving up and down several times before he continued. "When we got back in the fall, I ran out to the solarium and set the dish of milk and biscuits on the back stoop. I gave the whistle my squirrel had always responded to in the past, but he didn't come. I sat down next to the dish to wait, hoping he was being shy. I happened to look behind the hedges bordering the solarium. He was there, by the door, stiff as a board, his little body decomposing into the dirt."

Olivia's gut clenched, knowing what he would say next.

"The squirrel died there waiting for me to come back and feed it. It had never learned to fend for itself." Max took both her hands in his, but her fingers felt numb. "Olivia, I know you're trying to do the right thing by helping these orphans. But you wouldn't be doing them any favors. You would only make them dependent on your goodwill. If they are to survive, they must learn to fend for themselves."

"But they're people, Max. Brit is their leader, and he's brilliant and tries his best to protect the younger ones. Archie is clever and scrappy. Chip is only six years old, and he's been sick with a cough for months." Olivia could hear the pleading in her voice, but she didn't care. "Please, Max, they have no one!"

Max set his jaw and shook his head. "I will not perpetuate the homeless issue in this city by providing a handout. If any of the boys are old enough, perhaps we could consider them for a position here."

Hope flared in Olivia's chest, but quickly faded when she realized the only one old enough was Brit, and he would never abandon the other boys.

Max stood and held his hand out to her. "Come. We have much to celebrate."

Olivia swallowed the tears burning the back of her throat as she took his hand and allowed him to lead her along the path toward the four-story stone manor that was soon to be her home. In her wildest imaginings as a child, she had never dreamed of such a mansion. How could she live like a queen when her friends, the boys she'd come to love, were fighting for their lives?

As they reached the back portico, Max squeezed her hand and grinned down at her. Olivia pushed aside her emotions and tried to think logically. Becoming Mrs. Maxwell Grimwig would afford her a wealth of opportunities. Not least of all, ensuring Uncle Brownlow would spend the remainder of his days in peace and relative comfort.

She picked up her step, linked her arm through Max's elbow, and lifted her chin. She was doing the right thing by marrying him. If nothing else, the Grimwig mansion was a treasure trove of loot that no one would ever miss.

⁂

The rented hansom cab pulled up in front of the brownstone she shared with her uncle. It wasn't the four-story townhome with the pristine white exterior that they'd lived in when she was a child—they'd had to downsize years ago—but in many ways, she preferred this cozy home and smaller staff.

Descending from the carriage, a wave of exhaustion weighed down her steps. She longed to curl up in her bed and hide under the covers. She'd smiled and celebrated with the Grimwigs until her face hurt and her soul felt hollow. But as Thompson opened the door, blatant disapproval etched into his face, a restorative nap seemed highly unlikely. If Mrs. Foster had discovered the maid missing from her duties, the butler would be the first to know. But Thompson ignored the girl as she scurried up the stairs, instead turning his scowl on Olivia. "Miss Brownlow, your uncle is abed, but wishes to see you at dinner." She nodded in acknowledgement, sensing there was more. "And . . . you had a *gentleman* caller while you were out."

Olivia paused as she unbuttoned her coat, and met the butler's narrow gaze. She shrugged out of her wrapper and folded the soft velvet over her arm. When he offered no further information, she prompted, "Thompson, please don't make me drag it out of you. Did this caller leave a card?"

"No, Miss." Thompson turned to the salver on the hall table and plucked up a cream-colored envelope with the tips of his gloved fingers. "He left this."

The butler dropped the missive into her hand as if it were a stinking bit of rubbish. Olivia arched her eyebrows, her mouth tilting in amusement at his dramatics. "Was he really so terrible, then?"

The man's thin lips pressed together, his eyes shifting away. He was entirely too proper for his own good, Olivia thought as she turned toward the staircase. But his next words made her pause.

"The man is dangerous, Miss Olivia." Olivia rotated to face the old butler. She'd known him since coming to live with Uncle Brownlow, but this was the first time he'd shared anything resembling a personal opinion.

Thompson cleared his throat, and his face appeared pained, as if a struggle between his brain and his mouth preceded his next statement. "I do not trust the fellow. He looks the part, but . . . he's a wolf in sheep's clothing, is what he is." He cleared his throat again and turned away, pink staining his weathered cheeks.

Touched by the man's concern, Olivia gave his arm a brief squeeze. "Thank you, Thompson. I shall take that under advisement."

He nodded, but kept his face averted as she turned and mounted the stairs. A wolf in sheep's clothing, indeed. Olivia didn't need to look at the seal on the letter to know Thompson was referring to Jack MacCarron.

Unable to help herself, she paused on the staircase, turned the envelope over, and stared at her name written in decisive strokes. Her stomach did a funny little flip. The bold handwriting was exactly what she would've expected. Running the rest of the way, she made it to her bedroom, shut the door, and slumped against it, before she ripped open the envelope with shaking hands and began to read:

> *Olivia,*
> *I have come by some information concerning you, which is of an urgent nature. Meet me at Golden Square at midnight tonight. Come in disguise.*
> *Yours,*
> *Jack*

Olivia wandered over to the window, reading the short note again. *Yours?* Did this mean he'd forgiven her for her deception? Or was this his standard roguish salutation? She could picture him leaving notes at bedsides all over London. *Jolly good romp, luv. Until next time. Yours, Jack*

Why all the secrecy? Was it a ploy to get his money back? An excuse to see her?

Before she could stop herself, plans spun out in her head. She'd need at least twenty minutes to make it to Golden Square. Eleven thirty was earlier than she typically ventured out, but if she ensured Mrs. Foster's tea was spiked after dinner, perhaps she could— A light flashed in her eyes, stilling her thoughts. Max's ring, the heavy diamond capturing the sun, circled her finger like a tether.

Her stays seemed to tighten around her ribs as she read Jack's letter for a third time. As the future Mrs. Maxwell Grimwig, she could not keep secret assignations with unsavory gentlemen in the middle of the night. The sad fact was she couldn't trust herself around Jack any longer. Despite the questionable nature of his present vocation and his abandonment of her, she couldn't seem to stop seeing him as noble. The boy who'd rescued her off the streets had left too indelible a mark. Which meant the danger he posed to her heart and soul outweighed any information he could offer.

Before she changed her mind, Olivia rushed to the fireplace, crumpled the letter into a ball, and tossed it into the glowing embers. She watched the edges blacken and curl as her heart thrashed against her ribs. Her eyes closed as she tensed against the pain of loss. There would be no more sensual dances or kisses that left her breathless.

She would make the right choice this time.

CHAPTER 10

The moment Jack walked into the party, his eyes found Olivia. In her cream silk gown edged in black lace, and the sides of her hair braided and twisted up into a graceful fall of curls down her back, he couldn't fathom how this enticing young woman could be the same urchin he'd found sneaking out in the rain six nights past—or the orphan boy Oliver Twist, for that matter.

"So you finally deigned to grace us with your presence," a droll voice pronounced.

"Hullo, Topher." Jack didn't spare his counterfeit relative a glance, his gaze fastened to the sway of Olivia's skirts as she exited through the far door on the arm of an unknown gentleman.

"The ladies have been positively flummoxed by your absence, cousin. But I must admit, it has been amusing inventing excuses for you. One of my favorites was the creeping rash of unknown origin. That one should get a few marriage-minded maidens off your tail."

Jack turned to Topher with a sardonic smile. "Excellent. I can't thank ye enough."

"Don't mention it." Topher arched one brow. "Would you like to take my elbow, or shall I take yours? It seems our late arrival leaves us to escort each other into dinner."

Jack chuckled and shook his head as he followed

Christopher out of the room. The self-centered tosser was actually growing on him. When he wasn't digging into Jack's fabricated history, that is.

If the sheltered toff ever discovered the truth, it would make his perfectly pomaded hair stand on end. Hell, Jack would erase his past if he could. Being born on the wrong side of the blanket was bad enough, but when one's own mother attempted to sell her seven-year-old son to feed a raging opium addiction, one tended to avoid those memories at all costs.

Seated at the far end of one of the longest dining tables he'd ever seen, Jack glanced down the row of guests, but could not find Olivia. In fact, he'd been unable to catch her eye since arriving. His hand clenched in frustration. Speaking with her was the sole reason for his attendance at this god-forsaken crush.

He'd waited for her at Golden Square in the drizzling rain for three nights in a row. His notes were ignored, his attempts to call on her during the day met with the blasted butler refusing to even open the door to him. In the wee hours of the third night, he'd arrived at the Brownlow house intent on getting to her any way he could. But all the entrances were locked tight, and the trellis by her bedroom window had been removed from the building. He'd considered breaking in through a first-floor window, but with the butler on high alert, it was too risky.

Olivia's deception still sat in his gut like a rancid meat pie, but for some reason he couldn't bear the thought of that bludger Monks getting his claws into her. How much longer until the bloke realized Olivia was his sister? And what would he do once he figured it out?

"Jack, old man, I believe that mutton is already dead. No need to bludgeon it with your utensils."

Jack shot Topher a glare, but endeavored to calm his raging emotions. He knew from experience that losing control only made him vulnerable. He needed to approach this like a complex heist—pick it apart, analyze every piece of available information, and then lay out a plan.

By the time dinner ended, Jack had reached a place of cold determination. And when it was announced that a game of blindman's bluff would follow in the parlor, he knew exactly what he needed to do.

Jack rose from the table and waited by his seat as people filed out of the room, sluggish after the heavy meal. Topher followed Olivia's cousin, Francesca, as she passed by, worming his way between the girl and her escort. Toph had game, Jack had to give him that. One would *almost* think they were truly related.

A footman stood at the door, prompting each guest to draw a folded paper out of a hat. The unlucky one who drew the piece marked with a black dot would act as Seeker during the first round of tonight's entertainment. The parade paused while a giggling trio of young ladies made a spectacle of choosing their papers. Jack didn't care who found the black dot, as long as it wasn't Olivia or himself. He searched the crowd for his mark and found her almost directly across the table.

She turned and met his intense stare, jerking back as if seeing a ghost. Jack enjoyed an instant of satisfaction until that familiar honeyed gaze narrowed, and her pert nose lifted in an expression of blatant disdain. *So, that's how she wants to play it,* Jack thought as he returned her look with a glacial one of his own.

A squeal sounded from the doorway, and a girl with platinum hair waved a piece of black-dotted parchment in the air. With the Seeker chosen, and the need to select a paper unnecessary, the rest of the participants paraded out of the dining room quickly. In the parlor, Jack positioned himself in the shadows of a dark corner.

Olivia stood next to her escort and chatted with another couple. Jack watched the elegant movement of her hands, her animated expression, and the way the little group seemed enraptured by her every word. Where was Grimwig tonight? Had he given up his suit? If so, he was more of a nitwit than Jack thought. *No way would I give up so easily.* Hypothetically, of course.

"The best hiding spots are through the south door," a voice purred near his ear.

Jack turned to find Francesca Lancaster so close he could see the kohl lining her eyes and the stain of rouge on the apples of her cheeks. So much for going unnoticed. Feigning ignorance to her invitation, Jack said, "Thanks for the tip." Then turned to watch the hostess as she blindfolded the Seeker with a black silk cloth.

Francesca's fingers squeezed his forearm. "The most *fascinating* spots, that is." Her lashes beat like hummingbird wings as she gazed up into his face.

Jack suppressed a sigh of impatience and gave her his best roguish grin, hoping she would take it as a confirmation and move away. To her credit, she grasped the hint and headed toward the south entrance with a quick nod.

As footmen extinguished the lamps and candles, Jack's gaze slid back to Olivia. But she was gone. His breath caught as he scanned the room. The hostess began to spin the Seeker, and chaos erupted.

"Five!" Everyone joined in the countdown as they scurried to hide.

Surely, Olivia's light-colored dress would be easy to spot even in the partial darkness. "Four!"

Jack began to work his way around the perimeter of the room.

"Three!"

Where could she have gone? There! The swirl of light fabric behind a sofa. Jack rushed over, but found an older woman crouched with her back to him.

"Two!"

Jack turned in a circle, his pulse accelerating as he searched the nooks and crannies along a wall of bookcases. Could she have left the room?

"One!"

Spying a servant's entrance in a far corner, he headed in that direction, wondering if she could've slipped into the hallway. Then just to the right of the door, he spotted a twitch of cream silk behind a potted tree.

As the Seeker yelled, "Stop," and the guests froze in their hiding spots, Jack grasped Olivia's gloved arm, opened the side entrance and forced her through, the call of "Blindman's . . ." cutting off as he closed the door behind them.

"What are you doing?" Olivia hissed, attempting to pull herself from his grip.

But he was not letting go until he'd had his say. Pushing

open the first door they came to, he guided her into the room and released her long enough to turn the key and drop it into his pocket.

"Jack! This is highly inappropriate."

He leaned back against the closed door, crossed his arms over his chest, and waited for his eyes to adjust to the gloom. Details began to emerge, and it became clear they were in a water closet.

Olivia stood in the middle of the cramped room, her arms stick straight, hands clenched at her sides. He pushed off the door and advanced toward her. "Then perhaps next time you won't ignore my requests for a meeting."

"Give me one honest reason why I shouldn't scream." She propped her fists on her tiny waist and leaned forward. "Besides the fact that you're an arrogant prat who expects women to fall at his feet!"

"I may be arrogant, but you've been lying to me since the day we met. What right do you have to an honest response from *me*?" In two paces, he towered over her. "I thought we were friends."

"Friends are just enemies in disguise. You said that to me once, but I was too naive to know you were referring to yourself." She poked him hard in the chest. "We ceased being friends the day you deserted me so I'd take the fall for your crime. *Dodger.*" She sneered his old name like it left a bad taste in her mouth.

He stepped back and shoved a hand through his hair.

So that's what this was all about. She thought he'd betrayed her to the coppers that ancient day, and she still didn't trust him. That's why she hadn't responded to his notes or requests for a meeting. Buying time, he walked past her and opened the drapes, flooding the small space with moonlight.

When he turned, Olivia's eyes burned with gold fire, her hair glistening with flecks of starlight. And a long-buried memory struck him like a physical blow: The night he'd escaped from his mother, he had run until his legs refused to take him another inch. Lost and alone, he'd looked up into the glowing eyes of a stained glass angel, beckoning to him, offering shelter. He snuck into the church and curled up on a pew under her watchful gaze. She was the most beautiful thing he had ever seen.

Until now.

"Well?" she demanded.

Jack realized he'd been staring at her in silence for several moments. With a sigh, he glanced down at his boots. It was time to come clean. "I'm no bloody hero."

"Clearly."

He raised his head and met her gaze. "But I did not abandon you that day."

Olivia glared at Jack's heart-stoppingly gorgeous face and thought this must be what it felt like to be tempted by the devil. He stepped toward her, and the moonlight caught in his eyes, making them appear to glow an unearthly blue. His raven hair fell across his forehead, bringing back memories of the boy he had been. A boy she had trusted with her life. Part of her longed to hear him out, but he would just wrap her up in lies, as he always had.

"I have to go." She extended her hand. "Give me the key."

"Oll— I don't even know what to call you!" His left thumb rubbed across the pads of his fingers, betraying the vulnerability he tried so hard to hide.

But Olivia wasn't ready to make amends. "I'm Olivia. I might pretend to be a boy at times, but underneath I've always been a girl."

"I know what you are—who you are." He swallowed, the muscles in his broad throat constricting as he took another step. "But I swear I didn't abandon you."

Olivia closed her hand in a fist and dropped it to her side. "I saw you! After the copper caught me, you met my gaze and I knew I was saved. But then you turned tail and ran without a backward glance!"

"But you *were* saved . . . Your uncle—"

"You know that now—"

"Let me bloody well finish!" He reached for her, but then seemed to change his mind and shoved the hair off his forehead instead. "I wasn't familiar with the courthouses in that part of the city. So after they carted you away, I followed at a distance. I knew I couldn't help you if we were both pinched. I also knew my priors would ensure my own death sentence. I'd hoped with your youth and no prior record . . ."

He stared out the window a moment, lost in thought.

"Once I saw where they took you, I found that toff we robbed—your uncle—and gave him back his wallet, then led him to the courthouse. I stuck around until I knew he'd saved you from the drop, and then I ran before they could pin the crime on me."

"Why didn't you come find me after?"

"I did." He shrugged one shoulder. "I spied on the town-house for days. After I got my quota for the day, I'd sneak over to Kensington and hide in the park across the street. I wanted to check on you, at least speak to you once. But your uncle found me and convinced me you'd be better off with a clean break."

Olivia stood frozen to the spot. His story didn't add up. Why would her uncle never mention getting his wallet back or tell her he'd spoken to Jack?

"I don't believe you." She crossed her arms under her chest and lifted her chin. "You're not getting your money back. It's long gone. So you might as well save your pretty stories for one of those dimwitted debutants who think you can do no wrong."

He stared at her for several long moments, his face an impassive mask, before answering, "It's easy enough to ver-ify. Ask your uncle when you return home."

Olivia vehemently wished she could be as cold as he appeared. But standing this close to him—hyperaware of his every move, his every breath—she felt as bristly as an alley cat. With a sudden desperation, she knew she needed to get out of that tiny room. "The game has to be over by now. We'll be missed."

"They'll have chosen a new Seeker and started another round. We have time." He leaned back against the door and crossed one booted foot over the other. "Are you ready to hear me out?"

"Do I have a choice?"

"Oh, you always have a choice," Jack drawled, as his win-tery eyes lingered on her lips, a wicked half smile tilting one side of his mouth. "We could always do what everyone will assume we are doing."

Heat rushed through Olivia's veins and pooled in her gut. Her eyes swept over the finely molded lines of his body, highlighted by the precise cut of his suit—broad shoulders filling out his jacket, his waistcoat flat against his abdomen, and strong thighs outlined beneath his trousers.

She glanced at her hand for strength, but Max's ring wasn't there. They'd agreed to keep the engagement a secret until the ball. *Curses!*

The sooner Jack started talking, the sooner she could get away from him. "Fine. What is so blasted urgent that it can't wait?"

All signs of flirtation gone, a muscle ticked in the line of his jaw and some unreadable combination of emotions darkened his eyes. "Are you missing a locket, by chance?" He lifted his hand, forming an oval with his thumb and forefinger. "About yay big."

Olivia's heart stuttered, and she resisted the urge to clutch the empty spot against her breastbone. "How did you . . ." Her voice gave out, and she blinked at him in shock.

"A few nights back, I was gambling at Langdale's—"

"In Holborn?" she interrupted. Langdale's was a stone's throw from the Hill Orphans' hideout.

"Yes, the warehouse on Holborn." Then he told her about seeing the locket during his poker game. "Turns out, the bludger who bought your necklace goes by the name Monks."

Monks? The same Monks who was tormenting Brit and the others?

"I tried to buy the locket myself, but I couldn't meet Monks's price. So when he left, I followed him and listened as he boasted to his mate about the locket leading him to his long-lost sibling." He swallowed, and his right hand clenched into a fist. When he spoke again, his voice was strained. "He seemed extremely put out that his father had a child with the woman in the locket."

Olivia felt the blood drain from her body by slow degrees. "My mother . . ."

Jack's unguarded gaze met hers, the corners of his eyes wrinkling with apprehension. "He's planning to use the locket to track you down. For what purpose, I don't know, but it isn't good."

Olivia felt herself sway. She had a half brother she'd known nothing about.

Jack was across the room in two strides, an expression of alarm clouding his face. He took her by the shoulders and pulled her against him, wrapping his strong arms around her. "There's more, I'm afraid. I know him. We have a past history."

Barely registering his words, Olivia pulled back and asked, "What's his name? What's my brother's real name?"

"Edward Leeford."

"That's my father's surname. Monks is his blood son with another woman?"

Jack nodded, then he searched her face; satisfied with what he saw, he said, "Edward was a crime lord who took power a year or so after you went to live with your uncle. He vamped off all the gangs. Fagin was terrified of him. Gave him fifty percent of everything we earned. If Leeford even suspected the old man was holding out on him, he'd beat him or one of us. But he got greedy and began sending us on missions of his own. Risky ventures for big scores."

Her brain whirling, she stepped back from Jack and faced the window. Moonlight splashed over the perfect hedges of the garden, its brilliance reflecting on a koi pond surrounded by stone benches. Almost too perfect to be real. All these years she'd longed to have a family. She loved her uncle, but whenever she saw a mother and father playing with their children in the park or walking hand in hand, her heart splintered with grief.

Brother. She had a brother.

She spun to face Jack, who stood with both his hands shoved into his pockets. "Are you certain he isn't trying to find me so we can meet? Have a relationship?"

"I'm sorry, love, but of that, I'm certain. What I don't know is why he's looking for you."

Suddenly cold washed down Olivia's back. The boys. Monks had been stalking them for weeks, and if he followed the locket . . . "Jack, I need your help."

His eyes locked on hers with heated intensity. "Anything."

A cheer sounded from down the hall, signaling they were out of time.

She quickly told him about the Hill Orphans, why she'd had to sell the locket, and her concerns regarding Monks, then moved to the door. "Meet me tonight at Golden Square. Midnight."

His lips compressed, his brows lifting into his hair. "I believe I've been trying to make that arrangement for nigh on a week."

Loud conversation and laughter floated through the walls. "You said anything. Now give me the key."

He produced the key and set it in her palm, his large hand engulfing hers in a light embrace. "Do you believe me then? That I didn't abandon you?"

She blinked at their joined fingers, his touch buzzing through her veins. "I'll speak to my uncle."

He released her, and with a bow of his head stepped away from the door. "Tonight, then."

Olivia returned to the party. Jack did not. She kept up polite conversation for a few moments for the sake of appearances, and then, claiming a headache, left early. The entire cab ride home, one thought played over and over in her mind: Monks, the terror of the London streets, was her brother, and he was coming after her.

Chapter 11

"I hate that blasted getup," Jack grumbled, shooting Olivia a glare. "It's hard enough to reconcile my memories of you and Oliver without seeing you dressed like an overgrown bag-snatcher." Tucking a large black umbrella under his right arm, he shoved both hands into his pockets, and focused on the cobbles at his feet as if they might contain the answers of the universe.

Olivia almost laughed at the way he wrinkled his nose like a petulant child. "What would you suggest as an alternate disguise? No, wait, let me guess." Olivia shifted Bram's leash to her other hand and then tapped her finger against her lips, pretending to think. "Perhaps the blousy dress of a milkmaid?"

When he didn't respond, she went on. "Oh, I know! I saw a perfectly garish frock in Paul's Pawnbroker Shop. Purple silk edged with a profusion of black feathers. I believe I could pass for a lightskirt if I set my mind to it." She skipped ahead of him and gave an exaggerated sway to her hips.

Jack jogged up beside her and placed a hand on her shoulder. "Stop that, before you attract attention."

The streets were deserted, besides the stray drunk or homeless wanderer. But when he pulled his hand back like it burned, she refrained from pointing that out. A bubble of hurt swelled in Olivia's chest, dampening the elation she'd felt since Jack agreed to help. She realized now that she had no knowledge of his motivations.

When she'd returned home from the party, her uncle had been tucked into bed, but still awake. She'd asked him about the missing wallet all those years ago, and reluctantly he'd admitted Dodger's role in returning it and leading him to the courthouse where she was being sentenced. When she'd questioned him about Jack checking on her afterward, her uncle said he couldn't recall such a conversation.

But the more she thought about it, the more she felt he hadn't divulged the full truth. Growing up, he'd told her many times that he wished for her to have a clean slate; a fresh start as Miss Olivia Brownlow. When she would talk of her old life, Uncle encouraged her to think of her past as a nightmare; the less one spoke of it, the quicker it faded away.

"Tell me what you know about your parents," Jack requested, still staring straight ahead.

His words reminded her they had bigger problems to solve than sorting out their twisted past. Olivia took a deep breath and dove into her tragic tale. "This is all second-hand knowledge, from my uncle's point of view, you understand."

At Jack's nod, she continued. "My father's name was Edwin Leeford. He was a widower, an industrialist, and an inventor with a reputation for being brilliant but eccentric. When he met my mother, he pursued her with singular focus. His charm and persistence proved to be irresistible to her and they fell in love, but her parents would not approve the match. They felt that despite his success, he was not of respectable stock, and therefore not good enough for their daughter."

Brom stopped to sniff a discarded paper sack, jerking Olivia to an abrupt halt. Jack stepped close, took Brom's leash, and they walked on.

"Continue, please."

Olivia sorted through all the snippets of information she'd gained of her parents over the years and worked to put them in logical order. "My mother ran away with my father and they eloped in Scotland. My grandparents disowned her, refusing to even acknowledge her existence when someone mentioned her name. After they passed away, my uncle came into possession of a letter my mother had written to her parents several years after the elopement, begging for their help. She wrote of my father's personality taking a drastic turn, that he'd become obsessed with proper society not accepting him and took it out on her. He became abusive. And she was with child."

Olivia peeked over at Jack, but his profile remained stoic. "The best we can piece together is that she feared for my life, so she ran. We can't be sure why she wasn't wearing a wedding ring at the time of my birth and" —Olivia swallowed— "her death."

"Have you ever seen that letter?"

Olivia thought back and realized she hadn't. She only knew what her uncle had told her was written in it. "No, but I think I need to."

"Where does your half brother fit into all this?"

"I can only assume he was a product of my father's first marriage. I had no awareness of his existence until you spoke of him last night."

Jack seemed to consider this and then said, "He's a few years my senior, so he's in his mid to late twenties. Logically, it would follow that he did something to fall out of your father's good graces before you were born. Perhaps there's an inheritance he's looking to gain, but being the eldest, and a son, he should have first rights to it."

Olivia had no response to this conclusion. Her parents' tragedy still festered like an open wound, and she was too close to view it objectively. Her father had been abusive, and possibly insane. She doubted the existence of any inheritance at all.

Jack began to walk faster, forcing Olivia to jog to keep up. His profile was set like fired clay, but his thumb ran frantically over his fingers. When she caught up to him, she grasped the edge of his jacket. "Hey, stop."

He did, but when he turned, his eyes were focused above her head.

"What's going on with you? You won't even look at me."

His gaze lowered to her then, though his eyes narrowed in contemplation. "It confounds me how you've gotten away with this disguise for even one night."

Olivia quirked her lips, but before she could form a reply he handed her his umbrella, which turned out to be far sturdier than her frilly parasols. Then, he crossed the street and entered a squat corner tavern.

Olivia followed but paused at the door as Brom tugged on his leash. Olivia released him, knowing he wouldn't go far, then walked into the pub, her boots slipping on the sanded floor. She gained her balance and hung back in the doorway. The air, tainted with sour ale and years of snuff ground into every surface, brought unpleasant memories of Bumble the beadle's office at the workhouse. One visit to that chamber and you'd never want to go back.

Shaking off memories of the switch against her skin, Olivia took in the rest of the main room. The ceiling was low and bulged with a water-stained, patterned paper that peeled in strips. Faded, old-fashioned paintings hung on the walls. The nearest was of Queen Caroline, appearing severely put out in an enormous hat and feathers as she overlooked a shining Blackfriars Bridge.

A handful of patrons sat scattered at different tables nursing a tumbler of grog or snifter of amber whiskey. An old codger, his silver hair tied in a tail of the antiquated style, raised clouded eyes. Olivia tugged her cap lower, stiffened her spine, and shifted her gaze to where Jack squatted in front of the large hearth.

As she watched, he rose and wove his way through the round tables, his right fist closed tight, and exited the building. Olivia followed him outside and took a long draw of the crisp night air before asking, "What is it you're doing, exactly?"

"Come with me," he instructed as he rounded the corner and ducked into a narrow, cobblestoned alley.

Apprehension crawled across her shoulders as she walked into the dead-end passage. These dark, shadowed places were deathtraps she normally avoided at all costs. Overhead, silhouettes of outdoor staircases hung like hulking, black spiders, further tightening the space. A cool wind pushed against her back, fluttering the strands of her wig. She trailed the dark outline of Jack's broad shoulders and battered top hat with an acute sense of déjà vu. Following the Dodger on adventures through the streets of London had caused her no end of trepidation, but she'd never once turned back.

The rhythmic click of claws against stone announced

Brom's arrival, forcing her back into the present. Jack stopped, turned around, and pushed up the brim of his hat. The moment Olivia paused, her loyal pet sat, his warmth pressed against her leg, one paw resting on the top of her boot.

"Jack, what's this all about?"

Instead of answering, he stepped up to her, took the umbrella and burlap sack containing food for the boys out of her hands and set them on the ground. With brow furrowed in concentration, he moved in close. So close she could smell the scent of his skin as he brushed the brown hair away from her face. Then he reached up and drew a finger along the right side of her jaw. She gave a start.

"Stand still," he ordered gently before he traced a line under her cheek, his touch feather light.

Stunned, Olivia watched as he dipped his pointer finger into the black soot in his other palm, and then traced the ashes across her upper lip. The sharp scent of cinders tickled her nose and she swallowed a sneeze. Her eyes flickered to Jack's in question.

"The dirt you smudge on your cheeks isn't enough to disguise the delicate line of your jaw." His low voice rumbled through her spine as he continued to "draw" whiskers onto her face with short stippling motions.

His full lips tilted in an ironic expression. "Or that pert little chin."

She blinked up at him, and he was Dodger again. The rough-and-tumble street kid with the heart of gold. The boy who did everything within his power to protect his crew. She swallowed the burning in her throat and whispered, "I never thanked you for taking care of me . . . when we were kids."

His gaze darted down to his open hand, where he swirled the dark soot against his skin. "It was nothing," he muttered. Perhaps it was the angle of the moonlight, but she could've sworn his neck turned red.

As he began to work on the left side of her face, he stepped close, his arm brushing hers. His finger traced the sensitive skin beneath her jaw, and Olivia's heart raced like a runaway coach. She inhaled his enticing scent and closed her eyes. She only hoped he couldn't feel the heat of her flushed cheeks or see the frantic beat of her pulse beneath her skin.

When she dared glance back at him, their eyes locked for one heartbeat. *Two. Three . . .*

Did he feel what she felt? This visceral connection?

He cleared his throat, leaned back, and assessed her with a critical eye. "Much better. You should do this every time you're in disguise."

Instinctively, Olivia reached up to touch her cheek.

"Ach!" Jack captured her hand and held it away from her face. "You'll smudge my masterpiece."

He grinned, and she grinned back. His gaze shifted to her mouth. Then with a shake of his head, he dropped her hand. "Whatever you do, do *not* smile."

Olivia felt her face fall at his harsh words. But as he stepped around her and swiped his palms together, ash falling in a cloud to the ground, she heard him mumble, "Those dimples could kill a man."

With a chuckle, she snatched up her sack and practically skipped back out to the street.

As they neared the river, its eternal reek caused Olivia to endeavor to inhale through her mouth. A lone ferry whistle echoed through the fog, signaling the one o'clock boat, the last of the night, leaving from Warren's Blacking Factory. This was much earlier than Olivia usually dared venture out on her own.

As if to illustrate her point, a group of men exited Warren's, their boasting laughter preceding them down the sidewalk. Their clothes were stained such a flat, unrelenting black that the white of their faces appeared disembodied until they stepped into one of the sparse pools of lamplight.

Jack handed Olivia Brom's leash and then casually moved a hand inside his jacket, where she suspected he would have one of several knives. Olivia preferred not to carry weapons. Having no training to wield them, she relied on her intellect to get her out of sticky situations. Well, that and the mass of fur and muscle by her side.

The men drew closer, and from what Olivia could make out, their exuberance was in anticipation of a visit to the Golden Crown, a tavern known for their strong ale and pretty serving wenches. They seemed harmless enough, and Olivia knew how to go unnoticed. Keeping a firm hold on Brom's leash, she tugged her hat down and hunched her shoulders. Brom would follow her lead, unless someone gave him reason not to.

As the men approached, Olivia drifted toward the street to give them a wide berth. Jack, she noticed at the last second, moved around the group in the opposite direction, toward the river side of the path. Keeping her eyes fixed ahead, she calculated how much longer it would take to get to the Hill. She gasped when a thick arm blocked her path.

"I was talkin' to you, boy. Think yer too good for me or somethin'?" Olivia took a step back and followed the line of the burly arm to a face covered in orange muttonchops. Brom snarled, but Olivia gave his leash a quick yank to quiet him.

"I'm sorry, sir. I didn't hear you." Olivia dipped her head in a deferential nod.

"What are ye doin' out so late? Don'cha know there's a price for young ones like you?"

Olivia glanced around, noticing she was surrounded on three sides by men reeking of acrid, tar-like polish. She coughed as the smell stung the back of her throat. A warning rumble began in Brom's chest.

"Leave the boy. We've other business to attend to," one of the men suggested.

Gloved fingers reached out and grasped her face, tilting it up to the lamplight, and the stench of pitch almost made her gag. "Look at those eyes . . . like gold coins, and that delicate nose. I'm thinkin' old Kutzle would pay a pretty penny for a girly boy like this."

"Aye, or mayhaps enough credit to earn us all a night in heaven!" one of them shouted. All the men chortled in agreement.

With her heart pounding in her ears, Olivia jerked her face out of the man's hand and let go of Brom's leash. He snarled and leapt toward the bloke who'd touched her, knocking him to the ground. Olivia turned to run and crashed directly into a hard chest.

Almost blind with panic, it took her a moment to realize it was Jack who grasped her arms and steered her behind him.

"This boy's under my protection. Leave him be." Jack's steely voice gave the men pause.

They seemed to freeze for a moment, before glancing at

one another in question. As Brom returned to her side, Olivia prayed they would move on. There were four rough-looking factory workers, against one man, a girl, and her dog.

Muttonchops, back on his feet, clutched a bleeding wound on his arm and moved to the front of the group. "I've lost blood for this boy. Now, I'll 'ave him."

Jack pushed the hat back on his head and met the man's glare with one of his own. "We can do this the easy way or the hard way." He stepped into the slightly taller man's space and growled, "You choose."

Then, as if by some invisible signal, Jack moved like lightning. He tossed his umbrella up, caught it in his right hand, and slammed the handle into Muttonchop's chin with a loud crack. The man's head flew back as he crumpled to the ground, out cold. But Jack didn't stop. He punched the ruffian to his left in the mouth, and then twirled the brolly into his other hand, spun in a half circle, and rammed it into another man's gut. Brom jumped into the fray. Hackles raised and jaws snapping, he forced one of the men out into the street.

Jack faced the last man and brandished the pointed end of the umbrella like a sword. The man backed away, wide-eyed, then turned tail and ran.

The one Jack had hit in the stomach straightened and hurtled in Jack's direction.

"Watch out!" Olivia screamed.

He landed a blow to Jack's kidney before Jack whirled on his heel, his coattails flying in a wide arc. Using his momentum, he clutched the man by the throat and lowered to one knee, slamming the man into the ground with so much force that his head smacked loudly against the cobbles. Jack stood and pressed the umbrella handle against the man's throat. Afraid his skull had fractured, Olivia cautiously moved closer, but he groaned and rolled onto his side, only a slight trickle of blood staining his light hair.

Olivia just stared at the ruffians laid out around them. Like a dancer in a macabre play of death, Jack had defeated four powerful men with his fists and . . . a *brolly*?

"Let's go," he ordered.

Brom at her heels, Olivia clapped a hand on her cap and ran, cringing as icy water splashed into the holes in her shoes. They didn't slow until they reached the Temple Bar arch and the gloom of Fleet Street. She glanced over her shoulder more than once, staring into the shadows to make sure they weren't followed.

As they turned onto Chancery Lane, a chill wind blew against Olivia's face, and she clutched the collar of her coat tightly around her neck, her eyes flicking to the man beside her. The strong nose was familiar, the midnight hair resting against his neck as it had always been, but it would seem this Jack had become someone very different from the charming pickpocket she had once known.

The farther they walked in silence, the stronger her curiosity became. She needed answers. "How did you *do* that?"

"Do what?" Jack shrugged as if he'd just tied a neckcloth, instead of mopping the street with four grown men.

"You know exactly what I'm talking about! You took out those factory workers like they were featherweights. Since when do you know how to do *that*?"

They rounded a corner, and Jack's umbrella clattered to the ground as he pushed Olivia into a darkened doorway. His face a hairsbreadth from hers as he hissed, "Since the Dodger was forced to become a street lord just to survive. Since every gang in bloomin' Holborn looked to me for protection from your blasted brother. Since my fists, and whatever makeshift weapon I could get my hands on, were the only things standing between me and a slow, painful death." His palm smacked the wooden doorframe at her back, making her jump. "You think I chose to become this . . . this bloody bludger?"

Olivia met his eyes, something tortured and wild lurking in their depths. She could taste apples and spice as his panting breaths blew against her mouth. His body was so close it stole her words, her very thoughts.

When the tense silence between them became unbearable, she whispered, "I . . . I'm sorry." She wasn't sure what she was apologizing for, except perhaps that she'd escaped that life and he had not.

Jack's shoulders slumped as if the air had been knocked out of him, and he closed his eyes. Without volition, her hand lifted to his cheek, cradling the rough stubble along his jawline. "It's all right, Jack. You did what you had to do. As we both always have."

His eyes opened, spikey lashes a dark shadow against his skin, his expression completely unguarded. The hurt and fear, the resolve, and the need she read there made it clear this boy was no danger to her. The pad of her thumb brushed his cheekbone and she lifted on her toes, drawn to his lips. He leaned toward her, his eyes sweeping her face, and then he jerked back. Confusion flashed in his eyes before his countenance locked tight, closing her out.

"It's getting late." He stepped out of the doorway and clucked to Brom, who was sniffing around a nearby lamp pole.

Cheeks burning, she hefted her satchel back onto her shoulder. Something dark lurked just beneath Jack's surface and she'd seen it emerge tonight. Part of her wanted to dig deeper, help him exorcise his demons, but then she glanced down at her naked ring finger. She pushed out a sigh. Perhaps it would help if she tied a string there to remind her she was an engaged woman.

Jack followed Olivia and Brom into a dilapidated building, barely able to squeeze through the boards nailed to the window. The first level of the hovel was one open room, empty save for piles of refuse and several massive holes in the floor. A large rodent scurried across their path and down into one of the pits. Jack suppressed a shudder as his boot crunched a large bug, and memories took him back to a similar flea-ridden dump he'd huddled in for a few very long months before Fagin took him into his gang.

Olivia whistled, and feet pounded across the ceiling above their heads. A curly blond head appeared above them, a single candle clutched in his fist.

"Ollie! Yer early!"

Olivia grinned and waved up at the child as an unmistakable clearing of a throat sounded.

"Sorry. Whot's the password?"

"Katrina Van Tassel," Olivia answered in a jarringly rough voice.

Jack recognized the password as the coquette from "The Legend of Sleepy Hollow," and as he watched the giant mutt, Brom, run up a narrow board that had just been lowered from the opening in the ceiling, he felt a bit of the darkness lift from his heart. He'd never put it together before, but Olivia had chosen to name her beloved pet after the character Brom Bones, likely because she didn't subscribe to the widely held view of Brom as the villain of the story.

Looking past her ratty wig and ash-smudged cheeks, he met her honeyed gaze and his heart gave a squeeze. This girl insisted on seeing the best in everyone, even in the fictional world. Perhaps this explained a bit of her tolerance for him.

Their eyes locked for a moment, and then she motioned for him to follow her up the slender ramp. "I've brought a friend," she announced as she reached the landing.

Jack walked quickly up the slope, his days of scaling the rooftops and hidey-holes of London a physical memory not easily forgotten. Stepping into the upper room, he was met by eighteen pairs of wide eyes—if he counted correctly. He scanned the little faces, most of them open with curiosity. Until he reached a tall boy, arms crossed over his chest, feet spread wide, his dark eyes narrowed, chin lifted in challenge. This *had* to be Brit.

"Everyone, this is Jack. He's a good chum and he'd like to help." Olivia met Brit's gaze, mirrored his stance, and spoke her next words with deliberation. "You can trust him."

As if she'd uttered the magic code, Jack was surrounded and tugged over to the one fireplace in the open room, little hands grasping his fingers and his clothes. One of his knives appeared in a boy's hand and Jack snatched it back, making note to take stock of his pockets before he left. They led him through a path of pallets scattered on the floor, chattering like a nest of mice.

"How do ye know Ollie?"

"Have you gots kids?"

"How old are you?"

"Do you live wit' Ollie?"

At that, Jack met Olivia's amused gaze and arched a brow. She laughed and shrugged before kneeling to dig into the bag she'd brought with her. Realizing he was on his own, Jack took a deep breath and answered each of their questions. "We've known each other since we were children. No. Twenty. And absolutely not."

The boys were silent for a moment, digesting what he'd said, and then they converged on Olivia as she pulled random food items from her sack. Jack leaned against the warm bricks of the chimney and assessed his surroundings. A pile of tin dishes sat next to a cast-iron pot on the hearth, coats hung on a line of pegs on one wall, and boots and shoes were arranged in a neat row. There was even a beat-up table with six pieced-together chairs, a few books and slate tablets organized in the center.

Between the moonlight coming in from windows on both sides of the room—which surprisingly still held their glass panes—the fire, and several candles on the table, the room was far less gloomy than he'd expected. He could see why the boys were reluctant to move, despite the threat of Monks and his gang. *Leeford.* A pain shot through his jaw at the thought of the bloody menace.

Jack unclenched his teeth and focused on his goal. These boys were the key to taking the crime lord down once and for all. Why he felt compelled to do so, and what Olivia was to him, he could not easily identify, but he did know he couldn't let her brother succeed in his Machiavellian plans. Nor could he allow the dinger to terrorize and extort children all over Holborn.

Revenge had little to do with it.

At least that's what Jack told himself as he watched Olivia cut a loaf of bread and a wheel of cheese into rations, while chatting with the kids, ruffling hair, teasing and calling them by name. The little blond one, who Jack assumed was Chip, sat on her lap. The boys may be vital to finding Monks, but they were also Olivia's weakness. It was only a matter of time before her brother caught on to that fact as well.

Watching her now, it was clear she would never agree to walk away from them, even if it meant saving her own life. She was stubborn . . . and determined, and courageous. Jack cut short his thoughts. *Emotional detachment equals control.* He would have to find a way to lure Monks out, without exposing Olivia's vulnerability.

With that aim in mind, he turned his focus on Brit, who'd been throwing him furtive glances since he arrived. The kid's dark coloring fit the old pawnbroker's description of the one who'd sold him the locket. Between that and his unique name, it wouldn't take long for Monks to follow the trail.

Jack pushed off the wall and walked over to the young leader. "We need to talk." Brit gave a tight nod, and held Jack's unwavering gaze. The inner strength Jack saw in the boy's eyes gave him hope. Hope that what he was about to do would not be in vain.

It was time to go on the offense and resurrect a past he'd hoped to leave behind forever. The Dodger was coming out of retirement.

CHAPTER 12

Olivia held her hat in place as wind whipped the thick strands of her wig against her cheeks. The crisp scent of coming snow had her wishing for her fur-lined jacket and muff. Jack trudged along beside her, his ragged-looking coat little protection against the elements. The harsh turn in weather didn't allow for easy conversation, but that didn't stop the questions spinning in Olivia's head.

She'd just overheard Jack instruct Brit and the boys to tell anyone who would listen that the Dodger was back and he was their new kidsman. They'd all heard of the Dodger; he was a legend among the street folk. And tonight, watching him fight like a warrior, Olivia had witnessed a good part of the reason why.

Stunned silence had clouded her brain as the boys threw questions at Jack from every side. True to his nature, he avoided giving specific answers, all while rallying the boys around his plan—*If Monks wants a turf war, he'll get one!*

Then he'd helped them invent ideas to fortify the hide-out. Jack pointed out vulnerabilities, such as the accessible opening in the floor, and then led the boys through possible solutions. They'd agreed to build a hatch with a sturdy lock. As the little ones drifted off to their beds, Jack, Brit, and Archie addressed the windows, concocting an elaborate rope and pulley system that would dump wet paint on anyone who attempted to break in.

Before leaving, Jack had pulled the two older boys aside, handed them a wad of cash, and given them a list of supplies they would need to create the protective measures they'd discussed. That kind of cash flow would certainly gain attention, which seemed part of Jack's master plan.

The only problem being that, as far as Olivia knew, Jack "The Artful Dodger" MacCarron had left that life behind, going so far as to fake his own death. He was hiding something. She just couldn't figure out his angle—yet. Not that she wasn't grateful for his help. But had he thought through the possible repercussions? Resurrecting his past could jeopardize his new life, and if his current or past crimes came to light, it would land him behind bars . . . or worse.

Leaning into the wind, Olivia turned off the walk to cut through the park. Jack moved ahead of her and lifted branches out of her path as they wove through the trees. She knew he had a noble side—she'd witnessed it over and over again when they were children—but that still didn't explain the terrible risk he was taking by diving headfirst into his past. It only illustrated how very little Olivia knew about the person he had become. His whole life was a mystery, from his parents to his arrangement with Lois March.

At the gates of her garden, Jack touched his hat with a nod, propped the umbrella on his shoulder, and turned to go.

"Jack!" she yelled, but he either ignored her or couldn't hear over the wind. "Jack!" When he didn't respond, she caught up to him, looped her arm through his, and guided him toward the townhouse, doing her best to ignore the powerful curve of his bicep under her fingers. There was a place where three brick walls of the house formed an alcove. It was where she hid her stolen trinkets until she could take them to the boys.

When they reached the spot, she reluctantly removed her hand from the warmth of his arm and pushed aside the hedge that disguised the entrance. The moonlit niche got them out of the wind, but as they both squeezed in together, she realized it was much smaller than she remembered.

"If you want to get me alone, I could arrange a more comfortable meeting place," Jack quipped, a wicked glint in his eye.

Olivia's stomach did a tight flip as she shifted into the corner to create some much-needed space between them. "I simply want to talk."

Jack rolled his eyes and slumped back against the wall. "Must we?"

"Yes, we must." Olivia scratched her wig, longing to pull the itchy thing off her head, but instead she assumed her "boy stance" and crossed her arms. "What are you hiding?"

He remained silent.

"Why do you want to go after Monks?"

His eyes turned glacial.

She fired another question. "How did you end up with Lois March?"

The way Jack's brow lifted, she could tell her question surprised him. Good. He'd had her off balance since the day he walked back into her life.

He recovered quickly, a tiny smirk sliding across his lips. "She's my aunt. Or hadna ye heard I'm a wee orphan from Ireland?"

His accent was spot on, but his words were complete

twaddle. Her chest burned like it was filled with hot coals. How dare he treat her with such cavalier disregard? "I shared every sordid detail about my parents with you. And you can't be honest with me about this one thing?"

"I'm helping your *precious* orphans, so what does it matter?" he sneered.

"It matters, you insolent dolt, because by trotting out the Dodger like some diverting party trick, you're risking everything Lois has done for you! It could endanger your life!" She didn't realize she'd moved until she felt his hands circling her upper arms, holding her back.

"A party trick! You think I'm playing some blasted game?" He let go of her so suddenly that she fell back against the bricks, knocking the air out of her lungs. She'd meant to provoke a reaction out of him, but by the thunderous look on his face, she'd gone too far.

"Jack—"

"Do me a favor and leave off. Stay home tucked into your cozy feather bed," he spat. "And bury that foolish costume. I'll take care of the orphans. You're only making it harder for all of us."

Speechless, Olivia watched Jack crash through the hedge, the branches shuddering in his wake. She leaned against the cold bricks, her harsh breaths clouding the air in front of her eyes. Why the devil couldn't she just keep her mouth shut?

Snow began to fall; a trickle at first, and then a deluge. Fat flakes stuck to her lashes and melted on her already wet cheeks. She'd lashed out, desperate to see behind the mask he showed the rest of the world, but instead she may have pushed him away for good.

The next morning Olivia arrived at the tearoom early, a bell tinkling against the door as she entered. With a shiver, she wiped snow from her boots. The comforting scents of hot tea, wood smoke, and fresh baked goods welcomed her as a server indicated a variety of seats. She scanned the room, and noting that Vi and Francesca had yet to arrive, selected a cozy arrangement of overstuffed chairs draped in sunlight.

After ordering a pot of strong black tea, she settled in and stared blindly out the window. She'd awoken that morning with a melancholy she couldn't shake. It was as if she were drifting without a tether anchoring her to anything solid.

She removed her fur-lined gloves and placed them in her lap. Jack was right; her connection to Monks was putting the boys in more danger. Perhaps her days of gallivanting through the city as Ollie were at an end. If Jack promised to take care of the orphans, could she leave them in his hands? Her heart physically ached at the thought of never again seeing Chip's little face, or Archie's mischievous grin, or Brit—Olivia took a sip of tea and swallowed the lump in her throat—brilliant Brit, who took the weight of the world on his shoulders.

It wasn't a matter of trust, exactly. She was sure Jack could meet their needs and provide protection. But was he in it for the duration? Or would he forget all about the boys once the novelty of being their hero wore off?

The fact of the matter was, without those boys, Olivia had no idea who she was anymore. Was she the future Mrs. Maxwell Grimwig? Endeavoring to be the perfect society wife, her days filled with conversations about the latest wall-papering trends, the most frivolous hat designs, the grandest parties, and who was dallying with whom? God forbid!

Her cup clanged against its saucer, drawing the eyes of the few patrons in the shop. Olivia smiled wanly in apology and turned back to the window, where the foot traffic was picking up despite the snow-covered streets.

At least if she were going to become a wife, it would be not only for her uncle's guaranteed security, but to assist as many of the unfortunate as possible—and that included the Hill Orphans.

She'd let Jack serve his purpose and protect them with his reputation, but she refused to step aside quietly. Besides, if Monks hadn't deduced who she was by now, he was unlikely to link a street thug named Ollie with his lost little sister.

That morning, she'd worked up the nerve to ask Uncle Brownlow about Edward Leeford. He hadn't shown much of a reaction to her half brother's existence, but had assured her that her father's wealth had been squandered on asinine inventions and failed business ventures long ago. So Jack's theory that Monks sought to do her harm because of some long-lost fortune didn't hold weight.

The bell on the door tinkled and Fran and Vi rushed in, all rosy cheeks and laughter. Olivia waved, and Violet rushed over, rubbing her arms and shivering. Fran, much too sophisticated to show physical weakness, stamped her boots and swept over to the table wearing her perpetual smug smile.

"You'll never guess who we've just run into!" Violet proclaimed, taking a seat on the chair across from Olivia.

"Who?" Olivia asked, forcing herself out of her self-absorption for her best friend's sake.

"None other than Mr. Jack MacCarron," Fran pronounced as she hung her sable-trimmed jacket on a nearby coat tree.

Olivia swallowed a large gulp of hot tea and began to cough. Saints! Could she not escape the man for even a moment?

"Good heavens. Are you quite all right, Livie?" Violet handed her a napkin, which Olivia gracelessly snatched and pressed to her mouth as coughs racked her chest.

Francesca perched on the edge of her seat and poured her tea, ignoring Olivia's outburst. "Yes, Mr. MacCarron was on his way to Beakmans to have his final fitting for a suit of evening clothes."

"Just like us," Violet interjected, earning a scathing look from Fran, who wasn't finished gloating.

Since the Grimwigs' ball was next week, they'd planned to meet before heading to their ball gown fittings with the *fabulous* Madam Franchon. Olivia could only tolerate the pretentious woman in small doses, and never alone. She clucked around Olivia like a disapproving mother hen, shaking her head at Olivia's freckled skin and tsking at her sun-lightened hair.

Fran cleared her throat. "As I was saying, Jack made a point to inquire if I would be attending the ball."

Olivia arched a brow at Francesca's blatant use of his given name, and almost laughed out loud as she imagined what her sheltered cousin would do if she had witnessed Jack beating those men to bloody pulps in the street the previous night. An ungentlemanly practice to be sure.

"He inquired after both of us, Fran," Violet insisted, snatching a brown-butter cookie from the tray of sweets.

"I'm sure he was only asking *you* to be polite. Those evocative blue eyes didn't leave my face the entire conversation," Francesca replied.

Violet didn't respond, but Olivia could see her internal struggle as she pursed her lips and shoved the rest of the cookie into her mouth. Her best friend displayed commendable restraint, but knowing Vi as she did, it was only a matter of time before Fran found herself pushed from behind into a reeking pond. Olivia only hoped she'd be there to witness it.

"Speaking of the Grimwigs, how is a certain Mr. Grimwig these days?" Violet asked, wiggling her russet brows suggestively.

Only Uncle Brownlow and Max's parents knew of the engagement. But her cousins suspected Max's intentions, and were constantly prodding her for the latest information.

"I haven't seen him in several days. He's just returned from inspecting a property in Southampton with his father." Olivia leaned forward and selected a glistening apple-raisin tart from the tray. "I'm attending the theater with him tonight ..."

Olivia lifted the tart to her mouth, but before she could take a bite, the scent of spiced apples filled her head with visions of Jack, their breath mingling, his body pressing hers in the darkened doorway.

"Olivia?"

She blinked the wayward images out of her mind's eye and focused on Violet's pertly wrinkled nose. "Whyever do you have a string tied around your finger, Olivia dear?"

As she glanced down at the piece of black thread, heat rushed into her cheeks. She'd placed the string on her ring finger that morning as a reminder of her commitment to Max. She set the tart on her plate, untasted. "Um . . . it's to remind me of something . . . I . . . er . . . need to tell Maxwell this evening."

It wasn't a complete lie. Tonight, she was determined to show Max what a proper, devoted fiancée she could be to him. The theater was the perfect venue to spend some quality time and demonstrate her commitment, and at the very least, it was the one place she'd never run into Jack.

"If this is one of your little tests to gage my dedication, I'll tolerate it, but I promise I won't enjoy it." Jack stared across the shadowed interior of the carriage at Lois's pillowy face, her expression inscrutable—or devious, more like.

"The theater is not torture, my boy. It will do you good to gain a bit of culture. And this is not an examination, I simply needed your escort this evening."

"Right, and the queen of England is my long-lost sister," Jack muttered under his breath. Lois March never did anything without a precise purpose.

"What's that, my boy?" Lois asked over the creaking of the carriage.

"Nothing," he responded, slouching in his seat. "What play are we seeing?"

"*The Bohemian Girl.*" Lois twirled her fingers in a dismissive gesture. "The opera, you know."

"And why would I know?" Jack asked, lifting his brows in question.

"With your musical aptitude, I was sure you would've heard of it."

The carriage rumbled through a rough patch of snow and Lois gripped the hand strap and edge of her seat, softly cursing the perils of modern transportation. She preferred to walk whenever possible.

Even after the wheels found purchase and the ride smoothed out, Jack was unable to follow Lois's twisted logic. "To what musical aptitude are you referring?"

"The violin, of course. Your little impromptu performance at the Dells' musicale was inspired."

Jack grinned at her praise. He'd learned to play on a beat-up old fiddle he'd found in an abandoned Gypsy trunk. He'd picked up the instrument out of sheer boredom, but with a little instruction from Fagin, the music seemed to flow through him with ease. His performances had become a nightly entertainment on the Hill and a pure source of happiness for him.

"You should have seen how Little Miss Amethyst practically swooned at your feet that night."

Remembering the lovely set of amethyst jewels Lois referred to, Jack knew she spoke of Francesca Lancaster, Olivia's cousin. *Olivia.* Dark heat pulsed in his chest. How could she accuse him of being reckless? He'd weighed all the risks of dragging the Dodger out of the past. And he knew exactly what was at stake.

She was the one taking needless risks by wandering around the city in that thinly veiled disguise. A wig and dirt-smeared cheeks couldn't hide her innate grace and beauty. He'd never wanted to kiss and strangle someone in the same breath, but that incongruous and decidedly uncomfortable state had become the norm when he was with her.

Jack realized Lois was still talking and he'd tuned her out.

". . . an association?" Lois met his gaze expectantly as the carriage rolled to a halt.

Parting the curtains, Jack saw that they were still down the block from Drury Lane Theatre. They jerked back into motion, moving forward in the line. "What type of association?" Jack asked distractedly.

"Blast it, Jack! Where is your head? You disappear for days on end without a word, and don't think I haven't noticed that it's been several weeks since your last score."

Jack ran a hand through his hair; he'd known this interrogation was coming. "I thought it best to lay low for a bit. The Dells reported the theft, and the beaks launched a full investigation."

"Be that as it may, it's time to refocus our efforts. And if you'd been attending you would realize this next assignment is complicated, but . . . fruitful."

Now she had his attention. "I'm listening."

"As I was saying, the Emeralds'—" She stopped and shook her head. "I mean, the *Grimwigs'* ball is next week. It should be a huge crush and the perfect time for a heist. The gems are flawless, a total of fifty carats. I already have a potential buyer lined up in Calcutta."

"If they're so fabulous, how do you know Mrs. Grimwig won't be wearing them at the ball?"

The old woman leaned forward, her eyes glowing through the gloom. "I have it on good authority that she's had a scarlet dress designed for the occasion. Emeralds would clash horribly."

Jack nodded. If this hit was as big as Lois claimed, it would be their most lucrative yet.

"Here's the rub. For some inexplicable reason, we haven't received an invitation to the ball."

Jack didn't have to guess why. String-bean Grimwig didn't want Jack anywhere near Olivia. Little did Maxwell know that Jack didn't need a formal invitation to spend time with his girl.

"Wipe that smirk off your face and focus!" Lois gave his calf a whack with her cane. "And stop slouching."

Jack winced and rubbed his stinging leg as he straightened in his seat. The old woman was stronger than she appeared.

"Now, if you were to cultivate an association with the highly sought-after Francesca Lancaster, I'm sure we would receive an invitation post haste."

From the seductive looks Miss Lancaster had thrown his way that morning on the street, his attentions would be more than welcome. But he feared Francesca would take his interest to heart.

"I know you don't have an aversion to rich, beautiful women, so why the reluctance?"

Jack ran his thumb over the pads of his fingers in contemplation. He wanted to tell her no, that he wouldn't do it. But in this case, the ends more than justified the means. "I know Miss Lancaster rather well. It won't be a problem."

"Good. Because I invited her to the theater on your behalf, and she'll be sitting in our box tonight."

The woman worked fast, he had to give her that.

CHAPTER 13

"It occurred to me, Miss Brownlow," Maxwell said as he led Olivia to her seat in the second-tier balcony, "that I have been neglectful in my courtship duties." He spoke the words as if rehearsed. Or, more likely, prompted by his mother.

"Tonight qualifies as a courtship outing, does it not?" Olivia placed her gloved fingers on Max's dark coat sleeve and met his eyes.

He blinked down at her hand, his cheeks darkening. "Perhaps this courtship business isn't so bad after all." His solicitous comment made Olivia's throat constrict with guilt as she removed her hand from his arm and sat, fingering the small knot of string beneath the fabric of her glove, a reminder that her heart was divided.

Flustered, she raised her opera glasses to glance around the packed theater. They were seated in the Grimwigs' private box with his parents. The perch gave them an optimal view of not only the stage but the colorful crowd as well.

Movement in the box directly across the theater caught her eye, and she swung the glasses around until she landed on a couple, just in time to see the dark-haired man leaning over to kiss the extended hand of a petite brunette. As the glasses brought the couple into focus, the blood drained from Olivia's head and landed with a lump in her stomach. It was none other than Jack MacCarron and her blasted cousin

Francesca. Lowering the glasses, she sucked air in gulps, the stricture of her stays stifling.

"What is it, Miss Brownlow?" Max lifted his glasses to follow the direction of her gaze. "Is that MacCarron?"

"Why, yes," Martha Grimwig commented from the other side of Maxwell. "And Miss Lancaster. What a lovely couple they make. Don't you agree, Miss Brownlow?"

Olivia couldn't open her mouth for fear she might vomit. What was he doing here with *her*? Fran knew she was going to the theater this evening and hadn't mentioned a word of her plans to attend. It must have been a last-minute invitation following her meeting with Jack on the street that morning. What was it Fran had said? *Those evocative blue eyes didn't leave my face the entire conversation.* Olivia had dismissed it as her cousin's over-inflated opinion of herself. Apparently, she'd been wrong.

Like a spectator unable to resist the macabre pull of a bloody accident, Olivia lifted her glasses and watched Jack and Fran's dark heads tilt together in intimate conversation. She couldn't make out their expressions in the dim light, but it was clear by their body language that they were enjoying each other's company.

"Whyever did you ask me not to invite him to the ball?" Mrs. Grimwig asked Max in an annoyed tone.

"Mother, *please*. Let's not discuss this here," Max replied in a hiss.

Olivia forced herself to lower her glasses and focus on the conversation.

"He is always perfectly charming, and if Miss Lancaster deems him suitable then I shan't exclude him."

"Mother, you don't—"

The orchestra's discordant tuning swelled into organization, the smooth woodwinds melding with soaring strings and a roll of percussion, cutting off further conversation. Ushers garbed in gray from head to toe swarmed in like a flock of jays, extinguishing the lamps in formation. This dramatic prelude was Olivia's favorite part. But not even a rainbow of gypsies twirling across the stage, tambourines jingling, could distract her when her gut was churning with such violence.

She knew she had no claim on Jack and no cause to feel this jealousy, but that didn't change the fact she longed to be the one sitting beside him—his leg brushing hers, his breath stirring the tiny hairs by her ear, the very air around them pulsing with expectation. She glanced over at Max, his long legs crossed, his posture erect, very properly not touching her person. *This* was her fate and her future.

But who said it had to be? Why couldn't Olivia add excitement to her relationship with her betrothed? Shifting closer to Max, she placed her hand on top of his and pressed the length of their arms together. He didn't appear to notice, so she gave his fingers a squeeze. His brows scrunched as he tore his gaze from the stage and looked down at their joined hands. He pressed his lips together, his eyes shifting over to his mother. He gave Olivia's fingers a pat before extricating his hand from hers and resting it on his knee, directing his attention back to the performance.

A flush rose to heat Olivia's cheeks as she shifted away from the man beside her, ensuring that not even their clothing touched. Olivia was quite certain Jack and Francesca were not inhibited by such antiquated strictures of propriety, especially in the dim intimacy of the auditorium. A jittery energy coursed through her, her legs itching to move.

But she sat through what seemed like an endless number of songs, the dancers blurring before her eyes. Then all the frenetic movement stopped, and a lone woman stood center stage, singing lyrics that cut to Olivia's heart: *"The secret of my birth, to him is only known. The secret of a life whose worth perchance he will disown, disown . . ."* Would Max disown her if he knew all the secrets of *her* scandalous past? *Her present?*

Olivia leaned forward in her seat as a man joined in the song, his words unbeknownst to the woman: *"The secret of her birth to me is only known, the secret of a life whose worth I prize beyond mine own, beyond mine own."* Or would Max respond as the man and cherish her despite her past? She couldn't dismiss the fact there was one who knew all her secrets, yet protected her with his life—and he sat across the theater wooing her cousin.

Suddenly, the darkened box began to close in around her. Murmuring an excuse, she grabbed her reticule and stood, feeling her way along the brocade-covered wall and up the aisle stairs to the hallway. She didn't stop until she reached the mezzanine level. The large atrium was empty save for a few ushers replacing candles in the lowered chandeliers, their wavering light casting discordant shadows on the walls. Olivia rushed to a nearby ladies' washroom, ducked inside, and threw herself down at a vanity table.

She plucked off her gloves and stared at her own image in the mirror. From the sweetheart neckline of her rose-colored silk gown to the elaborate upsweep of her hair and the glint of paste jewels dangling from her ears, she was a lady of elegance and refinement. But a large part of her wanted to rip it all off. Tear the earbobs from her lobes, pluck the pins from her hair, and scream the truth of her identity to the world.

Instead, she unclenched her fists and lowered her face into her palms. She'd been hiding so long, she didn't even know who she was anymore.

"Miss? Are you all right?"

Olivia raised her head and looked up to find a woman standing behind her. The lady was unfamiliar, with dark eyes and hair streaked with silver. She held Olivia's gaze in the mirror, exuding poise and grace.

With a confidence she did not yet feel, Olivia answered, "Yes, I am . . . or at least, I will be."

"I've been there myself." A smile full of warmth and understanding lit her face, creasing the skin by her eyes. "I've found if one follows their heart, everything works out in the end."

"My heart?" Olivia gripped the reticule in her lap, hundreds of beads digging into her palms. If her mother's life had been any indication, the heart was far too fickle to follow.

The woman moved to the next vanity and leaned down to check her face. "You know, your intuition." She turned and looked at Olivia, a bit of challenge shining in her gaze. "That small inner voice that most women ignore because they're too concerned with living the life others expect."

Olivia returned the woman's stare for several seconds, wondering how she had read her thoughts. "I'll keep that in mind."

"Good. Well, if you've collected yourself, there's a gentleman waiting for you outside. He asked me to look in on you."

Max. He'd come after her! Perhaps they weren't so disconnected after all. Olivia rose to her feet, straightened her skirts, and dipped a quick curtsy to the woman. "Thank you for your kindness."

The woman nodded with a knowing smile as Olivia rushed out the door and into the shadowed hallway, and almost walked past Jack.

Jack?

She stopped and looked up and down the passageway. He was the only one there. She walked over to where he leaned with a shoulder against the wall, one booted foot crossed in front of the other, comfortable as you please, watching her with a disconcerting familiarity.

"Jack, what are you doing here?"

He responded with a sardonic lift of one brow, as if the answer should be obvious. "Checking on you." The deep timbre of his voice vibrated over her skin.

"Why? I—" Olivia stopped to swallow. "I thought you were angry with me."

"I am . . . was." A corner of his lips curled and he plucked off his top hat, dark hair falling into his eyes as he fidgeted with the ribbon around the brim. "But something was clearly wrong for you to leave in the middle of such an engaging performance."

"How did you— Wait. Were you watching me?"

"Plays bore me." He shrugged and met her gaze. "Besides, I don't believe opera glasses were intended for the stage."

"True enough." Olivia's heart skipped a beat as he confirmed he'd been watching her instead of the show. "What about Francesca?"

"What about her? I came to check on *you*." His words melted through her like warm brandy, leaving her light headed.

Jack shifted to lean with his back against the wall and studied his fingernails. "Do you want to go somewhere with me . . . to talk?" His eyes lifted, burning into hers, and Olivia stopped breathing.

"Where?"

"Anywhere."

"I . . ." Did she want to leave the theater in the middle of the performance? Abandon both their companions without a word? With Jack?

He looked down at the tip of his shoe, shoved a hand in his pocket and waited, giving her time to decide. She noticed he'd removed his cravat, displaying the strong column of his throat; his too-long hair brushed his collar, and stubble darkened the hard angle of his jaw. He was danger and temptation personified. And she'd never wanted anything more in her life than to allow him to lead her where he may.

She glanced up and down the hallway. They were still very much alone. Could she truly shut down the warnings in her head and follow her heart? Listen to her inner voice?

Olivia moved toward him and his eyes widened a fraction, his whole body tensing. A thrill of power coursed through her, and she knew the answer. She took another step and tilted her face up to his. "Yes."

Their gazes locked, his eyes sparking with mystery. "Then let's be off. The night awaits." He pushed off the wall, cupped the back of her neck, and pulled her in for a single searing kiss that curled her toes in her slippers.

When he lifted his head, she saw her own exhilaration reflected in his blue gaze. She could not conceive of his motivations, but for now, being with him was enough. He touched the back of her arm and guided her down the passage.

A bit dizzy, Olivia leaned into his strength. It wasn't as if they'd never been alone before, but this was somehow different. Perhaps because they weren't Ollie and Dodger on a mission or Miss Brownlow and Mr. MacCarron putting on airs at a party. They were simply Olivia and Jack, and being together felt like the most natural thing in the world.

Once they reached the atrium, ushers stood sentinel at every door. All the wall sconces and chandeliers had been lit and raised. Jack walked faster. The intermission was about to begin. As they rushed across the enormous space, the swish of Olivia's skirts whispered in time with her pulse and the diamond-patterned carpet stretched before them, giving the illusion that it moved beneath their feet.

When the intermission began, Max and Mr. and Mrs. Grimwig would search for her, panicked at her sudden disappearance. And when she couldn't be found, they would inform her uncle and possibly the constables to search the city. Uncle Brownlow would be frantic with worry. Olivia's steps slowed.

Jack continued past her, but his hand still held her elbow so that when she stopped, his arm stretched out behind him. He turned and met her gaze. Pressure building behind her eyes, she shook her head. The doors opened all around them, and the buzz of hundreds of voices, like a beehive exploding, assaulted her ears. She glanced behind Jack at the exit, so close. Her heart galloped in her chest, compelling her to flee.

"We can still make it, if we go *now*," Jack urged, his crystal-blue eyes imploring.

With a fortitude she didn't know she possessed, Olivia stepped back from his touch. "I cannot."

⌘

"Miss Brownlow!"

String-bean Grimwig rushed toward them, and Jack had to force his hands to unclench. *Blast it all!* Where was bloomin' Grimwig when Olivia fled the theater in distress? He was sitting on his pompous behind, too afraid to go against convention and follow her, that's where.

"Miss Brownlow, is something amiss? Why did you leave the performance?" Twin flags of red stained Grimwig's cheeks as he stopped in front of them, his gaze darting to Jack, and then back to Olivia. "What is *he* doing here?"

"I'm fine. I merely needed a spot of fresh air." Olivia's mouth twisted in an effort to smile, but she quickly abandoned the attempt and began to fiddle with her reticule. She looked lost, like a baby bird that had fallen out of its nest, and Jack longed to put his arms around her.

Grimwig's eyes narrowed in accusation. "I asked you what *MacCarron* is doing here."

"He was . . . I mean, I . . ." Olivia floundered, blinking rapidly.

"Olivia appeared distraught, and I was simply inquiring as to the lass's wellbeing." Jack worked to keep his tone light, when he longed to smash his fist into Grimwig's abnormally large nose.

"Olivia?" Maxwell's face turned a disturbing shade of mauve, his raised tone drawing several curious stares.

Jack suppressed a groan at his slip in address. What could he say? *I've actually known her since she was a child dressed like a boy and stealing on the streets to survive. So I believe I've earned the right to speak her bloody name.*

"It's quite all right, Max." Olivia attempted to placate Grimwig with a touch to his sleeve.

"Did you give MacCarron leave to use your given name?"

Jack clenched his teeth and took a step forward. Robbing this git was going to be one of the great pleasures of his life. But for Olivia's sake he would bury his anger and find a way to diffuse the situation. Before he could intervene, however, Olivia took Grimwig by the arm and began leading him away. "Max, you know how I despise formality . . ."

At that inopportune moment, Lois and Miss Lancaster approached. "What is going on, here?" Lois demanded. "Jack?"

Jack watched the graceful line of Olivia's back as she walked away. He couldn't blame her for changing her mind, but that didn't dissipate the disappointment scalding through him like a fever.

Turning to face his own disastrous situation, he pasted on a wide smile. "Ah, Auntie Lois and Miss Lancaster, so very good to see ye both! Please forgive my earlier absence," he cooed in his most seductive brogue as he took Miss Lancaster's hand and placed a lingering kiss on her gloved fingers. Her glare melted into a pout.

Lois arched a brow, but thankfully kept her mouth shut. By the way her hawklike gaze focused past his shoulder, he could guess she knew he'd been with Olivia Brownlow, and she wasn't pleased.

Turning his attention to his neglected companion, Jack apologized again and made his excuses for leaving the play. Soon, his irreverent critiques of the performance had her laughing, and they joined the line at the refreshment table. As they drank tiny cups of swill being passed off as lemonade, bells tinkled overhead, warning everyone to find their way back to their seats.

Joining the crush, Jack remained attentive to Francesca while covertly scanning the crowd for Olivia. Just ahead and to the right, he caught a glimpse of her dark-gold curls. He placed his hand on Francesca's back and maneuvered her through the maze of people. The airless passage wreaked of body odor, hair pomade, and cloying perfumes. Jack excused his way through a cluster of older ladies shuffling along at a snail's pace. He needed to reach Olivia before the hallway divided.

"Mr. MacCarron, do slow down. These shoes pinch my feet," Francesca whined as she struggled to stay at his side. Jack ignored the inane comment. The woman should purchase shoes that actually fit her bloomin' feet.

Just before reaching the split, Jack positioned himself directly behind Olivia. Utilizing one of his old pickpocketing moves, he feigned a trip, and his shoulder plowed into Olivia's arm, knocking the reticule from her hand. She turned and knelt to pick it up, but Jack was already there. Their eyes met and everything seemed to slow around them. "Meet me at the gate. Tonight. Two a.m."

Olivia blinked twice, frowned, and then gave a barely

perceptible shake of her head. Did she mean not at that time, or not tonight, or not ever? Jack handed the bag back to her, breathing in her sunshine and vanilla scent as they both stood.

The entire exchange lasted mere seconds and soon they rejoined their companions. Jack caught String-bean's glare, and returned it with a glacial smirk before leading Francesca down the opposite hall.

Olivia had been ready to go anywhere with him. He'd read the inclination in her eyes. What had changed in those short minutes after they'd parted? Jack rolled his shoulders and suppressed a sigh of frustration. He would have to put on a good show if he hoped to hold Francesca's interest. But after he fulfilled his duty and Lois was tucked away in her room, the night was his. He wasn't giving up on Miss Brownlow so easily.

Chapter 14

Olivia slipped out of the rose silk gown and gasped in relief as she unlaced her corset. Sitting on the bed, she rolled off her stockings, releasing a sigh as the air hit her bare skin. After hanging her gown in the wardrobe and placing her underthings in the dresser drawer, she fetched the key to the locked chest at the end of her bed and removed her costume.

She desperately needed to see the boys, but she would have to leave within the next quarter hour to avoid running into Jack. She had no doubt he would arrive at the designated time and place, despite her refusal. He was not one to take denial in stride. She yanked on a pair of trousers, the coarse material scratching against her bare legs.

Olivia finished winding the binding cloth around her chest, fastened the tiny metal clips down the side, and then shrugged into a cambric shirt, her fingers pausing on the second button. She could still meet him and they could go to the Hill together. Dressed as Ollie, who would know?

Absolutely not!

She hastily finished buttoning the shirt over her bound breasts. Her impetuous behavior at the theater had proved she could no longer trust herself around Jack. And as much as she hated to admit it, Max's warning earlier that evening had struck a chord: *If you believe a cad like Jack MacCarron has your best interest at heart, then you're sadly mistaken. I've heard stories about his past that would horrify you. The man is not only a user of women, but possibly a criminal. If you value your reputation—moreover, if you respect my family in the least—you'll stay well clear of that blackguard.*

Not that Olivia took it all to heart; she knew well of Jack's "horrifying" past. However, she had to admit he had behaved quite the rogue that evening. Escorting one woman to the theater—her dimwit cousin, no less—and then enticing Olivia to leave with him before the performance concluded. But even beyond Jack's deceitful actions, the underlying meaning behind Max's words chilled her to the bone. If he caught her with Jack in another compromising situation, he would break the betrothal.

Olivia stuffed a stray curl into her hairnet with extra vigor, the painful tug of the tiny hairs on her neck making her eyes sting. Once again she would do what was right and ignore her own wishes and desires. The woman in the washroom at the theater may have meant well, but she did not know of the inescapable prison Olivia had backed herself into.

She could hardly believe she'd been seconds away from taking the woman's advice, following Jack from the theater and throwing her whole future, not to mention her uncle's security, down the gutter. And for what? An alluring smile? A touch that shivered across her skin?

Olivia sighed and stared at the mousy wig clutched in her hands. It was true that when their lips met she felt it over every inch of her skin, but as much as she wished it so, her feelings for Jack were not merely physical.

When she'd asked for his help, before she could even explain what she needed, he had responded, *Anything.* No lectures on propriety. No questions asked. Because he knew the dark fear that drove her. It lived inside of him too.

Jack could match wits with her all while twirling her in a flawless waltz. He put on airs with the gentry of London, warming his hands by their hearths, consuming their sumptuous feasts, playing their games, all while hiding his true intentions, his true identity. Just as she did. They each had a foot in both worlds, but didn't fit into either.

But together, miraculously, they fit.

Perhaps she'd never stopped caring for the boy who'd once been her champion. But when he'd agreed to unbury his past to save the orphans, regardless of the risks to himself, her feelings had deepened to a dangerous level.

She collapsed into the hearth chair, something inside her disintegrating at the thought of never seeing him again. Their paths would cross at social events, but they would have to pretend they didn't share a history, pretend they meant nothing to one another. She stared into the dancing flames behind the grate. A life without Jack would be like a doused fire; ashy shades of gray washed of the light and heat that had created them.

Brom whined and set his head on her feet. She reached down and rubbed his ears. "I know, boy. I'm going to miss him too."

"Miss whom?"

Olivia hitched a breath and sprang out of her seat. Brom jumped up, tail wagging, and padded over to Jack as he shut the bedroom door softly behind him. He turned and grinned that cocky grin of his, and Olivia's heart flipped like a pancake on a skillet, a slow sizzle heating her blood.

"Jack! How did you get in here?" she hissed under her breath.

"I asked you a question first," he replied in his normal deep tone of voice.

"Hush!" Olivia lifted a finger to her lips, glancing at the ceiling. She'd had no time to slip a toddy in Mrs. Foster's tea, and the evil housekeeper's room was directly above hers. "Someone will hear you."

He shrugged a broad shoulder. "I'm confident in your skills of deception. If someone should come to the door, I'm sure you could manufacture a convincing lie."

His words, casual yet provoking, scraped across her frazzled nerves like an onion grater against flesh. "What is *that* supposed to mean?" She marched over to him, hands fisted on her hips.

He moved farther into the room, stopped in front of the fireplace, and inspected a porcelain doll on the mantel. "Do you still play with dolls?"

It was the first toy she'd ever owned—a reminder of her uncle's generosity. She snatched it out of his hands and placed it gently back on the mantel. "What are you doing here?"

"We have unfinished business." His gaze perused her outfit, and returned to her face with an amused lift of his brow. "I'm not sure what to call you right now, love. Being in mid-transformation as you are."

Olivia fought against the blush threatening to erupt across her skin. In baggy boy clothes, all her hair tucked into a tight net, she must look a fright. She blinked at Jack, the personification of masculine beauty, his athletic build evident even in his unrefined clothes, and she yanked the net off her head.

The rough motion sent pins clinking to the wood floor and her hair tumbling around her shoulders.

An appreciative smile spread across his face as he reached out and picked up one of her curls, letting it coil around his fingers. "I had no idea your hair was so long. *Beautiful*," he whispered as he tugged on the strand, leading her closer.

She came willingly, drawn into his snare. Every warning thought, every tug of conscience flew out of her head as he closed the space between them. His eyes, like blue flames, locked on hers, his hair falling over his brow. "I'm going to kiss you now, Olivia." The stirring melody of his voice flooded through her, washing away her fear and the last of her resistance. His arm wrapped around her waist and pulled her against him. "But only if you tell me that's what you want."

She nodded her head, unable to speak. He cupped the side of her face and leaned down, brushing aside her hair. Olivia inhaled sharply, his spicy scent flooding her senses as he tilted his head so that his lips grazed her ear. "You need to say it, love," he murmured.

A hard shiver wracked down Olivia's spine, and Jack brought her closer, his body heat soothing her chill.

"Yes."

His mouth hovered a hairsbreadth from hers. "Yes, what?"

"Kiss me now, blast it!" Olivia clasped the back of his neck and pressed her lips to his. At the touch of his mouth, lights burst behind her closed eyes. She shoved her fingers into the silken layers of his hair, gripping the strands as the entire world tilted on its axis.

His lips slid over hers and he took her head in his hands, his thumbs caressing her face. Olivia pressed closer still.

Responding to her urgency, he deepened the kiss and began to walk, pushing her backward, carrying her with one arm around her waist. The room tipped and spun until all that existed were his hands, his mouth, his skin, a blaze like starlight in her veins.

Then the back of her knees hit the bed and Olivia realized she couldn't breathe.

Pulling away from Jack, she pushed against his shoulder. "I . . . can't . . . brea—"

"That's normal, love." Still holding her around the waist, he lowered his mouth to the pulse hammering in her throat.

Now she *really* couldn't breathe! She arched back and wiggled until he dropped her to her feet. Frantic, she began tugging at the buttons of her shirt, gasping like a fish on the dock.

Jack flicked the hair out of his eyes and volunteered, "Let me help with that." His large hands reached for the tiny buttons, but she pushed him away. When she'd parted the sides of her shirt, he stared at her bound chest, his eyes darting in incomprehension.

Olivia reached around her side and released the metal fasteners that held the cloth in place. As soon as she'd unhooked the top two she drew in several exquisite gulps of air.

Jack grinned wickedly. "I thought you'd felt curvier before."

Her limbs shook with the effort, but she stepped back and drew the shirt closed. Her sense returning, she knew the next few moments could have irreversible consequences. "I care for you, Jack . . . but . . . I have my reputation to think about . . . my future."

Something desolate filled his eyes before he schooled his

expression. Olivia took several deliberate steps away from him, tears burning her throat.

Shoving the hair off his forehead, Jack stared at something beyond her shoulder. "Your future?" he asked, as if the thought of life after this moment had just occurred to him.

"Yes, I have to—"

He cut her off with a frosty look. "It's Grimwig, isn't it?" He shoved off the bed. "You're saving yourself for that idiotic dolt!"

Olivia refused to answer, her sorrow dissolving into a slow burn as she watched him pace in front of the window. He was so entitled! Never sharing anything with her about his own life, yet demanding answers from her every time she turned around. "Speaking of dolts, what were you doing with my cousin tonight?"

A bang sounded from overhead, and Brom growled from where he'd been sleeping by the fire. Jack and Olivia froze and stared up at the ceiling.

After several seconds of quiet, Jack glared at Olivia and hissed, "I care nothing for Francesca."

"Then why would you invite her to the theater?" she demanded as she felt the sting of her fingernails pressing into the flesh of her palms.

"I wouldn't."

Olivia suppressed a groan of frustration. He made no sense whatsoever. "You need not lie to me, Jack. Or have you forgotten that I saw you there *with her*?"

A predatory light sparked in his eyes, reminiscent of a lion with its tail twitching in the air as he stalked toward her. He backed her across the room and spoke with slow deliberation.

"Would it kill you to have a little faith in me? Just for once? To give me the benefit of the bloody doubt?"

Olivia stopped when her back hit the dresser. "I—"

He leaned in and braced a hand on either side of her, trapping her between his arms. Her pulse accelerated in time with the warning vein throbbing in his throat.

"Does Grimwig kiss you until you can't stand?" he demanded.

Olivia didn't move, words failing her.

"Can he make you lose your breath?" Jack's tone softened. "Can he?"

When she shook her head, all the tension left his arms and he took her chin between his fingers. Clearly, he wanted to kiss her, but something held him back.

She touched his hand and stared into those soul-searing blue eyes. "What is it you want, Jack?"

He blinked. And Olivia prayed he wouldn't run away, like every other time she'd asked him anything personal. She waited, holding her breath.

His hands dropped to his sides and he stepped back, his features slammed shut. "Nothing. There's nothing I want."

Olivia sighed. "Jack, I want to trust you. I do. But I know very little about you." She took his broad hand in hers, knowing she was about to scare the living daylights out of him but willing to take the chance. "What makes Jack MacCarron get up in the morning? What motivates him to plot his next brilliant heist? Do you want to be a jewel thief for the rest of your life? What do you want for your future?"

Jack froze like a statue of solid rock, the muscle ticking

in his jaw the only discernible movement. For someone who was constantly in motion, the contrast was . . . disconcerting.

Just when she thought he wouldn't answer, he said, "You don't understand. The goal *is* to want nothing." He swallowed and looked away. When he turned back it was with a brash half grin. "I have everything I need: the scent of London air, good food in my belly, and a soft place to rest my head. What else is there?"

It was the most personal admission she'd ever heard him make, but it was utter nonsense. Olivia let go of his hand, and turning her back on him, walked to the fireplace. She knelt down and began gathering the pins that had fallen from her hair. Brom opened one eye and watched her for a moment before falling back to sleep. How could a person want *nothing* for their future? It was completely counterintuitive that he went to such lengths to rob the rich, and yet claimed there was no motivation behind such a risk.

Sitting down at her vanity, she shoved pins into her hair and watched Jack in the mirror as he plucked his jacket off the floor and shrugged it on. Her face heated as she realized she'd removed that jacket from his shoulders just moments before. He then picked up his hat and angled it low over his eyes.

Would he leave without another word? She jerked her gaze back to her reflection, refusing to give in to the emotion building in her chest. Grabbing the hairnet, she tugged it onto her head, viciously tucking strands into the netting. If he wanted to go, then good riddance! She was done playing his game.

Warm fingers touched the back of her head as Jack coiled

up a section of curls and slid it beneath the net. Olivia jerked her head away from him, but when his soft touch brushed against the sensitive skin of her neck her resistance turned to mush. He gathered another section of hair, and tingles raced across her scalp. Her shoulders slumping in defeat, she closed her eyes and melted into his gentle ministrations.

Exhausted from many nights with little sleep, she couldn't motivate her jellylike muscles to move, even after he finished. As if in a dream, Olivia felt Jack's hands on her shoulders and his warm breath in her ear. "I didn't lie to you. There's no point in wanting something you can never have."

Her eyes flew open, searching for the meaning behind his words, but he'd already moved away. She turned, and he threw her mousy wig into her lap. "If you're still planning on going to the Hill tonight, we should leave now."

CHAPTER 15

The sharp scent of wood smoke swirled through the frosty night air, causing Olivia to long for a warm fire and a cozy blanket. Her eyes grew heavy as she pushed her feet to move faster. Jack had not spoken a word since they'd climbed through the dining room window—the one with the now broken lock.

As they turned onto the Strand, Jack blurted, "I killed a man once." The words overlapped and rushed out of him as if he could no longer take the pressure of keeping them inside.

Olivia nearly tripped over his confession. Only when she was sure she could conceal her shock did she venture a glance at his face. His eyes darted to hers and then away. When several seconds passed and he didn't elaborate, Olivia decided a bit of prompting couldn't hurt. She swallowed and endeavored to sound blasé, as if people confessed murder to her every other day. "What happened?"

After tucking his trusty umbrella under his arm, he pushed the hat back on his head then ran a hand over his face. "It was a few years after you went to live with your uncle. I was leading my own gang by then, and one of the boys disappeared. Daniel. He was the youngest of the group, around Chip's age. His mother had died, leaving him with an opium-addicted father who threatened to sell him at every turn. One day the father followed through on the threat, and Daniel ran. That's when I found him sleeping in the street." Jack paused and tugged the hat low over his eyes, his jaw set in a grim line. "Daniel had been with us a few months when he didn't return from picking. None of the other kids saw where he went, but I knew. Somehow I *knew* his father had found him."

Jack's stride slowed, and his next words seemed to scratch through his throat. "I made inquiries, and the clues led me to a brothel in Seven Dials."

Olivia sucked in an involuntary breath. Seven Dials was the point where seven crooked streets, narrow alleys, and obscure lanes met in an irregular square. But beyond its seemingly innocuous architecture, the district's heart was rotten to the core. If one sought to gorge himself on the most debased vices imaginable, Seven Dials more than fed their needs. But for an unprotected child, or even a street-wise young adult . . .

Olivia shivered so hard that Brom whined and butted her hand with his furry head. She clamped her fingers on Jack's arm. "Please tell me you did not go there alone."

He finally looked at her, his eyes unreadable in the shadowed street. "What would you have done?"

"Not go alone!"

Jack shoved his hands in his pants pockets and stared at his feet, kicking a pebble down the dark sidewalk. "When I reached the Dials, the brothel was heavily guarded. So, I snuck in through a broken window at the back of a public house two doors down, crossed the eaves, and entered through the attic. After reaching the second-floor hallway and picking lock after lock, I'd gotten an eyeful of flesh, but no Daniel."

Olivia was beginning to dread where the story was headed, but she kept her mouth shut. Jack obviously needed to get this off his chest. And she was honored, and not a little astonished, that he'd chosen to bare his soul to her.

"I'd reached the final door before the staircase, and as I jimmied the lock I heard heavy footfalls approaching. I slipped through the door. But instead of another bedroom, I found a staircase that I followed to a secluded third-floor chamber." Jack paused and drew a heavy breath before continuing. "Instinct prodded me to pick the lock quickly. I slammed into the room and found Daniel gagged and bound, a man flogging him with a whip."

Tendrils of horror wrapped themselves around Olivia's heart and squeezed. She didn't want to hear any more. Yet, she remained silent.

Jack stared ahead, his next words coming out in a rush. "It sounds crazy, but it was as if a red veil fell over my eyes and I lost control of my own actions. Like a wild animal, I tackled the man and began beating him. I got several good hits in before he turned on me and banged my head against the floor. He pulled a gun and shot, but I managed to dodge the bullet and . . . we scuffled again. The man had wrestled me to the floor. I managed to get away, and when I scrambled to my feet, he didn't move again. My knife was buried in his chest."

A crosswind blew the stench of the Thames across their path, curdling Olivia's stomach with the combination of human waste and dead fish. She swallowed hard and squeezed Jack's arm tighter, hoping to convey her understanding since she couldn't find her voice.

"After it was over, I noticed the man's fine clothes. He wasn't some lowlife, Dials scum. I killed a toff." Their eyes met and unshed tears hovered on Jack's dark lashes.

Olivia stopped in a shadowy spot between streetlamps, pulled him into her arms, and held him tight. "Jack," she said against his shoulder, "he may have been a gentleman, but he was the worst kind of human to have done that to a little boy. Just think of all the other children you likely saved from the same fate."

"I know. But that doesn't make it right," he whispered.

She leaned back, and seeing that he'd regained control of his emotions, asked, "What happened to Daniel?"

"That's the worst part." The edges of his mouth pulled down and he shook his head. "I took him straight to a crow, but he'd lost too much blood. He didn't make it. I didn't save him in time."

The tears Jack held in seemed to spill from Olivia's eyes. "I'm so sorry." She pressed her cheek against the warm skin of his neck and wept. She cried for Daniel. And she cried for the boy she'd known as Dodger, giving everything to protect others and losing himself along the way.

A squeak and crunch echoed down the street and Olivia felt Jack's body tense. Still holding her in his arms, he turned. Swiping the tears from under her eyes, she squinted through the haze and could just make out a spectral figure pushing a cart in their direction.

Jack released her, gripped the umbrella in his right hand, point out, and muttered, "Stay close."

She gave Brom's leash a firm yank, effectively cutting off the dog's growl. Then she scanned the area, but the man with the cart appeared to be alone. She grabbed Jack's coat and tried to pull him to the other side of the street. He didn't budge. The slow progress of the cart rumbled forward over the cobbles. "Come on," Olivia hissed.

"It's all right. I think I know him," Jack replied.

The costermonger passed through a pool of light, and Olivia gasped. Same flat-brimmed black hat, hawkish nose and wiry beard . . . it was their old kidsman, Fagin. How he was still alive, she couldn't fathom. She'd thought him ancient back when he'd taken her in all those years ago. Olivia shrunk behind Jack's shoulder. Fagin had acted the kindly old gentleman, but he could turn like a viper, striking when you least expected it.

"Care ta buy a bobble, my dears?" The craggy old man approached, leaning on his cart like a crutch. When he drew up under the nearest lamp, Olivia's hand flew to her mouth. Fagin's teeth were completely gone, his lips sunken in around his gums, and his eyes were covered with a thick, milky film. By the way he lifted his chin and turned his head from side to side, she could tell he'd lost most of his vision. No recognition dawned as his unfocused gaze settled in their direction.

"What have you got for sale, old man?" Jack asked.

The assortment of junk piled in his cart looked to have been plucked fresh from the garbage—a broken rattrap, chipped dishes, a few rotten pieces of fruit. Olivia spied a stained pallet tied to the side of the wagon and realized the old man must be homeless. Compassion sparked in her chest, despite her apprehension.

"Oh, this is prime merchandise, it is. How about a lovely apple or two, hm?"

Jack reached for a piece of fruit, but stopped just before touching the foul produce wriggling with maggots. He pulled back his hand and then paused. Olivia could see the tension leave his shoulders as a look of resignation settled over his countenance. He reached inside his coat and produced a wad of pound notes. Handing several bills to Fagin, he instructed, "Tuck this away and go get yourself a room where you can die in peace, old man. The Three Cripples will likely take you in."

Fagin took the cash and lifted his windfall to the meager light with trembling hands, straining to see as he shuffled through the notes. His lips began to quiver when the amount of his good fortune dawned.

Jack took Olivia's arm and steered her around the cart. When they drew even with the old man, Jack's hand whipped out and grasped both of Fagin's, lowering his arms. "Stash this before someone takes it from you, eh?"

Fagin turned leaky eyes to Jack, his voice barely a whisper. "Thank ye, my dear." He called everyone by the same endearment—boy, girl, or a little of both as had been her case.

Jack gave him a single nod before leading Olivia away. He set a quick pace, and she imagined he was as eager as she to leave that bit of their shared past behind.

After they'd rounded the corner, Jack released her arm and shoved his hands into his trouser pockets. His profile set into hard lines, his whole demeanor aloof.

Olivia felt the absence of his warmth all the way to her toes, but she followed suit and stuffed her hands into her jacket pockets. They'd made such strides tonight, she couldn't allow him to retreat inside himself again. She moved closer and caught his eye. "That was a very kind thing you just did."

After a brief silence, he said, "Not so much kind as guilt-driven."

She arched a brow in question.

"He called me his 'best worker,' and I left him behind." Jack shrugged both his shoulders.

"But you didn't owe him anything, Jack. He took from you for years."

"Perhaps, but he also taught me the craft, and where would I be now without it?" His voice had taken on a flat quality, and he'd maneuvered Brom so the dog walked between them.

"Monks, my . . . er . . ." Her mouth worked but it took a few tries for the title to emerge. "*My brother* was a big reason you went out on your own, right?"

He gave a tight nod. "Have you found any more information about Leeford . . . Monks, from your uncle?"

"He doesn't know any more than I do, and when I asked him to see the letter from my mother, he couldn't recall where he put it. I plan to search his study at the first opportunity."

"We need to figure out why that bludger is after you." He fingered the scar on his right cheekbone. "He's not to be underestimated."

"Why, Jack?" What wasn't he telling her? "Did he . . . hurt you?"

He jerked his hand back to his side and shoved it into his pocket, his fingers balled into a fist.

Olivia could sense him slipping away from her again, so she blurted, "I know you left Fagin because of Monks. But how did you end up working with Lois March?" After the words were out, she wished she could take them back. He'd shut her down before for asking precisely the same question.

"You need not answer. Sometimes I don't know when to leave off."

They were nearing the workhouse district, so she hoped it wouldn't seem too peculiar that she lifted her lavender-scented kerchief to cover her nose and mouth, surreptitiously disguising her heated cheeks. She increased her pace and pulled ahead, leaving Jack and Brom to follow.

Jack watched Olivia duck like a turtle into her neckcloth, and then speed ahead. He had no clue what was in that girl's head, but he was about to find out.

In two long strides, he reached her side.

"Hey," Jack whispered and pulled the ratty kerchief down, revealing her delicate nose and mouth. God in heaven, she was beautiful. She'd completely smudged the soot-whiskers he'd again painted on her cheeks. But he didn't even see the black streaks or the ratty wig anymore.

"I'm sorry, Jack, I didn't mean to pry. It's just that—"

"Shh. I was going to answer you, but you didn't give me the chance." He quirked one side of his mouth in a teasing grin.

She returned his smile, dimples appearing in both of her cheeks, and Jack had to fight the impulse to push her against a wall and kiss her senseless. Instead, he cleared his throat and glanced around the shadowed alley. "Let's keep moving."

Once they were on their way, he continued his tale. "After the incident with Daniel, I became like a machine. Taking on more and more kids, training them, saving every shilling I could scrape together. Protecting my turf with a vengeance.

All with the aim of escaping the life and making my way to the country. I didn't care a whit if I had to muck out stalls for the rest of my life . . . I knew I had to get out of that hellhole. It was around that time that I heard a rumor Leeford had been killed by a group of vigilante beaks, and with the reputation I was building, I feared I might be next.

"I'd saved just about enough, when I robbed an eccentric old woman who caught me red-handed."

"Lois March?" Olivia exclaimed, her eyes wide as teacups.

"Eh, she did. And no one was more shocked than I. But the old biddy is smart as a whip. Instead of turning me over to the beaks, she offered me a *position* in her household. If I would rob her toff friends and split the profits with her, she'd teach me how to be a gentleman and allow me to live in her posh townhouse as her long-lost nephew."

"But why would she do such a thing? She didn't need the money, did she?" Olivia tucked a clump of her wig behind her ear, exposing the fine lines of her cheekbone and jaw. It completely blew her disguise, but Jack didn't care. He couldn't seem to get enough of looking at her.

"Ah, but she did. Her husband died and left her with more gambling debt than she had the means to pay. When I moved in, she only had one servant left in her house. Clyde, the old butler, hadn't been paid in half a year, but stayed out of loyalty. They'd sold everything of value in the house, and were preparing to sell the place when I arrived." Jack laughed as he remembered those first few years. "My pickpocketing skills kept her out of debtor's prison, but I know she despaired of ever turning me into a gentleman. We got into some nasty rows, to be sure. Being proper is far too much work."

Olivia chuckled and nodded in agreement. "My uncle and I had some similar moments. It took him months just to teach me to walk and sit like a girl."

"I'll bet." He shook his head as he recalled the scrappy kid he had once known. She'd fooled him good, and that wasn't easy to do given observation was his profession. "It's still hard for me to think of you as that little urchin I saved from Madam Riceworth."

Her gaze swept over him, her lips curling up. "We may both look different, but deep down we're the same, aren't we? Still searching for acceptance and security."

Their gazes locked and Jack felt something unleash in his chest. She'd asked him earlier what he wanted. And he'd spouted the drivel he'd been telling himself for as long as he could remember. But she was right, he longed for so much more than just a place to rest his head.

"Finish your story, please," Olivia prompted, tugging his thoughts back to Lois.

"Er . . . yes." He forced himself to look away from her and back into his recent past. "Finally, one day, it all clicked. I realized if I ever wanted to put my old life behind me, I would have to become someone different. So I allowed Lois to shape me into the perfect Irish gentleman."

Desperate to lighten the mood, he jogged ahead and, umbrella in hand, swept into a deep bow. "Jack MacCarron the Third, at yer service, lassie."

"Oh, you're Scottish now?" Olivia laughed, and he felt a bit of the darkness that lived inside him fall away.

"Just a wee bit, on me mother's side."

She grinned up at him and looped her arm through his.

They walked side by side and a pleasant silence fell over them. Every moment he spent with her felt like a transformation. As if he were changing again, only this time he was becoming the person he was underneath the façade. With Olivia, he didn't have to be the Dodger, or the gentleman; he was just Jack. With her, he didn't have to hide.

He glanced at her profile, and his pulse throbbed a little faster, every place where she touched him buzzed with life. And he found himself wishing for the impossible. That he wasn't just a jewel thief with a manufactured lineage, but someone who could offer her the future she deserved.

Acceptance and security.

After he pulled off the Grimwig heist, he would have enough saved to purchase a small cottage, and he wasn't above doing hard work. Good Lord, he'd labor in the bloomin' fields if he could spend all his spare moments with Olivia. He could imagine their life together . . . long walks in the countryside, cozy evenings by the fire . . . no more stealing, or fear of the noose, just an honest life filled with laughter and love.

Love? The word smashed into his chest like a cannon ball. Who was he kidding? Every street kid knew love was nothing but a myth. But to have her by his side—to know she was his—would be enough.

Brom tugged on the leash as they neared the boys' hideout, and reality intruded into Jack's fantasies. Olivia would never leave the orphans behind, or her uncle for that matter. He let Brom go and watched the dog run the rest of the way, his dreams sinking as irretrievably as a coffer full of treasure in the ocean. He couldn't support them all.

A low growl followed by a rapid succession of barks reverberated from the orphans' building. Jack and Olivia ran for the boarded-up window as Jack handed her the brolly and pulled a knife from the holster at the small of his back. His heart pounding against his chest, he jumped through the opening.

And stopped cold. He double checked his surroundings to verify he was in the right place. Situated around the holes in the floor, groups of children huddled together for warmth around broken lanterns and candelabras. Twenty or more sets of eyes stared transfixed in Jack's direction.

Olivia whistled, and the new hatch door opened above them with a long creak. "Brit! What in the world is going on?" she hissed.

The boy hesitated for a moment, likely debating whether to ask for the password. Jack took a few steps back and shot the kid a warning glare, effectively loosening the boy's tongue. "It's all right, Ollie. These kids are here to pledge themselves to the Dodger."

A heaviness like a lead weight settled on his lungs. This was not a result he'd anticipated when he asked the Hill Orphans to spread the word that the Dodger was their new kidsman. But he should have. If he hadn't been so blasted eager to impress the girl standing beside him, he could have predicted this and headed it off.

"They're tired of bein' bullied by Monks and his gang, and they want yer protection."

When Jack looked back, all the kids in the room were staring at him like he was a knight come to slay the dragon. He sheathed his knife and swiped his sweaty face with an open palm. What the devil was he supposed to do with twenty orphans at his beck and call?

A small, familiar hand grasped his shoulder. He looked into Olivia's trusting eyes and came back to himself. If she believed in him, he could do anything—even if it meant donning a suit of armor and wielding a sword.

Suddenly, a crash of broken glass sounded overhead, followed by a heavy thunk, and then screams.

CHAPTER 16

"Lower the plank!" Jack's voice carried over the yells and clamoring feet above them. Seconds later, the board hissed over the edge and hit the ground with a bang. Olivia sprinted up to the second floor, closely followed by Jack and Brom. Her heart slammed in her ears as she met Brit's wide eyes.

"Help me with this," the boy pleaded as he struggled to raise the makeshift ramp.

After dragging the board up and locking the hatch, Olivia scanned the room. All the kids were gathered in a tight circle, staring at the floor. Glass shards glinted against the dark wood, a fist sized hole punched through a nearby window.

Jack elbowed a path through the cluster of boys and bent to pick up the object of their fascination. Chip made his way to Olivia's side, his blue eyes brimming with tears, and she hugged his thin shoulders. When Jack stood, he held out a large rock, a piece of folded parchment tied to it with a string. He strode over to the lantern, eighteen boys in his wake, all talking at once.

"What does it say?"

"Read it!"

"Who's it from?"

"Someone's gonna bloomin' pay," Archie grumbled as a cold wind blew through the shattered panes, ruffling his bright hair. But his freckles stood out around his ashen mouth and Olivia saw the fear dance across his face. She clasped his shoulder and gave it a squeeze. This was their home, their only safe haven in an insane world, and no one had ever breeched its boundaries. Until now.

Jack strode over to the piecemeal table and everyone, including Olivia, followed him. Each movement, from lighting the candles on the table to flicking out his coat as he sat, conveyed confidence. In the richest households of London, he displayed a relaxed poise, but this was something more; a swagger, scraped from paths of iniquity and cemented in his rise above those detrimental years to become a prince of his domain.

Jack lifted a hand, and the boys hushed their chatter.

Olivia watched as he flattened the note, his eyes scanning the words before he read them aloud, his tone deep and emotionless.

"To the one who claims to be the Artful Dodger." A corner of his mouth kicked up at the implied slur to his street name.

"Meet me at midnight three nights hence, on Blackfriars Bridge, or one orphan will disappear for every night you stand me up. Come alone. Let's settle ownership of the Hill once and for all."

Jack folded the letter in half and then half again, making it a tight square before he glanced up and said, "It's signed, Monks."

The room fell dead silent. Not a whisper of fabric or a shuffle of feet broke the quiet. Wide-eyed boys blinked like little owls, first at Jack, then at each other. Chip squirmed at Olivia's side, and she relaxed her hand where she'd been digging her fingers into his shoulder. The vilest thug to run the streets of London since Bill Sikes, and her blasted half brother, was challenging the man she loved . . .

Olivia gulped, a lump passing through her throat and lodging in her chest. *Love?* Did she love Jack? Her eyes landed on his dark head bent over the note, hair in his eyes, square jaw set in determination, and warmth spread through every inch of her body. Yes, she loved him. Perhaps she always had.

Then Brit, bless his sweet soul, whispered into the silence, "Don't go, Jack."

Jack's fierce blue eyes lifted to Brit and then softened. "I can handle myself, Brit, I assure you."

"I don't doubt ye. But Monks is the worst kind of bludger. He'll cheat. Lie. Do anythin' to win." Brit's hands clenched into fists at his sides. "He'll kill you."

Several of the boys nodded and shouted their agreement. As was typical, they spoke over one another, trying to be the one to tell Jack of all the blokes Monks had offed and the gory details of how he'd done it.

Jack let them ramble, but their commentary didn't change his expression. Lost in thought, he stared into space and rubbed a spot along his ribs.

"Besides," Brit's voice rose over the hubbub, "I've found a new hideout!" The others grew quiet to let the older boy speak. "It's large. Big enough for us *and* our new mates down-stairs. We'll move. Monks will never find us."

Jack leveled a steady gaze at the boy, his words slow and deliberate. "What makes you think he won't find you? He found you here—"

"Yes, but . . . we know how to hide better now. Don't we, boys?"

All the children concurred as Archie jumped into the conversation. "Aye, we're smarter now." He leaned toward Jack, cupping a hand around the side of his mouth as if in conspiracy. "I'd never be one to run from a fight, mind ye. But this Monks, he's . . . he's a dastardly git, if ye take my meanin'."

Olivia was so touched by the boys' unexpected valor, she longed to kiss each one of them on their sweet faces. She would've expected them to welcome the opportunity for Jack to sweep all their problems away with his fists. But instead, they were protecting him as one of their own. Altruism was not a trait even she would've expected from her boys.

"Jack, I agree," Olivia said, remembering to roughen her voice at the last moment. "Meeting Monks on his terms is a mistake. It's a trap. We need to find another way."

Jack's expression was unreadable when she met his gaze across the candlelit table. The rhythmic tick of Brit's beat-up pocket watch counted off the time. She could well imagine Jack's internal struggle, knowing she was right but longing to shut Monks down once and for all—not only for the boys, but because of the history they shared.

After several long seconds, Jack shook his head, a dry smile curling his lips. "All right, then. Where's this new hideout?"

The kids cheered, and an invisible weight lifted from Olivia's shoulders. They all drifted apart, the boys already plotting the best way to move without being detected. Archie worked with some of the older boys to board up the window, while Olivia sat at the table next to Brit. He explained where the new hideout was located and gave reasons why it would be more secure. But Olivia's mind kept drifting back to the note.

Jack's gaze locked with hers and she searched those unfathomable blue eyes, desperate to read his thoughts. Something about the tension in his neck and the grave set of his mouth told her this wasn't over. He'd conceded far too easily.

Olivia crouched under her uncle's desk as footsteps pounded overhead. *Mrs. Foster.* Olivia's pulse hammered in her ears. The woman had distrusted her from the day she'd come to live with them, going so far as calling her in front of Uncle Brownlow when anything, from cutlery to a tartlet, went missing in the house. As a child, trying desperately to become the young lady her uncle wished her to be, every accusation had been a blow to her fledgling confidence. Most times, the accusations had been empty. Except when tartlets were involved.

Olivia jerked her hat and wig off in one motion, then worked on the pins and net as the footfalls reached the first floor. She'd snuck into her uncle's study after returning from the Hill with the intention of finding information on her parents and, in turn, her half brother. If she could determine what Monks wanted from her, then perhaps she could negotiate freedom for her boys, and in doing so protect Jack. But she hadn't realized the late—or early, as the case may be—hour. Mrs. Foster rose before the sun to wake the rest of the staff, and if she found Olivia, dressed like a boy no less, snooping in Uncle Brownlow's things, well . . .

The bang of footfalls drew close and then paused. A door opened on squeaky hinges and Olivia jumped, sweat popping out on her brow. There was a clatter, followed by a squeal and a click. Olivia let out a slow breath. The broom closet. Of course; Mrs. Foster was gathering her cleaning implements.

Olivia scuttled backward from under the desk and rose to her feet. If the old housekeeper or anyone else found her going through her uncle's papers, Olivia would stand her ground. She was no longer that approval-seeking orphan girl who bawled when a spoon went missing.

And yet, she would still hurry. If she were caught, they would surely rat her out to her uncle. Even after all these years, his disapproval cut deep.

The flame of the single candle she'd lit flickered and smoked, managing to hide more than it revealed. But she didn't dare ignite one of the lamps or stoke the dim embers in the hearth for fear of discovery. Before ducking beneath the desk, she'd managed to search the files in the long cabinet beneath the window. She'd found nothing beyond financial papers, medical bills, and, the most interesting discovery, payments from an investment her uncle had made in a rock excavating company. The recompenses appeared to have dwindled over time and had grown farther apart. From her quick assessment, it appeared their bills would soon overtake their income.

Strictly speaking, they were broke.

Olivia pulled her collar away from her heated neck. The air felt warm and thick, as if a storm were brewing. She stuffed her wig and hairnet in her coat pockets and unbuttoned the top of her shirt. If she'd thought this through, she would've changed into her night rail and robe before conducting her search. As it was, the binding around her chest strangled her breath.

Ignoring her discomfort, she sat in the desk chair and began to search the row of drawers to her right. She'd half expected to find some of them locked, but they all opened easily. The drawers to her left were the same and contained nothing whatsoever to do with her or her parents. There had to be some clue that would help her understand why Monks would wish to do her harm. His search for her made no sense, especially when she'd never even met the man.

She was beginning to believe that her uncle had told the truth when he claimed he no longer possessed the fateful letter from her mother, until she opened the lap drawer and found a long, metal key shoved to the back. Holding the key to the candle flame, she made out an intricate looping design at one end. It appeared tarnished and ancient, like something out of a Shakespeare story. A glob of dried adhesive stuck to one side of the shaft, leading her to believe it had been glued to the underside of the desk at one time. She took the candle and leaned down. None of the desk drawers had such a large keyhole.

Voices droned low outside the door, and Olivia froze. Heavy footsteps clomped down the hall and then up the stairs. It must be Thompson, going to wake her uncle for his morning tonic. With renewed urgency, she jumped up and began to search the room for anything with a lock. She tilted every book and looked behind it. She opened each cabinet and searched through keepsakes and old pictures, a broken vase, a box containing her old toys. Her uncle had always been an intellectual, preferring his books to intimate relationships. Therefore, his accumulation of random baubles surprised her. He had never married—a decision she believed he regretted in later years.

She searched the bricks around the fireplace next, poking and prodding for a loose stone. She'd once overseen Fagin remove a small box of jewels and coins he'd stashed in an empty cavity behind the hearth. His *assurance*, he'd called it.

When she'd searched every nook and cranny, she stood in the center of the room and turned in a slow circle. A soft gold leaked around the drapes and slanted across the jade silk wallpaper. She was out of time.

She returned to the desk and slumped in the chair. Whyever would her uncle own a key that didn't fit anything? She leaned back and rubbed her burning eyes, realizing how little sleep she'd had in the past forty-eight hours. She fought to keep her mind alert by thinking over the night's events. Jack had walked her home from the Hill in contemplative silence. When she'd tried to breech the subject of Monks and his threats, he did little more than shrug. But his nonchalance didn't fool her for a heartbeat. He had a history with her brother, and she was beginning to suspect it to be more sinister than he let on.

If she could just find some hint of Monks's intentions towards her, perhaps she could save Jack from making a mistake. But to do that, she would need sleep. She opened her eyes and reached to open the lap drawer, when a tiny golden symbol just above her knee caught her eye. Three intertwining loops, the exact design of the metal on the key. Her heart gave a loud thump as she brought the candle closer and fingered the raised circles. She pressed it like a button. The wood gave a bit beneath her finger, but nothing happened.

She dropped to her knees and peered under the desk. The structure didn't make sense. Based on the drawers, there should've been more empty space. She leaned in close to the gold symbol and ran her fingers all around it. Giving the wood a strong push, the surface shifted beneath her fingers and moved to the left, revealing a large keyhole.

Something scratched against the study door and Olivia popped her head above the desk, ears straining. The scratch came again, followed by a low whine. Brom. If someone spotted him at the door, he would give her away. On light feet, she ran to the door and opened it an inch. Spying no one else in the hall, she let Brom in and shut the door.

She scrubbed his silky head. "You hush now."

He padded beside her back to the desk, where she sat in the chair and inserted the key. As soon as she turned the mechanism, a long, narrow drawer sprang out at her. Brom growled and shoved his nose against the wood. "My sentiments exactly," she murmured. It was beyond creepy.

Inside was a single yellowed envelope, *Mama and Papa* scrawled on the front in loopy script. Hand trembling, Olivia reached for the letter. When she'd spread the single page out on the desktop, her eyes jumped to the signature. *Agnes.*

Tears closed her throat as she ran her fingers over the words that her own mother had written, and noticed the perfect slant and long loops of her penmanship. Nothing like

Olivia's hasty scrawl. Would that have been different if she'd been raised by this woman? Loved and cherished? Educated from a young age with the best tutors? Attended the most prestigious finishing school? Perhaps. But she'd learned long ago not to play the "what if" game. It only broke her heart.

Straightening her spine, she moved the candle closer and began to read.

Dearest Mama and Papa,

I hope this letter finds you well, but I do not have the luxury of formalities, so I begin with the crux of the matter.

Something in my husband, Edwin, is broken. I fear, irreparably. His brilliance chases him like a dog after its tail. The disintegration of his mind, his descent into irrationality, has been horrifying to witness. He rants against the government, the ton, his investors, and more specifically, your rejection of our match. Honor and social standing have become his obsession. Last evening, he struck me and threatened our unborn child. This is why I must ask—no, beg—for your assistance.

I awoke this very morning to find my diamond and topaz wedding ring missing. I suspect Edward, Edwin's son from his first marriage. The boy has turned to opium to escape his father's abuses. He steals from us to feed his habit and then disappears for days. His beloved son's addiction has become the final break for Edwin. He rants about leaving his significant fortune to a child who does not besmirch his good name.

Before Edwin stole my ring, I had planned to pawn it and start a new future with this precious babe that grows within me. But even that avenue of escape has been taken from me.

I feel her, Mother. Just as you always said you could sense me before my birth. Her spirit is strong! I dream of her vivacity and fortitude—I know in my heart, she is much stronger than I.

Olivia's chest shuddered, and her mother's script blurred before her eyes. Strong was the last thing she felt at that moment. Brom's heavy head rested on her lap, his large tongue lapping at her knee. She clutched his furry neck and blinked rapidly at the ceiling, letting the tears burn down her face. This was why her uncle had hidden the letter from her; the reality hurt far worse than anything she had imagined. But she couldn't stop now. She had to read the rest.

Father, I beg your forgiveness. I dishonored our family and for that I am eternally sorry. If you allow me to return home, I will be the ideal daughter—all that is sweet and demure. I will live in the attic. Become a dutiful servant. Whatever you wish, is my command.

Just please, I beseech you, help us! If only for your unborn grandchild who does not deserve to live in the fear that I've come to know with every breath.

Your loving daughter
now and always,
Agnes

The night her grandparents had received the letter, they'd

flown to Leeford House, but it had been too late. Her mother had fled without a trace. Uncle Brownlow had once said they had searched for her, but to no avail. Olivia suspected they hadn't dared look so deep into the slums of London. At least not deep enough to find her.

Footsteps, clanking dishware, and hushed voices sounded in the house as she shoved the secret drawer back and locked it, replacing the panel with the golden emblem. Then, she returned the heavy key to where she'd found it, stood, and pushed in her uncle's chair. With a quick glance around the study, she confirmed that she'd returned everything to its approximate place.

No longer caring if anyone saw her wearing breeches, she exited the room with Brom on her heels, the letter held tight to her chest. Putting one foot in front of the other, she walked through the hallway and past a staring Thompson as she mounted the stairs.

Once in her room, Brom's warm comfort tucked beside her on the bed, she read the letter again, whispering the words aloud. Then, she read it again and again until she fell into a deep, dreamless sleep.

Following a solid eight hours of sleep and a good meal, Olivia's head was clear and she had a plan. With some assistance from the upstairs maid, she donned her chemise, drawers, corset, and several petticoats, along with her best day dress.

She ran her hands down the scarlet silk and arranged the panels to reveal the matte black-and-white-checked underskirt. Never mind that it was a hand-me-down from Frannie's last season wardrobe; with its striking colors and tailored fit, Olivia felt confident—something she would need to accomplish her upcoming errand.

She checked the mirror and adjusted the small ebony hat with scarlet feathers to a saucy angle. Looking smart and proper, she scooped up her reticule, her mother's letter tucked securely inside, and headed for the door.

Brom rose from where he'd been sleeping in front of the hearth and padded over to her side. "Sorry, boy, not this time." He gave a long, pathetic whine. She rubbed his soft ears and had to force her gaze from his huge liquid-brown eyes. "I promise we'll go to the park in the morning. Now go find Uncle Brownlow."

She gave him a dismissive pat, and he turned left down the hall toward her uncle's bedchamber. Shutting her door behind her, she shook her head with a smile. Sometimes she suspected Brom understood far more than she gave him credit for.

When she reached the front entryway, Thompson appeared, took her cashmere wrap and draped it around her shoulders. "Will Mrs. Cramstead be arriving to escort you, Miss Olivia?"

Violet's mother, her aunt Becky, served as her chaperone more often than not, but this was something she needed to do on her own. "I'm meeting Aunt Becky and Violet in Piccadilly at the new confectioner's shop. Apparently, they have hot cocoa served in tiny silver cups that's to die for!" The story slipped easily from her lips.

"Shall I call a maid to escort you, then?" His words had taken on that disdainful tone that implied her actions were not at all proper.

Having years of experience diverting her well-intentioned butler, she opened the door and replied breezily, "No thank you, Thompson. 'Tis not far, and I fancy a bit of a walk this fine afternoon."

When she stepped out onto the portico, the late-afternoon sun warmed her cheeks and an unseasonably mild breeze ruffled her skirts. That much, at least, had not been a lie—it was an uncommonly gorgeous November afternoon. So why were tears burning behind her eyes? She'd read her mother's letter until she'd memorized every heart-shattering word. For some reason, it made her feel more alone than ever.

Blinking up at the sun, she swallowed her emotion. Over the years, she'd accumulated vast experience putting on a brave face, and as a wise boy once told her, *Don't let the others see ya bawlin'. Tha's a good way to get trounced.* No way was she letting her half brother trounce her or anyone she loved. Ever again.

Plastering on a smile, she lifted her chin and stepped out of the gate and onto the walk. She turned right toward Piccadilly. That much had also been true. Her uncle's attorney, Mr. Appleton, kept offices there between a respectable tailor and an upholsterer's shop. Since she'd accompanied Uncle to the establishment on several occasions, she was certain the attorney would see her.

As she neared the corner of the block, a familiar ebony hansom cab rolled to a stop beside her.

"Olivia!" Violet leaned out and waved with a grin.

She walked over, quite happy for the distraction.

"I was going to pay you a visit, but it appears you are on a mission. May I join you?"

Olivia considered her options. She'd already determined that this particular job, which would require her to peer deep into her parents' sordid past, would be best accomplished alone. But seeing her cousin's sunny countenance, crimson curls framing her expectant smile, lifted a bit of the weight from her soul. With a decisive nod, she lifted her skirts and stepped into the open vehicle. "Actually, that would be wonderful."

After giving the address to the driver and making herself comfortable beside Vi on the single bench seat, she raised her voice to ask above the clop of the horse's hooves, "Where's Aunt Becky? I'm surprised she would let you take the cab out on your own."

"Yes, well." Violet smoothed her forest green skirts with gloved fingers. "She's been in bed with a chill for days, and I simply couldn't stay inside a moment longer."

Olivia grinned. "That's my girl."

"It's been a bit of a relief not to be trotted out to every dinner party like a sow to auction."

"Surely, not a sow." Olivia chuckled, her mood already lightened considerably.

"Well, a broodmare then. One would think that if I do not find a mate and produce children within the year, I might as well swear in as a nun!"

"I don't think one *swears in* as a nun. 'Tis more of a passionate commitment."

Violet waved the distinction away. "You know precisely what I mean."

Olivia did. Aunt Becky felt that at twenty years of age, Violet was doomed to spinsterhood if she did not find her a husband posthaste. But Violet's romantic nature would not allow her to settle for just any match, and thankfully, her parents were not prone to force her to choose based on convenience.

"I've lounged in the sunroom, read a book a day, and sipped coffee until my heart's content. Mother finds coffee uncivilized, you know."

"Yes," Olivia agreed. "I'm well aware." Aunt Becky didn't approve of Vi's voracious reading habits either.

"I've decided to marry a purveyor of books. How old would you suppose Mr. Snyder is?"

"The owner of the bookshop on Holywell Street? At least a hundred."

Violet gave her an arch look. "Well, it would be a peaceful life, at least."

Olivia burst out laughing.

When they'd finally sobered, Violet asked, "Why are we visiting the honorable Mr. Appleton?"

Olivia clutched the reticule in her lap. Her cousin knew of her origins in vague terms, but was too polite to ask for details. And even when Olivia had seen the curiosity brimming in Violet's eyes, she'd remained silent on the subject. Shame was a powerful motivator. But this discovery would drown her if she didn't share a bit of the burden.

She unfastened her purse, removed the letter, and handed it to her friend with a sigh. "I found this hidden in my uncle's office. It's from my mother."

Violet opened the folded paper and read, her body tensing as her cheeks turned red beneath her freckles. "Oh, Livie!"

Grasping her hand, she finished the letter and lifted

tearful eyes. "Your poor, poor mother! She left her family and everything she'd ever known for love, only to have it turn to tragedy."

Olivia took the letter back, folded it, and tucked it back into her purse.

Then Violet gasped in realization, "You have a brother!"

"A half brother," Olivia corrected. Violet, ever perceptive where emotional matters were concerned, searched her face. But she could not explain how her brother had become a street lord named Monks who was threatening her and those she cared about without divulging her double life. So she changed the subject. "I'm seeking Mr. Appleton's counsel on the will referenced in the letter."

Violet nodded. "The wording your mother used was decidedly peculiar. What do you think your father meant by leaving his fortune to a child who doesn't besmirch his good name?"

Recalling what Jack had overheard Monks say about asinine terms, Olivia imagined this was the heart of her brother's grievance toward her. Choosing her words carefully, Olivia explained, "I have reason to believe that Edward has only gone downhill over time and that he will attempt to discredit me somehow in order to inherit. I must confirm there is such a will, even if my uncle supposes there's no fortune to be had."

"Do you truly think your own relation would seek to harm you in some way?"

"Believe me when I tell you that if my half brother thinks there's the slightest possibility of gain, he will stop at nothing to acquire it." The carriage jerked to a stop and Olivia glanced outside. "We're here."

An hour and thirty minutes later, they were back out on the street with no more answers than when they'd arrived. Mr. Appleton had not been in the office and his secretary, Mr. Kit, had informed them that the office was not taking on any new clients, despite Olivia's insistence that Mr. Appleton knew her by association to Uncle Brownlow. Sure that if he met her again in person, he would take on her case, Olivia had determined to wait.

When Mr. Appleton did not return from court, his secretary politely but firmly kicked them out and closed the office.

Feeling useless and defeated, Olivia mounted Violet's family carriage and dropped down onto the bench. The busy thoroughfare of Piccadilly had quieted with the setting of the sun. Young lamplighters scampered up poles, igniting gas flames in neat rows up and down the street.

Violet gave Olivia's address to the driver, and sat beside her and tugged off her bonnet, playing with the ribbons as the vehicle set off with a jerk. "I'm sorry, Livie."

Olivia slumped down and pulled her wrap tighter. She didn't know what to do next. The orphans were moving that night, and she couldn't even help without endangering them further. She couldn't help her boys. She couldn't even help herself.

"We can go back to Mr. Appleton's office tomorrow," Violet suggested.

"You heard Mr. Kit. Appleton's not taking new clients. Ergo, no female clients."

Vi straightened, her green eyes flashing. "Then I'll ask Father to inquire on your behalf."

"No." She shook her head. "I'll have to ask my uncle."

Staring out at the passing street, Olivia clutched her purse to her chest, letting the implications sink in. "I'll need to confess to my uncle. Which will mean divulging breaking into his desk to find the letter." Perhaps it was time to come clean about all of it. How else would she explain that she knew Monks was after her without digging herself deeper in deceit? "It will break his heart that I've been . . ." *sneaking out and lying to him.* But she didn't say the rest, couldn't divulge her darkest secrets to the girl who'd always believed the best of her despite her past.

"Livie." Violet clutched her hand. "Let me help you. My family can keep you safe."

Keep me safe? Olivia met her dear friend's earnest gaze. She was so sweet and loyal and kind . . . and so very mistaken.

CHAPTER 17

Jack leaned his head back on the cushioned arm of the divan, the room spinning around him. He squeezed his eyes closed, but the nauseating rotation continued. Either he was suffering from sleep deprivation or he had finally taken the fast train to crazy town—which, considering his irrational actions of late, was highly probable.

Out of control. That's what his life had become.

He'd received a letter the previous evening from Olivia that explained why she believed her half brother was indeed after their father's supposed inheritance, and that she had things well in hand. She had forbid him to intervene. *Forbid him.*

So naturally, he'd spent the last twenty-four hours searching the streets of London for the blasted coward.

A part of him realized he was running from his feelings, the thoughts he couldn't escape . . . dreams that could never be. But instead of dulling his conscience, the lack of sleep had only served to sharpen his emotions until all the needs he'd worked so hard to ignore jabbed at him like tiny swords, leaving him raw and exposed.

The night before last, they'd walked under the same buttery moonlight. The same hazy stars that you couldn't see clearly unless you climbed above the smog of London, and yet *everything* had changed. With Olivia by his side, a weed sprouting between cracks of pavement signified hope.

The mist that swept through the streets, stealing the light, became a romantic backdrop. His lens on the world had shifted, seemingly overnight.

And apparently, sleep deprivation caused him to wax poetic.

How had he gone from a happily unencumbered bachelor with nothing to lose to this sniveling mess, pining over a young miss whose baggage included an ailing uncle and a gaggle of orphans? If anyone had told him a few weeks ago that he'd be racking his brain for a way to become everything one girl desired—even a girl as captivating as Olivia Brownlow—he would've laughed in their face.

Jack chuckled out loud, the lonely sound echoing around the empty room, mocking him. Perhaps he'd stayed busy to keep himself from chasing Olivia like a lovesick pup. To stop himself from begging her to choose him, even when he knew it was against her best interest.

He had to talk to her. Make sure she wouldn't go visit the boys on Turnbull Road. He began to rise, but stopped when the room tilted and spun. He would have to trust her.

The real question was . . . could he trust himself? Would he keep the vow he'd made to Olivia not to accept Monks's challenge? After all, he'd be killing two vultures with one stone, if he could strike a bargain to keep Olivia and the orphans safe *before* beating bloomin' Leeford to within an inch of his worthless life. Now that he was away from Olivia's hypnotizing gold eyes, he realized it was a promise he never should've made. If he broke it and saved the day, would she forgive him?

Blast it. He still had over twenty-four hours to decide. Blindly, he reached for the bottle on the table, and lifted the glass to his lips, the water cooling a welcome path down his parched throat and into his brain.

The library door opened behind him, but he couldn't seem to muster the energy, or the interest, to turn his head to see who had entered.

"Inebriated already, Jack?"

"Not yet." Jack pinched the top of his nose, Topher's grating voice triggering an instant headache. "What's it to you?"

Leather creaked and Jack caught a whiff of obnoxious cologne as Topher settled into the chair across from him.

"Gran Lois said you needed my help with something. Pray tell me you haven't summoned me to hold your hair back while you heave, because that goes beyond cousinly duties as far as I'm concerned."

Jack smiled despite himself, wishing a nursemaid was all he needed. They'd received the much-coveted invitation to the Grimwig Ball, but the card had very specifically excluded Jack's name. Apparently, none of the invitations—including the Lancasters'—allowed for uninvited guests. Which left Jack in quite the quandary.

He cracked open his eyes and sat up. Time to face the music. Gripping the arm of the sofa, he forced his swirling gaze to settle on Topher's blasé countenance. "It seems I require your superior social skills, old man."

Jack pegged his *cousin* with as level a stare as he could manage. "I need to pay a call on the Grimwigs tomorrow and would like for you to accompany me."

Topher's look of repugnance turned to shrewd interest, and the fingers he impatiently drummed against his knee stilled. "Why?"

Why, indeed. Lois had taken care of everything, down to a blueprint of the Grimwig estate marked with the exact location of the safe. She was peeved, to say the least, that Jack had flubbed up his part of the plan. But in Jack's muddled state, he seemed to be having trouble coming up with a plausible lie. He gripped his forehead and massaged his aching temples. "Because I need to get an invitation to their blasted ball."

Silence.

Jack glanced around his hand. Topher watched him with narrowed eyes, his long fingers steepled in front of him. "God only knows why, but you seem to have all the women of London society wrapped around your little finger. Why would you need *my* help?"

Jack sighed and sank back into the cushions. The buffoon was going to make him beg. "Because Grimwig bloody hates me, that's why."

That earned him a dry laugh as Topher sat straight in his chair. "Ah . . . his precious Miss Brownlow. Am I right?"

Jack met Topher's gray eyes. "String-bean thinks I'm after his girl, yes. But Olivia isn't his to own."

"So you *do* have a soft spot for the mysterious Miss Brownlow . . . Interesting. There's something . . . captivating about her, to be sure. Those melted-gold eyes, her gaze just a bit too direct. Her titillating wit, a smidge too candid." Topher leaned forward and lifted a pale brow. "The sway of her hips verging on improper."

Jack's muscles coiled, his hands closing into fists. Just as he was about to spring forward and smash Topher's pencil-thin nose, Toph chuckled.

The tosser was baiting him. Dragging a hand through

his hair, Jack forced himself to breathe. "The point is, *dear cousin*, it's imperative that I attend that ball, and I need your help to get back in String—I mean, Maxwell's good graces."

Topher pursed his lips and sat back. "No."

Jack arched a brow and waited for the explanation sure to follow.

Sure enough, Topher launched into a lecture. "You're not a good match for Miss Brownlow, and I refuse to pretend otherwise. I'm also not an idiot. I don't know what you're playing at, *cousin*, but until you truly tell me why it's so imperative you attend this particular ball, I have no intention of lending my assistance."

Jack had to unclench his teeth before he could reply, "You're a right git, you know that?"

Topher shrugged and smiled in reply, as if being a bloomin' prat was a point of pride. Some part of Jack could respect that. So perhaps it wasn't just the fishes swimming in his brain that convinced him that his counterfeit relative deserved to hear the truth—the full truth about Jack's role in the March fortune. Jack swallowed and then forced out the words before he changed his mind. "All right. I'll tell you who I really am and what I'm about."

Jack leaned forward and sloshed some water into a clean glass. "But I guarantee," he said, handing the drink to a slightly bemused Topher, "you're going to wish you had something stronger than this."

❧

The morning was unseasonably warm, and since the dining

room walls seemed to be closing in on her, Olivia took her breakfast to the garden. The trees were barren sticks, a few brittle leaves clinging to their branches, and the grass was dead and brown, but the air smelled of spring. November was a terrible tease. Olivia set down her tea, closed her eyes, and drew in a deep breath through her nose. Hints of living green, balmy air, and sunny skies tempted her away to adventure.

Vehemently, she blinked away visions of donning her disguise and running into the city, Jack by her side. Those days of freedom were speeding to an abrupt end, to be replaced by endless hours stuffed into a corset with a proper simper pasted on her face and only suitable words passing through her lips.

With a gulp of tea, she fought the panic that constricted like a corset pulled too tight. She'd decided at some point during the night that she would wait until her engagement to Max was official and then enlist his help with unearthing her father's will. It was the only sensible course of action.

A scrape and tap turned Olivia's attention to her uncle exiting the back door. A long-absent smile lifted his face, peeling back the years. "Good news, my darling girl! If I continue to feel this well, the doctor has approved my attendance at the Grimwigs' ball, and I'll be witness to your big announcement."

Olivia met her uncle's hopeful expression as he pulled out the wrought iron chair across from her with a rasp of metal against stone, reminiscent of the dull knife cutting open her chest. The ball, and subsequent proclamation of her engagement to Max, were only days away. And she hadn't told Jack.

Speaking the words and watching those flaming blue eyes frost over somehow made it deadly final. But even with all his pretty words, he'd never really offered her an alternative.

As her uncle settled across from her and leaned his cane against the table, she poured him a cup of tea. "That's wonderful, Uncle. I'm so relieved to hear you're feeling better."

"Yes, well, it's likely a temporary respite, but I'll take what I can get these days." He selected a biscuit from the tray and asked, "How are you, dear? Thompson told me he received delivery of your ball gown yesterday afternoon. Is it everything you'd hoped?"

Olivia met his expectant eyes and opened her mouth to make a positive reply, but her shoulders slumped, the lie she was about to tell burning in her throat.

"What is it, dear? If it's the dress, I can bring in a seamstress or buy one off the rack—"

Olivia shook her head, cutting off his words. Fran's family had paid for her gown and Uncle Brownlow could not afford another one. "No, sir. The dress is lovely." She stared past his head, fighting tears, ashamed to her core that she could be so blasted selfish. Her uncle was happier than she'd seen him in years, and all she could think about was her own heartache.

He reached across the table and took her hand in papery fingers. "There was a time when you shared everything with me. All the dreams of a little girl's heart." A faraway look entered his eyes as his voice lowered to a whisper. "Remember that night, soon after I found you, when you rushed into my bedroom after reading *Sleeping Beauty*? You were terrified to fall asleep." He shook his head, lost in memory. "You were afraid you might never wake up again because you hadn't yet found your true love. You asked me if he was really out there."

Tears flooded Olivia's eyes at the memory of a broken little girl who struggled to believe anyone could want her as much as a prince in a fairy tale. But the unconditional love of her uncle had opened her heart to the possibility that there was good in everyone.

He gave her hand a squeeze. "Have you found him, Olivia? Or are you settling?"

Sadly, she *had* found him, the one who would protect her with his life, who swept her off her feet with a single look, but her prince couldn't be bound by anything so mundane as love. For a brief instant she let herself imagine running away from it all—Maxwell, the Hill Orphans, her uncle. Even as the picture formed in her mind, she knew she could never leave them behind, even if Jack wanted to accompany her. It was time to accept that happily ever after was just a hopeless dream.

Olivia picked pieces off the biscuit on her plate, crumbling bits between her fingers. Her uncle let go of her other hand, and she looked up to find him searching her face with soft eyes. He'd always loved every part of her, but would he still look at her in the same way if she told him the truth? The full truth about Jack, about stealing from their friends, dressing as a boy and sneaking into the slums of London at night? What about the letter and the threats from her half brother?

She couldn't possibly burden him with the ugly truth. But perhaps, a portion would suffice.

"I . . ." Straightening her shoulders, she swiped away her tears. "Yes, to both of your questions. There *is* someone I love, and it isn't Max." She stopped and searched his face, waiting for the mask of disapproval, but instead, he smiled sadly.

"I suspected as much. But what I don't understand is why?" He shook his head, his white brows lowering. "Why would you settle for anything, my sweet girl? Surely—"

"He doesn't want me." Olivia cut him off and looked down at the dust she'd made of the biscuit on her plate. "At least not like that. Not enough to choose me or make a binding commitment."

"So you're settling for Maxwell?"

"Yes. It's for the best. This other gentleman is not . . . suitable, or financially stable." She nodded decisively. "Max loves me and I care deeply for him. It will be a . . . a pleasant life."

Uncle Brownlow straightened in his chair, clearly sensing that she was placating him. He leaned forward and looked her straight in the eyes. "That may be, but know this . . . if this boy, the one you love, has a change of heart, I will support your decision. I will not have you throwing your happiness away to support an old man. Do you hear me, young lady?"

Olivia nodded, wishing with all her heart it was that simple. She loved Jack, body and soul. But society separated them, just like her mother and father. And look how that had turned out. "Thank you, Uncle. I love you so." She rose and enfolded his thin shoulders in a hug, his comforting scent of soap and peppery tobacco enveloping her.

Tonight, she would tell Jack of the engagement and end things between them once and for all. Making an excuse to her uncle, she walked through the garden toward the house. A temperate breeze ruffled strands of her hair against her cheeks, but in her heart, it was the dead of winter.

CHAPTER 18

Jack turned from the passing cityscape to see Topher staring a hole into the carriage wall. The pompous kid had reacted better to the news of Jack's role in his family than expected. Luckily, Jack knew how to take a punch. He shifted his sore jaw and touched the bruise there with tentative fingers. Topher packed a wallop for such a skinny chap, but Jack figured he deserved one good hit, so he'd taken it with grace, before blocking the second and knocking the tosser on his backside.

Lois had not been happy with Jack's sudden need to spill his guts, but after a brief fit of histrionics, she had confirmed his story. The devastation written on Topher's face when he realized he was heir to a counterfeit fortune made Jack almost feel sorry for him. *Almost.* The spoilt prat wouldn't be living in his ancestral home, or have his precious Gran to take advantage of, if it weren't for Jack. But clearly, his *cousin* didn't see it that way.

The carriage rolled to a stop and Jack parted the curtains to view one of the largest homes he'd ever laid eyes on—all white-washed brick and stone, two-story columns flanking the massive front doors, no less than six chimneys spouting from its roof. The blueprints had prepared him for a substantial building, but not its grandeur. The driver opened the carriage door, and Topher turned to Jack with a look of narrow-eyed contempt. "Try not to embarrass yourself."

Jack lifted a wry brow before replying in his best Cockney

accent, "Don't you fret on 'at score, me covey. 'Tis yourself you should be worrit 'bout. Takes a good bit to mortify 'is chap." Jack wiggled his brows and arched a thumb at his chest.

"I can only imagine." Topher descended the vehicle stairs, a smile quirking one side of his mouth before he could hide it.

Jack jumped down from the carriage and stared up at the mansion looming above him. Evidently, he had underestimated the Grimwigs' wealth. Nervous energy and excitement swirled in his chest. This would be the biggest score he'd ever made, and if he had his way, it would be his last. Thieving was no kind of life. He hadn't quite figured out what he would do next, but there had to be a profession suited to his particular skills. One that didn't require risking his neck.

They mounted the stairs to the portico, and Jack focused on his objective. He would need to play the hapless dolt if he hoped to gain String-bean's favor. It would take swallowing his pride, not something he excelled at; but knowing he was doing it in order to rob the bloke made it infinitely easier.

Sinking his hands into his pockets, Jack lowered his shoulders and adopted the nonthreatening pose he'd perfected on the streets. An unassuming manner was the perfect disguise to throw one's quarry off guard.

On the front stoop, he grinned at the stained glass design adorning the entrance, a thin rodent that might have been a ferret or weasel welding a tiny sword; some sort of family crest, he presumed. In any case, the skittish-looking creature seemed to exemplify Maxwell Grimwig's nature.

The double front doors swung open on silent hinges, revealing a butler in his early thirties with an air that put the Brownlows' haughty servant to shame. "May I help you?"

Topher held out his calling card. "We are here to see Mr. Maxwell Grimwig. He's expecting us."

"Quite right." The butler sniffed and lifted his nose to such a severe degree that Jack wondered how he didn't get it stuck in the rafters. "Follow me, please."

They entered a grand two-story vestibule with granite columns anchoring a domed ceiling painted with clouds and fat cherubs. A red-carpeted staircase curved up to the second-floor walkway that Jack knew from the schematic branched off into the east and west wings of the manor. As they followed the butler down the cavernous hallway, Jack eyed the rare paintings and statuary. Any last bit of reticence he may have harbored about stealing from a friend of Olivia's drained away with each resounding tap of his shoes on the black-and-white marble floor.

They turned into a sumptuous parlor, all rich wood with accents of forest green and burgundy—very masculine—unlike the bloke leaning against the fireplace mantel playing Lord of the Manor. It was difficult, but Jack managed not to smirk.

After exchanging banal greetings, Max offered them a drink and then they all settled in chairs near the fire. Jack crossed his legs and hunched his shoulders, mimicking his host's tortoise-like posture. Since Topher and Max had been acquainted since childhood, Jack settled in, prepared to let Topher do the talking. Fixing a hangdog expression on his face, he anticipated a good bit of entertainment.

"What is it I can do for you, er . . ." Maxwell's gaze flicked to Jack and then slid away. "Gentlemen?"

"Yes, well, we're here to prevail upon your sense of romance, as it were," Topher replied.

Maxwell's brows met in the middle and he scratched one of his abnormally small ears. "You don't say."

"There is a certain young lady whom Jack, here"— Topher waved a hand in Jack's direction in case it wasn't clear which Jack he was referring to—"wishes to woo, and he fears if he cannot continue his suit at your ball—it being the social event of the year, of course—he will lose out to a more well-connected gentleman."

Jack stifled a groan as he watched Maxwell's posture straighten and sweat beads pop out on his forehead. Either Topher was being deliberately obtuse by omitting the name of the woman Jack intended to court, or he was a complete fool. Jack settled on the former as Topher leaned back in his seat, a smirk on his lips. Nothing like prodding a crocodile with a sharp stick before pushing your enemy into his swamp to extract a bit of revenge.

"And why should I lend my assistance with *his* personal affairs?" Max shot Jack a glare as he uncrossed his legs and then crossed them in the opposite direction.

"Mayhap because you believe in true love?" Topher's voice was as sappy as maple syrup. "Jack is simply heartsick over this girl. She's all he thinks about, all he talks about. Isn't that right, poor old chap?"

Jack nodded, unable to speak over the laughter stuck in his throat. Max squeezed the upholstered arms of his chair until finger bones threatened to poke through his skin. Clearly, as Topher had intended, their host believed the lady in question to be Olivia.

As delightful as torturing Grimwig was, Jack had to stop this runaway train before they all died in it. Tucking away his amusement, he wrinkled his brow and frowned in anguish. "'Tis true, Mr. Grimwig. I despair o' ever earning Miss Lancaster's affections. But if I cannot escort her to your ball . . ." Jack shook his head, then stared down at his clasped hands, clinching the role of the contrite Irish lad. "I fear she'll succumb to the pursuit o' another."

When Jack raised his eyes, Max looked like a different person. Relaxed, his entire body melted back into the chair.

"How could you deny a man the pursuit of love, Max?" Topher shook his head, nearly tsking in disappointment.

"Well, I—"

"Mr. MacCarron!" A female voice rang from the doorway. Jack turned to find the very wide, and extremely bejeweled, Mrs. Grimwig waddling into the room. "I couldn't help but overhear your sincere plea. You and Miss Lancaster make such a lovely couple."

"Thank you, ma'am." Jack grinned at the woman, sensing victory within his grasp.

"For shame, Max! How could you wish to prevent such a perfect match?"

"Of course . . . of course, I wouldn't," Maxwell stammered, and turned to Jack with a contrite expression. "Mr. MacCarron, I will procure an invitation posthaste."

"Thank you, sir. I will be ever in your debt." Jack stood and extended his hand to Max, only squeezing a bit harder than necessary before releasing his bony fingers. His muted brown eyes narrowed before Jack turned away to address Mrs. Grimwig with a deep bow and a kiss on her plump hand. She giggled like a girl. "I must excuse myself momentarily, *Miss* Grimwig, but I shall return."

He turned and strode out of the room, intent on doing a bit of reconnaissance. He'd stopped just outside the door to ask a maid the location of the nearest loo when he overheard words that chilled the blood in his veins.

"Won't it be nice that Miss Brownlow's cousin will be well settled when you announce your engagement at the ball? They are dreadfully competitive, you know . . ."

Engagement. Jack didn't hear the rest as his heartbeat thundered in his ears. Olivia and Max were engaged? To be married? She certainly had not bothered to tell him.

How long? Was she engaged when she'd almost left the theater with him? When he had poured his guts out to her about his past? When he'd kissed her until she couldn't breathe?

The grandiose hallway distorted around him like a drunken carousel. He strode toward the door, every painting and priceless statue mocking him as he passed. This haven of wealth and privilege would soon be Olivia's life.

How could he compete with that?

Jack pushed through the front doors and raced down the stairs, running from the image of Maxwell and Olivia in each other's arms, standing before a vicar, swearing to love one another for eternity.

His steps slowed and he saw clearly for the first time in weeks. Had Olivia ever cared for him? Or had she manipulated him into sacrificing himself to help her precious orphans? Righteous flames roared, cauterizing his pain. He embraced the fire and stoked it with memories of her pushing him away, telling him she had to think of her future—her future with a loaded prat who could give her the life of her dreams.

The blade carving into his heart twisted. He'd laid his

soul bare to her. Told her things he'd never shared with any-one. With the hopes of what? Making her *love* him? What a farce! He could well imagine the laugh she must have had as the street thief made a bloody idiot of himself in an attempt to impress her. His vision narrowed, and he clenched his hands into fists as they began to shake. He wanted to find her and make her hurt as much as he did. But blowing up at Olivia wouldn't do any good. She'd still belong to someone else.

However, there was another situation he *could* do some-thing about. He quickened his pace, his steps becoming more deliberate as he made his way to the carriage, threw open the door, and barked an order to the driver. Topher could find his own bloody way home.

Jack had an appointment to keep.

⁓⟋☙⟍⁓

Olivia stepped into the foyer of the Coxs' townhome behind Violet and her aunt Rebecca Cramstead. She loved Aunt Becky, but the woman watched her like a baker guarding a stall full of fresh buns. Getting away to find Jack, let alone a treasure or two for her boys, would be a challenge tonight.

As the footman took her wrap, she scanned the crowd for a dark head and broad shoulders. She knew Jack'd planned to be here, but as she entered the drawing room, his undefinable energy was absent. Olivia exhaled a slow breath and turned to find Violet pushing through the crush, her best friend's bril-liant hair making her hard to miss. *Best friend?* Guilt twisted in Olivia's stomach. She hadn't been much of a friend lately, wrapped up in her own drama.

She moved toward Vi, longing to feel the closeness they'd once had. But how? There was so little of her life she couldn't share. Or was she just not *willing* to share? Violet had never once judged her, never made her feel *less than* because of her background. Even after she'd read the scandalous letter from her mother, Vi had only shown empathy and support. Her cousin didn't know all the details of Olivia's life before Uncle Brownlow took her in, but she wasn't a fool—she'd seen the scars crossing Olivia's back and legs.

"Why did you rush off like that?" Violet asked as Olivia looped her arm through her friend's elbow.

"I thought I saw someone I knew—" The lie lodged in Olivia's throat. Why couldn't she just tell the truth for once? She met Vi's steady grass-green eyes and began to steer them to a quiet corner.

Her heart palpitated at the thought of opening up to her friend, letting someone else in and trusting them with her secrets. But another part, a larger part, felt exhilarated by the possibility. When they reached the isolated settee, Olivia drew Vi down beside her, smoothed her buttery yellow skirt and whispered, "I was looking for Jack."

Violet blinked in question, completely unaware of whom Olivia referred to.

"Jack MacCarron," she qualified, and watched a bright glow flood Vi's ivory cheeks. *Oh no, not her too!* Had he captivated every woman in London? Olivia sighed and glanced around to make sure they were still alone.

"I need to speak with J—Mr. MacCarron urgently. Can you help me distract Aunt Becky when he gets here?"

"Whyever for?"

Because I'm in love with him, but need to tell him I've chosen to marry Max and we're announcing our engagement at the ball tomorrow night . . . But that's not what she said. In fact, she didn't have to say a word; her face must have given her away, because Violet's eyes widened and her mouth fell open.

"You . . . you're . . . having an affair with him!" Vi accused, and squeezed Olivia's gloved arm in a death grip.

"No . . . not exactly."

"But you love him. I can see it all over your face. Oh, how wonderful!"

Olivia shook her head and bit the inside of her cheek to keep the tears at bay. "Vi, it's not like that. This isn't one of your gothic novels. I accepted Maxwell's proposal. The engagement will be announced tomorrow evening." Olivia's shoulders slumped at the devastated look on her friend's face.

"Livie, no." She shook her head, moisture shining in her eyes. "Please tell me you didn't agree to this for the money . . . for your uncle. Because you could—"

"It's more complicated than that," Olivia cut in before Violet offered some impulsive solution, like letting them move in with her family. "I promise to explain later, but right now I *must* speak with Jack. Max and I have kept it a secret, but I don't want Jack to find out from someone else."

"Does he love you? Jack, I mean." Vi rubbed her arm, making Olivia want to curl into a ball, lay her head on her friend's lap, and sob.

"I don't know." Was Jack even capable of love? The *forever* kind of love that every girl dreamed of? "I don't think so."

Remembering Jack's promises to do anything to help her,

how he'd protected her since they were children, and how his eyes lit like blue fire when he looked at her, Olivia was forced to concede, "But he does care for me, in his way."

"Then you have to fight for him!" Violet straightened her spine, her eyes raging with conviction. She'd always been a true believer in happily ever after. "You cannot marry Max."

"Vi, I must. You don't understand. There is no fairy tale ending for me." Olivia bit harder on her cheek, as that reality sunk deep into her soul.

"Well, I'm not settling. I don't care what my mother says. I *will* marry for love," Violet hissed, swiping at a tear that slipped down her cheek. "And if you aren't strong enough to defy society, then you can live with the consequences."

Olivia's lips lifted in a sad half smile. "Then I suppose I'll have to live vicariously through you."

"Good evening, Miss Brownlow."

Olivia and Vi both started and turned to find Topher March hovering over them. Olivia prayed he hadn't overheard their conversation.

After the girls stood and Olivia made the introductions, she glanced at Violet and was amazed at the transformation. Her friend showed no signs of her earlier emotional outburst, but from her pink cheeks to her crimson hair, appeared as serene as a sunset.

"It would seem I've the privilege of escorting you both into dinner since my cousin has not deigned to show his ugly face and we are at odd numbers," Topher said, his eyes twinkling with mischief.

Violet looped her arm through the blond gentleman's offered elbow, and Olivia followed behind them, noting how close Topher had pulled Violet, the dark wool of his suit blending with her lavender silk. Perhaps something good could come of this night.

As they moved into the dining room, Olivia searched the crowd, apprehension tightening her neck and shoulders. What could be keeping Jack?

After seven endless courses, and no Jack, Olivia could do nothing but sit and wring her hands in her lap. She was itching to ask Topher if he had any clue to Jack's whereabouts, but hadn't been able to get a word in the entire dinner. She'd never seen her cousin so animated. Topher appeared equally engaged, but as Olivia stared at the nearly gutted candles, her trepidation could no longer be contained.

"I find it extraordinarily diverting—"

"Excuse me, Mr. March, but would you have the time?" Olivia interrupted midsentence.

Topher turned his gray gaze on Olivia with a slow blink, as if he realized for the first time that she sat next to him. "Certainly." He reached into his coat, pulled out a gold pocket watch, and flipped open the cover. "'Tis nearly midnight. Are you planning to turn into a pumpkin soon, Miss Brownlow?"

His playful comment was lost on Olivia as her heartbeat slowed in her chest. *Midnight?* She clutched Topher's sleeve. "Did Jack tell you his plans for the evening?"

He stilled, the smile freezing on his face. "Jack does not confide his schedule to me."

Violet leaned forward and met Olivia's gaze with round eyes.

"Did he say *anything* at all that might give us a clue to his whereabouts? 'Tis vastly important," Olivia beseeched.

"Well, we weren't exactly speaking after he took the carriage and left me stranded at your fiancé's home this afternoon, but I overheard him arguing with Gran about keeping some appointment tonight."

"Wait." Blood rushed into Olivia's head, making the room spin. "You and Jack visited the Grimwigs?" At his nod, she rushed on. "Did Max tell you about the engagement?"

"His mother mentioned it in passing, but I don't think . . ." A light seemed to come on in Topher's eyes. "He must have overheard! That's why he left so suddenly."

"Oh no, no, no." Olivia pushed back her chair, her hands shaking in dread.

"What is it, Miss Brownlow?" Topher stood beside her, holding her elbow in a firm grip.

"I need to use your carriage, Mr. March. I must get to Blackfriars Bridge, without delay!"

CHAPTER 19

Ice ran through Jack's veins as he walked across the darkened bridge. Monks had chosen well. The railway tracks that ran along Blackfriars' east side and the trains that crossed with rumbling, smoke-belching regularity discouraged foot traffic and laggards. It was all the same to Jack. Witnesses or no, this ended tonight.

The beat of the umbrella's tip against the bridge echoed out around him as he walked. *Tap. Tap. Tap.* Street challenge rules dictated no weapons, but Jack didn't trust Leeford to comply. Besides, something as mundane as a brolly could hardly be considered a weapon.

Through the dense, churning fog, Monks and his gang appeared, and then disappeared. Jack kept walking.

Tap. Tap. Tap.

The haze shifted, coalescing around the legs of the six approaching men, making them seem more wraith than human, their shadowy figures propelled by the stiff breeze. Jack drew in the smells of the Thames, its familiar mixture of mud, salt, and rot bringing him courage. Perhaps he was daft to face this lot on his own, but at present he didn't much care what happened to him.

He had stewed in his anger all evening and begrudgingly admitted to himself that when it came to the orphans, Olivia's intentions had been true, if not her actions. But that didn't make her deception any less wounding. Jack was willing to bet his significant savings that Olivia had strong feelings for him, just not strong enough to turn down one of the wealthiest men in London. His hands clenched into fists as he stepped through a bank of smog, Monks and his gang materializing directly in front of him.

"Ah, if it isn't the street rat, the Artful Dodger back from the dead," Monks sneered, tipping his head in scrutiny. "You're not as tall as I imagined you'd be by now."

Ignoring the jab, Jack got to the point. "Give me the locket, Leeford. The gold one you bought at Langdale's off the old pawny."

Monks glowered suspiciously, and Jack noted his reptilian gaze bore no resemblance to the warm gold of his sister's.

"I'm well aware the locket belonged to your long-lost sibling and why you want it. I'm here to make you a deal."

Monks's laughter echoed through the night, soon mimicked by his band of misfit goons. "Yer offering *me* a deal? What makes you think you have anything to bargain with? I've stated my terms—"

"And now I'll state mine," Jack growled, stepping so close he could smell Monks's fishy breath. "You really didn't think I'd show up here just because you threatened me, did you? In case you haven't noticed, my boys have already moved on."

The hardening of Monks's face showed he knew he'd lost his leverage. "It's no matter. The Hill is my territory now, and if your boys work anywhere near it, they'll be paying me . . . or *else*." Monks lifted his chin and stared down his long nose in challenge.

Out of the corner of his eye, Jack saw Leeford's gang

position themselves in a circle around him. Stepping away from the dinger's noxious breath, Jack folded his arms over his chest. "You implied this to be a true street duel, a boon for a boon, but . . ." He glanced around at the ring of thugs and shrugged one shoulder. "I can see you're afraid you would lose to me one on one."

"Me afraid of you? I already killed you once." Monks snorted. "State your prize, pretty boy."

"I'll make this simple for you. If you fight me and win, you can have the entire city. I'll renounce my title as Street Lord and you'll be unchallenged. But if I win"—Jack let a slow, confident smile spread across his face—"you leave the Hill orphans alone for good, *and* you forget about your half sibling's inheritance."

Monks stalked forward, his face contorting as he grabbed a handful of Jack's shirt and yanked him forward. "What do you bloody know about my inheritance, street rat?"

It was what Leeford had always called him, but Jack refused to let the name take him back to those helpless days when he'd been forced to work for this bludger. He glanced down at Monks's hand on his shirt and pressed the umbrella handle into his sternum. When the half-wit realized he wouldn't get an answer by force, he let go and took a step back.

"I've learned enough to know your father squandered it into nonexistence," Jack bluffed as he jerked his shirt back into place. His patience at an end, he stepped forward. "If you agree to my terms, let's do this."

With a deadly glare and a nod to one of his mates, Monks lifted his fists in front of him.

Jack set the brolly near his feet, and moved into a fighting stance, bouncing on his toes and rolling his shoulders. The rage he'd held in check since learning of Olivia's engagement zipped through him like white lightning. He threw a right jab, connecting with his opponent's eye. Monks's head snapped back, but he quickly righted himself with a growl and circled, looking for an opening.

Feigning left, Monks punched with his right. Jack blocked with his forearm and threw an uppercut to the chin. His challenger staggered back. Unbidden, images flashed in Jack's head: Olivia smiling up at Max, his diamond on her finger. Olivia warm and waiting in his bed. Olivia and Max at the altar. With a rush of pain, he rammed a fist into Monks's gut. When he bent over, Jack followed with a slam to his left kidney. But the hurt came flooding back as quickly as he'd released it.

Monks straightened and smashed his fist into Jack's cheekbone. Stars exploded behind Jack's eye. Monks jabbed again, catching Jack on the chin in the precise spot where Topher had hit him the day before. Jack stumbled back a step, his vision darkening. He had to force Olivia from his mind and focus or risk losing everything.

Monks landed a jab to Jack's ribs. Clarifying pain bloomed. And as Monks crouched to deliver another hit, Jack grabbed the man's head and brought it up to meet his knee, crushing Monks's hawkish nose.

He cried out and clutched his face, blood pouring through his fingers.

The goons began closing in, but Monks waved them off. That's when Jack saw him slip a hand into his pocket, a blade catching a glint of the moon.

Jack stepped back, his eyes darting around for his umbrella as he said, "No weapons, Monks. Street challenge rules."

Then he found it. One of Leeford's goons clutched it in his fist and waved it back and forth with an admonishing grin.

"When have I ever played by the rules?" Monks roared as he charged.

Without a weapon, Jack was dead. He knew from experience, Leeford wouldn't hesitate to gut him if he got the chance. A phantom pain bloomed between his ribs, near paralyzing in its intensity.

His eyes darting from the razor-sharp blade to Monk's face, Jack calculated and ducked at the last second. He pushed Leeford's knife hand away as he drove his shoulder into his opponent's sternum, flipping him over his back. Fists at the ready, Jack spun and found Monks dazed on the ground. Jack kicked the knife out of his hand and watched it spin across the bridge. "Concede, Monks. It's over."

"Not quite," a voice growled from behind him.

Then a meaty arm looped around Jack's neck, crushing his windpipe as the rest of Monks's gang moved in, murder in their eyes.

Olivia's heart galloped in time with the horses' hooves as the carriage sped toward Blackfriars Bridge. Working hard to stay in her seat, she gripped the velvet cushion with one hand and the leather strap with the other as they bumped over the uneven streets. Topher March had stipulated that in order for her to use his carriage, he had to accompany her, muttering something about "insuring his future legacy." But Olivia insisted that Violet stay behind, not only for her own safety but to cover for her with Aunt Becky.

"What time is it?" Olivia asked, glancing out the window at the arches of Waterloo Bridge as they flew past. They were getting close, but not fast enough. Images of Jack, covered in blood and near death, flooded her with mind-numbing panic.

"Twelve thirty-two. Exactly two minutes after the last time you asked," Topher grumbled. "What on earth has Jack done that we have to speed to his bloomin' rescue?"

Olivia tried to shoot him a glare, but couldn't make it stick as they both jostled back and forth like eggs in a chicken cart. "Do you have a pistol hidden somewhere in this death trap?"

"What could you possibly do with it if I did?"

It was a good question. In theory, Olivia knew *how* to use a gun, but didn't know if she could actually shoot anyone. "As I explained—" The carriage hit a bump and knocked Olivia's head against the paneled wall. With a blink to refocus her vision, she continued, "The man Jack is meeting is corrupt and dangerous, and he won't be alone. Unless you have boxing skills of which I am unaware, we'll need more than your good looks to help him."

"What, fisticuffs?" Topher asked, incredulous, his voice raising a full octave.

Olivia couldn't tell if he was being facetious or serious. In any case, they were doomed.

They rounded a corner at breakneck speed, and the shadowy spires of Blackfriars Bridge came into view, its scarlet and gold paint a garish dark red in the muted moonlight. Olivia's mouth went dry. If anything were to happen to Jack, she would not survive it. Even if she couldn't be with him, she had to know he was out there somewhere plotting his next scheme, so charming that his victims thanked him for taking their most valuable treasures.

As the carriage slowed on Great Surrey Street, Olivia scooted to the edge of her seat and clutched the door handle, wishing heartily she'd had the time to rally an army of constables.

"Hold up," Topher said. "We can't just go charging out there without a plan."

Olivia glanced over her shoulder at Topher March. He pulled the cuffs down on his immaculate suit jacket and pushed a lock of blond hair back into place as if he were arriving at the opera. Fear tingled through Olivia's limbs, almost freezing her where she sat. What could she and Mr. Pompous Toff do against a band of street thugs?

"Just follow my lead and try not to get yourself killed," Olivia instructed as the wheels rolled to a stop and she jumped from the carriage. Not waiting, she lifted her skirt and ran toward the bridge. A dense haze obscured visibility, forcing her to slow. Topher jogged up beside her, and they crept forward into the cloud.

Sounds of a scuffle reached them just before the mist parted to reveal three men laid out in various stages of unconsciousness. Jack was in the center of it all, fighting three assailants at once. Olivia's hand flew to her mouth, and she screamed into her palm as two men charged Jack, one holding a wicked-looking knife.

In a blur of motion, Jack spun behind the knife-wielding thug, threw him off balance with a kick to the back of his knees, and grabbed his arm, thrusting the blade into the approaching attacker's arm. A third man rushed him. Olivia watched in amazement as Jack pivoted, punched him in the throat, and slammed his palm into the man's nose, sending him to his knees while bleeding and gasping for breath. The knife wielder returned, blood dripping from his blade as he stalked cautiously toward Jack. Jack's head swiveled between him and a bald giant who barreled out of the haze brandishing a club.

"I don't know which one to hit first," Topher said out of the side of his mouth. Olivia turned to see him swinging a pistol between Jack's accosters, trying to get a clear shot. The giant swung his club; Jack ducked and turned, taking the brunt of the hit to his shoulder.

"Give me that." Olivia grabbed the gun, cocked it, and fired up into the air. All three men froze. "The beaks are on their way. Take your wounded and go!" Her voice echoed back to her over the river, chanting the word, "Go . . . go . . . go."

Jack's gaze met hers as the goons began to scramble, but instead of gratitude, his eyes burned with fury. He stalked toward her, a slight hitch in his stride. "What have you done?" he ground out through clenched teeth. A shadow purpled his right cheekbone and blood oozed from his mouth and seeped from a cut on his bicep, soaking through the light material of his shirt.

A gasp escaped Olivia's throat, but his accusation and the rage on his face squashed her sympathy. "Last time I checked, I was saving your sorry hide!"

"Shut your mouth!" He grabbed her arm in a painful grip, took the pistol and thrust it, butt first, at Topher, who promptly began to reload it. "Get her out of here. Now." Jack whirled her around and gave her a push in the opposite direction. Olivia stumbled forward several steps, but something in her rebelled and she dug in her heels. After all they'd been through together, how dare he treat her like some damsel in distress!

"What a lovely gift you've brought me, Dodger." The voice was deep and intrinsically familiar.

The skin on Olivia's arms prickled into gooseflesh. She turned to find a man being held up by another, blood leaking from his nose and drying in rivulets around both sides of his mouth. He grinned in her direction. "You look just like your sweet, dead mama."

A shiver skittered down Olivia's spine. The man was tall and broad with dark blond hair, his leer showing long dimples in both his thin cheeks. *Her brother.* She'd been so focused on Jack's safety that she hadn't thought through the implications of coming to his rescue. If Monks recognized her, she'd condemned them all.

In her panic, one word scraped out of her throat. "Jack . . ."

Jack's fierce blue gaze met hers before he positioned himself in front of her, blocking her from view. "I beat you fair, Monks. If you don't keep our bargain, you can be beyond sure every street thief and costermonger from here to Newgate will know it. Without your reputation, you'll lose everything. Now scurry away to whatever hole you came from."

"All I want is a family reunion. What do you say, little sister?" Monks called out.

Jack grabbed the gun from Topher's hand, cocked it, and

leveled it at Monks's head. "Speak to her again and I'll end you right now."

Olivia looked around Jack's shoulder to see her brother's disdainful smirk. Not the reaction one would expect from someone being held at gunpoint. "What's stopping you, little street rat?" Monks taunted. "Mercy is for the weak. Surely when I drove the blade between your ribs and listened to your pathetic cries, you learned that lesson."

Jack's finger hovered over the trigger of the pistol and he took a step forward. Olivia could see the vein pulsing in the side of his throat. She prayed he wouldn't shoot. Although she doubted many would mourn her mad half brother, with so many witnesses, Jack would surely hang.

He took another step in Monks's direction, but her brother's next words froze him in place.

"You think you're the only one with a gun, *Mr. Dawkins*?" Two men appeared from behind the curtain of fog with pistols trained in their direction. "Or do you prefer your new name, *Mr. MacCarron*?"

Jack's shoulders jerked, likely in reaction to Monks knowing his dual identities. Olivia's thoughts tripped ahead. If Monks knew who Jack was, how much did he know about her? About her uncle? But none of that would matter if they didn't get out of this alive.

The sounds of clomping hooves and clattering wheels sounded on the bridge.

Monks and the man supporting him began backing away. "My men had orders to keep you alive, Jack, so you can enjoy every moment of what I have planned next." Monks shifted his gaze in Olivia's direction. "I'm so very pleased we were able to meet at last, dear sister. Too bad it will be the last time." And with that, he turned and hobbled away, his thugs following him into the fog.

A single seat buggy emerged from the mist, the driver's eyes fixed straight ahead, as if not seeing the scene on the bridge might keep him alive. He was possibly correct.

After all signs of Monks and his gang disappeared, Jack lowered his arms and turned around, his face ashen. "I hope you came in a bloody carriage, because I'm—" He blinked and crumpled.

Topher caught him under the shoulders, lowered him the rest of the way to the street, and positioned Jack's head on his knees.

"Jack!" Olivia knelt at his side, palming his pale cheek. "Jack?"

His dark lashes fluttered before he opened his eyes and focused on Olivia with a wry smile. "Must have lost more blood than I thought."

Olivia scanned his body, noting the blood stains that spattered his shirt and trousers. But she was fairly certain that was not his blood. Then she saw the gash in his side, his shirt soaked all the way to his waist. "Saints, Jack. Were you *trying* to get yourself killed?" she demanded as she lifted her skirt and ripped the entire bottom flounce from her petticoat.

Topher took off his jacket and tucked it under Jack's head. "I'll go fetch the carriage," he said as he stood and jogged away.

"I'm not a bloomin' invalid. It isn't deep. Nothing a good night's sleep won't fix."

Jack tried to sit up and Olivia put a hand on his chest,

pushing him back down. "Whoa. Let me take a look before you run off to slay more villains."

One side of his mouth kicked up as his incredible eyes caught hers. She gave him a gentle smile, trying to ignore the love bubbling in her chest and threatening to escape her lips. She brushed a lock of sweaty hair off his forehead, and drank in his pale, bruised, and *beautiful* face. "Jack, I'm so very sorry," she whispered.

"For what? Showing up here and almost getting us all killed? Or not leaving when I—"

"No, I'm sorry I didn't tell you myself . . . about the . . . the engagement."

His lips pressed together, and with a single nod, he averted his eyes, staring somewhere past her shoulder.

Olivia couldn't speak over the vise squeezing her throat. What could she say? There were no words that could make it better, that could soothe the hurt or repair his loss of trust in her, so she focused on tending his wound.

Gingerly, she pulled his shirttail from his trousers and lifted the blood-crusted material. His breath hissed through his teeth as the fabric separated from the wound with a soft tear. There was a long gash in the smooth flesh between his ribs, just below the puffy flesh of an old scar.

"I need to tie this around you to stop the bleeding. Can you sit up?" She put a hand on each of his shoulders. He sat up himself, and she snatched her hands away. Without looking at her, he held his shirt up to reveal a flat abdomen, all ribbed muscle and smooth skin. She leaned toward him, looped the cloth around his waist, and tied it in a knot at the indentation of his spine. The silence was like an insurmount-able wall, every second adding another brick between them.

Jack lowered his shirt and moved to stand. Olivia placed a hand under his arm to assist him, but he shook her off. "I'm fine."

Horses' hooves reverberated on the bridge, shaking the boards beneath their feet. The pounding echoed in Olivia's head like nails being hammered into a coffin. She glanced at Jack, but he wouldn't meet her gaze. Wringing her hands, she shut her eyes, willing back the tears. She refused to let him see her cry. She'd made her bed, now she had to lie in it—somewhat literally as it pertained to her pending nuptials. She cringed, the disturbing mental images causing her eyes to pop back open.

The carriage pulled to a stop beside them. Topher jumped down from the cabin and extended his arm to Jack. "Let me help you up, mate."

"Actually, I've decided to walk." Jack picked up his dis-carded umbrella, and with a slight wince, leaned on it as he turned and headed toward the street, hunched and stumbling.

"Jack, don't." Olivia picked up her skirts and chased after him. When she reached his side, she grabbed his sleeve, care-ful not to touch the knife wound on his arm. "I cannot allow you to walk home in this condition."

He stopped, but stared straight ahead, his jaw set in a hard line.

Olivia dropped her hand from his sleeve and said, "Unless, of course, you wish to endure the humiliation of the car-riage keeping pace with you all the way back to Saint James Square."

He turned toward her, an odd combination of sadness and amusement on his pale face. "You'd do it too, wouldn't you? Follow me all the way home?"

"You bet your trousers, I would." Olivia lifted her chin. Jack's gaze drilled down into hers, searching. Could he read her thoughts? Did he know that if she could, she would follow him to the ends of the earth?

He reached out and brushed aside a curl that had fallen across her face. His feather-soft touch pulled a shudder from deep within her. Still holding her gaze, he dropped his arm and whispered, "All right, Livie, I concede."

As he limped back toward the carriage and Olivia watched the defeated slope of his shoulders, she couldn't help but wonder if he referred to more than just the carriage ride home.

With a blink of stinging tears, Olivia followed Jack, wondering how in the world she was going to live her life without him.

CHAPTER 20

꧁꧂

ack tossed and turned, the freshly stitched wound in his
side burning with every movement. Sweat coated his skin.
The coverlet wrapped around his legs and dragged him into
a restless sleep. He could sense her there. As she always was.
But this dream was not the typical evocative yet elusive fan-
tasy. This was vivid, like being dropped into a memory . . .

Jack looked around at the park, lush and vibrant with the
brilliant greens of spring. A bed of pink and purple tulips surrounded by a ring of sunny daffodils waved on the soft breeze,
the occasional petal breaking loose and skittering across the
grass. He drew the air deep into his lungs. He couldn't be
sure where he was or why, but he might as well enjoy the
fine weather.

Sinking his hands into his pockets, he strolled along the
dirt path, still damp from a recent rain, and rounded a corner where he came upon a lovely picnic scene. The woman's
back was to him, but he knew the set of her slim shoulders
and the waves of her light caramel hair—Olivia.

Jack smiled, his pulse accelerating as it always did in her
presence. He took a step off the path, intent on saying hello,
and froze as she turned to the side, displaying a belly rounded
like a ripe watermelon beneath her dress. A dimpled grin
spread across her face as a dark-haired boy toddled toward
her, Brom keeping pace beside him.

Her voice drifted across the clearing as she scooped the child up in her arms. "Who's my strong boy? You are, that's who!" She nuzzled his tiny neck, and his sweet baby giggles rang through Jack's heart, bringing tears to his eyes. This was Olivia's family.

She had moved on without him.

Jack watched in fascination while she settled the boy beside her on the blanket, and the breeze ruffled through her curls as she opened a wicker basket. She sang a happy tune to the boy and set out three plates, loading two of them with fried chicken, ripe strawberries, and fresh carrots. Jack had never seen her more joyful or more beautiful. Some unknown feeling began to pulse inside him, expanding with every breath, as if a wild beast grew within his body. The animal shifted inward, grasping and clawing. He wanted to be the one to put that sparkle in her eyes, that incandescent glow on her skin. Jack clenched his hands into fists at his sides. Why couldn't it be him?

Then, from the other side of the glade, came a rustle of leaves. Brom gave a quick bark as the shrubbery parted and a man strode into the clearing.

"I found the other basket, Livie. Right where I left it on the porch." The man tossed dark hair out of his eyes, his crooked grin innately familiar. The park seemed to tilt on its axis. Jack had seen that face. Every day, looking back at him through the mirror.

"That's all right, darling. We've been having a fine time without you," Olivia taunted, tilting her chin in that adorably obstinate way of hers.

"Is that so?" Dream-Jack dropped to his knees and set

down the basket before stretching over to cup a hand behind her neck. "We'll have to see what we can do about that." He lowered his mouth to hers, and Jack felt his own lips pucker in anticipation . . .

He sat straight up in bed, his heart pounding so hard he could see the skin on his chest pulsing in time. What the devil was that?

And more importantly, how could he make it come true?

Stepping through the doors of the Grimwig mansion, Olivia felt a bit like Cinderella dressed in her magical finery, waiting for the stroke of midnight, when she'd turn back into plain old Olivia Brownlow. She watched the elite of society mill about the massive, two-story vestibule. Women in extravagant gowns of velvet and satin preened like exotic birds, the men perfect foils in their somber dark suits. Livered waiters circulated, offering flutes of bubbling champagne to the hundred or so guests. As Olivia took in the scene, she realized that her entire townhome could fit neatly into this front foyer. Would she ever feel comfortable in this palace?

If only her uncle were here to hold her hand and lend her courage. He had taken a turn for the worse, the doctor forbidding him to leave the house. At first, Olivia refused to go without him, but her uncle would have none of it. So, after she'd finished dressing for the ball, she'd swept into his bedroom to show off her elegant gown. His head had poked over the pile of quilts, tears gathering in his eyes, and he'd declared her his beautiful angel. Tugging on her hand, he'd asked her to sit beside him and whispered, "It isn't too late to change your mind, you know." Olivia had known he spoke of her engagement without having to ask. "Follow your heart, dearest." It was all he could say, before a coughing fit overtook him.

But she'd read the rest in his eyes: *I'm not long for this world. Don't plan your life around me.* Olivia suspected it was true, but the very thought of living without her uncle left her floating like a boat cut free of its anchor, tossed from wave to wave on a vast and turbulent ocean.

"Olivia, I simply cannot stop looking at you in that gown," Violet exclaimed, interrupting her morose thoughts. "The color is radiant on you!" Her cousin passed her wrap to the cloakroom attendant, revealing her own lovely emerald dress.

Begrudgingly, Olivia admitted Francesca's modiste had exceeded her expectations. As she handed over her cloak, she glanced down at her royal blue gown in wonder. The skirt fell from the tiny cinched waist in graceful folds, the hem and neckline embellished with embroidered leaves and a tasteful smattering of crystals that caught the light and glittered every time she moved. Capped sleeves fell over her arms, baring her shoulders. The exposure felt uncomfortable and liberating all at once.

"'Tis attractive, but I think the neckline is a tad bit revealing," Aunt Becky observed while deliberately staring at the woman's feathered hat in front of them.

"Mother, the gown was a last-minute cancelation. We were fortunate to find one so perfectly suited to Olivia."

Aunt Becky's face turned beet red as she glanced at Olivia's overflowing cleavage and then jerked her eyes past the receiving line to the ballroom entrance. "Quite right," came her strangled reply. As they drew closer to Mr. and Mrs. Grimwig, greeting each of their guests in turn, Olivia overheard her aunt whisper, "Stay close to her, Vi."

After being welcomed by their host and hostess with much hugging and winking, she and Vi followed the crowd to a part of the house that had been forbidden to them as children. Standing in the open doorway, the girls exchanged looks of amazement. The ballroom was a swirl of lights and sound. Enormous chandeliers dripped with mirrored glass, reflecting sparkles on the walls and twirling guests. One entire wall was composed of open French doors draped with strings of snow lilies and dinner plate dahlias, their white petals fluttering in the night air. A full orchestra, screened by a variety of tall, potted plants, took up the whole back of the room.

With Violet by her side, Olivia put one foot in front of the other and wiped the astonishment from her face. She searched for Maxwell's tall form, hoping to persuade him to get the announcement out of the way sooner rather than later. And in so doing, extinguish the tiny spark of hope her uncle's words had ignited within her. What better way to put impossible dreams to rest than to make her betrothal irreversibly official?

"Miss Brownlow, Miss Cramstead." Topher March bent in a deep bow over Violet's gloved hand and kissed it soundly. "Would you care to waltz with me, dear lady?"

Her friend curtsied and lit up like a Christmas tree covered in candles. "Yes, of course." She searched the area around them. "Olivia, I'm not sure where Mother's gotten off to . . ."

Pleased to her toes that her cousin might find her love match after all, she dismissed them with a sweep of her gloved hands. "Please go, Vi. I shall find the refreshment table and meet you there after your dance. I heard they have ice cream in seven different flavors, and I plan to sample them all." Topher gave her a nod, his gray eyes sparkling in thanks as he offered Violet his elbow. He was still a pompous toff, but he'd proven the night before that he wasn't nearly so useless as she had assumed. And besides, Vi brought out the best in him.

Olivia watched as they made their way to the dance floor, Topher's blond head tipped toward Violet's flaming curls. Something akin to a dark cloud passed across her soul—jealousy. *Surely not.* She could not be happier to see the obvious feelings growing between Mr. March and her cousin, yet a voice, quiet and small, tainted her joy. *What about me?*

Olivia pushed the question aside, knowing it was selfish in the extreme. She had a perfectly suitable arrangement with one of the wealthiest men in the city. Perhaps it wasn't a love match, but it was high time she accepted the future she'd chosen. Lifting her chin, she scanned the area again for her future husband.

Then she saw him—not Max, but *him*, the one who haunted her day and night—broad, athletic, his restless energy unmistakable as he turned and flicked his raven hair out of his face. *Jack.*

All the blood drained from Olivia's head as he turned, his gaze drilling into her from across the crowded room. He wasn't supposed to be here! Panic skittered over the exposed skin of her shoulders, leaving her fingers numb. It was too much to resist. *He* was too much.

She didn't realize she was moving until after she'd already taken several steps in his direction. He pushed through the throng to get to her. When they finally met, he took both her hands in his, the heat of his skin permeating the thin silk of her gloves. Jack leaned back, and the very air around him radiated intensity as he regarded her from her piled curls to her bejeweled slippers. His eyes returned to hers and she read something new there, a possessive confidence that melted her insides to pudding.

The laughter and music, the flowery scents of perfume and spicy cologne all faded as Olivia soaked in his face, noting that the dark bruise on his left cheekbone only added to his dangerous appeal. Something had changed in him. She couldn't define it; all she knew was that Jack stood before her, completely unguarded for the first time.

A tiny smile lifted one corner of his mouth. "Why is it that when you walk into a room, my world stops spinning?"

Olivia sucked in a breath, her pulse pounding in her ears until the dancers, the laughter, and the music all fell away. He'd asked her once what she wanted, and in that singular moment she knew. She wanted all of him; the gentleman, the street lord, the criminal—she didn't care anymore. Jack was her anchor. The brazen boy with the scruffy top hat had stolen her heart from the instant he'd plucked her off the streets and taken her under his wing. And Olivia couldn't imagine a single reason not to tell him. "Jack, I—"

"Jack," snipped a birdlike voice. Olivia started, having forgotten they were in a room packed with people. She turned and met the glassy eyes of a pheasant perched on top of Lois March's head. The old woman tapped her cane against the marble floor with a sharp crack. "I need your assistance, posthaste!"

Jack glanced down at the woman and then returned his glowing blue gaze to Olivia. Stepping close, he leaned in to whisper, "Please don't move, love. It's urgent that I speak with you." He gave her hands a firm squeeze before releasing them and turning to follow his impatient benefactor. But before he went, he glanced back at Olivia, white teeth flashing in the candlelight. The force of that smile nearly knocked her back on her heels.

"Excuse me. Are you Miss Olivia Brownlow?"

Olivia turned to find a young footman, his sandy brows scrunched in a troubled expression. "Yes," she answered.

"This urgent message arrived for you." The servant bowed, thrust a sealed envelope into her hand, and headed back the way he came. As he rushed through the crowd, Olivia noted that his uniform was mismatched and slightly rumpled, but worries for her uncle quickly turned her attention back to the letter.

She ripped into the missive with trembling fingers.

Ollie,
Brit missing. Come quick.
Archie

Talons gripped her heart. As if moving underwater, her senses muffled and sluggish, Olivia began to struggle through the crowd. She pushed past an older man, almost knocking him off his feet. Issuing a quick apology, she kept moving, all the while praying for God to keep Brit safe. Had he been mugged? Was he lying hurt and alone in the street? Or . . . A much more ominous thought sprang into her mind. *Monks.*

She stopped and turned in a circle, searching for Jack's

dark head. But he was nowhere to be found. There was no time. Picking up her skirts, she rushed out of the ballroom and into the corridor.

As she sped past the life-sized statuary and giant potted ferns, she formulated a plan—she would rent a hackney, stop at home to change out of her gown, and take the hack to Turnbull Road. She just hoped she could find the boys' new hideout.

Guilt and fear churned in Olivia's stomach. Why hadn't she visited the boys this week, despite Jack's warnings? What if she was too late? She glanced over her shoulder in indecision, wishing she had time to find Jack, and smacked into something solid. Stumbling back from the impact, Olivia blinked at the petite, purple-clad wall halting her progress.

Francesca, eyes narrowed, tapped her foot in annoyance. "I'd hoped such a lovely gown would lend you some civility. I can see that I was wrong."

No time for a retort, Olivia folded Archie's letter and stuffed it back into the envelope. "Fran, find Jack and give him this note. 'Tis most urgent." Olivia thrust the missive at her cousin, but Fran's arms stayed at her sides. "Please!"

"Jack?" Fran arched a dark brow in question.

"Bloody Jack MacCarron! You know exactly who I'm talking about," Olivia exclaimed as she grabbed Francesca's gloved hand and closed her fingers around the note.

Her cousin's eyes went wide, finally realizing Olivia meant business. "Yes, of course."

Olivia spun away and called a quick thank you over her shoulder.

The click of her heeled slippers echoed down the

seemingly never-ending hallway as she ran, her mind whirling with questions. If Monks had taken Brit, would he hurt
him? What could he possibly hope to gain by taking an innocent child? Was it a blackmail attempt to gain the missing
inheritance? Her lungs contracted. Her brother was more
unbalanced than she—

"Olivia?"

She turned her head and saw Maxwell rushing toward
her from a side hallway. *Thank God!*

She spun toward him, talking as she ran. "Max, I need
your help! I just received a note that one of the orphans—the
ones I told you about—has gone missing. We must—" She
sucked in air, as he took her shoulders in a firm grip. "We
must help him."

"Now? In the middle of our engagement ball?" Max held
her gaze, his brows scrunched together over his nose.

Olivia went very still. Surely he was not angry. She must
not have explained the situation properly. "Max, a child's life
is at stake."

He let out a long breath. "Olivia, street children are . . .
capricious by nature. How old is this boy?"

"He is twelve," Olivia answered, working hard not to cry
as she pictured Brit's serious dark eyes and freckled cheeks.

Max paused, a tight smile on his face. He looked past her
and then back again as if searching for the right words. "I'm
quite certain the boy was distracted by some form of iniqui-
tous amusement. He likely doesn't even want to be found.
Now, let's go back to the ball." He tipped her chin up, the
look on his face more condescending than beguiling. "We
haven't yet had our first dance."

Olivia jerked her chin out of his grasp and took a step back. "You are quite serious, aren't you? You expect me to return to the party as if I haven't a care in the world, when I've just received an urgent message that a child—a child I know and care for—is in danger!"

"Calm down, Olivia. You can check on the boy tomorrow." He took her arm and looped it through his, patting her hand as he steered her back down the corridor. "Let's find you one of those marmalade tarts you love so much."

Olivia's temper broke every last fetter. Heat rushed into her face, her heart pounding so violently it pulsed in her temples. She was not some petulant child to placate with the promise of a treat. Digging in her heels, she extricated her arm from his and met his startled gaze. "You're not at all who I thought you were, Maxwell Grimwig. You can go back to your fancy party, but I am going to find Brit, whether you approve or not!"

Olivia whirled on her heel and stalked toward the front doors.

"If you leave," Max called after her, his voice loud and trembling, "consider our engagement annulled."

Olivia stopped, but didn't turn around.

"Olivia!" Max barked her name like a command. "Where do you think you are going?"

She felt Max come up behind her. "I'm going to Turnbull Road."

"Turnbull Road? In the slums of Holborn? I forbid it!"

She turned back. "You *forbid* it?" Was this a hint of what her life would be like as the wife of an entitled gentleman? Him ordering her about, expecting her to obey without question?

To sit tucked within the drawing room, looking pretty like one of his possessions?

"Olivia, you cannot possibly choose a street rat over our relationship."

Street rat? She clenched her fist against the urge to slap his entitled face. "And you can't possibly expect me to marry you when all you care about is yourself and your blasted reputation!"

His brows lowered, his cheeks flaming red as he crossed his arms in front of his chest.

"That's what this is about, isn't it, Max? What people will think if I leave before we can make our big announcement?"

"Do you not have a care for propriety? Or your own safety?" he demanded, his face growing darker with every word. "A true lady would never—"

"Then I'm *not* a true lady! Nor do I wish to be, if it means sitting in this glorious mansion and ignoring the unimaginable suffering happening all around me!"

He swallowed hard, tipped his nose up, and glared at her.

She searched his face for some remorse, for some sign of her words breaking through his callous shell, but all she saw was a spoilt boy used to getting his way. Her voice barely a whisper, she said, "Goodbye, Max."

Without a second glance, she marched to the doors and out of Maxwell Grimwig's life.

CHAPTER 21

∾

ack slunk down the darkened hallway, his heart stampeding in his ears. But it wasn't fear that raced through his blood, it was anger. Lois had overheard a rumor that due to the recent rash of robberies, armed guards circulated throughout the mansion. In true Lois fashion, she'd panicked, forcing him to attempt the heist earlier than planned. Jack had no idea what difference it made, considering the guards would likely be there all night. He'd been on the verge of a breakthrough with Olivia. Any moment, Grimwig would pronounce his claim on the girl he loved, slamming shut Jack's window of opportunity. But instead of stopping Olivia from making the biggest mistake of her life, Jack was creeping through corridors like a blasted dog searching for a scrap of meat.

A rustle, followed by a muffled giggle, alerted Jack just before two shadows stretched around the corner. He ducked into a dim alcove and struggled to control the rapid rise and fall of his chest by sealing his lips. He didn't want to do this—not now and perhaps ever again. It was not . . . honorable. For the first time in his life, Jack longed to be moral and decent—to become the man he'd seen in his dream.

When the couple strolled by arm in arm and disappeared down the stairs, Jack closed his eyes and visualized his plan like a blueprint. He had to complete this one last heist if he ever wanted to earn his freedom. Steadily, he released the breath he'd been holding and opened his eyes.

Cold as a stone, Jack stepped into the corridor and continued on his way. He would make quick work of this job, hand the jewels off, and get back to Olivia before it was too late.

⌑

Olivia hopped from the carriage, prayed the driver would stay put as she'd paid him to, and then ran into the abandoned building on Turnbull Road. Thankful she'd taken the time to go back to Cavendish Square and change into her street clothes, she took the stairs two at a time. She reached the second-floor landing and nearly ran into empty space. She screeched to a halt, arms windmilling in the air at the edge of a two-story drop. In her haste, she'd forgotten Brit's plan to protect their third-floor hideout.

She took an unsteady step back from the ledge. Knowing that she must be in the right place, she began to search the walls for the hidden lever that would swing a board into place by rope and pulley, completing the broken staircase. She ran her fingers along the wood panels, but her hands trembled terribly and she didn't have a light. "You can do this, Olivia. Just calm down," she whispered aloud.

After what felt like hours of fruitless searching, she stopped and stood in the center of the landing. *What would Jack do right now?* He wouldn't waste time, she knew that much. Placing two fingers in her mouth, she let out her signature whistle. In moments, she heard muted footfalls and the grinding slide of a bolt.

"Whot's the password?" Archie's voice called from above.

Olivia cursed and stomped her boot in frustration. "Ichabod Crane. Brom Bones. Katrina Van Tassel," Olivia shouted in frustration. "I don't bloody know! Just let me up!"

"Ollie?"

"Yes, it's me!"

A thud, followed by a squeak, prompted Olivia to jump back as a dark outline lowered toward her. Brit was a genius. Of course, the control lever would only be accessible from the third floor. Before the ramp even slid into the grooves provided for it, Olivia's feet were on it. She ran up the steep incline and leapt onto the landing. "Why aren't you out looking for him?" she demanded as Archie spun the wheel backward, lifting the plank away from the staircase.

Archie's green eyes blinked at her, clearly confused. "How did you—"

"Because I'm here," croaked a voice from the doorway.

Unable to believe her ears, Olivia snatched a nearby lantern and thrust it toward the doorway. He was all right!

"Brit!" Olivia rushed forward and threw her arms around the boy, pushing him back into the room.

"Ouch. Ollie, leave off." Brit struggled and pulled back from her embrace.

"Are you hurt?" She released him and lifted the lantern. "What happ—" Her voice choked off at the sight of his face. His left eye was purple and swollen shut, his right cheek cut open, his lower lip busted and bleeding. "What happened to you?"

The bolt slammed into place and Archie joined them. "Ollie, how did you know Brit was in trouble?"

The hairs stood up on the back of Olivia's neck, a warning jangling over her skin. "I need to tend Brit's wounds and I'll explain."

Seated in front of the massive hearth, surrounded by what seemed like a hundred boys and at least two girls, Olivia cleaned Brit's face and began asking questions. From what she could gather, Brit had been kidnapped that afternoon by some of Monks's goons. They'd blindfolded him, taken him to their hideout, beat on him, and then released him. And most curious of all, Archie had never sent her a note. She knew Brit had shared her true identity with his second-in-command in case of an emergency, but Brit had returned before the boys had too much time to panic.

"So, they didn't give you any clues to why they would do this?" Olivia asked for the second time.

Brit winced as she dabbed a wet cloth against the gash on his cheek. "No."

"Was Monks there?"

"No, just heard the gits sayin' Monks would have their hides if he found out they let me go." Brit looked up at the ceiling before his solemn dark eyes met Olivia's and his brows wrinkled over his freckled nose. "I think they were meant to kill me."

A wave of such intense emotions rose inside Olivia that her hand hovered halfway to Brit's lip. She stared into the fire as her chin trembled. How could she protect them from someone so ruthless? *So utterly evil?* Not even Jack, with his cleverness and strength, could stop her half brother. Jack was only one man, after all.

Brit ordered the children to get their pallets laid out for

the night and then leaned in, whispering, "I'm all right, Ollie. These are just bruises."

She blinked back her tears and met Brit's gaze, his bravery so very like Jack's. "I know. But what about next time, Brit? I'm putting you all in danger and it has to stop."

"What does that blasted Monks have to do with you?"

Olivia threw a glance to the other children, but they were all busy preparing for the night. She took a deep breath and confessed, "Because he's my half brother, and he's using you to get to me."

A sharp vertical frown line creased Brit's smooth forehead, his eyes searching her face for several long seconds. "Then he's the one who sent you the note tellin' you I was missing. We just need to figure out why he wanted you to leave that ball."

Olivia shook her head and pulled Brit into a quick hug.

"Whot was that for?" He frowned, a blush rushing up his neck as he looked away and scratched his head.

Trying to buy time to reign in her emotions, she sat back and lifted a cloth from the bowl on the hearth, ringing out the pink-tinged water. "Hold this on your eye," she instructed, and handed him the damp material. "I'm going to miss you the most, you know."

Brit went very still, his unswollen eye locked on her face. "Ollie, no. We can fight this. What about Dodger?"

Finding an inner strength she didn't know she possessed, Olivia replied with a steady voice, "Jack will still come by. But I can't. It's too risky." She stood up and dusted the ashes from the seat of her trousers. "Besides, you don't need a den mother anymore."

Brit stood beside her, his one uncovered eye even with hers—and filled with tears. That almost broke her. Clenching her teeth until her jaw ached, she forced down her grief. To ensure this brilliant boy, and all the others, had a future, she would walk away. It was the only thing she could do to save them.

Olivia trudged down Oxford and turned onto Cavendish Square. When she'd left the hideout, the hackney had been long gone, but she didn't hire another. The walk would do her good, perhaps help her make some sense of what had happened that night. But she was no closer to finding any answers. Reaching the security of her familiar, tree-lined street, the dam on her tears broke free. She'd left without a word to the boys. Only Brit knew the truth.

And Max. She'd longed for freedom to be with the man she loved. But it was not at all how she'd wanted it to happen. Max had been her friend, and she'd hoped to have the time to explain her decision. But his ultimatum had taken the choice right out of her hands.

She cut behind a row of neighboring houses and then entered her garden through the back gate. Sobs hitched her chest as she slid open the dining room window to find Brom, tail wagging like a metronome, waiting to greet her. After climbing over the sill, she threw her arms around her dog's warm, solid body and buried her face in his coarse fur. She'd certainly made a mess of things. Guilt hammered on her brain until she thought her head might explode. She should have separated herself from the orphans weeks ago, when Jack advised the association had become too precarious. But instead, her pigheadedness had almost gotten Brit killed.

Brom stiffened, and a moment later banging reverberated through the house. Cautiously, she rose to her feet and moved toward the front door. It had to be after two o'clock in the morning, long past reasonable visiting hours. Another round of loud knocks filled the foyer as Olivia peeked between the curtains of a front window. Four coppers, in their black uniforms and helmets, stood on the front stoop, and a plain-clothed man approached from the street. Had her petty thefts finally caught up to her?

Olivia yanked the hat, wig, and net off her head, and stuffed them in the umbrella stand. She was removing her jacket when Thompson emerged from his apartments in the back of the house, grumbling and knotting the sash on his robe as he hurried to the entryway. Olivia sank back into the shadowy parlor as the butler opened the door.

"Is Miss Olivia Brownlow at home?" a clipped voice demanded.

Brom growled menacingly, and Thompson grabbed his collar to hold him back.

"She's abed. Come back in the morning." The butler moved to shut the door, but a club shoved into the jamb propped it open.

"This is a police matter." The door swung open, pushing Thompson back several steps. Brom strained against his collar, barks exploding out of his chest. "Do something with that canine, sir! It's urgent we speak with Miss Brownlow straightaway."

As Thompson tugged a ferocious Brom down the hall, likely to lock him in the broom closet, Olivia began to shake. There was no mercy for thieves and pickpockets. As if it were yesterday, she could feel the beak's rough hands latching her arms behind her back and carting her through the streets, the judge sentencing her to hang. Darkness edged in on her vision, but when Thompson returned, his next words snapped her back to herself.

"I'm sorry, sir. I had forgotten Miss Olivia is attending a ball at the Grimwig mansion this evening." The loyal butler straightened his robe and lifted his chin. "May I inquire what this is concerning?"

The man in the bowler and tweed coat stepped into the foyer and flashed his credentials at Thompson. "Inspector Martin, sir. And you are?"

"Thompson, sir. Burt Thompson, the Brownlows' butler."

"I must apologize for the late hour, but we have permission to search the premises." The detective moved into the house flanked by all four officers. "Have you seen Miss Brownlow this evening?"

Olivia crept backward on silent feet and ducked behind a curtain as she heard Thompson answer that he had not seen her since she left for the party. Olivia froze, praying her feet were not visible from beneath the drape. What could a detective want with her? If this was about the occasional stolen doorstop or silver fork, the regular constables would be sufficient to investigate.

Directly on the other side of the curtain, a voice said, "Please direct us to Miss Brownlow's bedchamber, Mr. Thompson, and then we'll let you return to your rest."

Olivia caught her breath, and a warning bell clanged in her head. Her ball gown was strewn across her bed, where she'd thrown it in her haste to find Brit. If they suspected her of some crime, that bit of evidence would destroy her alibi of being at the ball the entire evening.

Thompson's voice rose and cut into her thoughts. "Master Brownlow is gravely ill. If I wake him, he will be unnecessarily agitated. Surely this inspection can wait until morning."

"No, sir. It cannot," replied the curt voice of the inspector. "Miss Brownlow's wrap was found at the scene of the crime, and we've received a tip leading us to investigate her quarters. We cannot risk the evidence will not be tampered with. Now move aside."

Boots tromped on the wooden staircase like an army marching to battle. Olivia didn't know if she should sneak out the front door or turn herself in. But whatever they suspected her of, she imagined her male disguise would not be well received. She could sneak to Violet's house, pretend to have spent the night there, borrow one of her dresses, and return in the morning.

Deciding it was a sound plan, Olivia peered around the velvet drape. The parlor was empty, so she crept out, staying close to the wall. She tiptoed into the foyer and reached for the front doorknob, then heard the unmistakable tap and shuffle of her uncle's footsteps. Olivia stopped. She simply could not leave him to deal with whatever mess she'd unintentionally made. Turning, she caught her uncle's surprised gaze as he took in her attire. "Uncle, I can explain this later." Olivia swept a hand toward her clothes. "But right now, the constables are here because they think I've committed some crime. I can assure you—"

"Olivia," her uncle rasped. "Go. Go now!"

Olivia searched her uncle's alert eyes. Trust and love

mixed with fear. He was right, she had to go. Giving him a quick peck on the cheek, she spun on her heel and pulled open the front door.

"Halt!" Feet pounded on the stairs.

Framed in the entranceway, Olivia stopped and turned to see the inspector, his face a blank slate. He rushed toward her with an amethyst necklace clutched in his fist. The square violet gems and rose-cut diamonds winked in the flame of the lantern in his other hand. Olivia's stomach clenched. She had seen that necklace countless times. Because it was Fran's.

"Olivia Brownlow, you are under arrest for the murder of Francesca Lancaster."

CHAPTER 22

~~~

Jack's hackles were raised like a cat on its ninth life, making him wish he'd gone with his initial instinct and stolen a horse from the Grimwigs' massive stable. It wasn't as if they would miss the animal, but his thieving days were over. So he'd settled for renting a cab and hightailing it to Turnbull Road. But when he got there, Olivia was already gone. He rapped on the roof of the hackney with his brolly and shouted, "Get to Cavendish Square in the next ten minutes and there's an extra crown in it for you."

With a crack of leather against horsehide, the beast took off at a gallop, nearly catapulting Jack out of his seat. *That's more bloomin' like it*, he thought as he grasped the edges of the folded canopy. They sped past the river, the muddy ribbon nothing but a blur, and Jack worked through the night in chronological order, hoping to make some sense of it all. After cracking the Grimwigs' safe without a hitch, he'd passed the emeralds off to Topher as they'd planned, and then gone in search of Olivia. That's when Francesca found him, gave him "Archie's" note, reported that Olivia had run from the ball with the devil at her heels, and rather gleefully speculated that her cousin's engagement to Maxwell was off. There had been no time to digest that bit of happy news. Jack had rented a hackney, dropped Topher and the jewels off at March House, and raced to Turnbull Road. By the time he got there, Brit was safe, if not fully sound, and Olivia was gone.

Jack had inspected Brit's injuries while he gleaned as much about the kidnapping as the boy was willing to tell in his desolate state. Jack sensed something more than the boy's near brush with death caused his reticence. But when Jack attempted to buoy Brit's spirits by promising to return with Ollie the following night, the boy's solemn one-eyed gaze had gripped Jack's heart. He'd lowered his head and muttered, "She isn't comin' back. Not ever."

With every word the boy spoke, a terrible supposition grew—Olivia planned to run. If she left the orphans in order to protect them, what was to stop her from leaving London without a trace? The thought fueling him, Jack had torn out of there, intent on stopping her. Or saving her.

The hackney rounded the corner on two wheels, the gallop of hooves against cobblestones echoing in time with Jack's racing heart. They reached the tree-lined boulevard of Cavendish Square and the driver pulled back on the reins, the horse snorting into the quiet night.

"Just ahead on the right. Number Four." Jack pulled the coins from his pocket, ready to throw them and run. He would take Olivia out of the city himself—perhaps out of the country. Spirit her and her uncle away somewhere that bloody Monks would never find them.

They slowed to a stop behind a black police wagon. Jack paid the driver and jumped from the cab. Everything seemed to slow as if in a nightmare as the sky-blue door of Number Four opened and Olivia emerged. Jack rushed forward and then stopped dead as two constables, one restraining each of her shirt-clad arms, followed behind.

Olivia's stricken, tear-filled gaze met his and he stumbled

forward several steps. She shook her head almost imperceptibly as if warning him away—protecting him even as she was being hauled off to jail.

The coppers loaded her into the back of the wagon, chaining her to the seat like some deranged criminal. Pressure built in Jack's chest and burned behind his eyes as he watched, helpless. He couldn't let them take her, he had to do *something*. Just before they closed the doors, he sprinted forward. "Olivia! What's happened?"

"Francesca's been murdered. Jack, they think *I* did it." Her voice choked off in a sob.

"Stand back, sir." Hands tugged at his arms.

A constable climbed in and sat across from Olivia. The doors were closed and locked behind them.

Jack pushed away from the coppers restraining him and tripped forward, gripping the bars of the window. His eyes locked on Olivia's bewildered gaze through the darkness, a vow tearing from his throat. "I *will* save you, Olivia. I'll find a way, no matter what they say you've done."

"Jack, don't." Tears streamed down her cheeks as she shook her head. "There's nothing you can do."

The wagon pulled away, yanking the bars from Jack's numb fingers. He stood in the street and watched her face through the barred window until it shrank into the night, a piece of his soul ripping away and going with her.

"Young man!" It took Jack several seconds to realize the old man standing in the doorway of Olivia's house was her uncle and that he was talking to him. Jack focused on the bent figure.

"Young man, please come in and join me for tea."

With no clue what else to do, he followed the gent into the house, where they sat in the yellow parlor. Jack slumped on the divan, elbows on his knees, head in his hands. His mind felt oddly empty as he overheard Mr. Brownlow order tea and ask to have the fire lit in the hearth.

"I'm Charles Brownlow, Olivia's uncle and guardian."

Jack squeezed his temples between his thumb and fingers. "I know."

"Then I find I'm at a disadvantage, because I have no notion who you are."

Unsure who he was at the moment, Jack raised his eyes to the old man, who watched him with an empathy and a shared grief that drew him outside of himself. "I'm Jack MacCarron." Jack leaned over, extended his hand, and shook the man's knobby fingers.

"I must assume you are him."

Jack sat up straight. "Sir?"

"The man who's stolen my Olivia's heart."

A bit of light penetrated the dark saturating Jack's mind. Had he stolen Olivia's heart? If she'd admitted as much to her uncle, there had to be some truth to it. As if those words woke him from a dream, Jack jumped to his feet. "I have to go after her!"

He'd taken two long strides toward the door when a voice, more stern than he would've believed possible, bellowed from Mr. Brownlow. "Come sit back down!"

Jack stopped and turned around slowly.

"You will do her no good if you go racing down to the station half-cocked. We need to devise a plan."

He couldn't deny the old man's logic. With a quick nod

and a somewhat clearer mind, he returned to his seat. "Is Francesca Lancaster really dead?"

The man's eyes turned liquid, but his reply was steady. "It would appear so, and that someone has set Olivia up to take the fall."

"How?" Jack practically barked.

"The constables say they found Olivia's wrap at the scene of the crime, a servant spotted them together shortly before the murder was discovered, and . . ." He pressed his lips together and swallowed before continuing. "They found Frannie's amethyst necklace stashed in Olivia's dresser."

The stodgy butler arrived with their tea, shooting Jack a glare as he set the service on the table. In no mood, Jack stared the man down until he shifted his gaze to Mr. Brownlow.

"Will there be anything else, sir?"

"Yes, Thompson. Please go to Mr. Appleton's personal residence on Henrietta Street."

"I know the place, sir."

"Yes, wake him and explain what's happened. Please ask him to advocate for Olivia's bail and then come to me."

Thompson gave a bow, looked at Jack and then Mr. Brownlow and opened his mouth to speak, but the old man cut him off. "Go now."

As soon as the butler had gone, Jack said, "I think there are a few things you need to know."

Mr. Brownlow coughed, took a sip of tea, and then nodded for him to continue.

"I've known Olivia since she was a child living on the streets."

The old man's neck stretched out and his shoulders straightened.

"You see, I was the boy who took her in after she fled the workhouse, and I'm also the one who stole your wallet."

Tea halfway to his mouth, Mr. Brownlow froze. And then Jack explained his entire history from returning the wallet, to lurking around their house to check on his friend Ollie, to Monks almost killing him and that leading to him becoming a street lord. The old man didn't interrupt until Jack got to the part about Lois March.

"The Widow March trained you up as a gentleman for the sole purpose of you stealing for her?"

"Yes, sir, I'm not proud of it. But as you can surely see, her offer was irresistible."

A rough series of coughs racked the old man's entire body. Jack rose to come to his aid, but Olivia's uncle regained control and croaked, "Go on."

"Sir, I must ask your forgiveness." Jack perched on the edge of the sofa and stared into the cup clutched in both his hands, realizing this was the first time in his life he'd begged mercy from anyone. But for her, he would do anything.

"For what, son? I'm actually grateful for the day you stole from me, because it became the most joyful of my life."

"It's not that, sir . . . I've fallen irrevocably in love with your niece." He met the old man's gaze. "I know that I am not a suitable match, but she has become my world. Without her . . ." Emotion clogged his throat and he took a gulp of his tea, while images of Olivia in a prison cell morphed into her being dragged to the gallows. *No!*

He straightened. "Sir, Olivia has a half brother named

Edward Leeford, and I have reason to believe he's framed Olivia for Miss Lancaster's murder. He's known on the streets as Monks."

Brownlow's brow crinkled. "The crime lord who stabbed you?"

"Yes, sir. He believes Edwin Leeford left a significant fortune to the child who does not besmirch his good name. I overheard him threaten to defame his sibling—Olivia—so that he might inherit. He has considerable anger towards Olivia and her mother." He gestured toward the painting of Agnes Leeford looking down at them from above the hearth. "He blames her for driving his father insane."

"How do you know all of this?"

Realizing anything he said would implicate Olivia in any number of breeches in propriety, he answered, "That isn't important. But we need to find that will."

"Edwin Leeford died in Bedlam, penniless."

"Regardless, the only way we're going to have a hope of proving Monks set Olivia up for this crime is if we find the will, proving his motive."

The old man stared at him for several long moments, unblinking, and then said, "I believe you are right. I will engage Mr. Appleton to investigate all documents left behind by Edwin Leeford, if you'll do something for me."

"Of course." Jack's muscles tensed, ready to do anything he could to help.

"Use whatever connections you have, whatever nefarious skill, to hunt down this bloody character Monks. Do I make myself clear?"

"Yes, sir!" Jack jumped to his feet and headed toward the door.

"And one more thing."

Jack turned back and the old man's watery eyes locked on his. "For what it's worth, my boy, love never needs to be forgiven."

Jack shuffled down the cobbled lane, aimless. A week had passed, and while Jack couldn't be certain, he didn't think he'd slept in at least forty-eight hours. He'd scoured the city searching for Francesca's true killer, but no matter how many heads he'd banged together or how much money he'd thrown around, Monks eluded his reach. He hadn't found a single lead or scrap of evidence.

If only he could find the bludger, he'd drag him in front of the magistrate and throttle a confession from his scrawny neck. But it was as if the thug's entire operation had disappeared. The streets had gone silent. Everyone was so relieved that Monks had suspended his reign of terror that no matter what leverage Jack used, they refused to talk. The best he could figure, Monks had gone underground. It was what Jack would do.

He only hoped Mr. Brownlow was having better luck digging up Edwin Leeford's will.

Reaching inside his coat pocket for his watch, he flipped open the cover and stared at hands that refused to stop ticking forward no matter how hard he willed it. The timepiece showed less than five hours until Olivia's case was set to go before the judge. He was sorely tempted to throw the blasted thing to the ground and smash it into the cobbles. But it wouldn't help.

Nothing would.

Jack suppressed a growl of frustration, raked the hair out of his face, and gripped the strands, pulling until the pain lifted the fog from his brain. There had to be *something* he could do to clear her name. He released his hair and glanced around, realizing he'd wandered into a part of town he'd avoided for years. The slum of his origins—Southwark.

Glancing up, he met the golden eyes of an angel. The stained glass image beckoned him to shelter, just as it had that long-ago night he'd run from his mother. Once again out of options, Jack trudged up the worn stone stairs to an arched door and entered the dim sanctuary. Immediately, he was cocooned in the warmth of wood polish and burnt incense, the combination a balm to his frazzled nerves. The small, pew-lined church was empty, so he walked down the center aisle toward the candlelit altar and sunk down on the front bench. Hunching over, he folded his hands and stared into emptiness.

Passivity had never been his forte. He fixed things, changed outcomes, but this time his inability to stop and see the big picture had mucked up everything. If he just could have put the pieces of Monks's plan together a bit sooner, he could have saved Olivia.

Jack dropped his head into his hands. If he hadn't been so dead set on completing that last job, stealing from the man who had everything—wealth, privilege, respect, even Olivia—none of this would've happened. If he'd just stuck by her side at the ball . . .

Jack leaned his elbows on his knees and stared at the crucifix above the altar, a brutal depiction of the Son of God nailed to the cross, bloody and dying. An image Jack had never understood, even after all those Sundays in church with Lois. Wasn't life cruel enough without this glaring reminder?

Then he remembered what one of the nuns who'd taken him in had said when he'd become too old to stay in their care. *You have a good soul, Jack. If you're ever lost, look inside yourself for the answers you seek.*

Air whooshed out of Jack's lungs. Beseeching anyone who might listen, he whispered, "I've done everything in my power and it isn't enough. I don't know how—" His voice broke, so he cleared his throat and began again. "I'd do *anything* to save her."

Jack's thoughts stalled. The air around him felt heavy with significance, as if the answers he sought were just out of his grasp.

He straightened and stared at the altar and the cross, a truth settling deep into his soul—true love meant sacrifice. It meant putting that person above yourself. Jack had never known that kind of love. His own mother had not even been willing to give up her addiction for her only son. But what he felt for Olivia was vast, powerful; he loved her more than his own life.

The revelation flooded Jack's veins, his heart hammering and his skin tingling . . . exactly how he felt just before a fight.

CHAPTER 23

Olivia was suffocating.

Her eyes popped open to impenetrable darkness, pressing down on her chest like a thousand anvils. She sucked in rapid breaths only to choke on the stench of decades-old human filth ground into the floor and walls around her. The darkness seeped into the space between her bones, eating at her flesh. Draining her life.

She sat up and swung her feet over the side of the cot and gripped the icy metal bar under her legs, its solid mass grounding her and regulating the airflow to her lungs.

The seclusion in her cell was a blessing and a curse. She didn't have to fear that someone might harm her in her sleep, but another human, *any* other human, would reassure her that she wasn't utterly alone in the world. That she hadn't been forgotten.

Bread, gruel, and a tin cup of rust-tinged water were shoved into the room at regular intervals. But with no windows, or a watch to mark the passage of time, she couldn't tell if she'd been locked up for hours or weeks.

A scuttle of claws on cement and the trace scent of rotting meat announced the arrival of her near-constant companions. The sound tormented her. Just like in the workhouse, when those vicious, disgusting scavengers with their tiny claws and razor teeth had slithered out of the cracks in the walls to nibble ears or icy toes, drawing blood and cries of pain.

Goose bumps prickled over her flesh as she jerked her feet off the floor and hugged her legs to her chest. Rocking back and forth, she fervently wished they would bring her another candle. The vacant blackness on top of the isolation was too much to bear.

Sharp nails clinked against metal as the rat searched her dinner tray for any crumbs she may have left behind. Snuffling noises led to a hiss; another creature joining the hunt. The clicking of miniature talons and snapping of needle teeth combined with a hollow reverberation as the empty tin cup rolled across the stone floor.

Olivia buried her face in her knees, focusing on the familiar scent of home that still clung to her trousers. Her eyes burned, but she was too desiccated to cry. She attempted to swallow and draw moisture into her mouth, but instead it felt like she'd digested a handful of dried thorns, her tongue swollen like a puffy cluster of cotton. The first time they'd given her the lead-flavored water, she'd taken a sip and spat it across the room. She wouldn't make that mistake again.

The sounds of the rodents faded as they moved on to more fertile pastures. Olivia's eyes drifted shut and she began to mutter snippets of prayer. "Help me, Lord. Comfort my uncle, protect him. Aid Jack in his quest to find the real murderer. Please take Frannie's soul into heaven . . ." Grief knotted in her chest. It just couldn't be true. She'd spoken with Fran right before she left the ball. She'd been as vibrant and beautiful and annoying as ever. She simply *could not* be gone. There had to be some mistake.

Soon, she drifted into dreams.

"Olivia . . . Olivia . . ."

Waves of radiance and the lovely scent of roses and lilacs washed over her. She recognized that distinct fragrance, and as her eyes adjusted she observed the source. But seeing it defied belief. Swathed in layers of fluid lavender silk, her dark hair flowing down her back in perfect ringlets, stood a slightly translucent version of her cousin. "Francesca?"

"Who else do you think could magically appear in this dank cesspit? Yes, it's me."

With slow, careful movements, lest she wake from this sweet dream, Olivia unfolded her limbs and sat on the edge of her cot. "Frannie, what happened to you? Are you really . . ." Olivia swallowed the knot in her throat and whispered, "Dead?"

"Of course I'm dead, silly. I don't recall having the ability to enter your dreams in life." She laughed at her own joke as she fingered one of her diamond-and-amethyst earbobs, and Olivia knew it must truly be Fran . . . but Fran was dead.

Olivia began to shake as she repeated, "It's only a dream, it's only a dream."

"Don't be scared, Livie." Francesca leaned closer, and Olivia could see the gold flecks in her dark eyes. "I'm here to reassure you that I'm happy and that you will be too. But I need your help."

Olivia mustered her courage. "How? How can I help you when I'm locked in here? They think I killed you, Fran!"

The ethereal Francesca straightened and waved a hand in dismissal, her red lips twisting in disgust. "I know. Scotland Yard couldn't find the truth if it slapped them in the face. But you know." Fran pointed one perfectly shaped fingernail in Olivia's direction.

Olivia staggered to her feet, wishing with all her heart she could take her cousin's hand and hug her tight. "Fran, I don't know who killed you or why, but if I ever get out of here, I won't rest until I see justice done." Olivia's hands balled into fists at her sides. "I swear it!"

A slow, beautiful smile spread across Francesca's face and she began to fade.

Olivia stepped forward. "Frannie, don't go!"

"Miss Brownlow."

Olivia jerked awake. "Frannie . . ." she whispered, covering her eyes against a single blinding flame.

"Miss Brownlow, you're free to go. The bloke that did the murder turned 'imself in."

Olivia walked into the watery sunshine and lifted her face, soaking in the bittersweet rays of freedom. Fran would never again feel the glorious sun on her skin or smell the crisp winter wind or snuggle into a fur-lined cloak. Somehow it felt wrong to enjoy these simple pleasures.

Violet's hand slipped into hers and Olivia met her sorrowful green gaze. Seeing the cousin who had been the other part of their threesome was a stark reminder of what they had both lost. It was hard to believe Francesca was really gone, especially after Olivia's lifelike dream. She expected Fran to flounce down the walk at any moment, reminding her that her incarceration had damaged her reputation beyond repair.

Perhaps they hadn't been the best of friends, but Frannie had accepted Olivia despite her shady past, and had challenged her like no one else dared.

Even though she hadn't been the one to harm Frannie, guilt pressed hard on her shoulders as she glanced back at the imperial arches of Newgate, the doors guarded by gaping mouths full of iron teeth. She could almost hear their snapping as they tried to devour her.

"Livie?" Violet tugged on her fingers. "Is something wrong?"

With a slow exhale, she pushed out the darkness permeating her soul and blinked through her blurred vision. She'd endured countless horrors in her lifetime. This place would not defeat her. The real murderer had turned himself in, after all. She took a step and then another away from the prison, and walked hand in hand with Vi to the waiting carriage.

The driver held open the door, and Olivia stepped into the darkened interior to find her uncle tucked under a fur lap-blanket. "Uncle!" She sat beside him and threw her arms around his neck. "You came to get me."

"Of course I did, my darling girl. Those sawbones could not keep me away." He pulled back and gazed into her eyes, but something in his expression froze her to the spot.

"Uncle, what is it? Have the charges not been dropped against me?"

Violet had settled on the seat across from them, and when her uncle didn't reply Olivia's gaze darted to her best friend. "Violet, has something else happened? Besides—" Olivia swallowed hard and then whispered, "Besides Fran?"

Her uncle patted her knee as the carriage jolted into motion. "Your name has been cleared, my dear. You've been through so much. Let's just get you home, then we can have some tea and talk."

The tiny hairs on the back of her neck rose. "Wait. My half brother turned himself in, did he not? Why else would I be free?"

An oppressive silence pierced the atmosphere in the carriage. When she met Violet's tearful gaze, a shiver passed over her shoulders. "What is it, Vi?"

"The authorities really didn't tell you why the charges were dropped against you?"

"Yes, they said the real murderer turned himself in." Olivia's voice rose in pitch, her worry and impatience making her snappish. "I already told you that."

"Livie . . . he did turn himself in, but . . ." Vi paused and swiped at her wet cheeks. "It was Jack. Jack MacCarron confessed to killing Frannie."

Olivia grabbed the seat as the world tipped. "What?" She shook her head so hard she felt sick to her stomach. "No! Jack didn't do it! He would never—" Her words broke off in a sob. *No, no, no.* She wrapped her arms around her middle and bent in half.

Bony fingers gripped her arm. "Olivia!" Her uncle's authoritative voice cut through her moaning. "We *know* he did not do it."

Olivia stilled, her gaze swinging from her uncle to Violet. "You do?"

Vi nodded with a sad smile, tears still streaming down her cheeks. "He did it to save you, Livie. He told the police he hid the necklace in your room because he thought no one would ever think to look there. But we know he didn't . . ."

"He's been scouring the city for your half brother and his goons, but to no avail," her uncle said as he rubbed her back in slow circles. "He came to the house early this morning and told me his plan. Perhaps it was selfish, but I did not try to stop him."

Then it hit her like a house crumbling on top of her brick by brick; he'd lied to protect her, and if the authorities found out about Jack's past as the Artful Dodger, he would hang for certain. "Oh, God," Olivia cried out, praying she would wake up from this nightmare. She doubled over again, whimpers tearing from her gut. "Why? Why would he do this?"

"I'm fairly certain I know why he did it, my dear," her uncle soothed. "But we're not giving up. We will do everything we can to help him."

But Olivia knew that if Jack hadn't been able to find the real killer, using all his skill and connections, they had no chance. It was over and she'd never told him how she felt . . . never told Jack that she loved him.

Olivia woke from a restless sleep, the covers tangled around her waist. Disoriented, she rose on her elbows and turned her head to the window, the gray light edging the curtains only deepening her confusion. She was home in her own bed, but a monstrous darkness hovered at the edge of her mind like a demon ready to pounce. Her heartbeat accelerated, and a fine layer of sweat broke out over her skin.

When the memories hit, they knocked her on her back like waves. Brit had been beaten and almost killed. Frannie was gone; Jack in prison for her murder. Olivia curled onto her side and clutched a pillow to her face to muffle a sob. She couldn't breathe. Couldn't live.

She couldn't go on knowing Jack was sacrificing his life for hers. She yanked the fabric away from her mouth and fought for air, but the waves of pain were unrelenting. Her evil brother's blood-drenched face flooded her mind as he told Jack he'd kept him alive so that Jack could enjoy every moment of what he had planned next. Another wave of horror crashed down.

It was all because of her.

She sank deeper, her fingers clawing at the heavy water, her petticoats tangled around her arms, liquid flooding her lungs. Olivia sucked in a ragged breath. And then she stilled. That day in the Grimwigs' pond when she'd believed her life was over, all she'd had to do was put down her feet.

Her breathing calmed as she sat up and swung her legs over the side of the bed.

This was not over. She was not a bloody princess waiting for someone else to save the day. As her blasted brother was about to find out. She swiped at her useless tears and put her feet down.

It was time to stand up.

⁂

Olivia ran through the double doors of the courthouse behind Christopher March. She prayed they would make it in time. If it hadn't been for Uncle Brownlow's attorney, Mr. Appleton, they never would have known Jack's trial had been moved up to today.

Topher's testimony was their last hope. It was flimsy at best, but even with the Hill Orphans' help and Olivia flaunting herself around the streets of London as bait for the last week, Monks had not come out of hiding. And while Mr. Appleton had discovered a stash of her father's papers, all he'd found thus far were boxes of invention blueprints and patent paperwork.

The man behind the reception counter greeted them with a sharp tone. "May I assist you?"

"We need to see Judge Perkins right away, sir," Olivia answered. "'Tis a matter of life and death."

The man pressed his lips together and glanced down at his desk with a shake of his head. "It always is."

Olivia checked the urge to climb over the counter and shake the information out of the pompous clerk. She calmed herself by counting the ticks of the clock on the wall behind him.

One, two, three, four . . .

The man ran his finger along what looked to be a schedule.

Ten, eleven, twelve, thirteen . . .

Olivia bounced on the balls of her feet. When she got to twenty, she cleared her throat, loudly.

The man lifted his head with a glare. "The judge is in chambers, miss." He gestured to a uniformed constable Olivia hadn't noticed until that moment. "Jones, escort these people to room two eleven."

As they followed Jones's steady gate up a flight of stairs and down an endless hallway, Olivia longed to push past him and run. Topher must have seen her impatience, because he placed a restraining hand on her shoulder and met her eyes with a warning. Olivia took a deep breath and clenched her teeth. She could crawl faster than this git was walking!

Finally, they reached room 211 and Jones knocked, poking his head in to announce them.

Olivia rushed past the guard, speaking before she was fully into the room. "Judge Perkins, we have evidence that could exonerate Jack MacCarron."

The man sat behind a wide desk wearing the ceremonial white wig, frizzy ringlets draping over his robed shoulders, along with a decidedly uninviting expression on his face.

Topher removed his hat and clutched it in front of him. "Sir, I'm Christopher March, Jack's . . . er . . . cousin."

Olivia cringed as the lie stuttered out of Topher's mouth. She prayed the judge wouldn't see through him and throw them both out on their behinds.

"Your Honor, I was with Jack MacCarron the night of the murder." When the judge didn't speak, Topher continued. "I witnessed him conversing with Francesca Lancaster at the Grimwigs' ball."

The judge's face shifted, his brows hitching into his wig.

Topher barreled on. "Immediately after I saw him speak with Miss Lancaster, we left the ball together and took a rented hackney to March House."

This was the sketchy part, because although Topher did return to March House in order to stash the Grimwig emeralds, Jack never went into the house with him. From what she could gather, he'd gone straight to Turnbull Road to find Brit.

"Why did you rent a hackney?" Judge Perkins asked in a bored tone, scratching his shaggy, auburn muttonchops.

"My aunt, Lois March, was still at the party. I left early because I wasn't feeling well."

Olivia's heart pounded into the silence that followed.

The judge pierced Topher with dark, beady eyes. "Did Mr. MacCarron stay at March House after you returned?"

Olivia felt Topher stiffen beside her. "I . . . I believe so, sir . . . er . . . Your Honor."

"Did you not see him after your return?" The judge's voice was so deep, it reverberated inside Olivia's already aching head.

Topher glanced down at the hat he was ringing in his hands. "'Tis a large house, Your Honor." He looked up, his expression earnest. "But I know Jack did not commit this crime."

Judge Perkins, his face like a slate wiped clean, sat back in his chair. "That is of no consequence. MacCarron has already stood trial and been judged guilty."

Olivia swayed on her feet, Topher's fingers digging into her arm the only thing keeping the darkness at bay.

"With all respect, Your Honor, I was unable to testify because I did not know the trial had moved. Surely you can take my account into consideration."

Olivia stared at the judge, willing him to have a heart and praying harder than she'd ever prayed in her life that he would change his mind. He set his arms on the desk, folded his hands, and fixed his gaze on his linked fingers. Olivia's limbs shook uncontrollably. She gripped the back of a chair, effectively propping herself up lest her knees should fail her.

The judge frowned, deep grooves bracketing either side of his thin lips. "I would not have considered the testimony of a relative, in any case." His eyes shifted to Olivia. "Mr.

MacCarron was transferred to Newgate after his sentencing. I'll grant you a visitation before the execution."

Execution? Olivia's vision dimmed. She could almost hear the bang of a gavel as this one man sealed Jack's fate. She wanted to scream and rip her hair out like a madwoman. Or better yet, scream and rip *his* hair out. But instead, she took several cleansing breaths and channeled Jack's deadly calm in a crisis.

"It wasn't Jack, it was my half brother, Edward Leeford, who killed my cousin." The words rushed out of Olivia.

"Ah." Judge Perkins leaned back and pressed the tips of his fingers together in a point. "You must be Olivia Brownlow, the girl they originally arrested for Francesca Lancaster's murder."

"Yes, Your Honor. My brother goes by Monks—he is a street lord. He framed me so that he could collect the inheritance our father purportedly left to me."

The judge bolted into a perfectly straight posture. "Where is this will? And why has it not appeared in my court?"

Olivia let go of the chair and folded her hands in front of her to disguise their shaking. "I do not have it, sir. In fact, I've never seen it. It would seem Monks . . . I mean, my brother, Edward, has a copy."

"And how does this vindicate Jack MacCarron?" Judge Perkins asked, his lips pressing together.

"Jack confessed to the murder only to protect me, Your Honor." Olivia's voice trembled with emotion, and the tears she'd held back squeezed her throat.

"Why would he do such a thing?"

"To protect the one he loves, sir," Topher declared, and wrapped an arm around Olivia's shoulders.

The judge's face was no longer passive; in fact, his mouth hung open slightly, his eyes soft and distant. After a moment, he snapped his jaw shut and ordered, "Find the last will and testament of your father and bring it to me—"

"Oh, thank yo—"

"And then"—the judge cut off Olivia's gush of gratitude with a wave of his hand—"we will see about declaring a mistrial. That does not clear Mr. MacCarron of charges, you understand. The hanging is set a week from Friday, but if I can see a copy of this will, his execution will be delayed pending further investigation."

"Yes, sir!" Topher and Olivia said in unison.

Olivia wished she could take a moment to weep, or scream, but there was no time to lose.

CHAPTER 24

Olivia tugged down her cap to shield her eyes from the setting sun and leaned a shoulder against the wall, pretending to study her nails—which she had bitten to the quick. After a week of searching, they'd finally caught a break; Brit had spotted one of his kidnappers ducking into a pub near Temple Bar and one of the other boys had seen a man fitting her half brother's description nearby. So, Olivia and a few of the orphans were casing the area night and day.

Unfortunately, that meant a lot of idle waiting, which left nothing much to do but ponder and reminisce. Olivia grinned at her nubby nails as a distant memory surfaced. Her second night with Dodger and Fagin's gang, a boy had taken one of her socks and flung it into the fire. It had been her only pair. Dodger had found her crying in the corner, her icy-cold toes curled against the hardwood. He'd draped his arm around her shoulders and said, *"Buck up, mate. Second rule of the streets—never lose control."* And he'd tossed her a sock with a wink and a grin. Later, she'd noticed the boy who'd burned her sock was missing one of his own.

Jack's execution was set for the day after tomorrow, at dawn. Olivia's knees nearly buckled under the weight of her fear. She pushed it away and pressed her shoulder harder into the rough brick wall. Only at night, when she was alone in her room, did she allow herself to indulge in her grief. Her dreams were haunted by his tormented expression growing smaller and smaller as the paddy wagon took her away, the strong lines of his beautiful face crumpling, his brilliant blue eyes shining with tears. Jack had always been protective of her, but could Topher and her uncle be right? Did he love her?

Olivia shifted, changing her angle, constantly scanning the street. She couldn't bear the thought of Jack locked in a dark, airless cell, but the visitation pass Judge Perkins had given her sat unused on her nightstand. She'd been waiting until she could bring some speck of hope with her; the good news that they'd found the will or some evidence against Monks. Olivia pushed out a ragged sigh. Tomorrow, she would go, if only to thank him and say goodbye.

The swish and whisper of an approaching street sweeper pulled Olivia back to the task at hand. She pushed off the wall, shoved a hand in her pocket, and ambled over to a vendor selling books and newspapers. She purchased a rag, and then perched on a stone windowsill directly across from the entrance to Nemo's Pub. Flicking open the paper, her eyes focused just over the top of the pages. Brit had said the man who'd abducted him was tall and wore a gold hoop in his left ear and a blue knit cap over his bald head.

Olivia turned the page with a crinkle and snap. An unsolved murder headline caught her attention and reminded her of what she'd learned the night before. Mr. Appleton had called in a favor and received a copy of Francesca's autopsy report. As difficult as it had been, Olivia had read every word, twice. Fran had been killed by a single bullet to the chest, but the thing that interested Olivia the most was the list of items found with the body. Not only had the amethyst necklace been missing, but the matching earbobs as well. Olivia suppressed a shiver and pushed aside memories of the vision she'd had in prison, knowing now it had been nothing more than a dream, or perhaps her subconscious mind's way of telling her the jewelry could be a clue to finding the truth. But the valuable earrings were still unaccounted for, and Olivia was willing to bet her greedy half brother had taken them.

Her gaze was drawn to a lanky man nervously glancing over his shoulder. He wore a blue knit cap, and as he opened the door to Nemo's, she caught a flash of gold in his ear. The kidnapper! Olivia forced herself to take several breaths before she folded her paper, stood up, and signaled to Brit, who was stationed under the Temple Arch. He moved out of the shadows and jogged over.

After telling him the plan, she darted around a passing carriage and crossed the street to Nemo's. She stopped inside the doorway, waiting for her eyes to adjust to the gloom within. Sparse sunlight penetrated the windows stained with years of smoke. A long wooden counter flanked the right side of the narrow room, and round tables with mismatched chairs were scattered around the rest of the floor. The sharp scents of tobacco and fermented spirits flooded Olivia's nose as she sauntered up to the bar, as if she frequented dingy pubs every day, and ordered a pint. The barkeep raised an eyebrow at her grungy appearance, but when she flipped him an extra shilling, he turned with a shrug and brought her a frothy mug.

Olivia hunched over her drink, tucked a strand of wig behind her ear, and glanced around the room. Baldy had removed his hat and sat alone at a table near the front door. His back was to her, so she sauntered over to the table behind him and took a seat. From what she could see from the corner of her eye, he was reading a book. What kind of thug snuck into a pub to read?

Carefully, she drew her knife and turned it so she could press the blunt hilt into his back—revolver style. She roughened her voice, letting her anger punctuate every word. "Do exactly as I say and I won't blow a hole through your ribcage."

The man straightened one vertebra at a time and began to turn his head.

"Stop," she ordered. He froze midturn as Olivia pressed the knife harder into his side, keeping the weapon hidden behind his coat. "Stand up slowly and walk out the front door."

With careful movements, he set the book on the table and rose. When they reached the street, Brit and the others fell in around them. They turned onto a side street and then into a deserted alley. Olivia spun the man by his shoulder and pushed him up against the wall. Getting a good look at his face for the first time, she was jarred with the recognition that he was one of the men who'd harassed her at Paul's Pawnbroker Shop. "Critch?"

"How do ye know my name?" he demanded, warily eying the knives Brit and Archie held on him.

Olivia took her stroke of luck and ran with it. "I know a lot about you, Critch. Including that you kidnapped my mate." Olivia nodded to Brit. The boy grabbed Critch's arm and pressed the tip of his blade against the man's throat. When their captive met Brit's still-bruised face, he swallowed, his hazel eyes widening.

"I also know that gold in your ear is new, and means you've sold your soul to a devil named Monks."

"Whot do ye want from me?"

Olivia tucked her weapon into her pocket and began to pace in front of him. "Just a bit of information is all." She stopped and pinned him with a narrow stare. "Unless you want to hang for kidnapping."

"I spared the boy. 'E's supposed to be floatin' in the Thames!" Critch jerked away from the wall. Archie grabbed his other arm and poked his blade in the man's stomach. Critch froze.

"It's no matter." Olivia tilted her head to the side. "If you tell me what I want to know, it will all be forgotten."

Critch only stared, seemingly afraid to move as a thin line of red trickled down his throat. Brit was angry; she could see it in his coiled posture and clenched jaw. She just hoped the kid could hold it together. Jack's life depended on it.

"Your boss is in possession of a specific document that I am in need of. A last will and testament. Just tell me where he keeps it and you're free to get back to your reading."

As Olivia spoke, the color slowly leached from Critch's face. "I can't tell ye *that*. Monks would kill me!"

Olivia's heart thumped against her ribs. He knew where the will was hidden! But he feared her half brother more than the blades pressed into his flesh, or the threat of persecution. She paced to the other side of the alley. There was one other thing she knew he dreaded, and could only pray it would be enough. With her back to him, she pulled off her hat and wig and then slipped the hairnet off, freeing her long curls with a shake of her head. After scrubbing at the ash on her cheeks, she turned and walked toward Critch, letting a sneer slide across her face. "Remember me? From Paul's shop?"

Critch blinked several times as if not believing his own eyes. "Yer . . . Yer D . . . Dodger's girl."

Closing the distance between them, she ran a finger down the side of his sweat-covered face and whispered, "Yes—and if you don't tell me what I want to know, the Dodger will rip you limb from limb. With pleasure."

Critch raised his eyes to heaven, his hands balling into fists. Brit sensed their captive's tension and slanted his knife across the cords of Critch's throat. Olivia waited, unmoving, praying he hadn't heard of Jack's arrest.

Finally, Critch met her gaze, a kind of defeat written in his eyes. "I . . . I . . . don't know for certain, but . . . but Monks has a safe box at Tellson's Bank . . . where he keeps all 'is valuables." He sealed his lips and Archie gave him a poke between the ribs.

Critch glanced down and saw the blood blooming on his shirt. His next words rushed out in a jumble. "He goes on Tuesdays and . . . and sometimes Thursdays to make 'is deposits. Tha's all I know. I swear it!"

Tellson's was right around the corner, which would explain why Monks had been seen in the area. Satisfied that Critch was telling the truth, Olivia gave him a hard pat on the cheek. "Thank you, sir. I'll be sure to give Dodger your regards." Then, she slammed her fist into his gut. Air whooshed out of his lungs as he doubled over, and Olivia smashed her knee into his nose with a crack, dropping him to the ground. "That's for hurting Brit, you bloody blighter."

Olivia gave the signal and they all sprinted for the street.

The following afternoon, Olivia's fingers drummed against her thigh in time with a troubadour whose steps triggered a bang on his drum as he tooted on a trumpet and strummed a tiny harp strapped to his side. She watched Archie fall in behind him as he rounded a corner. The one-man musician's pockets were prime for picking.

It was after four o'clock, the sun had sunk behind the buildings, creating long shadows, and Monks had yet to make an appearance.

Not for the first time, Olivia wished for the comfort and security of having Brom by her side, but she couldn't risk Monks recognizing the dog. Clearly, he'd been watching her activity for weeks. With that in mind, she'd borrowed a suit of her uncle's clothes and disguised herself as a gentleman of leisure. She'd only had to make slight alterations to the suit, since he'd become so thin. But the shoes were a different matter. Her feet were sweating something awful in the layers of hose and socks she'd donned in order to keep his shoes from slipping from her heels. As a final touch, she'd used her kohl pencil to thicken her eyebrows and enhance her fake beard and mustache.

Giving her paper a flick, Olivia folded it and tucked it under her arm as she stood. She strolled with wide, confident steps and shoulders back down the aisle of vendors and paused at a bakery cart, reminding herself to peruse the selections slowly. Toffs had all the time in the world.

But hers was running out. Jack would hang in the morning. The thought fired into her soul like a cannon blast.

With every blink of her eyes, memories flashed: that first night, grown-up and so handsome she couldn't help but stare; his hands caressing her face as he kissed her until she didn't know her own name; the earnest promise in his gaze as he swore he'd do *anything* to help her; the boy with the ragged top hat and too big coat; the warrior who'd protected her with only an umbrella and his fists. This man reveled in the true, unguarded person she'd never been with anyone else. She loved him beyond reason. And deep in her soul, she knew he felt the same.

As she looked over the loaves and pastries, fear boiled inside of her. A stark terror that told her they would never find Monks in time. That pictured Jack, back straight, chin up, walking to the gallows. A noose tightening around his neck, until her own heart exploded inside her chest.

Heat built in her head until she had to hide behind the baker's canopy to press her fingers against her eyes. Jack burned so bright and beautiful, no one could hope to own him. But . . . *If I could have just one more chance, I'll make sure he never doubts how much he is loved.*

"The bank'll close up in less than an hour. What if he don't show?" Brit's words jolted her out of her morose thoughts. Time to put on her mask. She swallowed the madness boiling inside of her and selected a sack of day-old sticky buns, then moved to the next stall, positioning herself so she could see the bank across the street. She handed Brit the sack of bread and answered with a confidence she didn't feel, "He'll show." *He has to.*

Just then, there was a break in the traffic, and Olivia spotted a tall man with a blond ponytail entering the bank. "That's him."

Thank you, God.

Squaring her shoulders, she strode across the street and darted through a group of young women selling flowers, narrowly remembering to tip her hat.

With a deep breath, she entered the bank. The interior was bright, every surface polished and sterile. Monks stood at the counter with his back to her. She couldn't hear what he said, but he pulled a key from his pocket as the clerk plunked a heavy-looking box in front of him. She strode forward and stood behind him as if waiting for her turn. She'd never entered a bank in her life, so she had no sense of what the procedure might be, but she had to get a look inside that box.

Monks unlocked the safe and took a wad of pound notes and a small sack of coins from his pocket. Olivia stepped closer, trying to see over his shoulder. But he was taller than she by half a head and his broad back blocked her view.

"May I help you with something, sir?"

Olivia only just kept herself from starting as the man behind the counter directed his question toward her. She stepped back and jerked her eyes to the slate board that listed the bank's rates and services. "One moment, please," she grumbled with an off-putting frown.

After a few seconds had passed, she clasped her shaking hands behind her back and sidled up to the counter right next to Monks. "I need information on acquiring a safe box."

"What size, sir?"

Olivia glanced back at the rate chart, but in her jittery state the words and numbers read like gibberish. Under the guise of assessing its size, she pointed her chin toward the box Monks sifted through and allowed her gaze to linger.

Monks shot a glare at the clerk. "Is there somewhere more private I might go?"

There!

Monks snapped the box closed, but not before Olivia

spied a distinctive glitter. Shoved into the far corner of the safe, as if they were of no consequence, rested a very familiar pair of amethyst-and-diamond earbobs.

Unexpected tears closed Olivia's throat as Fran's beautiful face filled her mind. She swallowed hard and turned back to the clerk. "I've changed my mind. Thank you." She tipped her hat, turned, and rushed out the door.

When she reached the street, she leaned back against the wall and reined in her emotion. The bell on the door clanged and Monks strode into the street. She knew what she had to do.

Olivia fell into step behind him and nodded to Archie, who was loitering against a nearby windowsill.

"Two loaves for a shilling!" the baker called from across the street. "A bag o' sweet buns for a crown!"

Monks stopped and glanced over his shoulder at the vendor. Olivia kept walking past him, but when he jogged across the street, she turned and followed. Brit stood leaning against a wall near the cart. Olivia met his eyes, and he gave an almost imperceptible nod.

"Please, sir, do ye have any buns for a starvin' orphan?" It was Archie, begging with his hat in his hands.

Monks picked up two loaves and fished in his pocket. "I'll take these."

Olivia's eyes darted back to Brit. They couldn't let Monks leave. Archie kept up his tirade, getting on his knees. "Please, sir."

"Get up, boy. I ain't got nothing for a street rat," the baker barked.

Monks tried to shove the shilling into the baker's hand, just as Brit unlatched the end of the cart, spilling bread and rolls all over the street. Kids swarmed like insects from the walls, converging on the windfall. The baker yelled and attempted to swat them away. In the confusion, Olivia stepped up to Monks, dipped her hand into his pocket, and extracted the key.

Her half brother whirled, gripped her throat, and slammed her against a wall. "What'd you take, you greedy little toff?" he spit through clenched teeth, his face a hairbreadth from hers. "I saw ye in the bank eyeballin' my safe."

Olivia couldn't breathe or speak. Her brother's yellow eyes, paler than hers but still a similar tone, bore into her face. Would he see the resemblance too? Recognize her for who she was?

He squeezed her throat tighter. "I said, whot did you take?"

Olivia moved her mouth, but nothing came out. Digging blindly in her trouser pocket, she produced the key. He gave her another slam against the bricks, then released her and grabbed the key. "You're lucky there are so many witnesses, or this would be the last thing you ever did."

With a final shove, her brother glanced around and then stalked away.

Her pulse pounding so hard she could feel it in the tips of her fingers, Olivia turned and rushed down the street, every muscle in her body straining to run. When she finally rounded the corner, and looked behind her, Monks was nowhere in sight. Jogging forward, she hailed the nearest hackney. "I need to reach the Old Bailey courthouse, posthaste!"

The driver nodded and Olivia hoisted herself into the buggy. A moment later, when the carriage lurched into traffic, she fell back against the seat and pulled the tiny key from her jacket pocket. Thank God, Brit had thought to give her a fake. He'd done his research and created a similar key fob out of sturdy paper. By the time Monks noticed the switch, she would be long gone.

Twenty agonizing minutes later, Olivia slammed through the double doors of the courthouse. She dashed past the reception desk and toward the stairs.

"Sir! You can't go up there unescorted!"

Olivia heard the clerk shout for the guard, but she wasn't about to stop now. She couldn't take the chance that the judge would leave for the night—if he was in his office at all. She hit the stairs at a sprint.

"Halt this instant!"

The guard's boots pounded on the steps behind her, but Olivia just ran faster. Leaping up the last two stairs, she darted around the corner, room 211 in her sight.

"Sir, you must stop!"

Not on your bloody life.

As she reached Judge Perkins's office, she didn't slow, but crashed against the door and stumbled inside. The judge sprang from his seat. Olivia turned and threw the lock behind her.

"What is the meaning of this?"

Olivia bent over and sucked in air, her lungs burning like fire.

The guard slammed into the locked door, vibrating the opaque glass.

"Your Honor." Olivia reached for her hat, but it was long gone. "It's me." She drew in another breath, tugging the wig and net off her head. "Olivia Brownlow."

"What in all that's holy—" The outrage on his face rivaled a drawing she'd once seen of Zeus.

"Sir, I . . . have the evidence to vindicate Jack MacCarron."

The guard gave the door a mighty kick, the frame splintering in response. Judge Perkins rushed around his desk and unbolted the lock. The guard flew into the room, tripping forward, and only stopped when he hit the back of a chair.

Olivia met Judge Perkins's annoyed gaze, pleading with her eyes. "Please, sir, hear me out."

The judge shifted his attention to the panting guard. "There's no threat here, as you can see." He swept his hand toward Olivia. "You're dismissed."

Olivia let out a slow breath and ran her fingers through the tangled strands of her hair. The guard shot her a withering glare before exiting the room.

Judge Perkins stared at her thoughtfully for several seconds before gesturing to the chairs in front of his desk. "Have a seat, Miss Brownlow. But be warned, this better be legitimate, or you could find yourself in contempt."

Olivia perched on the edge of a hardwood seat, her leg muscles quivering like jam.

The judge sat and removed his own wig, revealing thin spikes of reddish-gray hair. "Well, let's hear it."

In a deluge of words, Olivia explained how she'd followed Monks to Tellson's and what she'd seen inside his safe box.

The judge leaned forward. "How can you be *sure* these earrings were Miss Lancaster's?"

"Your Honor, they were her favorites. She wore them at least once a week." Olivia had to swallow before she could continue. "The ones I saw in Monks's safe had square amethysts and rose-cut diamonds. They were identical to Fran's. The very same ones I saw her wearing at the Grimwig Ball."

The judge sat unmoving, his face an impassive mask. Olivia waited, butterflies the size of crows rioting in her stomach.

"If we can prove that your half brother is in possession of your cousin's jewels, the case against Mr. MacCarron will be thrown out." The judge tapped a finger against his chin. "But a warrant to break into a personal box at Tellson's could take time."

Olivia pulled the safe key from her pocket and held it out with a grin. "That's precisely why I alleviated Monks of *this* when he was otherwise occupied."

Judge Perkins stared at the key dangling from her fingers and then shook his head, his lips curling into his red mutton-chops. "I'll pretend as if I did not hear that last bit."

Olivia stood and handed the key to the judge, lifting her chin in challenge. "The tag says it's for box number 160. Surely, a man of your great esteem could get the bank to reopen tonight."

Jack hunched on the edge of his cot, his elbows on his knees, hands supporting his aching head. Although he couldn't see outside, he sensed that the sun would be up soon. He tried to pray for his soul, but he didn't know if he had one. Everything inside him felt hollow, his heart cracked open like an empty safe. Olivia hadn't even come to see him. Perhaps he'd misinterpreted her feelings for him. Likely she'd already reconciled with that git, Grimwig, and they were planning their wedding.

He should've been happy for her, but he couldn't help wishing he hadn't returned the Grimwigs' precious emeralds before turning himself in. When he'd dropped the anonymous package in the post, it had felt like the right thing to do. One final act of good. And he had to admit, once she married into the family, those jewels *would* look lovely against Olivia's honeyed skin.

Heck, she looked good enough to eat with a ratty wig on her head and soot smeared on her face. Jack sighed, the visual bringing back all the emotion he'd locked away. If he could have kissed her lips one last time, he would feel absolved from everything he'd done wrong in his short but eventful life. He pushed the heels of his hands into his burning eyes. "I'm sorry, God. If I had another chance, I'd do it all so much differently."

"Well then, today's yer lucky day, isn't it?"

Jack jerked upright as the key rattled in the lock and a guard opened the door with a screech. A wig-free Judge Perkins, what was left of his reddish hair sticking out in disarray all over his head, stood in the open doorway. "Took half the night and one very angry bank owner, but you're free to go, Mr. MacCarron."

Jack rose, his legs trembling beneath him.

"I try to run a just court, so when someone confesses to a crime they did not commit, I'm bound by the law to find the truth."

Jack stood rooted to the spot. "And what would the truth be in this case?"

"That a heinous criminal plotted to frame his own sister for murder, in order to claim her inheritance for himself." The judge paused and ran a hand over his sparse strands of hair, meeting Jack's eyes. "And it would seem one extremely noble individual sacrificed himself to save an innocent young woman."

Jack couldn't speak, couldn't move. Was he dreaming?

"If you don't mind, Mr. MacCarron, I'd like to spend an hour or two in my bed this night." The judge swept his hand in an ushering motion.

Without a backward glance, Jack rushed from his cell. "How did you know, sir? That it wasn't me?"

Judge Perkins clapped Jack on the shoulder as they walked through the maze of dank prison corridors. "Let's just say you're in love with one tenacious little lady."

"Olivia," Jack said under his breath.

The judge chuckled as they emerged into the darkened administrative wing. "Miss Brownlow's methods may be a bit unconventional, but I can't deny that they are effective. She appeared in my office this afternoon dressed as a gentleman." The judge shook his head with an incredulous laugh. "She was right, though. That Monks character had Miss Lancaster's missing earbobs, and a copy of a will that gave him motive for framing his sister. All of it was stashed in a personal safe that Miss Brownlow discovered and brought to my attention."

Jack walked in stunned silence. The realization that she hadn't abandoned him, but had been working to free him, sparked a warmth inside his chest that seemed to grow larger by the second.

They rounded a corner, entering the prison lobby and the judge continued, "A warrant has been issued for Monks's arrest. With all the evidence against him, it should be an open-and-shut case."

They reached the front door and Judge Perkins extended his hand. "Godspeed to you, Mr. MacCarron. I hope you don't take offense when I say I hope to never see you again."

Jack shook the judge's hand with a wide smile. "No worries, Your Honor. I have a very good reason to stick to the straight and narrow."

Walking out of Newgate, Jack stared up at a sky bursting with stars. He breathed in the fragrance of London—rot and coal smoke laced with a bit of clean frost—and knew he meant every word he'd just said. He wouldn't so much as lift a lost coin from the gutter. After hearing everything Olivia had done to save him, he would never dare jeopardize her faith by falling back into his old ways.

Jack set off down the street at a jog. He had a lot to do before he could rest. His past life as a thief may be over, but one of his biggest heists loomed before him—to win the prize of one brave, beautiful girl's heart.

CHAPTER 25

Olivia awoke to music, the sweet, sweeping notes of a song mixing with the remnants of her dreams. Soft sunlight slanted through her window and across her coverlet as she stretched an arm over her head and smiled. She'd been dreaming of Jack.

Jack!

Excitement propelled her out of bed. When they'd opened Monks's safe box, Judge Perkins had assured her Jack's conviction would be overturned and he'd be free before morning. Which had now arrived!

She was tugging her trousers on under her nightgown when a pinging sound drew her eyes to the window. The haunting strains of the song began again. In a daze, Olivia walked toward the sound, the music hauntingly familiar. It was a song from *The Bohemian Girl*, the opera she and Jack had attended.

Almost tripping over her pants as they fell around her ankles, she kicked her feet free, ran the rest of the way to the window, and threw open the curtains. Just below her, in the garden, she spied a familiar dark head tilted over a violin. With a wordless cry of joy, Olivia pushed up the window and leaned out. "Jack!"

He stopped playing and lifted his head. White teeth contrasting against ruddy skin, he flashed the most beautiful grin she'd ever seen in her life. "Princess Olivia, please come down," he called.

Olivia flew out of her room and down the stairs, not bothering with a wrap. She flung open the front door and there he was, leaning against the jamb, hands shoved in his pockets, as if he hadn't a care in the world.

Her heart ready to explode, she forced herself to pause in the doorway and mirror his posture, quipping, "Where's your trusty brolly this morning, Mr. MacCarron?"

His shimmering blue gaze caught hers, his voice low. "It doesn't much look like rain, Miss Brownlow."

No, it didn't. In fact, the skies shone a dusty pink as the sun rose on the most perfect of days. Olivia had a feeling their storms were behind them.

Unable to take it a moment longer, she rushed out and threw her arms around Jack's neck. She kissed his chin, his cheek, his hair, and breathed deep of his skin—the scents of spring rain and soap and that indescribable energy that was pure Jack. A fragrance she thought to never savor again.

He pulled back, the wicked grin she loved slanting his mouth. "I guess this means you're happy to see me?"

"Yes, you dolt!" She pulled out of their embrace and smacked his arm.

He made a face. "Ow! That hurts me, it does."

She shook her head. The sight of him stung her eyes. She couldn't believe he was real. "How long have you been free?"

"Not long." All humor gone, he took her face in his hands and lowered his head. "I came to you as soon as I could."

Olivia blinked up at him, her next words a breathless rush. "I love you, Jack."

His mouth took hers and she laced her fingers into the silk of his hair. As he kissed her, tingles skittered up and down her spine, settling low in her back.

Jack's mouth slid to her cheek and then her ear. "How do you feel about marrying a traveling musician?"

A daze of joy and passion clouding her brain, Olivia leaned back in his arms. "What?"

He placed one more open-mouthed kiss on her neck, causing her brain to momentarily lapse. "'Tis how I plan to make an honest living." He turned with her in his arms and gestured toward the fiddle leaning up against the banister.

Olivia blinked at the violin and then back at Jack's tense expression. Was he serious?

"I would lower to one knee, but I can't bear to let you go." He met her gaze and tucked a strand of hair behind her ear, brushing his knuckles along her cheek.

As his meaning began to sink in, Olivia trembled against him, every bone in her body melting.

"Olivia Brownlow, I would do *anything* for you. I love you more than my own life. Will you marry me?"

She gazed at him for several moments, letting his words fill her heart. "Yes, Jack. Yes, I'll marry you!" Then she kissed him soundly on the mouth.

But he pulled back, concern clouding his gaze. "I can't steal anymore, Olivia. You deserve better. Even though living off my music will be a struggle, if I can find a position with a theater company, I know I can provide for you."

"Jack, I would follow you anywhere." His face shone with such happiness, Olivia had to swallow before she could continue. "I would marry you if we had to live in a gypsy wagon and eat gruel for every meal. But . . ." She let a teasing grin flit across her lips. "That won't be necessary."

He arched a dark brow.

"Turns out my father didn't squander his fortune. In fact, it's been growing larger every year from all the inventions he had patented before he died."

Jack froze, motionless save for the vein throbbing in his neck.

"Mr. Appleton discovered my father's accounts last week. We just needed the missing will. Which Monks conveniently provided in his safe box, and Judge Perkins had delivered here last evening."

Jack stepped back from her, blinking like a startled barn owl.

Olivia took both his hands in hers. "Jack, if you want to open a theater and play your fiddle every night, I'll be a happy woman. But I have a better idea . . ."

A slow smile spread across Jack's face, a chuckle rumbling up from his chest. He pulled her against him, his laughter shaking through Olivia's body and lighting up her soul. After a moment, he grew quiet and cocked his head to one side. "What's your *better* idea?"

"How do you feel about kids?" Olivia grinned. "Lots of them!"

EPILOGUE

1861
The outskirts of London, Hill Orphanage

The mansion vibrated with the pounding of feet as the children ran along the second-floor gallery. Olivia counted twenty-one boys, five girls, and one massive dog tromping down the main staircase. Chip led the pack, leaping from the second step and landing with a grin at her feet. "Miss Livie! Aren't you playing with us?" The boy eyed Olivia's skirts.

She tousled Chips silky blond curls. "Did Miss Bridgett finish with your studies already?"

"Yep, she did!" Chip pursed his little mouth and shook his head before correcting himself. "I mean . . . yes, Miss Livie, on account of the beautiful day, Miss Bridgett let us out early for a bit of exercise."

Children surged around them and scampered down the hallway, presumably headed for the back garden. Several of them called for Olivia to join their team for a cricket match.

"That was perfect, Chip." She grinned and bent to kiss his baby-soft cheek. "You're becoming quite the little gentleman."

"Thank you, Miss Livie!" Chip called over his shoulder as he joined the fray.

Olivia turned back toward the staircase to see Brit and Jack bringing up the rear. Dark heads tilted together, their hair almost identical in shade, except Brit's curled at his collar. From their good-natured ribbing, it would seem they were both team captains for the pending match.

"That's not fair. You got her last game!" Brit complained as they reached the bottom of the staircase.

"Well then, let's ask her whose team she wants to be on, shall we?" Jack replied before he stalked forward, his gaze locked on hers.

Olivia's heart skipped a beat and then galloped forward. Amazed that he could still send her pulse racing with just a look, she closed the distance between them and wrapped her fingers around the exposed muscles of his arm beneath his short-sleeved jersey. It was safe to say, cricket had become one of her favorite pastimes.

"Good afternoon, Mrs. MacCarron." His voice was husky as he leaned in and kissed her lips.

"Oh, brother! You don't play fair, Mr. Jack." Brit's nose crinkled and his mouth twisted like he'd just eaten a rank turnip. He spun away and jogged down the hall calling, "Archie's mine!"

Jack's arm looped around Olivia's waist and he pulled her close. "I need you, my sweet. But you're going to have to get out of those clothes first."

She turned into him and threaded her fingers into the hair resting against his broad neck. "You'll have to play without me today. I have guests arriving. If Aunt Becky saw me in trousers and wielding a cricket bat, she might have a conniption."

Jack grinned devilishly. "That might be interesting. Are you sure I can't persuade you?"

"Excuse me, Mr. MacCarron."

They turned to see Thompson approach, his face carefully blank, but a joyful spark shone in his eyes. "Will you be requiring my services this afternoon?"

"Of course, Thompson. We couldn't play without your precise refereeing skills. It would be a bloodbath out there." Jack winked at Olivia before turning back to the butler. "And if you would be so kind as to escort Mrs. March to the field, Olivia will need company in the cheering section."

"Yes, sir. Right away, sir," Thompson responded with enthusiasm just as the front bell sounded.

The butler stepped quickly to the door and opened it to Topher and Violet. The newly engaged couple entered the house arm in arm. Topher had asked for her cousin's hand as soon as he'd been able to gather the funds to purchase March House. Lois had moved into the Hill Orphanage and greatly enjoyed teaching decorum to all the children. She loved to remind Jack that if she could turn the Artful Dodger into a gentleman, these children didn't stand a chance at remaining street urchins.

"I'm so glad you're here, old man." Jack clapped Topher on the shoulder. "I'm down a cricket player."

Olivia looked past Violet's bright coiffure as Thompson shut the door. "Where is Aunt Becky?"

Violet's meadow-green eyes widened before she explained, "Mother isn't much for long carriage rides, you know. And doesn't get out of the city often . . ." She trailed off and looked around the foyer. "I really like what you've done—"

"She still hasn't forgiven me, has she?" Olivia's shoulders slumped. Between the murder scandal, her unconventional marriage to Jack, not to mention the wildly unpopular notion of taking in street kids and starting her own orphanage, Olivia had been shunned from London society with a speed akin to lightning. And her ultra-proper Aunt Becky had followed suit.

Vi took Olivia's hand and shook her head with a sad smile. "I'm sorry, Livie."

Olivia glanced away from her best friend so she wouldn't see her eyes welling up. It wasn't that she missed the fancy parties or even the favor of society; she mourned the loss of the woman who'd accepted her like a daughter. On top of losing Uncle Brownlow, it was almost too much to bear. Her uncle had passed on in peace, trusting that his sister would watch over Olivia after he was gone. Olivia had allowed him the misconception because she believed Aunt Becky simply required time, and that she cared about her beyond society's predications.

"Violet, I need a moment with my wife, please," Jack said before he turned to Topher. "If you could head out back and organize the teams, I'll join you momentarily."

After Violet and Topher left, Jack took Olivia's hand in his large, warm fingers. "I have something for you. Wait right here." He planted a quick kiss on her lips and then sprinted up the stairs.

Olivia sank down on the foyer bench. Some days her uncle's absence was like a physical ache, but he hadn't left her alone. He'd blessed her union with Jack and had been able to see the orphanage grow into a home bursting with joy and love.

Jack skipped down the stairs, his right arm tucked behind his back. He came to her and lowered to one knee, his raven hair falling over his eyes. He raked the lock off his face with an impatient, but perfectly familiar gesture, and smiled. "I was going to save this for your next birthday, but now seems an appropriate time to give it to you." He handed her a small, velvet-covered box.

Having no earthly idea what he could give her that she didn't already have, Olivia lifted the lid and gasped. There, nestled in a bed of scarlet silk, was a gold, egg-shaped locket. "Is this . . ." Her words deserted her as she lifted the familiar weight and unlatched the tiny clasp with trembling fingers. Her mother's angelic face stared back at her from the tiny portrait.

"Jack! However did you find it?" Her eyes flooded with tears as she grasped the beloved piece of her past to her chest.

"Well, I thought it was high time I used my talents to do some good. I've been tracking it for months. Finally, I followed the trail to an old woman who wouldn't part with it until I told her the entire sordid tale and why the locket was important to you." He shrugged one shoulder. "Then she refused to let me pay her for it."

Olivia gazed at the beloved portrait again and Jack moved to sit beside her, looking over her shoulder.

"I'm certain she would be proud of you, Livie. And all that you've done with your father's money."

"All *we* have done, Jack." Olivia smiled into his eyes. She had so very much to be thankful for. "It's a fine life we have, isn't it?"

A whisper of Jack's old intensity captured her gaze as he brushed a tear from her cheek. "I couldn't imagine a finer life than spending every day with you, Olivia MacCarron."

And just like that, the Artful Dodger stole her heart, again.

ACKNOWLEDGMENTS

ometimes authors declare a certain story is "the book of their heart." *Olivia Twist* is that to me and more: this story has been thirty-five years in the making. Yes, you read that right ... *thirty-five years*.

After seeing the musical *Oliver!* as a child, I fell in love with the Artful Dodger and the orphan Oliver—who, in my peculiar mind, was always a girl in disguise. I would sit in my bedroom for hours and stare at the album cover as I listened to the soundtrack, belted the songs at the top of my lungs, and then let my imagination run wild as I created further adventures for these beloved characters.

Years later, I read the Dickens novel, *Oliver Twist*, and although it didn't line up with the romanticized vision of the musical, it introduced me to the hideously selfish Monks. At this point, I had all the elements of a great book: the altruistic orphan, the reluctant hero, and the evil villain. What I didn't have were the skills to bring my story to the page.

That changed over many years of study and practice, and in 2011 I began researching the Victorian era and writing the first draft of this novel. I worked on Olivia and Jack's story in between writing the Doon series, and finally finished it in 2013. But the young adult publishing world wasn't ready for a historical novel without steampunk elements or vampires, and I received rejection after rejection. But I didn't give up hope, I had faith that this book would find its place in the world, and I have many of you to thank for that...

My superstar agent, Nicole Resciniti, for being the first to fall in love with this story and for never giving up on it!

I am beyond grateful to my publishing team at Blink; Annette Bourland, Matt Saganski, Sara Bierling, Sara Merritt, Marcus Drenth, Liane Worthington, Jacque Alberta, the design team, the sales team, and everyone at Blink who worked to bring this story to life.

Love and thanks to my family, the Lunekes and the Moeggenbergs. Your encouragement and support continues to be my safe place to land!

To my sons, Ben and Alex, for falling in love with the musical *Oliver!* and quoting it even more than I do. *"Whot did you say?"*

To the friends who keep me sane: Jennifer Osborn, Laurie Pezzot, Mindee Arnett, Tricia Lacey, Angie Knopp, Brenda Hess, Deanna Miller, Amy Wolf, Maryann Murad, Jennifer Dilly, Lisa Litz, Jennifer Egbert, JR. Forasteros, and my Southbrook Bible study crew!

Thanks to my early readers: Jessica Lemmon (who was surprised that historical could be funny), Sienna Condy, Jennifer Stark, and Jennifer Osborne.

To my book besties and critique partners, Carey Corp and Melissa Landers, for being the best travel buddies a girl could have. And most of all, for not letting me turn this book into *Oliver Twist* "With Magic Mother &#^%@*!" I love you both!

Thanks to Kirk DouPonce for using your artistic brilliance to design a cover that says, "This is not your grandmother's historical!"

A big thank you to Marisa Miller, Lee Slater, Lilly Santiago, and Sasha Alsberg for your support and inspiration.

Thanks to the band One Republic for the music that stitched Jack "the Artful Dodger" MacCarron together in my mind. (If you'd like to hear the full playlist for *Olivia Twist*, please visit my website, www.LorieLangdon.com, for the link.)

To my readers, I am grateful for each and every one of you! Thank you for the letters, art, book photos, for coming to my events, spreading the word about my books, and welcoming my characters into your hearts. You are the reason why I love writing young adult literature!

A special thank you goes out to my Grandma Joyce, who started this whole journey by taking me to see a revival of *Oliver!* in the theater. And to my Grandpa Leon, who left us the week I typed "The End" on this book. Our story will continue one day when I'm with you both in eternity.

And last, but always first, my Father God, who has given me more than I could ask or think possible!